Petticoat Rule

Baroness Emmuska Orczy

Petticoat Rule

The present edition is a reproduction of previous publication of this classic work. Minor typographical errors may have been corrected without note, however, for an authentic reading experience the spelling, punctuation, and capitalization have been retained from the original text.

ISBN: 978-1-64799-119-7

CONTENTS

PART I
THE GIRL

CHAPTER
I	A Farewell Banquet	1
II	The Rulers of France	5
III	Pompadour's Choice	13
IV	A Woman's Surrender	19
V	The First Trick	27
VI	A False Position	31
VII	The Young Pretender	35
VIII	The Last Trick	44
IX	The Winning Hand	50

PART II
THE STATESMAN

X	The Beggar on Horseback	56
XI	La Belle Irène	61
XII	The Promises of France	66
XIII	The Weight of Etiquette	76
XIV	Royal Favours	81
XV	Diplomacy	89
XVI	Strangers	96

PART III
THE WOMAN

XVII	Splendid Isolation	107
XVIII	Clever Tactics	110
XIX	A Crisis	120
XX	A Farewell	127
XXI	Royal Thanks	128
XXII	Paternal Anxiety	132
XXIII	The Queen's Soirée	136
XXIV	Gossip	139
XXV	The First Doubt	142
XXVI	The Awful Certitude	146
XXVII	A Fall	160
XXVIII	Husband and Wife	165

XXIX	The Fate of the Stuart Prince	177
XXX	M. de Stainville's Seconds	185
XXXI	The Final Disappointment	193
XXXII	The Dawn	197
XXXIII	The Ride	201
XXXIV	"Le Monarque"	204
XXXV	The Stranger	210
XXXVI	Revenge	216
XXXVII	The Letter	223
XXXVIII	The Home in England	226

PART I

THE GIRL

CHAPTER I

A FAREWELL BANQUET

"D'Aumont!"

"Eh? d'Aumont!"

The voice, that of a man still in the prime of life, but already raucous in its tone, thickened through constant mirthless laughter, rendered querulous too from long vigils kept at the shrine of pleasure, rose above the incessant babel of women's chatter, the din of silver, china and glasses passing to and fro.

"Your commands, sire?"

M. le Duc d'Aumont, Marshal of France, prime and sole responsible Minister of Louis the Well-beloved, leant slightly forward, with elbows resting on the table, and delicate hands, with fingers interlaced, white and carefully tended as those of a pretty woman, supporting his round and somewhat fleshy chin.

A handsome man M. le Duc, still on the right side of fifty, courtly and pleasant-mannered to all. Has not Boucher immortalized the good-natured, rather weak face, with that perpetual smile of unruffled amiability forever lurking round the corners of the full-lipped mouth?

"Your commands, sire?"

His eyes—gray and prominent—roamed with a rapid movement of enquiry from the face of the king to that of a young man with fair, curly hair, worn free from powder, and eyes restless and blue, which stared moodily into a goblet full of wine.

There was a momentary silence in the vast and magnificent dining hall, that sudden hush which—so the superstitious aver—descends three times on every assembly, however gay, however brilliant or thoughtless: the hush which to the imaginative mind suggests the flutter of unseen wings.

Then the silence was broken by loud laughter from the King.

"They are mad, these English, my friend! What?" said Louis

the Well-beloved with a knowing wink directed at the fair-haired young man who sat not far from him.

"Mad, indeed, sire?" replied the Duke. "But surely not more conspicuously so to-night than at any other time?"

"Of a truth, a hundred thousand times more so," here interposed a somewhat shrill feminine voice—"and that by the most rigid rules of brain-splitting arithmetic!"

Everyone listened. Conversations were interrupted; glasses were put down; eager, attentive faces turned toward the speaker; this was no less a personage than Jeanne Poisson now Marquise de Pompadour; and when she opened her pretty mouth Louis the Well-beloved, descendant of Saint Louis, King of France and of all her dominions beyond the seas, hung breathless upon those well-rouged lips, whilst France sat silent and listened, eager for a share of that smile which enslaved a King and ruined a nation.

"Let us have that rigid rule of arithmetic, fair one," said Louis gaily, "by which you can demonstrate to us that M. le Chevalier here is a hundred thousand times more mad than any of his accursed countrymen."

"Nay, sire, 'tis simple enough," rejoined the lady. "M. le Chevalier hath need of a hundred thousand others in order to make his insanity complete, a hundred thousand Englishmen as mad as April fishes, to help him conquer a kingdom of rain and fogs. Therefore I say he is a hundred thousand times more mad than most!"

Loud laughter greeted this sally. Mme. la Marquise de Pompadour, so little while ago simply Jeanne Poisson or Mme. d'Étioles, was not yet blasée to so much adulation and such fulsome flattery; she looked a veritable heaven of angelic smiles; her eyes blue—so her dithyrambic chroniclers aver—as the dark-toned myosotis, wandered from face to face along the length of that gorgeously spread supper table, round which was congregated the flower of the old aristocracy of France.

She gleaned an admiring glance here, an unspoken murmur of flattery there, even the women—and there were many—tried to look approvingly at her who ruled the King and France. One face alone remained inscrutable and almost severe, the face of a woman—a mere girl—with straight brow and low, square forehead, crowned with a wealth of soft brown hair, the rich tones of which peeped daringly through the conventional mist of powder.

Mme. de Pompadour's sunny smile disappeared momentarily when her eyes rested on this girl's face; a frown—oh! hardly that; but a shadow, shall we say?—marred the perfect purity of her brow. The next moment she had yielded her much-beringed hand to her royal worshipper's eager grasp and he was pressing a kiss on each rose-tipped finger, whilst she shrugged her pretty shoulders.

"Brrr!" she said, with a mock shiver, "here is Mlle. d'Aumont frowning stern disapproval at me. Surely, Chevalier," she asked, turning to the young man beside her, "a comfortable armchair in your beautiful palace of St. Germain is worth a throne in mist-bound London?"

"Not when that throne is his by right," here interposed Mlle. d'Aumont quietly. "The palace of St. Germain is but a gift to the King of England, for which he owes gratitude to the King of France."

A quick blush now suffused the cheeks of the young man, who up to now had seemed quite unconscious of Mme. de Pompadour's sallies or of the hilarity directed against himself. He gave a rapid glance at Mlle. d'Aumont's haughty, somewhat imperious face and at the delicate mouth, round which an almost imperceptible curl of contempt seemed still to linger.

"La! Mademoiselle," rejoined the Marquise, with some acerbity, "do we not all hold gifts at the hands of the King of France?"

"We have no sovereignty of our own, Madame," replied the young girl drily.

"As for me," quoth King Louis, hastily interposing in this feminine passage of arms, "I drink to our gallant Chevalier de St. George, His Majesty King Charles Edward Stuart of England, Scotland, Wales, and of the whole of that fog-ridden kingdom. Success to your cause, Chevalier," he added, settling his fat body complacently in the cushions of his chair; and raising his glass, he nodded benignly toward the young Pretender.

"To King Charles Edward of England!" rejoined Mme. de Pompadour gaily.

And "To King Charles Edward of England!" went echoing all around the vast banqueting-hall.

"I thank you all," said the young man, whose sullen mood seemed in no way dissipated at these expressions of graciousness and friendship. "Success to my cause is assured if France will lend me the aid she promised."

"What right have you to doubt the word of France, Monseigneur?" retorted Mlle. d'Aumont earnestly.

"A truce! a truce! I entreat," here broke in King Louis with mock concern. "Par Dieu, this is a banquet and not a Council Chamber! Joy of my life," he added, turning eyes replete with admiration on the beautiful woman beside him, "do not allow politics to mar this pleasant entertainment. M. le Duc, you are our host, I pray you direct conversation into more pleasing channels."

Nothing loth, the brilliant company there present quickly resumed the irresponsible chatter which was far more to its liking than talk of thrones and doubtful causes. The flunkeys in gorgeous liveries made the round of the table, filling the crystal glasses with wine. The atmosphere was heavy with the fumes of past good cheer, and the scent of a thousand roses fading beneath the glare of innumerable wax-candles. An odour of perfume, of powder and cosmetics hovered in the air; the men's faces looked red and heated; on one or two heads the wig stood awry, whilst trembling fingers began fidgeting with the lace-cravats at the throat.

Charles Edward's restless blue eyes searched keenly and feverishly the faces around him; morose, gloomy, he was still reckoning in his mind how far he could trust these irresponsible pleasure-lovers, that descendant of the great Louis over there, fat of body and heavy of mind, lost to all sense of kingly dignity whilst squandering the nation's money on the whims and caprices of the ex-wife of a Parisian victualler, whom he had created Marquise de Pompadour.

These men who lived only for good cheer, for heady wines, games of dice and hazard, nights of debauch and illicit pleasures, what help would they be to him in the hour of need? What support in case of failure?

"What right have you to doubt the word of France?" was asked of him by one pair of proud lips—a woman's, only a girl's.

Charles Edward looked across the table at Mlle. d'Aumont. Like himself, she sat silent in the midst of the noisy throng, obviously lending a very inattentive ear to the whisperings of the handsome cavalier beside her.

Ah! if they were all like her, if she were a representative of the whole nation of France, the young adventurer would have gone to his hazardous expedition with a stauncher and a lighter heart. But, as matters stood, what could he expect? What had he got as a serious asset in this gamble for life and a throne? A few vague promises from that flabby, weak-kneed creature over there on whom the crown of Saint Louis sat so strangely and so ill; a few smiles from that frivolous and vain woman, who drained the very heart's blood of an impoverished nation to its last drop, in order to satisfy her costly whims or chase away the frowns of ennui from the brow of an effete monarch.

And what besides?

A farewell supper, ringing toasts, good wine, expensive food offered by M. le Duc d'Aumont, the Prime Minister of France—a thousand roses, now fading, which had cost a small fortune to coax into bloom; a handshake from his friends in France; a "God-speed" and "Dieu vous garde, Chevalier!" and a few words of stern encouragement from a girl.

With all that in hand, Chevalier St. George, go and conquer your kingdom beyond the sea!

CHAPTER II

THE RULERS OF FRANCE

Great activity reigned in the corridors and kitchens of the old château. M. le Chef—the only true rival the immortal Vatel ever had—in white cap and apron, calm and self-possessed as a field-marshal in the hour of victory, and surrounded by an army of scullions and wenches, was directing the operations of dishing-up—the crowning glory of his arduous labours. Pies and patties, haunches of venison, trout and carp from the Rhine were placed on gold and silver dishes and adorned with tasteful ornaments of truly architectural beauty and monumental proportions. These were then handed over to the footmen, who, resplendent in gorgeous liveries of scarlet and azure, hurried along the marble passages carrying the masterpieces of culinary art to the banqueting-hall beyond, whilst the butlers, more sedate and dignified in sober garb of puce or brown, stalked along in stately repose bearing the huge tankards and crystal jugs.

All of the best that the fine old Château d'Aumont could provide was being requisitioned to-night, since M. le Duc and Mlle. Lydie, his daughter, were giving a farewell banquet to Charles Edward Stuart by the grace of God—if not by the will of the people—King of Great Britain and Ireland and all her dependencies beyond the seas.

For him speeches were made, toasts drunk and glasses raised; for him the ducal veneries had been ransacked, the ducal cellars shorn of their most ancient possessions; for him M. le Chef had raged and stormed for five hours, had expended the sweat of his brow and the intricacies of his brain; for him the scullions' backs had smarted, the wenches' cheeks had glowed, all to do honour to the only rightful King of England about to quit the hospitable land

5

of France in order to conquer that island kingdom which his grandfather had lost.

But in the noble salle d'armes, on the other hand, there reigned a pompous and dignified silence, in strange contrast to the bustle and agitation of the kitchens and the noise of loud voices and laughter that issued from the banqueting hall whenever a door was opened and quickly shut again.

Here perfumed candles flickered in massive candelabra, shedding dim circles of golden light on carved woodwork, marble floor, and dull-toned tapestries. The majestic lions of D'Aumont frowned stolidly from their high pedestals on this serene abode of peace and dignity, one foot resting on the gilded shield with the elaborate coat-of-arms blazoned thereon in scarlet and azure, the other poised aloft as if in solemn benediction.

M. Joseph, own body servant to M. le Duc, in magnificent D'Aumont livery, his cravat a marvel of costly simplicity, his elegant, well-turned calves—encased in fine silk stockings—stretched lazily before him, was sprawling on the brocade-covered divan in the centre of the room.

M. Bénédict, equally resplendent in a garb of motley that recalled the heraldic colours of the Comte de Stainville, stood before him, not in an attitude of deference of course, but in one of easy friendship; whilst M. Achille—a blaze of scarlet and gold—was holding out an elegant silver snuff-box to M. Joseph, who, without any superfluous motion of his dignified person, condescended to take a pinch.

With arm and elbow held at a graceful angle, M. Joseph paused in the very act of conveying the snuff to his delicate nostrils. He seemed to think that the occasion called for a remark from himself, but evidently nothing very appropriate occurred to him for the moment, so after a few seconds of impressive silence he finally partook of the snuff, and then flicked off the grains of dust from his immaculate azure waistcoat with a lace-edged handkerchief.

"Where does your Marquis get his snuff?" he asked with an easy graciousness of manner.

"We get it direct from London," replied M. Achille sententiously. "I am personally acquainted with Mme. Véronique, who is cook to Mme. de la Beaume and the sweetheart of Jean Laurent, own body-servant to General de Puisieux. The old General is Chief of Customs at Havre, so you see we pay no duty and get the best of snuff at a ridiculous price."

"Ah! that's lucky for you, my good Eglinton," said M. Bénédict, with a sigh. "Your Marquis is a good sort, and as he is not personally acquainted with Mme. Véronique, I doubt not but he pays full price for his snuff."

"One has to live, friend Stainville," quoth Achille solemnly—"and I am not a fool!"

"Exactly so; and with an English milor your life is an easy one, Monsieur."

"Comme-ci! comme-ça!" nodded Achille deprecatingly.

"Le petit Anglais is very rich?" suggested Bénédict.

"Boundlessly so!" quoth the other, with conscious pride.

"Now, if perchance you could see your way to introducing me to Mme. Véronique. Eh? I have to pay full price for my Count's snuff, and he will have none but the best; but if I could get Mme. Véronique's protection——"

Achille's manner immediately changed at this suggestion, made with becoming diffidence; he drew back a few steps as if to emphasize the distance which must of necessity lie between supplicant and patron. He took a pinch of snuff, he blew his nose with stately deliberation—all in order to keep the petitioner waiting on tenterhooks.

Finally he drew up his scarlet and gold shoulders until they almost touched his ears.

"It will be difficult, very, very difficult my good Stainville," he said at last, speaking in measured tones. "You see, Mme. Véronique is in a very delicate position; she has a great deal of influence of course, and it is not easy to obtain her protection. Still, I will see what I can do, and you can place your petition before her."

"Do not worry yourself, my good Eglinton," here interposed M. Bénédict with becoming hauteur. "I thought as you had asked me yesterday to use my influence with our Mlle. Mariette, the fiancée of Colonel Jauffroy's third footman, with regard to your nephew's advancement in his regiment, that perhaps—— But no matter—no matter!" he added, with a deprecatory wave of the hand.

"You completely misunderstood me, my dear Stainville," broke in M. Achille, eagerly. "I said that the matter was difficult; I did not say that it was impossible. Mme. Véronique is beset with petitions, but you may rely on my friendship. I will obtain the necessary introduction for you if you, on the other hand, will bear my nephew's interests in mind."

"Say no more about it, my good Eglinton," said Bénédict, with easy condescension; "your nephew will get his promotion on the word of a Stainville."

Peace and amity being once more restored between the two friends, M. Joseph thought that he had now remained silent far longer than was compatible with his own importance.

"It is very difficult, of course, in our position," he said pompously, "to do justice to the many demands which are made on our influence and patronage. Take my own case, for instance—my Duke leaves all appointments in my hands. In the morning, whilst I shave him, I have but to mention a name to him in connection with any post under Government that happens to be vacant, and immediately the favoured one, thus named by me, receives attention, nearly always followed by a nomination."

"Hem! hem!" came very discreetly from the lips of M. Bénédict.

"You said?" queried Joseph, with a slight lifting of the right eyebrow.

"Oh! nothing—nothing! I pray you continue; the matter is vastly entertaining."

"At the present moment," continued M. Joseph, keeping a suspicious eye on the other man, "I am deeply worried by this proposal which comes from the Parliaments of Rennes and Paris."

"A new Ministry of Finance to be formed," quoth M. Achille. "We know all about it."

"With direct control of the nation's money and responsible to the Parliaments alone," assented Joseph. "The Parliaments! Bah!" he added in tones of supreme contempt, "bourgeois the lot of them!"

"Their demands are preposterous, so says my milor. 'Tis a marvel His Majesty has given his consent."

"I have advised my Duke not to listen to the rabble," said Joseph, as he readjusted the set of his cravat. "A Ministry responsible to the Parliaments! Ridiculous, I say!"

"I understand, though," here interposed M. Achille, "that the Parliaments, out of deference for His Majesty are willing that the King himself shall appoint this new Comptroller of Finance."

"The King, my good Eglinton," calmly retorted M. Joseph— "the King will leave this matter to us. You may take it from me that we shall appoint this new Minister, and an extremely pleasant post it will be. Comptroller of Finance! All the taxes to pass through the Minister's hands! Par Dieu! does it not open out a wide field for an ambitious man?"

"Hem! hem!" coughed M. Bénédict again.

"You seem to be suffering from a cold, sir," said M. Joseph irritably.

"Not in the least," rejoined Bénédict hastily—"a slight tickling in the throat. You were saying, M. Joseph, that you hoped this new appointment would fall within your sphere of influence."

"Nay! If you doubt me, my good Stainville——" And M. Joseph

rose with slow and solemn majesty from the divan, where he had been reclining, and walking across the room with a measured step, he reached an escritoire whereon ink and pens, letters tied up in bundles, loose papers, and all the usual paraphernalia commonly found on the desk of a busy man. M. Joseph sat down at the table and rang a handbell.

The next moment a young footman entered, silent and deferential.

"Is any one in the ante-room, Paul?" asked Joseph.

"Yes, M. Joseph."

"How many?"

"About thirty persons."

"Go tell them, then, that M. Joseph is not receiving to-night. He is entertaining a circle of friends. Bring me all written petitions. I shall be visible in my dressing room to those who have a personal introduction at eleven o'clock to-morrow. You may go!"

Silently as he had entered, the young man bowed and withdrew.

M. Joseph wheeled round in his chair and turned to his friends with a look of becoming triumph.

"Thirty persons!" he remarked simply.

"All after this appointment?" queried Achille.

"Their representatives, you see," explained M. Joseph airily. "Oh! my ante-chamber is always full—You understand? I shave my Duke every morning; and every one, it seems to me, is wanting to control the finances of France."

"Might one inquire who is your special protégé?" asked the other.

"Time will show," came with cryptic vagueness from the lips of M. Joseph.

"Hem! hem!"

In addition to a slight tickling of the throat, M. Bénédict seemed to be suffering from an affection of the left eye which caused him to wink with somewhat persistent emphasis:

"This is the third time you have made that remark, Stainville," said Joseph severely.

"I did not remark, my dear D'Aumont," rejoined Bénédict pleasantly—"that is, I merely said 'Hem! hem!'"

"Even so, I heard you," said Joseph, with some acerbity; "and I would wish to know precisely what you meant when you said 'Hem! hem!' like that."

"I was thinking of Mlle. Lucienne," said Bénédict, with a sentimental sigh.

"Indeed!"

"Yes! I am one of her sweethearts—the fourth in point of favour. Mlle. Lucienne has your young lady's ear, my good D'Aumont, and we all know that your Duke governs the whole of France exactly as his daughter wishes him to do."

"And you hope through Mlle. Lucienne's influence to obtain the new post of Comptroller for your own Count?" asked M. Joseph, with assumed carelessness, as he drummed a devil's tattoo on the table before him.

A slight expression of fatuity crept into the countenance of M. Bénédict. He did not wish to irritate the great man; at the same time he felt confident in his own powers of blandishments where Mlle. Lucienne was concerned, even though he only stood fourth in point of favour in that influential lady's heart.

"Mlle. Lucienne has promised us her support," he said, with a complacent smile.

"I fear me that will be of little avail," here interposed M. Achille. "We have on our side, the influence of Mme. Auguste Baillon, who is housekeeper to M. le Docteur Dubois, consulting physician to Mlle. d'Aumont. M. le Docteur is very fond of haricots cooked in lard—a dish in the preparation of which Mme. Baillon excels—whilst, on the other hand, that lady's son is perruquier to my Eglinton. I think there is no doubt that ours is the stronger influence, and that if this Ministry of Finance comes into being, we shall be the Chief Comptroller."

"Oh, it will come into being, without any doubt," said Bénédict. "I have it from my cousin François, who is one of the sweethearts of Mlle. Duprez, confidential maid to Mme. Aremberg, the jeweller's wife, that the merchants of Paris and Lyons are not at all pleased with the amount of money which the King and Mme. de Pompadour are spending."

"Exactly! People of that sort are a veritable pestilence. They want us to pay some of the taxes—the corvée or the taille. As if a Duke or a Minister is going to pay taxes! Ridiculous!"

"Ridiculous, I say," assented Achille, "though my Marquis says that in England even noblemen pay taxes."

"Then we'll not go to England, friend Eglinton. Imagine shaving a Duke or a Marquis who had paid taxes like a shopkeeper!"

A chorus of indignation from the three gentleman rose at the suggestion.

"Preposterous indeed!"

"We all know that England is a nation of shopkeepers. M. de Voltaire, who has been there, said so to us on his return."

M. Achille, in view of the fact that he represented the Marquis of Eglinton, commonly styled "le petit Anglais," was not quite sure

10

whether his dignity demanded that he should resent this remark of M. de Voltaire's or not.

Fortunately he was saved from having to decide this delicate question immediately by the reëntry of Paul into the room.

The young footman was carrying a bundle of papers, which he respectfully presented to M. Joseph on a silver tray. The great man looked at Paul somewhat puzzled, rubbed his chin, and contemplated the papers with a thoughtful eye.

"What are these?" he asked.

"The petitions, M. Joseph," replied the young man.

"Oh! Ah, yes!" quoth the other airily. "Quite so; but—I have no time to read them now. You may glance through them, Paul, and let me know if any are worthy of my consideration."

M. Joseph was born in an epoch when reading was not considered an indispensable factor in a gentleman's education. Whether the petitions of the thirty aspirants to the new post of Comptroller of Finance would subsequently be read by M. Paul or not it were impossible to say; for the present he merely took up the papers again, saying quite respectfully:

"Yes, M. Joseph."

"Stay! you may take cards, dice, and two flagons of Bordeaux into my boudoir."

"Yes, M. Joseph."

"Have you dismissed every one from the ante-chamber?"

"All except an old man, who refuses to go."

"Who is he?"

"I do not know; he——"

Further explanation was interrupted by a timid voice issuing from the open door.

"I only desire five minutes' conversation with M. le Duc d'Aumont."

And a wizened little figure dressed in seedy black, with lean shanks encased in coarse woollen stockings, shuffled into the room. He seemed to be carrying a great number of papers and books under both arms, and as he stepped timidly forward some of these tumbled in a heap at his feet.

"Only five minutes' conversation with M. le Duc."

His eyes were very pale, and very watery, and his hair was of a pale straw colour. He stooped to pick up his papers, and dropped others in the process.

"M. le Duc is not visible," said M. Joseph majestically.

"Perhaps a little later——" suggested the lean individual.

"The Duke will not be visible later either."

"Then to-morrow perhaps; I can wait—I have plenty of time on my hands."

"You may have, but the Duke hasn't."

In the meanwhile the wizened little man had succeeded in once more collecting his papers together. With trembling eager hands he now selected a folded note, which evidently had suffered somewhat through frequent falls on dusty floors; this he held out toward M. Joseph.

"I have a letter to Monsieur le valet de chambre of the Duke," he said humbly.

"A letter of introduction?—to me?" queried Joseph, with a distinct change in his manner and tone. "From whom?"

"My daughter Agathe, who brings Monsieur's chocolate in to him every morning."

"Ah, you are Mlle. Agathe's father!" exclaimed Joseph with pleasant condescension, as he took the letter of introduction, and, without glancing at it, slipped it into the pocket of his magnificent coat. Perhaps a thought subsequently crossed his mind that the timorous person before him was not quite so simple-minded as his watery blue eyes suggested, and that the dusty and crumpled little note might be a daring fraud practised on his own influential personality, for he added with stern emphasis: "I will see Mlle. Agathe to-morrow, and will discuss your affair with her."

Then, as the little man did not wince under the suggestion, M. Joseph said more urbanely:

"By the way, what is your affair? These gentlemen"—and with a graceful gesture he indicated his two friends—"these gentlemen will pardon the liberty you are taking in discussing it before them."

"Thank you, Monsieur; thank you, gentlemen," said the wizened individual humbly; "it is a matter of—er—figures."

"Figures!"

"Yes! This new Ministry of Finance—there will be an auditor of accounts wanted—several auditors, I presume—and—and I thought——"

"Yes?" nodded M. Joseph graciously.

"My daughter does bring you in your chocolate nice and hot, M. Joseph, does she not?—and—and I do know a lot about figures. I studied mathematics with the late M. Descartes; I audited the books of the Société des Comptables of Lyons for several years; and—and I have diplomas and testimonials——"

And, carried away by another wave of anxiety, he began to fumble among his papers and books, which with irritating perversity immediately tumbled pell-mell on to the floor.

"What in the devil's name is the good of testimonials and

diplomas to us, my good man?" said M. Joseph haughtily. "If, on giving the matter my serious consideration, I come to the conclusion that you will be a suitable accountant in the new Ministerial Department, ma foi! my good man, your affair is settled. No thanks, I pray!" he added, with a gracious flourish of the arm; "I have been pleased with Mlle. Agathe, and I may mention your name whilst I shave M. le Duc to-morrow. Er—by the way, what is your name?"

"Durand, if you please, M. Joseph."

The meagre little person with the watery blue eyes tried to express his gratitude by word and gesture, but his books and papers encumbered his movements, and he was rendered doubly nervous by the presence of these gorgeous and stately gentlemen, and by the wave of voices and laughter which suddenly rose from the distance, suggesting that perhaps a brilliant company might be coming this way.

The very thought seemed to completely terrify him; with both arms he hugged his various written treasures, and with many sideway bows and murmurs of thanks he finally succeeded in shuffling his lean figure out of the room, closely followed by M. Paul.

CHAPTER III

POMPADOUR'S CHOICE

M. Durand's retreat had fortunately occurred just in time; men's voices and women's laughter sounded more and more distinct, as if approaching toward the salle d'armes.

In a moment, with the swiftness born of long usage, the demeanour of the three gentlemen underwent a quick and sudden change. They seemed to pull their gorgeous figures together; with practised fingers each readjusted the lace of his cravat, reëstablished the correct set of his waistcoat, and flickered the last grain of dust or snuff from the satin-like surface of his coat.

Ten seconds later the great doors at the east end of the hall were thrown open, and through the embrasure and beyond the intervening marble corridor could be seen the brilliantly lighted supper-room, with its glittering company broken up into groups.

Silent, swift and deferential, MM. Joseph, Bénédict, and Achille glided on flat-heeled shoes along the slippery floors, making as little noise as possible, effacing their gorgeous persons in window recesses or carved ornaments whenever a knot of gentlemen or ladies happened to pass by.

Quite a different trio now, MM. Joseph, Bénédict, and Achille—just three automatons intent on their duties.

From the supper-room there came an incessant buzz of talk and laughter. M. Joseph sought his master's eye, but M. le Duc was busy with the King of England and wanted no service; M. Achille found his English milor, "le petit Anglais," engaged in conversation with his portly and somewhat overdressed mamma; whilst M. Bénédict's master was nowhere to be found.

The older ladies were beginning to look wearied and hot, smothering yawns behind their painted fans. Paniers assumed a tired and crumpled appearance, and feathered aigrettes nodded dismally above the high coiffures.

Not a few of the guests had taken the opportunity of bringing cards or dice from a silken pocket, whilst others in smaller groups, younger and not yet wearied of desultory talk, strolled toward the salle d'armes or the smaller boudoirs which opened out of the corridor.

One or two gentlemen had succumbed to M. le Duc's lavish hospitality; the many toasts had proved too exacting, the copious draughts altogether too heady, and they had, somewhat involuntarily, exchanged their chairs for the more reliable solidity of the floor, where their faithful attendants, stationed under the table for the purpose, deftly untied a cravat which might be too tight or administered such cooling antidotes as might be desirable.

The hot air vibrated with the constant babel of voices, the frou-frou of silk paniers, and brocaded skirts, mingled with the clink of swords and the rattle of dice in satinwood boxes.

The atmosphere, surcharged with perfumes, had become overpoweringly close.

His Majesty, flushed with wine, and with drowsy lids drooping over his dulled eyes, had pushed his chair away from the table and was lounging lazily toward Mme. de Pompadour, his idle fingers toying with the jewelled girdle of her fan. She amused him; she had quaint sayings which were sometimes witty, always daring, but which succeeded in dissipating momentarily that mortal ennui of which he suffered.

Even now her whispered conversation, interspersed with

profuse giggles, brought an occasional smile to the lips of the sleepy monarch. She chatted and laughed, flirting her fan, humouring the effeminate creature beside her by yielding her hand and wrist to his flabby kisses. But her eyes did not rest on him for many seconds at a time; she talked to Louis, but her mind had gone a-wandering about the room trying to read thoughts, to search motives or divine hidden hatreds and envy as they concerned herself.

This glitter was still new to her; the power which she wielded seemed as yet a brittle toy which a hasty movement might suddenly break. It was but a very little while ago that she had been an insignificant unit in a third-rate social circle of Paris—always beautiful, but lost in the midst of a drabby crowd, her charms, like those of a precious stone, unperceived for want of proper setting. Her ambition was smothered in her heart, which at times it almost threatened to consume. But it was always there, ever since she had learnt to understand the power which beauty gives.

An approving smile from the King of France, and the world wore a different aspect for Jeanne Poisson. Her whims and caprices became the reins with which she drove France and the King. Why place a limit to her own desires, since the mightiest monarch in Europe was ready to gratify them?

Money became her god.

Spend! spend! spend! Why not? The nation, the bourgeoisie—of which she had once been that little insignificant unit—was now the well-spring whence she drew the means of satisfying her ever-increasing lust for splendour.

Jewels, dresses, palaces, gardens—all and everything that was rich, beautiful, costly, she longed for it all!

Pictures and statuary; music, and of the best; constant noise around her, gaiety, festivities, laughter; the wit of France and the science of the world all had been her helpmeets these past two years in this wild chase after pleasure, this constant desire to kill her Royal patron's incurable ennui.

Two years, and already the nation grumbled! A check was to be put on her extravagance—hers and that of King Louis! The parliaments demanded that some control be exercised over Royal munificence. Fewer jewels for Madame! And that palace at Fontainebleau not yet completed, the Parc aux Cerfs so magnificently planned and not even begun! Would the new Comptroller put a check on that?

At first she marvelled that Louis should consent. It was a humiliation for him as well as for her. The weakness in him which had served her own ends seemed monstrous when it yielded to pressure from others.

He had assured her that she should not suffer; jewels, palaces, gardens, she should have all as heretofore. Let Parliament insist and grumble, but the Comptroller would be appointed by D'Aumont, and D'Aumont was her slave.

D'Aumont, yes! but not his daughter—that arrogant girl with the severe eyes, unwomanly and dictatorial, who ruled her father just as she herself, Pompadour, ruled the King.

An enemy, that Lydie d'Aumont! Mme. la Marquise, whilst framing a witticism at which the King smiled, frowned because in a distant alcove she spied the haughty figure of Lydie.

And there were others! The friends of the Queen and her clique, of course; they were not here to-night; at least not in great numbers; still, even the present brilliant company, though smiling and obsequious in the presence of the King, was not by any means a close phalanx of friends.

M. d'Argenson, for instance—he was an avowed enemy; and Marshal de Noailles, too—oh! and there were others.

One of them, fortunately, was going away; Charles Edward Stuart, aspiring King of England; he had been no friend of Pompadour. Even now, as he stood close by, lending an obviously inattentive ear to M. le Duc d'Aumont, she could see that he still looked gloomy and out of humour, and that whenever his eyes rested upon her and the King he frowned with wrathful impatience.

"You are distraite, ma mie!" said Louis, with a yawn.

"I was thinking, sire," she replied, smiling into his drowsy eyes.

"For God's sake, I entreat, do not think!" exclaimed the King, with mock alarm. "Thought produces wrinkles, and your perfect mouth was only fashioned for smiles."

"May I frame a suggestion?" she queried archly.

"No, only a command."

"This Comptroller of Finance, your future master, Louis, and mine——"

"Your slave," he interrupted lazily, "and he values his life."

"Why not milor Eglinton?"

"Le petit Anglais?" and Louis's fat body was shaken with sudden immoderate laughter. "Par Dieu, ma mie! Of all your witty sallies this one hath pleased us most."

"Why?" she asked seriously.

"Le petit Anglais!" again laughed the King. "I'd as soon give the appointment to your lapdog, Marquise. Fido would have as much capacity for the post as the ornamental cypher that hangs on his mother's skirts."

"Milor Eglinton is very rich," she mused.

16

"Inordinately so, curse him! I could do with half his revenue and be a satisfied man."

"Being a cypher he would not trouble us much; being very rich he would need no bribe for doing as we wish."

"His lady mother would trouble us, ma mie."

"Bah! we would find him a wife."

"Nay! I entreat you do not worry your dainty head with these matters," said the King, somewhat irritably. "The appointment rests with D'Aumont; an you desire the post for your protégé, turn your bright eyes on the Duke."

Pompadour would have wished to pursue the subject, to get something of a promise from Louis, to turn his inveterate weakness then and there to her own account, but Louis the Well-beloved yawned, a calamity which the fair lady dared not risk again. Witty and brilliant, forever gay and unfatigued, she knew that her power over the monarch would only last whilst she could amuse him.

Therefore now with swift transition she turned the conversation to more piquant channels. An anecdote at the expense of the old Duchesse de Pontchartrain brought life once more into the eyes of the King. She was once more untiring in her efforts, her cheeks glowed even through the powder and the rouge, her lips smiled without intermission, but her thoughts drifted back to the root idea, the burden of that control to be imposed on her caprices.

She would not have minded Milor Eglinton, the courteous, amiable gentleman, who had no will save that expressed by any woman who happened to catch his ear. She felt that she could, with but very little trouble, twist him round her little finger. His dictatorial mamma would either have to be got out of the way, or won over to Mme. la Marquise's own views of life, whilst Milor could remain a bachelor, lest another feminine influence prove antagonistic.

Pompadour's bright eyes, whilst she chatted to the King, sought amidst the glittering throng the slim figure of "le petit Anglais."

Yes, he would suit her purpose admirably! She could see his handsome profile clearly outlined against the delicate tones of the wall; handsome, yes! clear-cut and firm, with straight nose and the low, square brow of the Anglo-Saxon race, but obviously weak and yielding; a perfect tool in the hands of a clever woman.

Elegant too, always immaculately, nay daintily dressed, he wore with that somewhat stiff grace peculiar to the English gentleman the showy and effeminate costume of the time. But there was weakness expressed in his very attitude as he stood now talking to Charles Edward Stuart: the kindly, pleasant expression of his

17

good-looking face in strange contrast to the glowering moodiness of his princely friend.

One Lord Eglinton had followed the deposed James II into exile. His son had risked life and fortune for the restoration of the old Pretender, and having managed by sheer good luck to save both, he felt that he had done more than enough for a cause which he knew was doomed to disaster. But he hated the thought of a German monarch in England, and in his turn preferred exile to serving a foreigner for whom he had scant sympathy.

Immensely wealthy, a brilliant conversationalist, a perfect gentleman, he soon won the heart of one of the daughters of France. Mlle. de Maille brought him, in addition to her own elaborate trousseau and a dowry of three thousand francs yearly pin-money, the historic and gorgeous chateau of Beaufort which Lord Eglinton's fortune rescued from the hands of the bailiffs.

Vaguely he thought that some day he would return to his own ancestral home in Sussex, when England would have become English once again; in the meanwhile he was content to drift on the placid waters of life, his luxurious craft guided by the domineering hand of his wife. Independent owing to his nationality and his wealth, a friend alike of the King of France and the Stuart Pretender, he neither took up arms in any cause, nor sides in any political intrigue.

Lady Eglinton brought up her son in affluence and luxury, but detached from all partisanship. Her strong personality imposed something of her own national characteristics on the boy, but she could not break the friendship that existed between the royal Stuarts and her husband's family. Although Charles Edward was her son's playmate in the gardens and castle of Beaufort, she nevertheless succeeded in instilling into the latter a slight measure of disdain for the hazardous attempts at snatching the English crown which invariably resulted in the betrayal of friends, the wholesale slaughter of adherents, and the ignominious flight of the Pretender.

No doubt it was this dual nationality in the present Lord Eglinton, this detachment from political conflicts, that was the real cause of that inherent weakness of character which Mme. de Pompadour now wished to use for her own ends. She was glad, therefore, to note that whilst Charles Edward talked earnestly to him, the eyes of "le petit Anglais" roamed restlessly about the room, as if seeking for support in an argument, or help from a personality stronger than his own.

Lady Eglinton's voice, harsh and domineering, often rose

above the general hum of talk. Just now she had succeeded in engaging the Prime Minister in serious conversation.

The King in the meanwhile had quietly dropped asleep, lulled by the even ripple of talk of the beautiful Marquise and the heavily scented atmosphere of the room. Pompadour rose from her chair as noiselessly as her stiff brocaded skirt would allow; she crossed the room and joined Lady Eglinton and M. le Duc d'Aumont.

She was going to take King Louis's advice and add the weighty influence of her own bright eyes to that of my lady's voluble talk in favour of the appointment of Lord Eglinton to the newly created Ministry of Finance.

CHAPTER IV

A WOMAN'S SURRENDER

In a small alcove, which was raised above the level of the rest of the floor by a couple of steps and divided from the main banqueting hall by a heavy damask curtain now partially drawn aside, Mlle. d'Aumont sat in close conversation with M. le Comte de Stainville.

From this secluded spot these two dominated the entire length and breadth of the room; the dazzling scene was displayed before them in a gorgeous kaleidoscope of moving figures, in an ever-developing panorama of vividly coloured groups, that came and went, divided and reunited; now forming soft harmonies of delicate tones that suggested the subtle blending on the palette of a master, anon throwing on to the canvas daring patches of rich magentas or deep purples, that set off with cunning artfulness the masses of pale primrose and gold.

Gaston de Stainville, however, did not seem impressed with the picturesqueness of the scene. He sat with his broad back turned toward the brilliant company, one elbow propped on a small table beside him, his hand shielding his face against the glare of the candles. But Lydie d'Aumont's searching eyes roamed ceaselessly over the gaily plumaged birds that fluttered uninterruptedly before her gaze.

With one delicate hand holding back the rich damask curtain, the other lying idly in her lap, her white brocaded gown standing out in stiff folds round her girlish figure, she was a picture well worth looking at.

Lydie was scarcely twenty-one then, but already there was a certain something in the poise of her head, in every movement of her graceful body, that suggested the woman accustomed to dominate, the woman of thought and action, rather than of sentiment and tender emotions.

Those of her own sex said at that time that in Lydie's haughty eyes there was the look of the girl who has been deprived early in life of a mother's gentle influence, and who has never felt the gentle yet firm curb of a mother's authority on her childish whims and caprices.

M. le Duc d'Aumont, who had lost his young wife after five years of an exceptionally happy married life, had lavished all the affection of his mature years on the girl, who was the sole representative of his name. The child had always been headstrong and self-willed from the cradle; her nurses could not cope with her babyish tempers; her governesses dreaded her domineering ways. M. le Duc was deaf to all complaints; he would not have the child thwarted, and as she grew up lovable in the main, she found her father's subordinates ready enough to bend to her yoke.

From the age of ten she had been the acknowledged queen of all her playmates, and the autocrat of her father's house. Little by little she obtained an extraordinary ascendancy over the fond parent, who admired almost as much as he loved her.

He was deeply touched when, scarce out of the school room, she tried to help him in the composition of his letters, and more than astonished to see how quick was her intelligence and how sharp her intuition. Instinctively, at first he took to explaining to her the various political questions of the day, listening with paternal good-humour, to her acute and sensitive remarks on several important questions.

Then gradually his confidence in her widened. Many chroniclers aver that it was Lydie d'Aumont who wrote her father's celebrated memoirs, and those who at that time had the privilege of knowing her intimately could easily trace her influence in most of her father's political moves. There is no doubt that the Duc himself, when he finally became Prime Minister of France, did very little without consulting his daughter, and even l'Abbé d'Alivet, in his "Chroniques de Louis XV," admits that the hot partisanship of France for the Young Pretender's ill-conceived expeditions was mainly due to Mlle. d'Aumont's influence.

When Vanloo painted her a little later on, he rendered with

consummate and delicate skill the haughty look of command which many of Lydie's most ardent admirers felt to be a blemish on the exquisite purity and charm of her face.

The artist, too, emphasized the depth and earnestness of her dark eyes, and that somewhat too severe and self-reliant expression which marked the straight young brow.

Perhaps it was this same masterful trait in the dainty form before him that Gaston de Stainville studied so attentively just now; there had been silence for some time between the elegant cavalier and the idolized daughter of the Prime Minister of France. She seemed restless and anxious, even absent-minded, when he spoke. She was studying the various groups of men and women as they passed, frowning when she looked on some faces, smiling abstractedly when she encountered a pair of friendly eyes.

"I did not know that you were such a partisan of that young adventurer," said Gaston de Stainville at last, as if in answer to her thoughts, noting that her gaze now rested with stern intentness on Charles Edward Stuart.

"I must be on the side of a just cause," she rejoined quietly, as with a very characteristic movement of hers she turned her head slowly round and looked M. de Stainville full in the face.

She could not see him very well, for his head was silhouetted against the dazzling light beyond, and she frowned a little as she tried to distinguish his features more clearly in the shadow.

"You do believe, Gaston, that his cause is just?" she asked earnestly.

"Oh!" he replied lightly; "I'll believe in the justice of any cause to which you give your support."

She shrugged her shoulders, whilst a slightly contemptuous curl appeared at the corner of her mouth.

"How like a man!" she said impatiently.

"What is like a man?" he retorted. "To love—as I love you?"

He had whispered this, hardly above his breath lest he should be overheard by some one in that gay and giddy throng who passed laughingly by. The stern expression in her eyes softened a little as they met his eager gaze, but the good-humoured contempt was still apparent, even in her smile; she saw that as he spoke he looked through the outspread fingers of his hand to see if he was being watched, and noted that one pair of eyes, distant the whole length of the room, caught the movement, then was instantly averted.

"Mlle. de Saint Romans is watching you," she said quietly.

He seemed surprised and not a little vexed that she had noticed, and for a moment looked confused; then he said carelessly:

"Why should she not? Why should not the whole world look on, and see that I adore you?"

"Meseems you protest over-much, Gaston," she said, with a sigh.

"Impossible!"

"You talk of love too lightly."

"I am in earnest, Lydie. Why should you doubt? Are you not beautiful enough to satisfy any man's ardour?"

"Am I not influential enough, you mean," she said, with a slight tremor in her rich young voice, "to satisfy any man's ambition?"

"Is ambition a crime in your eyes, Lydie?"

"No; but——"

"I am ambitious; you cannot condemn me for that," he said, now speaking in more impressive tone. "When we were playmates together, years ago, you remember? in the gardens at Cluny, if other lads were there, was I not always eager to be first in the race, first in the field—first always, everywhere?"

"Even at the cost of sorrow and humiliation to the weaker ones."

He shrugged his shoulders with easy unconcern.

"There is no success in life for the strong," he said, "save at the cost of sorrow and humiliation for the weak. Lydie," he added more earnestly, "if I am ambitious it is because my love for you has made me humble. I do not feel that as I am, I am worthy of you; I want to be rich, to be influential, to be great. Is that wrong? I want your pride in me, almost as much as your love."

"You were rich once, Gaston," she said, a little coldly. "Your father was rich."

"Is it my fault if I am poor now?"

"They tell me it is; they say that you are over-fond of cards, and of other pleasures which are less avowable."

"And you believe them?"

"I hardly know," she whispered.

"You have ceased to love me, then?"

"Gaston!"

There as a tone of tender reproach there, which the young man was swift enough to note; the beautiful face before him was in full light; he could see well that a rosy blush had chased away the usual matt pallor of her cheeks, and that the full red lips trembled a little now, whilst the severe expression of the eyes was veiled in delicate moisture.

"Your face has betrayed you, Lydie!" he said, with sudden vehemence, though his voice even now hardly rose above a whisper.

"If you have not forgotten your promises made to me at Cluny—in the shadow of those beech trees, do you remember? You were only thirteen—a mere child—yet already a woman, the soft breath of spring fanned your glowing cheeks, your loose hair blew about your face, framing your proud little head in a halo of gold—you remember, Lydie?"

"I have not forgotten," she said gently.

"Your hand was in mine—a child's hand, Lydie, but yours for all that—and you promised—you remember? And if you have not forgotten—if you do love me, not, Heaven help me! as I love you, but only just a little better than any one else in the world; well, then, Lydie, why these bickerings, why these reproaches? I am poor now, but soon I will be rich! I have no power, but soon I will rule France, with you to help me if you will!"

He had grown more and more vehement as he spoke, carried along by the torrent of his own eloquence. But he had not moved; he still sat with his back to the company, and his face shaded by his hand; his voice was still low, impressive in its ardour. Then, as the young girl's graceful head drooped beneath the passionate expression of his gaze, bending, as it were, to the intensity of his earnest will, his eyes flashed a look of triumph, a premonition of victory close at hand. Lydie's strong personality was momentarily weakened by the fatigue of a long and arduous evening, by the heavy atmosphere of the room; her senses were dulled by the penetrating odours of wine and perfumes which fought with those of cosmetics.

She seemed to be yielding to the softer emotions, less watchful of her own dignity, less jealous of her own power. The young man felt that at this moment he held her just as he wished; did he stretch out his hand she would place hers in it. The recollections of her childhood had smothered all thoughts of present conflicts and of political intrigues. Mlle. d'Aumont, the influential daughter of an all-powerful Minister, had momentarily disappeared, giving way to madcap little Lydie, with short skirts and flying chestnut curls, the comrade of the handsome boy in the old gardens at Cluny.

"Lydie, if you loved me!" whispered Stainville.

"If I loved you!" and there was a world of pathos in that girlish "if."

"You would help me instead of reproaching."

"What do you want me to do, Gaston?"

"Your word is law with your father," he said persuasively. "He denies you nothing. You said I was ambitious; one word from you— this new Ministry——"

He realized his danger, bit his lip lest he had been too precipitate. Lydie was headstrong, she was also very shrewd; the master-mind that guided the destinies of France through the weak indulgence of a father was not likely to be caught in a snare like any love-sick maid. Her woman's instinct—he knew that—was keen to detect self-interest; and if he aroused the suspicions of the wealthy and influential woman before he had wholly subjugated her heart, he knew that he would lose the biggest stake of his life.

Lately she had held aloof from him, the playmates had become somewhat estranged; the echoes of his reckless life must, he thought, have reached her ears, and he himself had not been over-eager for the companionship of this woman, who seemed to have thrown off all the light-heartedness of her sex for the sake of a life of activity and domination.

She was known to be cold and unapproachable, rigidly conscientious in transacting the business of the State, which her father with easy carelessness gradually left on her young shoulders, since she seemed to find pleasure in it.

But her influence, of which she was fully conscious, had rendered her suspicious. Even now, when the call of her youth, of her beauty, of the happy and tender recollections of her childhood loudly demanded to be heard, she cast a swift, inquiring glance at Gaston.

He caught the glance, and, with an involuntary movement of impatience, his hand, which up to now had so carefully masked the expression of his face, came crashing down upon the table.

"Lydie," he said impetuously, "in the name of God throw aside your armour for one moment! Is life so long that you can afford to waste it? Have you learned the secret of perpetual youth that you deliberately fritter away its golden moments in order to rush after the Dead Sea fruit of domination and power? Lydie!" he whispered with passionate tenderness; "my little Lydie of the crisp chestnut hair, of the fragrant woods around Cluny, leave those giddy heights of ambition; come down to earth, where my arms await you! I will tell you of things, my little Lydie, which are far more beautiful, far more desirable, than the sceptre and kingdom of France; and when I press you close to my heart you will taste a joy far sweeter than that which a crown of glory can give. Will you not listen to me, Lydie? Will you not share with me that joy which renders men the equal of God?"

His hand had wandered up the damask curtain, gently drawing its heavy folds from out her clinging fingers. The rich brocade fell behind him with a soft and lingering sound like the murmured "Hush—sh—sh!" of angels' wings shutting out the noise and glare beyond, isolating them both from the world and its conflicts, its passions, and its ceaseless strife.

Secure from prying eyes, Gaston de Stainville threw all reserve from him with a laugh of pride and of joy. Half kneeling, wholly leaning toward her, his arms encircled her young figure, almost pathetic now in its sudden and complete abandonment. With his right hand he drew that imperious little head down until his lips had reached her ear.

"Would you have me otherwise, my beautiful proud queen?" he whispered softly. "Should I be worthy of the cleverest woman in France if my ambition and hopes were not at least as great as hers? Lydie," he added, looking straight into her eyes, "if you asked me for a kingdom in the moon, I swear to God that I would make a start in order to conquer it for you! Did you, from sheer caprice, ask to see my life's blood ebbing out of my body, I would thrust this dagger without hesitation into my heart."

"Hush! hush!" she said earnestly; "that is extravagant talk, Gaston. Do not desecrate love by such folly."

"'Tis not folly, Lydie. Give me your lips and you, too, will understand."

She closed her eyes. It was so strange to feel this great gladness in her heart, this abasement of all her being; she, who had so loved to dictate and to rule, she savoured the inexpressible delight of yielding.

He demanded a kiss and she gave it because he had asked it of her, shyly wondering in her own mind how she came to submit so easily, and why submission should be so sweet.

Up to now she had only tasted the delights of power; now she felt that if Gaston willed she would deem it joy to obey. There was infinite happiness, infinite peace in that kiss, the first her vestal lips had ever granted to any man. He was again whispering to her now with that same eager impetuosity which had subjugated her. She was glad to listen, for he talked much of his love, of the beautiful days at Cluny, which she had feared that he had wholly forgotten.

It was sweet to think that he remembered them. During the past year or two when evil tongues spoke of him before her, of his recklessness, his dissipations, his servility to the growing influence of the Pompadour, she had not altogether believed, but her heart, faithful to the child-lover, had ached and rebelled against his growing neglect.

Now he was whispering explanations—not excuses, for he needed none, since he had always loved her and only jealousies and intrigues had kept him from her side. As he protested, she still did not altogether believe—oh, the folly of it all! the mad, glad folly!— but he said that with a kiss she would understand.

He was right. She did understand.

25

And he talked much of his ambitions. Was it not natural? Men were so different to women! He, proud of his love for her, was longing to show her his power, to rule and to command; she, half-shy of her love for him, felt her pride in submitting to his wish, in laying down at his feet the crown and sceptre of domination which she had wielded up to now with so proud and secure a hand.

Men were so different. That, too, she understood with the first touch of a man's kiss on her lips.

She chided herself for her mistrust of him; was it not natural that he should wish to rule? How proud was she now that her last act of absolute power should be the satisfaction of his desire.

That new Ministry? Well, he should have it as he wished. One word from her, and her father would grant it. Her husband must be the most powerful man in France; she would make him that, since she could: and then pillow her head on his breast and forget that she ever had other ambitions save to see him great.

Smiling through her tears, she begged his forgiveness for her mistrust of him, her doubts of the true worth of his love.

"It was because I knew so little," she said shyly as her trembling fingers toyed nervously with the lace of his cravat; "no man has ever loved me, Gaston—you understand? There were flatterers round me and sycophants—but love——"

She shook her head with a kind of joyous sadness for the past. It was so much better to be totally ignorant of love, and then to learn it—like this!

Then she became grave again.

"My father shall arrange everything this evening," she said, with a proud toss of her head. "To-morrow you may command, but to-night you shall remain a suppliant; grant me, I pray you, this fond little gratification of my overburdened vanity. Ask me again to grant your request, to be the means of satisfying your ambition. Put it into words, Gaston, tell me what it is you want!" she insisted, with a pretty touch of obstinacy; "it is my whim, and remember I am still the arbiter of your fate."

"On my knees, my queen," he said, curbing his impatience at her childish caprice; and, striving to hide the note of triumph in his voice, he put both knees to the ground and bent his head in supplication. "I crave of your bountiful graciousness to accord me the power to rule France by virtue of my office as Chief Comptroller of her revenues."

"Your desire is granted, sir," she said with a final assumption of pride; "the last favour I shall have the power to bestow I now confer on you. To-morrow I abdicate," she continued, with a strange little sigh, half-tearful, half-joyous, "to-morrow I shall own a master. M. le Comte de Stainville, Minister of the Exchequer of France, behold your slave, Lydie, bought this night with the priceless currency of your love! Oh, Gaston, my lord, my husband!" she said, with a sudden uncontrollable outburst of tears, "be a kind master to your slave—she gives up so much for your dear sake!"

CHAPTER V

THE FIRST TRICK

A shrill laugh suddenly broke on their ears. So absorbed had Lydie been in her dream that she had completely forgotten the other world, the one that laughed and talked, that fought and bickered on the other side of the damask curtain which was the boundary of her own universe.

Gaston de Stainville, we may assume, was not quite so unprepared for interruption as the young girl, for even before the shrill laugh had expended itself, he was already on his feet, and had drawn the damask curtain back again, interposing the while his broad figure between Lydie d'Aumont and the unwelcome intruder on their privacy.

"Ah! at last you are tracked to earth, mauvais sujet," said Mme. de Pompadour, as soon as the Comte de Stainville stood fully revealed before her. "Faith! I have had a severe task. His Majesty demanded your presence a while ago, sir, and hath gone to sleep in the interval of waiting. Nay! nay! you need make neither haste nor excuses. The King sleeps, Monsieur, else I were not here to remind you of duty."

She stood at the bottom of the steps looking up with keen, malicious eyes at Gaston's figure framed in the opening of the alcove, and peering inquisitively into the sombre recesses, wherein already she had caught a glimpse of a white satin skirt and the scintillation of many diamonds.

"What say you, milady?" she added, turning to the florid, somewhat over-dressed woman who stood by her side. "Shall we listen to the excuses M. de Stainville seems anxious to make; meseems they are clad in white satin and show a remarkably well-turned ankle."

But before Lady Eglinton could frame a reply, Lydie d'Aumont had risen, and placing her hand on Stainville's shoulder, she thrust him gently aside and now stood smiling beside him, perfectly self-possessed, a trifle haughty, looking down on Jeanne de Pompadour's pert face and on the older lady's obviously ill-humoured countenance.

"Nay, Mme. la Marquise," she said, in her own quiet way, "M. le Comte de Stainville's only excuse for his neglect of courtly duties stands before you now."

"Ma foi, Mademoiselle!" retorted the Marquise somewhat testily. "His Majesty, being over-gallant, would perhaps be ready enough to accept it, and so, no doubt, would the guests of M. le Duc, your father—always excepting Mlle, de St. Romans," she added, with more than a point of malice, "and she is not like to prove indulgent."

But Lydie was far too proud, far too conscious also of her own worth, to heed the petty pinpricks which the ladies of the Court of Louis XV were wont to deal so lavishly to one another. She knew quite well that Gaston's name had oft been coupled with that of Mlle. de St. Romans—"la belle brune de Bordeaux," as she was universally called—daughter of the gallant Maréchal just home from Flanders. This gossip was part and parcel of that multifarious scandal to which she had just assured her lover that she no longer would lend an ear.

Therefore she met Mme. de Pompadour's malicious look with one of complete indifference, and ignoring the remark altogether, she said calmly, without the slightest tremor in her voice or hint of annoyance in her face:

"Did I understand you to say, Madame, that His Majesty was tired and desired to leave?"

The Marquise looked vexed, conscious of the snub; she threw a quick look of intelligence to Lady Eglinton, which Lydie no doubt would have caught had she not at that moment turned to her lover in order to give him a smile of assurance and trust.

He, however, seemed self-absorbed just now, equally intent in avoiding her loving glance and Mme. de Pompadour's mocking gaze.

"The King certainly asked for M. de Stainville a while ago," here interposed Lady Eglinton, "and M. le Chevalier de Saint George has begun to make his adieux."

"We'll not detain Mlle. d'Aumont, then," said Mme. de Pompadour. "She will wish to bid our young Pretender an encouraging farewell! Come, M. de Stainville," she added authoritatively, "we'll to His Majesty, but only for two short minutes, then you shall be released man, have no fear, in order to make your peace with la belle brune de Bordeaux. Brrr! I vow I am quite frightened; the minx's black eyes anon shot daggers in this direction."

She beckoned imperiously to Gaston, who still seemed ill at ease, and ready enough to follow her. Lydie could not help noting with a slight tightening of her heartstrings with what alacrity he obeyed.

"Men are so different!" she sighed.

She would have allowed the whole world to look on and to sneer whilst she spent the rest of the evening beside her lover, talking foolish nonsense, planning out the future, or sitting in happy silence, heedless of sarcasm, mockery, or jests.

Her eyes followed him somewhat wistfully as he descended the two steps with easy grace, and with a flourishing bow and a "Mille grâces, Mlle. Lydie!" he turned away without another backward look, and became merged with the crowd.

Her master and future lord, the man whose lips had touched her own! How strange!

She herself could not thus have become one of the throng. Not just yet. She could not have detached herself from him so readily. For some few seconds—minutes perhaps—her earnest eyes tried to distinguish the pale mauve of his coat in the midst of that ever-changing kaleidoscope of dazzling colours. But the search made her eyes burn, and she closed them with the pain.

Men were so different!

And though she had learned much, understood much, with that first kiss, she was still very ignorant, very inexperienced, and quite at sea in those tortuous paths wherein Gaston and Mme. de Pompadour and all the others moved with such perfect ease.

In the meanwhile, M. de Stainville and the Marquise had reached the corridor. From where they now stood they could no longer see the alcove whence Lydie's aching eyes still searched for them in vain; with a merry little laugh Madame drew her dainty hand away from her cavalier's arm.

"There! am I not the beneficent fairy, you rogue?" she said, giving him a playful tap with her fan. "Fie! Will you drive in double harness? You'll come to grief, fair sir, and meseems 'twere not good to trifle with either filly."

"Madame, I entreat!" he protested feebly, wearied of the jest. But he tried not to scowl or to seem impatient, for he was loth to lose the good graces of a lady whose power and influence were unequalled even by Lydie d'Aumont.

Pompadour had favoured him from the very day of her first

entry in the brilliant Court of Versailles. His handsome face, his elegant manners, and, above all, his reputation as a consummate mauvais sujet had pleased Mme. la Marquise. Gaston de Stainville was never so occupied with pleasures or amours, but he was ready to pay homage to one more beautiful woman who was willing to smile upon him.

But though she flirted with Gaston, the wily Marquise had no wish to see him at the head of affairs, the State-appointed controller of her caprices and of the King's munificence. He was pleasant enough as an admirer, unscrupulous and daring; but as a master? No.

The thought of a marriage between Mlle. d'Aumont and M. de Stainville, with its obvious consequences on her own future plans, was not to be tolerated for a moment; and Madame wondered greatly how far matters had gone between these two, prior to her own timely interference.

"There!" she said, pointing to an arched doorway close at hand; "go and make your peace whilst I endeavour to divert His Majesty's thoughts from your own wicked person; and remember," she added coquettishly as she bobbed him a short, mocking curtsey, "when you have reached the blissful stage of complete reconciliation, that you owe your happiness to Jeanne de Pompadour."

Etiquette demanded that he should kiss the hand which she now held extended toward him; this he did with as good a grace as he could muster. In his heart of hearts he was wishing the interfering lady back in the victualler's shop of Paris; he was not at all prepared at this moment to encounter the jealous wrath of "la Belle brune de Bordeaux."

Vaguely he thought of flight, but Mme. de Pompadour would not let him off quite so easily. With her own jewelled hand she pushed aside the curtain which masked the doorway, and with a nod of her dainty head she hinted to Gaston to walk into the boudoir.

There was nothing for it but to obey.

"Mlle. de Saint Romans," said the Marquise, peeping into the room in order to reassure herself that the lady was there and alone, "see, I bring the truant back to you. Do not be too severe on him; his indiscretion has been slight, and he will soon forget all about it, if you will allow him to make full confession and to do penance at your feet."

Then she dropped the curtain behind Gaston de Stainville, and, as an additional precaution, lest those two in there should be interrupted too soon, she closed the heavy folding doors which further divided the boudoir from the corridor.

"Now, if milady plays her cards cleverly," she murmured, "she and I will have done a useful evening's work."

CHAPTER VI

A FALSE POSITION

"Gaston!"

M. de Stainville shook off his moodiness. The vision of la belle Irène standing there in the satin-hung boudoir, the soft glow of well-shaded candles shedding an elusive, rosy light on the exquisite figure, with head thrown back and arms stretched out in a gesture of passionate appeal, was too captivating to permit of any other thought having sway over his brain, for the next second or two at any rate.

"I thought you had completely forgotten me to-night," she said as he came rapidly toward her, "and that I should not even get speech of you."

She took his hand and led him gently to a low divan; forcing him to sit down beside her, she studied his face intently for a moment or two.

"Was it necessary?" she asked abruptly.

"You know it was, Irène," he said, divining her thoughts, plunging readily enough now into the discussion which he knew was inevitable. His whole nature rebelled against this situation; he felt a distinct lowering of his manly pride; his masterful spirit chafed at the thought of an explanation which Irène claimed the right to demand.

"I told you, Irène," he continued impatiently, "that I would speak to Mlle. d'Aumont to-night, and if possible obtain a definite promise from her."

"And have you obtained that definite promise?" she asked.

"Yes."

"Lydie d'Aumont promised you that you should be the new State-appointed Minister of Finance?" she insisted.

"Yes! I have her word."

"And—what was the cost?"

"The cost?"

"Yes, the cost," she said, with what was obviously enforced calm. "Lydie d'Aumont did not give you that promise for nothing; you gave her or promised her something in return. What was it?"

Her lips were trembling, and she had some difficulty in preventing her nervous fingers from breaking into pieces the delicate mother-of-pearl fan which they held. But she was determined to appear perfectly calm, and that he should in no way suspect her of working up to a vulgar scene of jealousy.

"You are foolish, Irène!" he said, with his characteristic nonchalant shrug of the shoulders.

"Foolish?" she repeated, still keeping her temper well under control, though it was her voice which was shaking now. "Foolish? Ma foi! when my husband obtains——"

"'Sh! 'sh! 'sh!" he said quickly, as with rough gesture he grasped her wrist, and gave it a warning pressure.

"Bah!" she retorted; "no one can hear."

"The walls have ears!"

"And if they have? I cannot keep up this deception for ever, Gaston."

"'Twere worse than foolish to founder within sight of port."

"You trust Lydie d'Aumont's word then?"

"If you will do nothing to spoil the situation!" he retorted grimly. "Another word such as you said just now, too long a prolongation of this charming tête-à-tête, and Mlle. d'Aumont will make a fresh promise to some one else."

"I was right, then?"

"Right in what?"

"Mlle. d'Aumont promised you the appointment because you made love to her."

"Irène!"

"Why don't you tell me?" she said with passionate vehemence. "Can't you see that I have been torturing myself with jealous fears? I am jealous—can I help it? I suffered martyrdom when I saw you there with her! I could not hear your words, but I could see the earnestness of your attitude. Do I not know every line of your figure, every gesture of your hand? Then the curtain fell at your touch, and I could no longer see—only divine—only tremble and fear. Mon Dieu! did I not love you as I do, were my love merely foolish passion, would I not then have screamed out the truth to all that jabbering crowd that stood between me and you, seeming to mock me with its prattle, and its irresponsible laughter? I am unnerved, Gaston," she added, with a sudden breakdown of her self-control, her voice trembling with sobs, the tears welling to her eyes, and her hands beating against one another with a movement of petulant nervosity. "I could bear it, you know, but for this secrecy, this false position; it is humiliating to me, and—Oh, be kind to me—be kind to me!" she sobbed, giving finally way to a fit of weeping. "I have spent such a miserable evening, all alone."

Stainville's expressive lips curled into a smile. "Be kind to me!"—the same pathetic prayer spoken to him by Lydie a very short while ago. Bah! how little women understood ambition! Even Lydie! Even Irène!

And these two women were nothing to him. Lydie herself was only a stepping-stone; the statuesque and headstrong girl made no appeal to the essentially masculine side of his nature, and he had little love left now for the beautiful passionate woman beside him, whom in a moment of unreasoning impulse he had bound irrevocably to him.

Gaston de Stainville aspired to military honours a couple of years ago; the Maréchal de Saint Romans, friend and mentor of the Dauphin, confidant of the Queen, seemed all-powerful then. Unable to win the father's consent to his union with Irène—for the Maréchal had more ambitious views for his only daughter and looked with ill-favour on the young gallant who had little to offer but his own handsome person, an ancient name, and a passionate desire for advancement—Gaston, who had succeeded in enchaining the young girl's affections, had no difficulty in persuading her to agree to a secret marriage.

But the wheel of fate proved as erratic in its movements as the flights of Stainville's ambition. With the appearance of Jeanne Poisson d'Étioles at the Court of Versailles, the Queen's gentle influence over Louis XV waned, and her friends fell into disfavour and obscurity. The Maréchal de Saint Romans was given an unimportant command in Flanders; there was nothing to be gained for the moment from an open alliance with his daughter. Gaston de Stainville, an avowed opportunist, paid his court to the newly risen star and was received with smiles, but he could not shake himself from the matrimonial fetters which he himself had forged.

The rapid rise of the Duc d'Aumont to power and the overwhelming ascendancy of Lydie in the affairs of State had made the young man chafe bitterly against the indestructible barrier which he himself had erected between his desires and their fulfilment. His passion for Irène did not yield to the early love of his childhood's days; it was drowned in the newly risen flood of more boundless ambition. It was merely the casting aside of one stepping-stone for another more firm and more prominent.

Just now in the secluded alcove, when the proud, reserved girl

33

had laid bare before him the secrets of her virginal soul, when with pathetic abandonment she laid the sceptre of her influence and power at his feet, he had felt neither compunction nor remorse; now, when the woman who had trusted and blindly obeyed him asked for his help and support in a moral crisis, he was conscious only of a sense of irritation and even of contempt, which he tried vainly to disguise.

At the same time he knew well that it is never wise to tax a woman's submission too heavily. Irène had yielded to his wish that their marriage be kept a secret for the present only because she, too, was tainted with a touch of that unscrupulous ambition which was the chief characteristic of the epoch. She was shrewd enough to know that her husband would have but little chance in elbowing his way up the ladder of power—"each rung of which was wrapped in a petticoat," as M. de Voltaire had pertinently put it—if he was known to be dragging a wife at his heels; Gaston had had no difficulty in making her understand that his personality as a gay and irresponsible butterfly, as a man of fashion, and a squire of dames, was the most important factor in the coming fight for the virtual dominion of France.

She had accepted the position at first with an easy grace; she knew her Gaston, and knew that he must not be handled with too tight a curb; moreover, her secret status pleased her, whilst he remained avowedly faithful to her she liked to see him court and smile, a preux chevalier with the ladies; she relished the thought of being the jailer to that gaily-plumaged bird, whom bright eyes and smiling lips tried to entice and enchain.

But to-night a crisis had come; something in Gaston's attitude toward Lydie had irritated her beyond what she was prepared to endure. His love for her had begun to wane long ago; she knew that, but she was not inclined to see it bestowed on another. Stainville feared that she was losing self-control, and that she might betray all and lose all if he did not succeed in laying her jealous wrath to rest. He was past master in the art of dealing with a woman's tears.

"Irène," he said earnestly, "I have far too much respect for you to look upon this childish outburst of tears as representing the true state of your feelings. You are unnerved—you own it yourself. Will you allow me to hold your hand?" he said with abrupt transition.

Then as she yielded her trembling hand to him he pressed a lingering kiss in the icy cold palm.

"Will you not accept with this kiss the assurance of my unswerving faith and loyalty?" he said, speaking in that low, deep-toned voice of his which he knew so well how to make tender and appealing to the heart of women. "Irène, if I have committed an indiscretion to-night, if I allowed my ambition to soar beyond the bounds of prudence, will you not believe that with my ambition my thoughts flew up to you and only came down to earth in order to rest at your feet?"

He had drawn her close to him, ready to whisper in her ear, as he had whispered half an hour ago in those of Lydie. He wanted this woman's trust and confidence just a very little while longer, and he found words readily enough with which to hoodwink and to cajole. Irène was an easier prey than Lydie. She was his wife and her ambitions were bound up with his; her mistrust only came from jealousy, and jealousy in a woman is so easily conquered momentarily, if she be beautiful and young and the man ardent and unscrupulous.

Gaston as yet had no difficult task; but every day would increase those difficulties, until he had finally grasped the aim of his ambitious desires and had rid himself of Lydie.

"Irène!" he whispered now, for he felt that she was consoled, and being consoled, she was ready to yield. "Irène, my wife, a little more patience, a little more trust. Two days—a week—what matter? Shut your eyes to all save this one moment to-night, when your husband is at your feet and when his soul goes out to yours in one long, and tender kiss. Your lips, ma mie!"

She bent her head to him. Womanlike, she could not resist. Memory came to his aid as he pleaded, the memory of those early days on the vine-clad hills near Bordeaux, when he had wooed and won her with the savour of his kiss.

CHAPTER VII

THE YOUNG PRETENDER

And Lydie d'Aumont's eyes had watched his disappearing figure through the crowd, until she could bear the sight no longer, and closed them with the pain.

An even, pleasant, very courteous voice roused her from her reverie.

"You are tired, Mlle. d'Aumont. May I—that is, I should be very proud if you would allow me to—er——"

35

She opened her eyes and saw the handsome face of "le petit Anglais" turned up to her with a look of humility, a deprecatory offer of service, and withal a strange mingling of compassion which somehow at this moment, in her sensitive and nervous state, seemed to wound and sting her.

"I'm not the least tired," she said coldly; "I thank you, milor. The colours and the light were so dazzling for the moment, my eyes closed involuntarily."

"I humbly beg your pardon," said Eglinton with nervous haste; "I thought that perhaps a glass of wine——"

"Tush child!" interposed Lady Eglinton in her harsh dry voice; "have you not heard that Mlle. d'Aumont is not fatigued. Offer her the support of your arm and take her to see the Chevalier de Saint George, who is waiting to bid her 'good-bye.'"

"Nay! I assure you I can walk alone," rejoined Lydie, taking no heed to the proffered arm which Lord Eglinton, in obedience to his mother's suggestion, was holding out toward her. "Where is His Majesty the King of England?" emphasizing the title with marked reproof, and looking with somewhat good-natured contempt at the young Englishman who, with a crestfallen air, had already dropped the arm which she had disdained and stepped quickly out of her way, whilst a sudden blush spread over his good-looking face.

He looked so confused and sheepish, so like a chidden child, that she was instantly seized with remorse, as if she had teased a defenseless animal, and though the touch of contempt was still apparent in her attitude, she said more kindly:

"I pray you forgive me, milor. I am loth to think that perhaps our gallant Chevalier will never bear his rightful title in his own country. I feel that it cheers him to hear us—who are in true sympathy with him—calling him by that name. Shall we go find the King of England and wish him 'God-speed'?"

She beckoned to Lord Eglinton, but he had probably not yet sufficiently recovered from the snub administered to him to realize that the encouraging glance was intended for him, and he hung back, not daring to follow, instinctively appealing to his mother for guidance as to what he should do.

"He is modest," said Lady Eglinton, with the air of a proud mother lauding her young offspring. "A heart of gold, my dear Mlle. d'Aumont!" she whispered behind her fan, "under a simple exterior."

Lydie shrugged her shoulders with impatience. She knew whither Lady Eglinton's praises of her son would drift presently. The pompous lady looked for all the world like a fussy hen, her stiff brocaded gown and voluminous paniers standing out in stiff folds each side of her portly figure like a pair of wings, and to Lydie d'Aumont's proud spirit it seemed more than humiliating for a man, rich, young, apparently in perfect health, to allow himself to be domineered over by so vapid a personality as was milady Eglinton.

Instinctively her thoughts flew back to Gaston; very different physically to "le petit Anglais;" undoubtedly not so attractive from the point of view of manly grace and bearing, but a man for all that! with a man's weaknesses and failings, and just that spice of devilry and uncertainty in him which was pleasing to a woman.

"So unreliable, my dear Mlle. d'Aumont," came in insinuating accents from Lady Eglinton. "Look at his lengthy entanglement with Mlle. de Saint Romans."

Lydie gave a start sudden; had she spoken her thoughts out loudly whilst her own mind was buried in happy retrospect? She must have been dreaming momentarily certainly, and must have been strangely absent-minded, for she was quite unconscious of having descended the alcove steps until she found herself walking between Lord Eglinton and his odious mother, in the direction of the corridors, whilst milady went prattling on with irritating monotony:

"You would find such support in my son. The Chevalier de Saint George—er—I mean the King of England—trusts him absolutely, you understand—they have been friends since boyhood. Harry would do more for him if he could, but he has not the power. Now as Comptroller of Finance—you understand? You have such sympathy with the Stuart pretensions, Mademoiselle, and a union of sympathies would do much towards furthering the success of so just a cause; and if my son—you understand——"

Lydie's ears were buzzing with the incessant chatter. Had she not been so absorbed in her thoughts she would have laughed at the absurdity of the whole thing. This insignificant nonentity beside her, with the strength and character of a chicken, pushed into a place of influence and power by that hen-like mother, and she—Lydie—lending a hand to this installation of a backboneless weakling to the highest position of France!

The situation would have been supremely ridiculous were it not for the element of pathos in it—the pathos of a young life which might have been so brilliant, so full of activity and interest, now tied to the apron-strings of an interfering mother.

Lydie herself, though accustomed to rule in one of the widest spheres that ever fell to woman's lot, wielded her sceptre with discretion and tact. In these days when the King was ruled by Pompadour, when Mme. du Châtelet swayed the mind of Voltaire, and Marie Thérèse subjugated the Hungarians, there was nothing of the blatant petticoat government in Lydie's influence over her father. The obtrusive domination of a woman like milady was obnoxious and abhorrent to her mind, proud of its feminity, gentle in the consciousness of its strength.

Now she feared that, forgetful of courtly manners, she might say or do something which would offend the redoubtable lady. There was still the whole length of the banqueting-hall to traverse, also the corridor, before she could hope to be released from so unwelcome a companionship.

Apparently unconscious of having roused Lydie's disapproval, milady continued to prattle. Her subject of conversation was still her son, and noting that his attention seemed to be wandering, she called to him in her imperious voice:

"Harry! Harry!" she said impatiently. "Am I to to be your spokesman from first to last? Ah!" she added, with a sigh, "men are not what they were when I was wooed and won. What say you, my dear Mlle. Lydie? The age of chivalry, of doughty deeds and bold adventures, is indeed past and gone, else a young man of Lord Eglinton's advantages would not depute his own mother to do his courting for him."

A shriek of laughter which threatened to be hysterical rose to Lydie's throat. How gladly would she have beaten a precipitate retreat. Unfortunately the room was crowded with people, who unconsciously impeded progress. She turned and looked at "le petit Anglais," the sorry hero of this prosaic wooing, wondering what was his rôle in this silly, childish intrigue. She met his gentle eyes fixed upon hers with a look which somehow reminded her of a St. Bernard dog that she had once possessed; there was such a fund of self-deprecation, such abject apology in the look, that she felt quite unaccountably sorry for him, and the laughter died before it reached her lips.

Something prompted her to try and reassure him; the same feeling would have caused her to pat the head of her dog.

"I feel sure," she said kindly, "that Lord Eglinton will have no need of a proxy once he sets his mind on serious wooing."

"But this is serious!" retorted Lady Eglinton testily. Lydie shook her head:

"As little serious as his lordship's desire to control the finances of France."

"Oh! but who better fitted for the post than my son. He is so rich—the richest man in France, and in these days of bribery and corruption—you understand, and—and being partly English—not wholly, I am thankful to say—for I abominate the English myself;

38

but we must own that they are very shrewd where money is concerned—and——"

"In the name of Heaven, milady," said Lydie irritably, "will you not allow your son to know his own mind? If he has a request to place before M. le Duc my father or before me, let him do so for himself."

"I think—er—perhaps Mlle. d'Aumont is right," here interposed Lord Eglinton gently. "You will—er—I hope, excuse my mother, Mademoiselle; she is so used to my consulting her in everything that perhaps—— You see," he continued in his nervous halting, way, "I—I am rather stupid and I am very lazy; she thinks I should understand finance, because I—but I don't believe I should; I——"

Her earnest eyes, fixed with good-humoured indulgence upon his anxious face, seemed to upset him altogether. His throat was dry, and his tongue felt as if it were several sizes too large for his parched mouth. For the moment it looked as if the small modicum of courage which he possessed would completely give out, but noting that just for the moment his mother was engaged in exchanging hasty greetings with a friend, he seemed to make a violent and sudden effort, and with the audacity which sometimes assails the preternaturally weak, he plunged wildly into his subject.

"I have no desire for positions which I am too stupid to fill," he said, speaking so rapidly that Lydie could hardly follow him; "but, Mademoiselle, I entreat you do not believe that my admiration for you is not serious. I know I am quite unworthy to be even your lacquey, though I wouldn't mind being that, since it would bring me sometimes near you. Please, please, don't look at me—I am such a clumsy fool, and I daresay I am putting things all wrong! My mother says," he added, with a pathetic little sigh, "that I shall spoil everything if I open my mouth, and now I have done it, and you are angry, and I wish to God somebody would come and give me a kick!"

He paused, flushed, panting and excited, having come to the end of his courage, whilst Lydie did not know if she should be angry or sorry. A smile hovered round her lips, yet she would gladly have seen some manlike creature administer chastisement to this foolish weakling. Her keenly analytical mind flew at once to comparisons.

Gaston de Stainville—and now this poor specimen of manhood! She had twice been wooed in this self-same room within half an hour; but how different had been the methods of courting. A look of indulgence for the weak, a flash of pride for the strong, quickly lit up her statuesque face. It was the strong who had won, though womanlike, she felt a kindly pity for him who did not even dare to ask for that which the other had so boldly claimed as his right—her love.

Fortunately, the tête-à-tête, which was rapidly becoming embarrassing—for she really did not know how to reply to this strange and halting profession of love—was at last drawing to a close. At the end of the corridor Charles Edward Stuart, surrounded by a group of friends, had caught sight of her, and with gracious courtesy he advanced to meet her.

"Ah! the gods do indeed favour us," he said gallantly in answer to her respectful salute, and nodding casually to Lady Eglinton, who had bobbed him a grudging curtsey, "We feared that our enemy, Time, treading hard on our heels, would force us to depart ere we had greeted our Muse."

"Your Majesty is leaving us?" she asked. "So soon?"

"Alas! the hour is late. We start to-morrow at daybreak."

"God speed you, Sire!" she said fervently.

"To my death," he rejoined gloomily.

"To victory, Sire, and your Majesty's own kingdom!" she retorted cheerily. "Nay! I, your humble, yet most faithful adherent, refuse to be cast down to-night. See," she added, pointing to the group of gentlemen who had remained discreetly in the distance, "you have brave hearts to cheer you, brave swords to help you!"

"Would I were sure of a brave ship to rescue me and them if I fail!" he murmured.

She tossed her head with a characteristic movement of impatience.

"Nay! I was determined not to speak of failure to-night, Sire."

"Yet must I think of it," he rejoined, "since the lives of my friends are dependent on me."

"They give their lives gladly for your cause."

"I would prefer to think that a good ship from France was ready to take them aboard if evil luck force us to flee."

"France has promised you that ship, Monseigneur," she said earnestly:

"If France meant you, Mademoiselle," he said firmly, "I would believe in her."

"She almost means Lydie d'Aumont!" retorted the young girl, with conscious pride.

"Only for a moment," broke in Lady Eglinton spitefully; "but girls marry," she added, "and every husband may not be willing to be held under the sway of satin petticoats."

"If France fails you, Monseigneur," here interposed a gentle voice, "I have already had the honour of assuring you that there is enough Eglinton money still in the country to fit out a ship for your safety; and—er——"

Then, as if ashamed of this outburst, the second of which he had been guilty to-night, "le petit Anglais" once more relapsed into silence. But Lydie threw him a look of encouragement.

"Well spoken, milor!" she said approvingly.

With her quick intuition she had already perceived that milady was displeased, and she took a malicious pleasure in dragging Lord Eglinton further into the conversation. She knew quite well that milady cared naught about the Stuarts or their fate. From the day of her marriage she had dissociated herself from the cause, for the furtherance of which her husband's father had given up home and country.

It was her influence which had detached the late Lord Eglinton from the fortunes of the two Pretenders; justly, perhaps, since the expeditions were foredoomed to failure, and Protestant England rightly or wrongly mistrusted all the Stuarts. But Lydie's romantic instincts could not imagine an Englishman in any other capacity save as the champion of the forlorn cause; one of the principal reasons why she had always disliked the Eglintons was because they held themselves aloof from the knot of friends who gathered round Charles Edward.

She was, therefore, not a little surprised to hear "le petit Anglais" promising at least loyal aid and succour in case of disaster, since he could not give active support to the proposed expedition. That he had made no idle boast when he spoke of Eglinton money she knew quite well, nor was it said in vain arrogance, merely as a statement of fact. Milady's vexation proved that it was true.

Delighted and eager, she threw herself with all the ardour of her romantic impulses into this new train of thought suggested by Lord Eglinton's halting speech.

"Ah, milor," she said joyously, and not heeding Lady Eglinton's scowl, "now that I have an ally in you my dream can become a reality. Nay, Sire, you shall start for England with every hope, every assurance of success, but if you fail, you and those you care for shall be safe. Will you listen to my plan?"

"Willingly."

"Lord Eglinton is your friend—at least, you trust him, do you not?"

"I trust absolutely in the loyalty of his house toward mine," replied Charles Edward unhesitatingly.

"Then do you agree with him, and with him alone, on a spot in England or Scotland where a ship would find you in case of failure."

"That has been done already," said Eglinton simply.

"And if ill-luck pursues us, we will make straight for that spot and await salvation from France."

Lydie said no more; she was conscious of a distinct feeling of disappointment that her own plan should have been forestalled. She had fondled the notion, born but a moment ago, that if her own influence were not sufficiently great in the near future to induce King Louis to send a rescue ship for the Young Pretender if necessary, she could then, with Lord Eglinton's money, fit out a private expedition and snatch the last of the Stuarts from the vengeance of his enemies. The romantic idea had appealed to her, and she had been forestalled. She tried to read the thoughts of those around her. Lady Eglinton was evidently ignorant of the details of the plan; she seemed surprised and vastly disapproving. Charles Edward was whispering a few hasty words in the ear of his friend, whom obviously he trusted more than he did the word of France or the enthusiasm of Mlle. d'Aumont.

"Le petit Anglais" had relapsed into his usual state of nervousness, and his eyes wandered uneasily from Lydie's face to that of his royal companion, whilst with restless fingers he fidgeted the signet ring which adorned his left hand. Suddenly he slipped the ring off and Charles Edward Stuart examined it very attentively, then returned it to its owner with a keen look of intelligence and a nod of approval.

Lydie was indeed too late with her romantic plan; these two men had thought it all out before her in every detail—even to the ring. She, too, had thought of a token which would be an assurance to the fugitives that they might trust the bearer thereof. She felt quite childishly vexed at all this. It was an unusual thing in France these days to transact serious business without consulting Mlle. d'Aumont.

"You are taking it for granted, Sire, that France will fail you?" she said somewhat testily.

"Nay! why should you say that?" he asked.

"Oh! the ring—the obvious understanding between you and milor."

"Was it not your wish, Mademoiselle?"

"Oh! a mere suggestion—in case France failed you, and I were powerless to remind her of her promise."

"Pa ma foi," he rejoined gallantly, "and you'll command me, I'll believe that contingency to be impossible. The whole matter of the ring is a whim of Eglinton's, and I swear that I'll only trust to France and to you."

"No, no!" she said quickly, her own sound common sense coming to the rescue just in time to rout the unreasoning petulance

42

of a while ago, which truly had been unworthy of her. "It was foolish of me to taunt, and I pray your Majesty's forgiveness. It would have been joy and pride to me to feel that the plans for your Majesty's safety had been devised by me, but I gladly recognize that milor Eglinton hath in this matter the prior claim."

Her little speech was delivered so simply and with such a noble air of self-effacement that it is small wonder that Charles Edward could but stand in speechless admiration before her. She looked such an exquisite picture of proud and self-reliant womanhood, as she stood there, tall and erect, the stiff folds of her white satin gown surrounding her like a frame of ivory round a dainty miniature. Tears of enthusiasm were in her eyes, her lips were parted with a smile of encouragement, her graceful head, thrown slightly back and crowned with the burnished gold of her hair, stood out in perfect relief against the soft-toned gold and veined marble of the walls.

"I entreat you, Mademoiselle," said the Young Pretender at last, "do not render my departure too difficult by showing me so plainly all that I relinquish when I quit the fair shores of France."

"Your Majesty leaves many faithful hearts in Versailles, none the less true because they cannot follow you. Nay! but methinks Lord Eglinton and I will have to make a pact of friendship, so that when your Majesty hath gone we might often speak of you."

"Speak of me often and to the King," rejoined Charles Edward, with a quick return to his former mood. "I have a premonition that I shall have need of his help."

Then he bowed before her, and she curtsyed very low until her young head was almost down to the level of his knees. He took her hand and kissed it with the respect due to an equal.

"Farewell, Sire, and God speed you!" she murmured. He seemed quite reluctant to go. Gloom had once more completely settled over his spirits, and Lydie d'Aumont, clad all in white like some graceful statue carved in marble, seemed to him the figure of Hope on which a relentless fate forced him to turn his back.

His friends now approached and surrounded him. Some were leaving Versailles and France with him on the morrow, others accompanied him in spirit only with good wishes and anxious sighs. Charles Edward Stuart, the unfortunate descendant of an unfortunate race, turned with a final appealing look to the man he trusted most.

"Be not a broken reed to me, Eglinton," he said sadly. "Try and prevent France from altogether forgetting me."

Lydie averted her head in order to hide the tears of pity which had risen to her eyes.

"Oh, unfortunate Prince! if thine only prop is this poor weakling whose dog-like affection has no moral strength to give it support!"

When she turned once more toward him, ready to bid him a final adieu, he was walking rapidly away from her down the long narrow corridor, leaning on Eglinton's arm and closely surrounded by his friends. In the far distance King Louis the Well-beloved strolled leisurely toward his departing guest, leaning lightly on the arm of Mme. la Marquise de Pompadour.

CHAPTER VIII

THE LAST TRICK

The noise of talk and laughter still filled the old château from end to end. Though the special guest of the evening had departed and royalty no longer graced the proceedings, since His Majesty had driven away to Versailles after having bidden adieu to the Chevalier de Saint George, M. le Duc d'Aumont's less important visitors showed no signs as yet of wishing to break up this convivial night.

The sound of dance music filled the air, and from the salle d'armes the merry strains of the gavotte, the tripping of innumerable feet, the incessant buzz of young voices, reached the more distant corridor like an echo from fairyland.

Lydie had remained quite a little while leaning against the cool marble wall, watching with eager intentness the group of gallant English and Scotch gentlemen congregated round their young Prince. Louis the Well-beloved, with that graciousness peculiar to all the Bourbons, had, severally and individually bidden "good-bye" to all. Each in turn had kissed the podgy white hand of the King of France, who had been so benignant a host to them all. None understood better than Louis XV, the art of leaving a pleasing impression on the mind of a departing friend. He had a smile, a jest, a word of encouragement for each whilst Jeanne de Pompadour, with one dainty hand on the King's shoulder, the other flirting her fan, emphasized each token of royal goodwill and of royal favour.

"Ah! milor Dunkeld, a pleasing journey to you. M. le Marquis de Perth, I pray you do not, amidst the fogs of England, forget the sunshine of France. Sir André Seafield, your absence will bring many tears to a pair of blue eyes I wot of."

She pronounced the foreign names with dainty affectation, and Louis had much ado to keep his eyes away from that bright, smiling face, and those ever-recurring dimples. Lydie felt a strange nausea at sight of these noble, high-born gentlemen paying such reverential homage to the low-born adventuress, and a deep frown appeared between her eyes when she saw Charles Edward Stuart bending as low before Jeanne Poisson as he had done just now before her—Lydie, daughter of the Duc d'Aumont.

Bah! what did it matter, after all? This world of irresponsible butterflies, of petty machinations and self-seeking intrigues: would she not quit it to-morrow for a land of poetry and romance, where women wield no sceptre save that of beauty, and where but one ruler is acknowledged and his name is Love?

She made a strenuous attempt to detach herself mentally from her surroundings; with a great effort of her will she succeeded in losing sight of the individuality of all these people round her. Lady Eglinton still talking at random beside her, Mme. de Pompadour yielding her hand to the kiss of a Stuart Prince, that fat and pompous man, whom duty bade her call "Your Majesty," all became mere puppets—dolls that laughed and chatted and danced, hanging on invisible strings, which the mighty hand of some grim giant was dangling for the amusement of his kind.

How paltry it seemed all at once! What did it matter if France was ruled by that vapid King or by that brainless, overdressed woman beside him? What did it matter if that young man with the shifty blue eyes and the fair, curly hair succeeded in ousting another man from the English throne?

What did matter was that Gaston was not faithless, that he loved her, and that she had felt the sweetness of a first kiss!

Happily back in dreamland now, she could once more afford to play her part amongst the marionettes. She was willing to yield the string which made her dance and talk and move into the hands of the fiercely humorous giant up aloft. No doubt it was he who pulled her along the corridor, made her join the group that congregated round departing royalty.

M. le Duc d'Aumont—the perfect courtier and gentleman— was already formulating his adieux. His Majesty the King of France would, by the rigid rule of etiquette, be the first to leave. Accompanied by Mme. de Pompadour and followed by M. le Duc, he was commencing his progress down the monumental staircase which led to the great entrance hall below.

Lydie, still made to move no doubt by that invisible giant

45

hand, found it quite simple and easy to mingle with the crowd, to take the King's arm, being his hostess, whilst M. le Duc her father and Mme. de Pompadour followed close behind.

With her spirit wandering in dreamland, she was naturally somewhat distraite—not too much so, only sufficiently to cause Louis XV to make comparisons betwixt his sprightly Jeanne and this animated statue, whose cold little hand rested so impassively on the satin of his coat.

At the foot of the perron the King's Flemish horses, as round of body and heavy of gait as himself, were impatiently pawing the ground. The opening of the great gates sent a wave of sweet-scented air into the overheated château. Lydie was glad that her duty demanded that she should accompany the King down the steps to the door of his coach. The cool night breeze fanned her cheeks most pleasingly, the scent of June roses and of clove carnations filled the air, and from below the terraced gardens there came the softly-murmuring ripple of the Seine, winding her graceful curves toward the mighty city of Paris beyond.

Far away to the east, beyond the grim outline of cedar and poplar trees, a fair crescent moon appeared, chaste and cold.

"An emblem of our fair hostess to-night," said Louis with clumsy gallantry and pointing up to the sky, as Lydie bent her tall figure and kissed the royal hand.

Then she stood aside, having made a cold bow to Mme. de Pompadour; the fair Marquise was accompanying His Majesty to Versailles; she stepped into the coach beside him, surrounded by murmurs of flattery and adulation. Even Charles Edward made her a final speech of somewhat forced gallantry; he was the last to kiss her hand, and Lydie could almost hear the softly whispered words of entreaty with which he bade her not to forget.

And Jeanne Poisson—daughter of a kitchen wench—was condescendingly gracious to a Stuart Prince; then she calmly waved him aside, whilst the King apparently was content to wait, and called Lady Eglinton to the door of the coach.

"You are wasting too much time," she whispered quickly; "an you don't hurry now, you will be too late."

At last the departure was effected; the crowd, with backbone bent and tricornes sweeping the ground, waited in that uncomfortable position until the gilded coach and the men in gorgeous blue and gold liveries were swallowed in the gloom of the chestnut avenue; then it broke up into isolated groups. Lydie had done her duty as hostess; she had taken such leave as etiquette demanded from Charles Edward Stuart and his friends. Coaches and chairs came up to the perron in quick succession now, bearing the adventurers away on this, the first stage of their hazardous expedition. When would they sup again in such luxury? when would the frou-frou of silk, the flutter of fans, the sound of dance music once more pleasantly tickle their ears? To-morrow, and for many a long day to come it would be hurried meals in out-of-the-way places, the call to horse, the clink of arms.

Puppets! puppets all! for what did it matter?

Lydie would have loved to have lingered out on the terrace awhile longer. The oak-leaved geraniums down at the foot of the terrace steps threw an intoxicating lemon-scented fragrance in the air, the row of stunted orange trees still bore a few tardy blossoms, and in the copse yonder, away from the din and the bustle made by the marionettes, it must be delicious to wander on the carpet of moss and perchance to hear the melancholy note of a nightingale.

"Do you think not, Mademoiselle, that this night air is treacherous?" said Lord Eglinton, with his accustomed diffidence. "You seem to be shivering; will you allow me the honour of bringing your cloak?"

She thanked him quite kindly. Somehow his gentle voice did not jar on her mood. Since Gaston was not there, she felt that she would sooner have this unobtrusive, pleasant man beside her than any one else. He seemed to have something womanish and tender in his feeble nature which his mother lacked. Perhaps milady had divested herself of her natural attributes in order to grace her son with them, since she had been unable to instil more manly qualities into him.

But Lydie's heart ached for a sight of Gaston. The clock in the tower of the old château chimed the hour before midnight. It was but half an hour since she had parted from him on the steps of the alcove; she remembered quite distinctly hearing the bracket clock close by strike half-past ten, at the same moment as Pompadour's shrill laugh broke upon her ear.

Half an hour? Why, it seemed a lifetime since then; and while she had made her bow to the Stuart Prince and then to King Louis, while she had allowed the unseen giant to move her from place to place on a string, perhaps Gaston had been seeking for her, perhaps his heart had longed for her too, and a sting of jealousy of her multifarious social duties was even now marring the glory of happy memories.

Without another moment's hesitation she turned her back on the peaceful gloom of the night, on the silver crescent moon, the fragrance of carnations and orange-blossoms, and walked quickly up the perron steps with a hasty: "You are right, milor, the night air

47

is somewhat chilling and my guests will be awaiting me," thrown over her shoulder at her bashful cavalier.

Beyond the noble entrance doors the vast hall was now practically deserted, save for a group of flunkeys, gorgeous and solemn, who stood awaiting the departure of their respective masters. At the farther end which led to the main corridor, Lydie, to her chagrin, caught sight of Lady Eglinton's brobdingnagian back.

"What an obsession!" she sighed, and hoped that milady would fail to notice her. Already she was planning hasty flight along a narrow passage, when a question authoritatively put by her ladyship to a magnificent person clad in a purple livery with broad white facings arrested her attention.

"Is your master still in the boudoir, do you know?"

"I do not know, Mme. la Marquise," the man replied. "I have not seen M. le Comte since half an hour."

The purple livery with broad white facings was that of the Comte de Stainville.

"I have a message for M. le Comte from Mme. de Pompadour," said Lady Eglinton carelessly. "I'll find him, I daresay."

And she turned into the great corridor.

Lydie no longer thought of flight; an unexplainable impulse caught her to change her mind, and to follow in Lady Eglinton's wake. She could not then have said if "le petit Anglais" was still near her not. She had for the moment forgotten his insignificant existence.

There was an extraordinary feeling of unreality about herself and her movements, about the voluminous person ahead clad in large-flowered azure brocade and closely followed by a stiff automaton in purple and white; they seemed to be leading her along some strange and unexpected paths, at the end of which Lydie somehow felt sure that grinning apes would be awaiting her.

Anon Lady Eglinton paused, with her hand on the handle of a door; she caught sight of Mlle. d'Aumont and seemed much surprised to see her there. She called to her by name, in that harsh voice which Lydie detested, whilst the obsequious automaton came forward and relieved her from the trouble of turning that handle herself.

"Allow me, milady."

The door flew open, the flunkey at the same moment also drew a heavy curtain aside.

Lydie had just come up quite close, in answer to Lady Eglinton's call. She was standing facing the door when Bénédict threw it open, announcing with mechanical correctness of attitude:

48

"Mme. la Marquise d'Eglinton, M. le Comte!"

At first Lydie only saw Gaston as he turned to face the intruders. His face was flushed, and he muttered a quickly-suppressed oath. But already she had guessed, even before Lady Eglinton's strident voice had set her every nerve a-tingling.

"Mlle. de Saint Romans!" said milady, with a shrill laugh, "a thousand pardons! I had a message from Mme. de Pompadour for M. le Comte de Stainville, and thought to find him alone. A thousand pardons, I beg—the intrusion was involuntary—and the message unimportant—I'll deliver it when Monsieur is less pleasantly engaged."

Lydie at that moment could not have stirred one limb, if her very life had depended on a movement from her. The feeling of unreality had gone. It was no longer that. It was a grim, hideous, awful reality. That beautiful woman there was reality, and real, too, were the glowing eyes that flashed defiance at milady, the lips parted for that last kiss which the flunkey's voice had interrupted, the stray black curls which had escaped from the trammels of the elaborate coiffure and lay matted on the damp forehead.

And those roses, too, which had adorned her corsage, now lying broken and trampled on the floor, the candles burning dimly in their sockets, and Gaston's look of wrath, quickly followed by one of fear—all—all that was real!

Real to the awful shame of it all—milady's sneer of triumph, the oath which had risen to Gaston's lips, the wooden figure of the lacquey standing impassive at the door!

Instinctively Lydie's hand flew to her lips; oh, that she could have wiped out the last, lingering memory of that kiss. She, the proud and reserved vestal, a Diana chaste and cold, with lips now for ever polluted by contact with those of a liar. A liar, a traitor, a sycophant! She lashed her haughty spirit into fury, the better to feel the utter degradation of her own abasement.

She did not speak. What could she say! One look at Gaston's face and she understood that her humiliation was complete; his eyes did not even seek her pardon, they expressed neither sorrow nor shame, only impotent wrath and fear of baffled ambition. Not before all these people would she betray herself, before that beautiful rival, or that vulgar intrigante, not before Gaston or his lacquey, and beyond that mechanical movement of hand to lips, beyond one short flash of unutterable pride and contempt, she remained silent and rigid, whilst her quick eyes took in a complete mental vision of that never to-be-forgotten picture—the dimly-lighted boudoir, the defiant figure of Irène de Saint Romans, the crushed roses on the floor.

Then with a heart-broken sigh unheard by the other actors in this moving tableaux, and covering her face with her hands, she began to walk rapidly down the corridor.

CHAPTER IX

THE WINNING HAND

But Lydie d'Aumont had not gone five paces before she heard a quick, sharp call, followed by the rustle of silk on the marble floor.

The next moment she felt a firm, hot grip on her wrist, and her left hand was forcibly drawn away from her face, whilst an eager voice spoke quick, vehement words, the purport of which failed at first to reach her brain.

"You shall not go, Mlle. d'Aumont," were the first coherent words which she seemed to understand—"you cannot—it is not just, not fair until you have heard!"

"There is nothing which I need hear," interrupted Lydie coldly, the moment she realized that it was Irène de Saint Romans who was addressing her; "and I pray you to let me go."

"Nay! but you shall hear, you must!" rejoined the other without releasing her grasp on the young girl's wrist. Her hand was hot, and her fingers had the strength of intense excitement. Lydie could not free herself, strive how she might.

"Do you not see that this is most unfair?" continued Irène with great volubility. "Am I to be snubbed like some kitchen wench caught kissing behind doorways? Look at milady Eglinton and her ill-natured sneer. I'll not tolerate it, nor your looks of proud contempt! I'll not—I'll not! Gaston! Gaston!" she now exclaimed, turning to de Stainville, who was standing, silent and sullen, whilst he saw his wife gradually lashing herself into wrathful agitation at his own indifference and Lydie's cold disdain. "If you have a spark of courage left in you, tell that malicious intrigante and this scornful minx that if I were to spend the whole evening in the boudoir en tête-à-tête with you, aye! and behind closed doors if I chose who shall have a word to say, when I am in the company of my own husband?"

"Your husband!"

The ejaculation came from Lady Eglinton's astonished lips. Lydie had not stirred. She did not seem to have heard, and certainly Irène's triumphant announcement left her as cold, as impassive as before. What did it matter, after all, what special form Gaston's lies to her had assumed? Nothing that he or Irène said or did could add to his baseness and infamy.

"Aye, my husband, milady!" continued the other more calmly, as she finally released Lydie's wrist and cast it, laughing, from her. "I am called Mme. la Comtesse de Stainville, and will be called so in the future openly. Now you may rejoin your guests, Mlle. d'Aumont; my reputation stands as far beyond reproach as did your own before you spent a mysterious half hour with my husband behind the curtains of an alcove."

She turned to de Stainville, who, in spite of his wife's provocative attitude, had remained silent, cursing the evil fate which had played him this trick, cursing the three women who were both the cause and the witnesses of his discomfiture.

"Your arm, Gaston!" she said peremptorily; "and you, Benedict, call your master's coach and my chair. Mlle. d'Aumont, your servant. If I have been the means of dissipating a happy illusion, you may curse me now, but you will bless me to-morrow. Gaston has been false to you—he is not over true to me—but he is my husband, and as such I must claim him. For the sake of his schemes, of his ambitions, I kept our marriage a secret so that he might rise to higher places than I had the power to give him. When your disdainful looks classed me with a flirty kitchen-wench I rebelled at last. I trust that you are proud enough not to vent your disappointment on Gaston; but if you do, 'tis no matter; I'll find means of consoling him."

She made the young girl a low and sweeping curtesy in the most approved style demanded by the elabourate etiquette of the time. There was a gleam of mocking triumph in her eyes, which she did not attempt to conceal, and which suddenly stung Lydie's pride to the quick.

It is strange indeed that often at a moment when a woman's whole happiness is destroyed with one blow, when a gigantic cataclysm revolutionises with one fell swoop her entire mode of thought, dispels all her dreams and shatters her illusions, it is always the tiny final pin-prick which causes her the most acute pain and influences the whole of her subsequent conduct.

It was Irène's mocking curtsey which roused Lydie from her mental torpor, because it brought her—as it were—in actual physical contact with all that she would have to endure openly in the future, as apart from the hidden misery of her heart.

Gaston's shamed face was no longer the only image which seared her eyes and brain. The world, her own social world, seemed all at once to reawaken before her. That world would sneer even as Irène de Stainville sneered; it would laugh at and enjoy her own discomfiture. She—Lydie d'Aumont—the proud and influential daughter of the Prime Minister of France, whom flatterers and sycophants approached mentally on bended knees, for whom suitors hardly dared even to sigh, she had been tricked and fooled like any silly country mouse whose vanity had led to her own abasement.

Half an hour ago in the fullness of her newly-found happiness she had flaunted her pride and her love before those who hated and envied her. To-morrow—nay, within an hour—this humiliating scene would be the talk of Paris and Versailles. Lydie's burning ears seemed even now to hear the Pompadour retailing it with many embellishments, which would bring a coarse laugh to the lips of the King and an ill-natured jest to those of her admirers; she could hear the jabbering crowd, could feel the looks of compassion or sarcasm aimed at her as soon at this tit-bit of society scandal had been bruited abroad.

The scene itself had become real and vivid to her; the marble corridor, the flickering candles, the flunkey's impassive face; she understood that the beautiful woman before her was in fact and deed the wife of Gaston de Stainville. She even contrived to perceive the humour of Lady Eglinton's completely bewildered expression, the blank astonishment of her round, bulgy eyes, and close to her she saw "le petit Anglais," self-effaced as usual, and looking almost as guilty, as shamefaced as Gaston.

Lydie turned to him and placed a cool, steady hand upon his sleeve.

"Madame la Comtesse de Stainville," she then said with perfect calm, "I fear me I must beg of your courtesy to tarry awhile longer, whilst I offer you an explanation to which I feel you are entitled. Just now I was somewhat surprised because your news was sudden—and it is my turn to ask your pardon, although my fault—if fault there be—rests on a misapprehension. M. le Comte de Stainville's amours or his marriage are no concern of mine. True, he begged for my influence and fawned upon my favour just now, for his ambition soared to the post of High Controller of the Finances of France. That appointment rests with the Duc, my father, who no doubt will bestow it on him whom he thinks most worthy. But it were not fair to me, if you left me now thinking that the announcement of your union with a gentleman whose father was the friend of mine could give me aught but pleasure. Permit me to congratulate you, Madame, on the choice of a lord and master, a helpmeet no doubt. You are indeed well matched. I am all the more eager to offer you my good wishes as I have been honoured to-night with a proposal which has greatly flattered me. My lord the Marquis of Eglinton has asked me to be his wife!"

Once more she turned her head toward the young Englishman and challenged a straight look from his eyes. He did not waver and she was satisfied. Her instinct had not misled her, for he expressed no astonishment, only a sort of dog-like gratitude and joy as, having returned her gaze quite firmly, he now slowly raised his arm bringing her hand on a level with his lips.

Lady Eglinton also displayed sufficient presence of mind not to show any surprise. She perhaps alone of all those present fully realized that Lydie had been wounded to the innermost depths of her heart, and that she herself owed her own and her son's present triumph to the revolt of mortified pride.

What Gaston thought and felt exactly it were difficult to say. He held women in such slight esteem, and his own vanity was receiving so severe a blow, that, no doubt, he preferred to think that Lydie, like himself, had no power of affection and merely bestowed her heart there where self-interest called.

Irène, on the other hand, heaved a sigh of relief; the jealous suspicions which had embittered the last few days were at last dispelled. Hers was a simple, shallow nature that did not care to look beyond the obvious. She certainly appeared quite pleased at Lydie's announcement, and if remorse at her precipitancy did for one brief second mar the fullness of her joy, she quickly cast it from her, not having yet had time to understand the future and more serious consequences of her impulsive avowal.

She wanted to go up to Lydie and to offer her vapid expressions of goodwill, but Gaston, heartily tired of the prolongation of this scene, dragged her somewhat roughly away.

From the far distance there came the cry of the flunkeys.

"The chair of Mlle. de Saint Romans!"

"The coach of M. le Comte de Stainville!"

M. Bénédict, resplendent in purple and white, reappeared at the end of the corridor, with Irène's hood and cloak. Gaston, with his wife on his arm, turned on his heel and quickly walked down the corridor.

Milady, puzzled, bewildered, boundlessly overjoyed yet fearing to trust her luck too far, had just a sufficient modicum of tact left in her to retire discreetly within the boudoir.

Lydie suddenly found herself alone in this wide corridor with the man whom she had so impulsively dragged into her life. She looked round her somewhat helplessly, and her eyes encountered those of her future lord fixed upon hers with that same air of dog-like gentleness which she knew so well and which always irritated her.

"Milor," she said very coldly, "I must thank you for your kind coöperation just now. That you expressed neither surprise nor resentment does infinite credit to your chivalry."

"If I was a little surprised, Mademoiselle," he said, haltingly, "I was too overjoyed to show it, and—and I certainly felt no resentment."

He came a step nearer to her. But for this she was not prepared, and drew back with a quick movement and a sudden stiffening of her figure.

"I hope you quite understood milor, that there is no desire on my part to hold you to this bond," she said icily. "I am infinitely grateful to you for the kind way in which you humoured my impulse to-night, and if you will have patience with me but a very little while, I promise you that I will find an opportunity for breaking, without too great a loss of dignity, these bonds which already must be very irksome to you."

"Nay, Mademoiselle," he said gently, "you are under a misapprehension. Believe me, you would find it well-nigh impossible to—to—er—to alter your plans now without loss of dignity, and—er—er—I assure you that the bonds are not irksome to me."

"You would hold me to this bargain, then?"

"For your sake, Mademoiselle, as well as mine, we must now both be held to it."

"It seems unfair on you, milor."

"On me, Mademoiselle?"

"Yes, on you," she repeated, with a thought more gentleness in her voice; "you are young, milor; you are rich—soon you will regret the sense of honour which ties you to a woman who has only yielded her hand to you out of pique! Nay, I'll not deceive you," she added quickly, noting the sudden quiver of the kind little face at her stinging words. "I have no love for you, milor—all that was young and fresh, womanly and tender in my heart was buried just here to-night."

And with a mournful look she glanced round at the cold marble of the walls, the open door to that boudoir beyond, the gilded sconces which supported the dimly-burning candles. Then, smitten with sudden remorse, she said eagerly, with one of those girlish impulses which rendered her domineering nature so peculiarly attractive:

"But if I can give you no love, milor, Heaven and my father's indulgence have given me something which I know men hold far greater of importance than a woman's heart. I have influence, boundless influence, as you know—the State appointed Controller of Finance will be the virtual ruler of France, his position will give him power beyond the dreams of any man's ambition. My father will gladly give the post to my husband and—"

But here a somewhat trembling hand was held deprecatingly toward her.

"Mademoiselle, I entreat you," said Lord Eglinton softly, "for the sake of your own dignity and—and mine, do not allow your mind to dwell on such matters. Believe me, I am fully conscious of the honour which you did me just now in deigning to place your trust in me. That I have—have loved you, Mlle. Lydie," he added, with a nervous quiver in his young voice, "ever since I first saw you at this Court I—I cannot deny; but"—and here he spoke more firmly, seeing that once again she seemed to draw away from him, to stiffen at his approach, "but that simple and natural fact need not trouble you. I could not help loving you, for you are more beautiful than anything on earth, and you cannot deem my adoration an offence, though you are as cold and pure as the goddess of chastity herself. I have seen Catholics kneeling at the shrine of the Virgin Mary; their eyes were fixed up to her radiant image, their lips murmured an invocation or sometimes a hymn of praise. But their hands were clasped together; they never even raised them once toward that shrine which they had built for her, and from which she smiled whilst listening coldly to their prayers. Mlle. d'Aumont, you need have no mistrust of my deep respect for you; you are the Madonna and I the humblest of your worshippers. I am proud to think that the name I bear will be the shrine wherein your pride will remain enthroned. If you have need of me in the future you must command me, but though the law of France will call me your husband and your lord, I will be your bondsman and serve you on my knees; and though my very soul aches for the mere touch of your hand, my lips will never pollute even the hem of your gown." His trembling voice had sunk down to a whisper. If she heard or not he could not say. From far away there came to his ears the tender melancholy drone of the instruments playing the slow movement of the gavotte. His Madonna had not stirred, only her hand which he so longed to touch trembled a little as she toyed with her fan.

And, like the worshippers at the Virgin's shrine, he bent his knee and knelt at her feet.

PART II

THE STATESMAN

CHAPTER X

THE BEGGAR ON HORSEBACK

Monsieur le Marquis d'Eglinton, Comptroller-General of Finance, Chevalier of the Order of St. Louis, Peer of England and of France, occupied the west wing of the Château of Versailles. His Majesty the King had frequent and urgent need of him; Mme. de Pompadour could scarce exist a day without an interview behind closed doors with the most powerful man in France: with him, who at the bidding of the nation, was set up as a bar to the extravagances of her own caprice.

And le petit lever of M. le Contrôleur was certainly more largely attended than that of M. le Duc d'Aumont, or even—softly be it whispered—than that of His Majesty himself. For although every one knew that M. le Marquis was but a figurehead, and that all graces and favours emanated direct from the hand of Mme. la Marquise Lydie, yet every one waited upon his good pleasure, for very much the same reason that those who expected or hoped something from the King invariably kissed the hand of Mme. de Pompadour.

M. le Contrôleur very much enjoyed these petits levers of his, which were considered the most important social events in Versailles. He was very fond of chocolate in the morning, and M. Achille—that prince of valets—brought it to his bedside with such inimitable grace and withal the beverage itself so aromatic and so hot, that this hour between ten and eleven each day had become extremely pleasant.

He had no idea that being Comptroller-General of Finance was quite so easy and agreeable an occupation, else he had not been so diffident in accepting the post. But in reality it was very simple. He governed France from the depths of his extremely comfortable bed, draped all round with rich satin hangings of a soft azure colour, embroidered with motifs of dull gold, which were vastly pleasing to the eye. Here he was conscious of naught save fine linen of a remarkably silken texture, of a lace coverlet priceless in value, of the scent of his steaming chocolate, and incidentally of a good many pleasant faces, and some unamiable ones, and of a subdued hive-like buzz of talk, which went on at the further end of the room, whilst M. Achille administered to his comforts and Mme. de Pompadour or Mme. la Comtesse de Stainville told him piquant anecdotes.

Yes, it was all very pleasant, and not at all difficult. A wave of the hand in the direction of Mme. la Marquise, his wife, who usually sat in a window embrasure overlooking the park, was all that was needed when petitioners were irksome or subjects too abstruse.

Lydie was so clever with all that sort of thing. She had the mind of a politician and the astuteness of an attorney, and she liked to govern France in an energetic way of her own which left milor free of all responsibility if anything happened to go wrong.

But then nothing ever did go wrong. France went on just the same as she had done before some of her more meddlesome Parliaments insisted on having a Comptroller of Finance at the head of affairs. Mme. de Pompadour still spent a great deal of money, and the King still invariably paid her debts; whereupon, his pockets being empty, he applied to M. le Contrôleur for something with which to replenish them. M. le Contrôleur thereupon ordered M. Achille to bring one more cup of aromatic chocolate for Mme. de Pompadour, whilst His Majesty the King spent an uncomfortable quarter of an hour with Mme. la Marquise d'Eglinton.

The usual result of this quarter of an hour was that His Majesty was excessively wrathful against Mme. Lydie for quite a fortnight; but no one could be angry with "le petit Anglais," for he was so very amiable and dispensed such exceedingly good chocolate.

Par ma foi! it is remarkably easy to govern a country if one happen to have a wife—that, at least, had been milor's experience—a wife and a perfect valet-de-chambre.

M. Achille, since his Marquis's elevation to the most important position in France, had quite surpassed himself in his demeanour. He stood on guard beside the azure and gold hangings of his master's bed like a veritable gorgon, turning the most importunate petitioners to stone at sight of his severe and repressive visage.

Oh! Achille was an invaluable asset in the governing of this kingdom of France. Achille knew the reason of each and every individual's presence at the petit lever of milor. He knew who was the most likely and most worthy person to fill any post in the country that happened to be vacant, from that of examiner of stars and planets to His Majesty the King down to that of under-scullion in the kitchen of Versailles.

Had he not been the means of introducing Baptiste Durand to the special notice of M. le Marquis? Durand's daughter being girl-in-waiting to M. Joseph, valet-de-chambre to M. le Duc d'Aumont, and personal friend of M. Achille, what more natural than, when milor wanted a secretary to make notes for him, and to—well, to be present if he happened to be wanted—that the worthy Baptiste should with perfect ease slip into the vacant post?

And Baptiste Durand was remarkably useful.

A small ante-chamber had been allotted for his occupation, through which all those who were on their way to the petit lever held in milor's own bedchamber had of necessity to pass; and Baptiste knew exactly who should be allowed to pass and who should not. Without venturing even to refer to His Majesty, to Mme. de Pompadour, to Monseigneur le Dauphin, or persons of equally exalted rank, the faithful chroniclers of the time tell us that no gentleman was allowed a private audience with M. le Contrôleur-Général if his valet-de-chambre was not a personal friend of Monsieur Durand.

There sat the worthy Baptiste enthroned behind a secretaire which was always littered with papers, petitions, letters, the usual paraphernalia that pertains to a man of influence. His meagre person was encased in a coat and breeches of fine scarlet cloth, whereon a tiny fillet of gold suggested without unduly flaunting the heraldic colours of the house of Eglinton. He wore silk stockings—always; and shoes with cut-steel buckles, whilst frills of broidered lawn encircled his wrists and cascaded above his waistcoat.

He invariably partook of snuff when an unknown and unrecommended applicant presented himself in his sanctum. "My good friend, it is impossible," he was saying on this very morning of August 13, 1746, with quiet determination to a petitioner who was becoming too insistent. "Milor's chamber is overcrowded as it is."

"I'll call again—another day perhaps; my master is anxious for a personal interview with yours."

Whereupon M. Durand's eyebrows were lifted upward until they almost came in contact with his perruque; he fetched out a voluminous handkerchief from his pocket and carefully removed a few grains of dust from his cravat. Then he said, without raising his voice in the slightest degree or showing impatience in any way at the man's ignorance and stupidity—

"My good—— What is your name? I forgot."

"I am Hypolite François, confidential valet to M. le Maréchal de Coigni and——"

M. Durand's thin and delicately veined hand went up in gentle deprecation.

"Ma foi! my worthy Coigni, 'tis all the same to me if you are a maréchal or a simple lieutenant. As for me, young man," he added, with dignified severity, "remember in future that I serve no one. I assist M. le Contrôleur-Général des Finances to—to——"—he paused a second, waving his hand and turning the phrase over in his mouth, whilst seeking for its most appropriate conclusion—"to, in fact, make a worthy selection amidst the hundreds and thousands of petitions which are presented to him."

And with a vague gesture he indicated the papers which lay in a disordered heap on his secretaire.

"For the rest, my good Coigni," he added, with the same impressive dignity, "let me assure you once again that M. le Marquis's bedchamber is overcrowded, that he is busily engaged at the present moment, and is likely to be so for some considerable time to come. What is it your maréchal wants?"

"His pension," replied Hypolite curtly, "and the vacant post in the Ministry of War."

"Impossible! We have fourteen likely applicants already."

"M. le Maréchal is sure that if he could speak with M. le Contrôleur——"

"M. le Contrôleur is busy."

"To-morrow, then——"

"To-morrow he will be even more busy than to-day."

"M. Durand!" pleaded Hypolite.

"Impossible! You are wasting my time, my good Coigni; I have hundreds to see to-day."

"Not for your daughter's sake?"

"My daughter?"

"Yes; didn't you know? You remember Henriette, her great friend?"

"Yes, yes—little Henriette Dessy, the milliner," assented M. Durand with vast condescension. "A pretty wench; she was at the Ursulines convent school with my daughter; they have remained great friends ever since. What about little Henriette?"

"Mlle. Henriette is my fiancée," quoth the other eagerly, "and I thought——"

"Your fiancée? Little Henriette Dessy?" said M. Durand gaily. "Pardieu my good Coigni, why did you not tell me so before? My daughter is very fond of Henriette—a pretty minx, par ma foi! Hé! hé!"

"You are very kind, M. Durand."

"Mais non, mais non," said the great man, with much

affability; "one is always ready to oblige a friend. Hé, now! give me your hand, friend Coigni. Shoot your rubbish along—quoi!—your Maréchal; he may pass this way. Anything one can do to oblige a friend."

With the affairs of M. le Maréchal de Coigni the present chronicle hath no further concern; but we know that some ten minutes later on this same August 13, 1746, he succeeded in being present at the petit lever of M. le Contrôleur-Général des Finances. Once within the secret precincts of the bedchamber he, like so many other petitioners and courtiers, was duly confronted by the stony stare of M. Achille, and found himself face to face with an enormous bedstead of delicately painted satinwood and ormulu mounts, draped with heavy azure silk curtains which hung down from a gilded baldachin, the whole a masterpiece of the furniture-maker's art.

The scent of chocolate filled his nostrils, and he vaguely saw a good-looking young man reclining under a coverlet of magnificent Venetian lace, and listening placidly to what was obviously a very amusing tale related to him by well-rouged lips. From the billowy satins and laces of the couch a delicate hand was waved toward him as he attempted to pay his respects to the most powerful man in France; the next moment the same stony-faced gorgon clad in scarlet and gold beckoned to him to follow, and he found himself being led through the brilliantly dressed crowd toward a compact group of backs, which formed a sort of living wall, painted in delicate colours of green and mauve and gray, and duly filled up the approach to the main window embrasure.

It is interesting to note from the memoirs of M. le Comte d'Argenson that the Maréchal de Coigni duly filled the post of State Secretary to the Minister of War from the year 1746 onward. We may, therefore, presume that he succeeded in piercing that wall of respectful backs and in reaching sufficiently far within the charmed circle to attract the personal attention of Mme. la Marquise Lydie d'Eglinton née d'Aumont.

He had, therefore, cause to bless the day when his valet-de-chambre became the fiancé of Mlle. Henriette Dessy, the intimate friend of M. Baptiste Durand's dearly beloved daughter.

CHAPTER XI

LA BELLE IRÈNE

Monsieur Durand had indeed not exaggerated when he spoke of M. le Contrôleur's bedchamber being overcrowded this same eventful morning.

All that France possessed of nobility, of wit and of valour, seemed to have found its way on this beautiful day in August past the magic portal guarded by Baptiste, the dragon, to the privileged enclosure beyond, where milor in elegant robe de chambre reclined upon his gorgeous couch, whilst Madame, clad in hooped skirt and panniers of dove-gray silk, directed the affairs of France from the embrasure of a window.

"Achille, my shoes!"

We must surmise that his lordship had been eagerly awaiting the striking of the bracket clock which immediately faced the bed, for the moment the musical chimes had ceased to echo in the crowded room he had thrown aside the lace coverlet which had lain across his legs and called peremptorily for his valet.

"Only half-past ten, milor!" came in reproachful accents from a pair of rosy lips.

"Ma foi, so it is!" exclaimed Lord Eglinton, with well-feigned surprise, as he once more glanced up at the clock.

"Were you then so bored in my company," rejoined the lady, with a pout, "that you thought the hour later?"

"Bored!" he exclaimed. "Bored, did you say, Madame? Perish the very thought of boredom in the presence of Mme. la Comtesse de Stainville!"

But in spite of this gallant assertion, M. le Contrôleur seemed in a vast hurry to quit the luxuriance of his azure-hung throne. M. Achille—that paragon among flunkeys—looked solemnly reproachful. Surely milor should have known by now that etiquette demanded that he should stay in bed until he had received every person of high rank who desired an intimate audience.

There were still some high-born, exalted, and much beribboned gentlemen who had not succeeded in reaching the inner precincts of that temple and fount of honours and riches—the bedside of M. le Contrôleur. But Monseigneur le Prince de Courtenai was there—he in whose veins flowed royal blood, and who spent a strenuous life in endeavouring to make France recognize this obvious fact. He sat in an arm-chair at the foot of the bed, discussing the unfortunate events of June 16th at Piacenza and young Comte de Maillebois's subsequent masterly retreat on Tortone, with Christian Louis de Montmorenci, Duc de Luxembourg, the worthy son of an able father and newly created Marshal of France.

Close to them, Monsieur le Comte de Vermandois, Grand Admiral of France, was intent on explaining to M. le Chancelier d'Aguesseau why England just now was supreme mistress of the seas. M. d'Isenghien talked poetry to Jolyot Crébillon, and M. le Duc d'Harcourt discussed Voltaire's latest play with ex-comedian and ex-ambassador Néricault-Destouche, whilst Mme. la Comtesse de Stainville, still called "la belle brune de Bordeaux" by her many admirers, had been endeavouring to divert M. le Contrôleur's attention from this multiplicity of abstruse subjects.

Outside this magic circle there was a gap, a barrier of parquet flooring which no one would dare to traverse without a distinct look of encouragement from M. Achille. His Majesty had not yet arrived, and tongues wagged freely in the vast and gorgeous room, with its row of tall windows which gave on the great slopes of the Park of Versailles. Through them came the pleasing sound of the perpetual drip from the monumental fountains, the twitter of sparrows, the scent of lingering roses and of belated lilies. No other sound from that outside world, no other life save the occasional footstep of a gardener along the sanded walks. But within all was chatter and bustle; women talked, men laughed and argued, society scandals were commented upon and the newest fashions in coiffures discussed. The men wore cloth coats of sober hues, but the women had donned light-coloured dresses, for the summer was at its height and this August morning was aglow with sunshine.

Mme. de Stainville's rose-coloured gown was the one vivid patch of colour in the picture of delicate hues. She stood close to M. le Contrôleur's bedside and unceremoniously turned her back on the rest of the company; we must presume that she was a very privileged visitor, for no one—not even Monseigneur le Prince de Courtenai—ventured to approach within earshot. It was understood that in milor's immediate entourage la belle Irène alone was allowed to be frivolous, and we are told that she took full advantage of this permission.

All chroniclers of the period distinctly aver that the lady was vastly entertaining; even M. de Voltaire mentions her as one of the sprightliest women of that light-hearted and vivacious Court. Beautiful, too, beyond cavil, her position as the wife of one of the most brilliant cavaliers that e'er graced the entourage of Mme. de Pompadour gave her a certain dignity of bearing, a self-conscious

62

gait and proud carriage of the head which had considerably added to the charms which she already possessed. The stiff, ungainly mode of the period suited her somewhat full figure to perfection; the tight corslet bodice, the wide panniers, the ridiculous hooped skirt—all seemed to have been specially designed to suit the voluptuous beauty of Irène de Stainville.

M. d'Argenson when speaking of her has described her very fully. He speaks of her abnormally small waist, which seemed to challenge the support of a masculine arm, and of her creamy skin which she knew so well how to veil in transparent folds of filmy lace. She made of dress a special study, and her taste, though daring, was always sure. Even during these early morning receptions, when soft-toned mauves, tender drabs or grays were mostly in evidence, Irène de Stainville usually appeared in brocade of brilliant rosy-red, turquoise blue, or emerald green; she knew that these somewhat garish tones, mellowed only through the richness of the material, set off to perfection the matt ivory tint of her complexion, and detached her entire person from the rest of the picture.

Yet even her most ardent admirers tell us that Irène de Stainville's vanity went almost beyond the bounds of reason in its avidity for fulsome adulation. Consciousness of her own beauty was not sufficient; she desired its acknowledgment from others. She seemed to feed on flattery, breathing it in with every pore of her delicate skin, drooping like a parched flower when full measure was denied to her. Many aver that she marred her undoubted gifts of wit through this insatiable desire for one sole topic of conversation—her own beauty and its due meed of praise. At the same time her love of direct and obsequious compliments was so ingenuous, and she herself so undeniably fascinating, that, in the hey-day of her youth and attractions, she had no difficulty in obtaining ready response to her wishes from the highly susceptible masculine element at the Court of Louis XV.

M. le Contrôleur-Général—whom she specially honoured with her smiles—had certainly no intention of shirking the pleasing duty attached to this distinction, and, though he was never counted a brilliant conversationalist, he never seemed at a loss for the exact word of praise which would tickle la belle Irène's ears most pleasantly.

And truly no man's heart could be sufficiently adamant to deny to that brilliantly-plumaged bird the tit-bits which it loved the best. Milor himself had all the sensitiveness of his race where charms—such as Irène freely displayed before him—were concerned, and when her smiling lips demanded acknowledgment of her beauty from him he was ready enough to give it.

"Let them settle the grave affairs of State over there," she had said to him this morning, when first she made her curtsey before him. And with a provocative smile she pointed to the serious-looking group of grave gentlemen that surrounded his bedside, and also to the compact row of backs which stood in serried ranks round Mme. la Marquise d'Eglinton in the embrasure of the central window. "Life is too short for such insignificant trifles."

"We only seem to last long enough to make love thoroughly to half a dozen pretty women in a lifetime," replied M. le Contrôleur, as he gallantly raised her fingers to his lips.

"Half a dozen!" she retorted, with a pout. "Ah, milor, I see that your countrymen are not maligned! The English have such a reputation for perfidy!"

"But I have become so entirely French!" he protested. "England would scarce know me now."

And with a whimsical gesture he pointed to the satin hangings of his bed, the rich point lace coverlet, and to his own very elaborate and elegant robe de chambre.

"Is that said in regret?" she asked.

"Nay," he replied, "there is no more place for regret than there is for boredom in sight of smiles from those perfect lips."

She blushed, and allowed her hands—which were particularly beautiful—to finger idly the silks and laces which were draped so tastefully about his person. As her eyes were downcast in dainty and becoming confusion, she failed to notice that M. le Contrôleur was somewhat absent-minded this morning, and that, had he dared, he would at this juncture undoubtedly have yawned. But of this she was obviously unconscious, else she had not now murmured so persuasively.

"Am I beautiful?"

"What a question!" he replied.

"The most beautiful woman here present?" she insisted.

"Par ma foi!" he protested gaily. "Was ever married man put in so awkward a predicament?"

"Married man? Bah!" and she shrugged her pretty shoulders.

"I am a married man, fair lady, and the law forbids me to answer so provoking a question."

"This is cowardly evasion," she rejoined. "Mme. la Marquise, your wife, only acknowledges one supremacy—that of the mind. She would scorn to be called the most beautiful woman in the room."

"And M. le Comte de Stainville, your lord, would put a hole right through my body were I now to speak the unvarnished truth."

Irène apparently chose to interpret milor's equivocal speech in the manner most pleasing to her self-love. She looked over her shoulder toward the window embrasure. She saw that Mme. la Marquise d'Eglinton's court was momentarily dismissed, and that M. le Duc d'Aumont had just joined his daughter. She also saw that Lydie looked troubled, and that she threw across the room a look of haughty reproof.

Nothing could have pleased Irène de Stainville more.

Apart from the satisfaction which her own inordinate vanity felt at the present moment by enchaining milor's attention and receiving his undivided homage in full sight of the élite of aristocratic Versailles, there was the additional pleasure of dealing a pin-prick or so to a woman who had once been her rival, and who was undoubtedly now the most distinguished as she was the most adulated personality in France.

Irène had never forgiven Lydie Gaston's defalcations on that memorable night, when a humiliating exposure and subsequent scene led to the disclosure of her own secret marriage, and thus put a momentary check on her husband's ambitious schemes.

From that check he had since then partially recovered. Mme. de Pompadour's good graces which she never wholly withdrew from him had given him a certain position of influence and power, from which his lack of wealth would otherwise have debarred him. But even with the uncertain and fickle Marquise's help Gaston de Stainville was far from attaining a position such as his alliance with Lydie would literally have thrown into his lap, such, of course, as fell to the share of the amiable milor, who had succeeded in capturing the golden prey. In these days of petticoat government feminine protection was the chief leverage for advancement; Irène, however, could do nothing for her husband without outside help; conscious of her own powers of fascination, she had cast about for the most likely prop on which she could lean gracefully whilst helping Gaston to climb upward.

The King himself was too deeply in the toils of his fair Jeanne to have eyes for any one save for her. M. le Duc d'Aumont, Prime Minister of France, was his daughter's slave; there remained M. le Contrôleur-Général himself—a figure-head as far as the affairs of State were concerned, but wielding a great deal of personal power through the vastness of his wealth which Lydie rather affected to despise.

Irène, therefore—faute de mieux—turned her languishing eyes upon M. le Contrôleur. Her triumph was pleasing to herself, and might in due course prove useful to Gaston, if she succeeded presently in counterbalancing Lydie's domineering influence over milor. For the moment her vanity was agreeably soothed, although "la belle brune de Bordeaux" herself was fully alive to the fact that,

65

while her whispered conversations at milor's petits levers, her sidelong glances and conscious blushes called forth enough mischievous oglings and equivocal jests from the more frivolous section of society butterflies, Lydie only viewed her and her machinations with cold and somewhat humiliating indifference.

"And," as M. d'Argenson very pertinently remarked that self-same morning, "would any beautiful woman care to engage the attentions of a man unless she aroused at the same time the jealousy or at least the annoyance of a rival?"

CHAPTER XII

THE PROMISES OF FRANCE

Indeed, if Irène de Stainville had possessed more penetration, or had at any rate studied Lydie's face more closely, she would never have imagined for a moment that thoughts of petty spite or of feminine pique could find place in the busiest brain that ever toiled for the welfare of France.

History has no doubt said the last word on the subject of that brief interregnum, when a woman's masterful hand tried to check the extravagances of a King and the ruinous caprices of a wanton, and when a woman's will tried to restrain a nation in its formidable onrush down the steep incline which led to the abyss of the Revolution.

Many historians have sneered—perhaps justly so—at this apotheosis of feminity, and pointed to the fact that, while that special era of petticoat government lasted, Louis XV in no way stopped his excesses nor did Pompadour deny herself the satisfaction of a single whim, whilst France continued uninterruptedly to groan under the yoke of oppressive taxation, of bribery and injustice, and to suffer from the arrogance of her nobles and the corruption of her magistrates.

The avowed partisans of Lydie d'Eglinton contend on the other hand that her rule lasted too short a time to be of real service to the country, and that those who immediately succeeded her were either too weak or too self-seeking to continue this new system of government instituted by her, and based on loftiness of ideals and purity of motives, a system totally unknown hitherto. They also insist on the fact that while she virtually held the reins of government over the heads of her indolent lord and her over-indulgent father, she brought about many highly beneficent social reforms which would have become firmly established had she remained several years in power; there is no doubt that she exercised a wholesome influence over the existing administration of justice and the distribution of the country's money; and this in spite of endless cabals and the petty intrigues and jealousies of numberless enemies.

Be that as it may, the present chronicler is bound to put it on record that, at the moment when Irène de Stainville vaguely wondered whether Madame la Marquise was looking reprovingly at her, when she hoped that she had at last succeeded in rousing the other woman's jealousy, the latter's mind was dwelling with more than usual anxiousness on the sad events of the past few months.

Her severe expression was only the outcome of a more than normal sense of responsibility. The flattering courtiers and meddlesome women who surrounded her seemed to Lydie this morning more than usually brainless and vapid. Her own father, to whose integrity and keen sense of honour she always felt that she could make appeal, was unusually absent and morose to-day; and she felt unspeakably lonely here in the midst of her immediate entourage—lonely and oppressed. She wanted to mix more with the general throng, the men and women of France, arrogant nobles or obsequious churls, merchants, attorneys, physicians, savants, she cared not which; the nation, in fact, the people who had sympathy and high ideals, and a keener sense of the dignity of France.

While these sycophants were for ever wanting, wanting, wanting, standing before her, as it were, with hands outstretched ready to receive bribes, commissions, places of influence or affluence, Charles Edward Stuart, lately the guest of the nation, the friend of many, whom France herself little more than a year ago had feasted and toasted, to whom she had wished "God-speed!" was now a miserable fugitive, hiding in peasants' huts, beneath overhanging crags on the deserted shores of Scotland, a price put upon his head, and the devotion of a few helpless enthusiasts, a girl, an old retainer, as sole barrier 'twixt him and death.

And France had promised that she would help him. She promised that she would succour him if he failed, that she would not abandon him in his distress—neither him nor his friends.

And now disaster had come—disaster so overwhelming, so appalling, that France at first had scarce liked to believe. Every one was so astonished; had they not thought that England, Scotland and

Ireland were clamouring for a Stuart? That the entire British nation was wanting him, waiting for him, ready to acclaim him with open arms? The first successes—Falkirk, Prestonpans—had surprised no one. The young Pretender's expedition was bound to be nothing but a triumphal procession through crowded streets, decorated towns and beflagged villages, with church bells ringing, people shouting, deputations, both civic and military, waiting hat in hand, with sheaves of loyal addresses.

Instead of this, Culloden, Derby, the hasty retreat, treachery, and the horrible reprisals. All that was common property now.

France knew that the young prince whom she had fêted was perhaps at this moment dying of want, and yet these hands which had grasped his were not stretched out to help him, the lips which had encouraged and cheered him, which had even gently mocked his gloomy mood, still smiled and chatted as irresponsibly as of yore, and spoke the fugitive's name at careless moments 'twixt a laugh and a jest.

And this in spite of promises.

She had dismissed her entourage with a curt nod just now, when her father first joined her circle. At any rate, her position of splendid isolation should give her the right this morning to be alone with him, since she so wished it. At first glance she saw that he was troubled, and her anxious eyes closely scanned his face. But he seemed determined not to return her scrutinizing glance, and anon, when one by one M. de Coigni, the Count de Bailleul, and others who had been talking to Lydie, discreetly stepped aside, he seemed anxious to detain them, eager not to be left quite alone with his daughter.

Seeing his manœuvres, Lydie's every suspicion was aroused; something had occurred to disturb her father this morning, something which he did not intend to tell her. She drew him further back into the window embrasure and made room for him close to her on the settee. She looked up impatiently at the Dowager Lady Eglinton, who had calmly stood her ground whilst the other intimates were being so summarily dismissed. Miladi appeared determined to ignore her daughter-in-law's desire to be alone with her father, and it even seemed to Lydie as if a look of understanding had passed between the Duke and the old lady when first they met.

She felt her nervous system on the jar. Thoroughly frank and open in all political dealings herself, she loathed the very hint of a secret understanding. Yet she trusted her father, even though she feared his weakness.

She talked of Charles Edward Stuart, for that was her chief preoccupation. She lauded him and pitied him in turn, spoke of his predicament, his flight, the devotion of his Scotch adherents, and finally of France's promise to him.

"God grant," she said fervently, "that France may not be too late in doing her duty by that ill-starred prince."

"Nay, my dear child, it is sheer madness to think of such a thing," said the Duke, speaking in tones of gentle reproof and soothingly, as if to a wilful child.

"Hé! pardieu!" broke in miladi's sharp, high-pitched voice: "that is precisely what I have been trying to explain to Lydie these past two weeks, but she will not listen and is not even to be spoken to on that subject now. Do you scold her well, M. le Duc, for I have done my best—and her obstinacy will lead my son into dire disgrace with His Majesty, who doth not favour her plans."

"Miladi is right, Lydie," said the Duke, "and if I thought that your husband——"

"Nay, my dear father!" interrupted Lydie calmly; "I pray you do not vent your displeasure on Lord Eglinton. As you see, Mme. la Comtesse de Stainville is doing her best to prevent his thoughts from dwelling on the fate of his unfortunate friend."

It was the Duke's turn to scrutinize his daughter's face, vaguely wondering if she had spoken in bitterness, not altogether sorry if this new train of thought were to divert her mind from that eternal subject of the moribund Stuart cause, which seemed to have become an obsession with her. He half-turned in the direction where Lydie's eyes were still fixed, and saw a patch of bright rose colour, clear and vivid against the dull hangings of M. le Contrôleur's couch, whilst the elegant outline of a woman's stately form stood between his line of vision and the face of his son-in-law.

The Duc d'Aumont dearly loved his daughter, but he also vastly admired her intellectual power, therefore at sight of that graceful, rose-clad figure he shrugged his shoulders in amiable contempt. Bah! Lydie was far too clever to dwell on such foolish matters as the vapid flirtations of a brainless doll, even if the object of such flirtations was the subjugation of milor.

Lady Eglinton had also perceived Lydie's fixity of expression just now when she spoke of Irène, but whilst M. le Duc carelessly shrugged his shoulders and dismissed the matter from his mind, miladi boldly threw herself across her daughter-in-law's new trend of thought.

"My son for once shows sound common sense," she said decisively; "why should France be led into further extravagance and entangle herself, perhaps, in the meshes of a hopeless cause by——"

"By fulfilling a solemn promise," interrupted Lydie quietly, whilst she turned her earnest eyes on her mother-in-law in the manner so characteristic of her—"a promise which the very hopelessness of which you speak has rendered doubly sacred."

"His Majesty is not of that opinion," retorted the older woman testily, "and we must concede that he is the best judge of what France owes to her own honour."

To this challenge it was obviously impossible to reply in the negative, and if Lydie's heart whispered "Not always!" her lips certainly did not move.

She looked appealingly at her father; she wanted more than ever to be alone with him, to question him, to reassure herself as to certain vague suspicions which troubled her and which would not be stilled. She longed, above all, to be rid of her mother-in-law's interfering tongue, of the platitudes, which she uttered, and which had the knack of still further jarring on Lydie's over-sensitive nerves.

But the Duke did not help her. Usually he, too, was careful to avoid direct discussions with Lady Eglinton, whose rasping voice was wont to irritate him, but this morning he seemed disinclined to meet Lydie's appealing eyes. He fidgeted in his chair, and anon he crossed one shapely leg over the other and thoughtfully stroked his well-turned calf.

"There are moments in diplomacy, my dear child——" he began, after a moment of oppressive silence.

"My dear father," interrupted Lydie, with grave determination, "let me tell you once for all that over this matter my mind is fully made up. While I have a voice in the administration of this Kingdom of France, I will not allow her to sully her fair name by such monstrous treachery as the abandonment of a friend who trusted in her honour and the promises she made him."

Her voice had shaken somewhat as she spoke. Altogether she seemed unlike herself, less sure, less obstinately dominant. That look of understanding between her father and Lady Eglinton had troubled her in a way for which she could not account. Yet she knew that the whole matter rested in her own hands. No one—not even His Majesty—had ever questioned her right to deal with Treasury money. And money was all that was needed. Though the final word nominally rested with milor, he left her perfectly free, and she could act as she thought right, without let or hindrance.

Yet, strangely enough, she felt as if she wanted support in this matter. It was a purely personal feeling, and one she did not care to analyse. She had no doubt whatever as to the justice and righteousness of her desire, but in this one solitary instance of her masterful administration she seemed to require the initiative, or at least the approval, of her father or of the King.

Instead of this approval she vaguely scented intrigue.

She rose from the settee and went to the window behind it. The atmosphere of the room had suddenly become stifling. Fortunately the tall casements were unlatched. They yielded to a gentle push, and Lydie stepped out on to the balcony. Already the air was hot, and the sun shone glaringly on the marble fountains, and drew sparks of fire from the dome of the conservatories. The acrid, pungent smell of cannas and of asters rose to her nostrils, drowning the subtler aroma of tea roses and of lilies; the monotonous drip of the fountains was a soothing contrast in her ear to the babel of voices within.

At her feet the well-sanded walks of the park stretched out like ribbons of pale gold to the dim, vast distance beyond; the curly heads of Athenian athletes peeped from among the well-trimmed bosquets, showing the immaculate whiteness of the polished marble in the sun. A couple of gardeners clad in shirts of vivid blue linen were stooping over a bed of monthly roses, picking off dead leaves and twigs that spoilt the perfect symmetry of the shrubs, whilst two more a few paces away were perfecting the smoothness of a box hedge, lest a tiny leaflet were out of place.

Lydie sighed impatiently. Even in this vastness and this peace, man brought his artificiality to curb the freedom of nature. Everything in this magnificent park was affected, stilted and forced; every tree was fashioned to a shape not its own, every flower made to be a counterpart of its fellow.

This sense of unreality, of fighting nature in its every aspect, was what had always oppressed her, even when she worked at first in perfect harmony with her father, when she still had those utopian hopes of a regenerate France, with a wise and beneficent monarch, an era of truth and of fraternity, every one toiling hand-in-hand for the good of the nation.

What a child she had been in those days! How little she had understood this hydra-headed monster of self-seeking ambition, of political wire-pulling, of petty cabals and personal animosities which fought and crushed and trampled on every lofty ideal, on every clean thought and high-minded aspiration.

She knew and understood better now. She had outgrown her childish ideals: those she now kept were a woman's ideals, no less pure, no less high or noble, but lacking just one great quality—that of hope. She had continued to work and to do her best for this country which she loved—her own beautiful France. She had—with no uncertain hand—seized the reins of government from the diffident fingers of her lord, she still strove to fight corruption, to curb excesses and to check arrogance, and made vain endeavours to close her eyes to the futility of her noblest efforts.

This attitude of King Louis toward the Young Pretender had brought it all home to her; the intrigues, the lying, the falseness of everything, the treachery which lurked in every corner of this sumptuous palace, the egoism which was the sole moving power of those overdressed dolls.

Perhaps for the first time since—in all the glory and pride of her young womanhood—she became conscious of its power over the weaker and sterner vessel, she felt a sense of discouragement, the utter hopelessness of her desires. Her heart even suggested contempt of herself, of her weak-minded foolishness in imagining that all those empty heads in the room yonder could bring forth one single serious thought from beneath their powdered perruques, one single wholly selfless aspiration for the good of France; any more than that stultified rose-tree could produce a bloom of splendid perfection or that stunted acacia intoxicate the air with the fragrance of its bloom.

Solitude had taken hold of Lydie's fancy. She had allowed her mind to go roaming, fancy-free. Her thoughts were melancholy and anxious, and she sighed or frowned more than once. The air was becoming hotter and hotter every moment, and a gigantic bed of scarlet geraniums sent a curious acrid scent to her nostrils, which she found refreshing. Anon she succeeded in shutting out from her eyes the picture of those gardeners maiming the rose-trees and bosquets, and in seeing only that distant horizon with the vague, tiny fleecy clouds which were hurrying quite gaily and freely to some unknown destination, far, no doubt, from this world of craft and affectation. She shut her ears to the sound of miladi's shrill laugh and the chatter of senseless fools behind her, and only tried to hear the rippling murmur of the water in the fountains, the merry chirrup of the sparrows, and far, very far away, the sweet, sad note of a lark soaring upward to the serene morning sky.

The sound of a footstep on the flag-stones of the balcony broke in on her meditations. Her father, still wearing that troubled look, was coming out to join her. Fortunately miladi had chosen to remain indoors.

Impulsively now, for her nerves were still quivering with the tension of recent introspection, she went straight up to this man whom she most fully trusted in all the world, and took his hands in both hers.

"My dear, dear father," she pleaded, with her wonted earnestness, "you will help me, will you not?"

He looked more troubled than ever at her words, almost pathetic in his obvious helplessness, as he ejaculated feebly:

"But what can we do, my dear child?"

"Send Le Monarque to meet Prince Charles Edward," she urged; "it is so simple."

"It is very hazardous, and would cost a vast amount of money. In the present state of the Treasury——"

"My dear father, France can afford the luxury of not selling her honour."

"And the English will be furious with us."

"The English cannot do more than fight us, and they are doing that already!" she retorted.

"The risks, my dear child, the risks!" he protested again.

"What risks, father dear?" she said eagerly. "Tell me, what do we risk by sending Le Monarque with secret orders to the Scottish coast, to a spot known to no one save to Lord Eglinton and myself, confided to my husband by the unfortunate young Prince before he started on this miserable expedition? Captain Barre will carry nothing that can in any way betray the secret of his destination nor the object of his journey—my husband's seal-ring on his finger, nothing more; this token he will take on shore himself—not even the ship's crew will know aught that would be fatal if betrayed."

"But the English can intercept Le Monarque!"

"We must run that risk," she retorted. "Once past the coast of England, Scotland is lonely enough. Le Monarque will meet no other craft, and Captain Barre knows the secrets of his own calling— he has run a cargo before now."

"This is childish obstinacy, Lydie, and I do not recognize the statesman in this sentimental chit, who prates nonsense like a schoolgirl imbued with novel-reading," said the Duke now with marked impatience; "and pray, if His Majesty should put a veto on your using one of his ships for this privateering expedition?"

"I propose sending Le Monarque to-morrow," rejoined Lydie quietly. "Captain Barre will have his orders direct from the Ministry of Finance; and then we'll obtain His Majesty's sanction on the following day."

"But this is madness, my child!" exclaimed the Duke. "You cannot openly set at defiance the wishes of the King!"

"The wishes of the King?" she cried, with sudden vehemence. "Surely, surely, my dear, dear father, you cannot mean what you suggest! Think! oh, think just for one moment! That poor young man, who was our guest, whom we all liked—he broke bread with us in our own house, our beautiful château de la Tour d'Aumont, which has never yet been defiled by treachery. And you talk of leaving him there in that far-off land which has proved so inhospitable to him? Of leaving him there either to perish miserably of want and starvation or to fall into the hands of that Hanoverian butcher whose name has become a by-word for unparalleled atrocities?"

She checked herself, and then resumed more calmly:

"Nay, my dear father, I pray you let us cease this argument; for once in the history of our happy life together you and I look at honour from opposite points of view."

"Yes, my dear, I see that, too," he rejoined, speaking now with some hesitation. "I wish I could persuade you to abandon the idea."

"To abandon the unfortunate young Prince, you mean, to break every promise we ever made to him—to become the by-word in our turn for treachery and cowardice in every country in Europe—and why?" she added, with helpless impatience, trying to understand, dreading almost to question. "Why? Why?"

Then, as her father remained silent, with eyes persistently fixed on some vague object in the remote distance, she said, as if acting on a sudden decisive thought:

"Father, dear, is it solely a question of cost?"

"Partly," he replied, with marked hesitation.

"Partly? Well, then, dear, we will remove one cause of your unexplainable opposition. You may assure His Majesty in my name that the voyage of Le Monarque shall cost the Treasury nothing."

Then as her father made no comment, she continued more eagerly:

"Lord Eglinton will not deny me, as you know; he is rich and Charles Edward Stuart is his friend. What Le Monarque has cost for provisioning, that we will immediately replace. For the moment we will borrow this ship from His Majesty's navy. That he cannot refuse! and I give you and His Majesty my word of honour that Le Monarque shall not cost the Treasury one single sou—even the pay of her crew shall be defrayed by us from the moment that she sails out of Le Havre until the happy moment when she returns home with Prince Charles Edward Stuart and his friends safe and sound aboard."

There was silence between them for awhile. The Duc d'Aumont's eyes were fixed steadily on a distant point on the horizon, but Lydie's eyes never for a second strayed away from her father's face.

"Will Le Monarque have a long journey to make?" asked the Duke lightly.

"Yes!" she replied.

"To the coast of Scotland?"

"Yes."

"The west coast, of course?"

"Why should you ask, dear?"

She asked him this question quite casually, then, as he did not reply, she asked it again, this time with a terrible tightening of her heart-strings. Suddenly she remembered her suspicions, when first she caught the glance of intelligence which passed swiftly from him to miladi.

With a quick gesture of intense agitation she placed a hand on his wrist.

"Father!" she said in a scarce audible murmur.

"Yes, my dear. What is it?"

"I don't know. I—I have been much troubled of late. I do not think that my perceptions are perhaps as keen as they were—and as you say, this matter of the Stuart Prince has weighed heavily on my mind. Therefore, will you forgive me, dear, if—if I ask you a question which may sound undutiful, disloyal to you?"

"Of course I will forgive you, dear," he said, after a slight moment of hesitation. "What is it?"

He had pulled himself together, and now met his daughter's glance with sufficient firmness, apparently to reassure her somewhat, for she said more quietly:

"Will you give me your word of honour that you personally know of no act of treachery which may be in contemplation against the man who trusts in the honour of France?"

Her glowing eyes rested upon his; they seemed desirous of penetrating to the innermost recesses of his soul. M. le Duc d'Aumont tried to bear the scrutiny without flinching but he was no great actor, nor was he in the main a dishonourable man, but he thought his daughter unduly chivalrous, and he held that political considerations were outside the ordinary standards of honour and morality.

Anyway he could not bring himself to give her a definite reply; her hand still grasped his wrist—he took it in his own and raised it to his lips.

"My father!" she pleaded, her voice trembling, her eyes still fixed upon him, "will you not answer my question?"

"It is answered, my dear," he replied evasively. "Do you think it worthy of me—your father—to protest mine honesty before my own child?"

She looked at him no longer, and gently withdrew her hand from his grasp. She understood that, indeed, he had answered her question.

CHAPTER XIII

THE WEIGHT OF ETIQUETTE

Perhaps certain characteristics which milor the Marquis of Eglinton had inherited from his English grandfather caused him to assume a more elaborate costume for his petit lever than the rigid court etiquette of the time had prescribed.

According to every mandate of usage and fashion, when, at exactly half-past ten o'clock, he had asked M. Achille so peremptorily for his shoes and then sat on the edge of his bed, with legs dangling over its sides, he should have been attired in a flowered dressing gown over a lace-ruffled chemise de nuit, and a high-peaked bonnet-de-coton with the regulation tassel should have taken the place of the still absent perruque.

Then all the distinguished gentlemen who stood nearest to him would have known what to do. They had all attended petits levers of kings, courtisanes, and Ministers, ever since their rank and dignities entitled them so to do. Mme. la Comtesse de Stainville, for instance, would have stepped aside at this precise juncture with a deep curtsey and mayhap a giggle or a smirk—since she was privileged to be frivolous—whereupon M. Achille would with the proper decorum due to so solemn a function have handed M. le Contrôleur's day shirt to the visitor of highest rank there present, who was privileged to pass it over milor's head.

That important formality accomplished, the great man's toilet could be completed by M. le valet-de-chambre himself. But who had ever heard of a Minister's petit-lever being brought to a close without the ceremony of his being helped on with his shirt by a prince of the blood, or at least a marshal of France?

However, le petit Anglais had apparently some funny notions of his own—heirlooms, no doubt, from that fog-ridden land beyond the seas, the home of his ancestors—and vainly had Monsieur Achille, that paragon among flunkeys, tried to persuade his Marquis not to set the hitherto inviolate etiquette of the Court of France quite so flagrantly at defiance.

All his efforts had been in vain.

Monsieur d'Argenson, who was present on this 13th of August, 1746, tells us that when milor did call for his shoes at least ten minutes too soon, and was thereupon tenderly reproached by Madame la Comtesse de Stainville for this ungallant haste, he was already more than half dressed.

True, the flowered robe-de-chambre was there—and vastly becoming, too, with its braided motifs and downy lining of a contrasting hue—but when milor threw off the coverlet with a boyish gesture of impatience, he appeared clad in a daintily frilled day-shirt, breeches of fine faced cloth, whilst a pair of white silk stockings covered his well-shaped calves.

True, the perruque was still absent, but so was the regulation cotton night-cap; instead of these, milor, with that eccentricity peculiar to the entire British race, wore his own hair slightly powdered and tied at the nape of the neck with a wide black silk bow.

Monsieur Achille looked extremely perturbed, and, had his rigorous features ventured to show any expression at all, they would undoubtedly have displayed one of respectful apology to all the high-born gentlemen who witnessed this unedifying spectacle. As it was, the face of Monsieur le valet-de-chambre was set in marble-like rigidity; perhaps only the slightest suspicion of a sigh escaped his lips as he noted milor's complete unconsciousness of the enormity of his offense.

Monsieur le Contrôleur had been in the very midst of an animated argument with Madame de Stainville anent the respective merits of rose red and turquoise blue as a foil to a mellow complexion. This argument he had broken off abruptly by calling for his shoes. No wonder Irène pouted, her pout being singularly becoming.

"Had I been fortunate enough in pleasing your lordship with my poor wit," she said, "you had not been in so great a hurry to rid yourself of my company."

"Nay, madame, permit me to explain," he protested gently. "I pray you try and remember that for the last half-hour I have been the happy yet feeble target for the shafts aimed at me by your beauty and your wit. Now I always feel singularly helpless without my waistcoat and my shoes. I feel like a miserable combatant who, when brought face to face with a powerful enemy, hath been prevented from arming himself for the fray."

"But etiquette——" she protested.

"Etiquette is a jade, madame," he retorted; "shall not you and I turn our backs on her?"

In the meantime M. Achille had, with becoming reverence, taken M. le Contrôleur's coat and waistcoat in his august hands, and stood there holding them with just that awed expression of countenance which a village curé would wear when handling a reliquary.

With that same disregard for ceremony which had

characterized him all along, Lord Eglinton rescued his waistcoat from those insistent hands, and, heedless of Achille's look of horror, he slipped it on and buttoned it himself with quick, dexterous fingers, as if he had never done anything else in all his life.

For a moment Achille was speechless. For the first time perhaps in the history of France a Minister of Finance had put his waistcoat on himself, and this under his—Achille's—administration. The very foundations of his belief were tottering before his eyes; desperately now he clung to the coat, ready to fight for its possession and shed his blood if need be for the upkeep of the ancient traditions of the land.

"Will milor take his coat from the hands of Monseigneur le Prince de Courtenai—prince of the blood?" he asked, with a final supreme effort for the reëstablishment of those traditions, which were being so wantonly flouted.

"His Majesty will be here directly," interposed Irène hastily.

"His Majesty never comes later than half-past ten," protested milor feebly, "and he has not the vaguest idea how to help a man on with his coat. He has had no experience and I feel that mine would become a heap of crumpled misery if his gracious hands were to insinuate it over my unworthy shoulders."

He made a desperate effort to gain possession of his coat, but this time M. Achille was obdurate. It seemed as if he would not yield that coat to any one save at the cost of his own life.

"Then it is the privilege of Monseigneur le Prince de Courtenai," he said firmly.

"But M. de Courtenai has gone to flirt with my wife!" ejaculated Lord Eglinton in despair.

"In that case no doubt M. le Duc de Luxembourg will claim the right——"

"Mais comment donc?" said the Duke with great alacrity, as, in spite of milor's still continued feeble protests, he took the coat from the hands of M. Achille.

M. de Luxembourg was very pompous and very slow, and there was nothing that Lord Eglinton hated worse than what he called amateur valeting. But now there was nothing for it but forbearance and resignation; patience, too, of which le petit Anglais had no more than a just share. He gathered the frills of his shirt sleeves in his hands and tried not to look as if he wished M. de Luxembourg at the bottom of the nearest pond; but at this very moment Monseigneur le Prince de Courtenai, who, it appeared, had not gone to flirt with Madame la Marquise, since the latter was very much engaged elsewhere, but had merely been absorbed in political discussions with M. de Vermandois, suddenly realized that one of his numerous privileges was being encroached upon.

Not that he had any special desire to help M. le Contrôleur-Général on with his coat, but because he was ever anxious that his proper precedence as quasi prince of the blood should always be fully recognized. So he gave a discreet cough just sufficiently loud to attract M. Achille's notice, and to warn M. le Duc de Luxembourg that he was being presumptuous.

Without another word the coat was transferred from the hands of the Maréchal to those of the quasi-royal Prince, whilst Eglinton, wearing an air of resigned martyrdom, still waited for his coat, the frills of his shirt sleeves gripped tightly in his hands.

Monseigneur advanced. His movements were always sedate, and he felt pleased that every one who stood close by had noticed that the rank and precedence, which were rightfully his, had been duly accorded him, even in so small a matter, by no less a personage than M. le Contrôleur-Général des Finances.

He now held the coat in perfect position, and Lord Eglinton gave a sigh of relief, when suddenly the great doors at the end of the long room were thrown wide open, and the stentorian voices of the royal flunkeys announced:

"Messieurs, Mesdames! His Majesty the King!"

The buzz of talk died down, giving place to respectful murmurs. There was a great rustle of silks and brocades, a clink of dress swords against the parquet floor, as the crowd parted to make way for Louis XV. The various groups of political disputants broke up, as if scattered by a fairy wand; soon all the butterflies that had hovered in the further corners of the room fluttered toward the magic centre.

Here an avenue seemed suddenly to form itself of silken gowns, of brocaded panniers, of gaily embroidered coats, topped by rows of powdered perruques that bent very low to the ground as, fat, smiling, pompous, and not a little bored, His Majesty King Louis XV made slow progress along the full length of the room, leaning lightly on the arm of the inevitable Marquise de Pompadour, and nodding with great condescension to the perruqued heads as he passed.

Near the window embrasure he met la Marquise d'Eglinton and M. le Duc d'Aumont, her father. To Lydie he extended a gracious hand, and engaged her in conversation with a few trivial words. This gave Mme. de Pompadour the opportunity of darting a quick glance, that implied an anxious query, at the Duc d'Aumont, to which he responded with an almost imperceptible shake of the head.

All the while M. le Contrôleur-Général des Finances was still standing, shirt frills in hand, his face a picture of resigned despair, his eyes longingly fixed on his own coat, which Monseigneur de Courtenai no longer held up for him.

Indeed, Monseigneur, a rigid stickler for etiquette himself, would never so far have forgotten what was due to the house of Bourbon as to indulge in any pursuit—such as helping a Minister on with his coat—at the moment when His Majesty entered a room.

He bowed with the rest of them, and thus Louis XV at the end of his progress, found the group around milor's bedside; his cousin de Courtenai bowing, Monsieur Achille with his nose almost touching his knees, and milor Eglinton in shirt sleeves looking supremely uncomfortable, and not a little sheepish.

"Ah! ce cher milor!" said the King with charming bonhomie, as he took the situation in at a glance. "Nay, cousin, I claim an ancient privilege! Monsieur le Contrôleur-Général, have you ever been waited on by a King of France?"

"Never to my knowledge, Sire," stammered le petit Anglais.

Louis XV was quite delightful to-day; so fresh and boyish in his movements, and with an inimitable laisser aller and friendliness in his manner which caused many pairs of eyes to stare, and many hearts to ponder.

"Let this be an epoch-making experience in your life, then," he said gaily. "Is this your coat?"

And without more ado he took that much-travelled garment from Monseigneur de Courtenai's hands.

Such condescension, such easy graciousness had not been witnessed for years! And His Majesty was not overfond of that State-appointed Ministry of Finance of which milor was the nominal head.

"His Majesty must be sorely in need of money!" was a whispered comment which ran freely enough round the room.

Withal the King himself seemed quite unconscious of the wave of interest to which his gracious behaviour was giving rise. He was holding up the coat, smiling benevolently at M. le Contrôleur, who appeared to be more than usually nervous, and now made no movement toward that much-desired portion of his attire.

"Allons, milor, I am waiting," said King Louis at last.

"Er—that is," murmured Lord Eglinton pitiably, "could I have my coat right side out?"

"Ohé! par ma foi!" quoth the King with easy familiarity, "your pardon, milor, but 'tis seldom I hold such an article in my hands, and I believe, by all the saints in the calendar, that I was holding it upside down, wrong side out, sleeves foremost, and collar awry!"

He laughed till his fat sides ached, and tears streamed from his eyes; then, amidst discreet murmurs of admiration at so much condescension, such gracious good humour, the ceremony of putting on M. le Contrôleur's coat was at last performed by the King of France, and milor, now fully clothed and apparently much relieved in his mind, was able to present his respects to Madame de Pompadour.

CHAPTER XIV

ROYAL FAVOURS

Apparently there was to be no end to royal graciousness this morning, as every one who looked could see. Hardly was the coat on M. le Contrôleur's shoulders than the King engaged him in conversation, whilst Mme. de Pompadour dropped into the armchair lately vacated by Monseigneur de Courtenai. The well-drilled circle of courtiers and ladies, including la belle Irène herself, retired discreetly. Once more there was a barrier of emptiness and parquet flooring round the inner group, now composed of His Majesty, of M. le Contrôleur-Général, and of Mme. de Pompadour. Into these sacred precincts no one would have dared to step. Lydie, having paid her respects to His Majesty, had not joined that intimate circle, and it seemed as if Louis XV had noted her absence, and was duly relieved thereat.

Anon M. le Duc d'Aumont approached the King, offering him a chair. Louis took it, and in the act of so doing he contrived to whisper four quick words in his Prime Minister's ear.

"Eh bien! Your daughter?"

Lord Eglinton just then was busy trying to find a suitable place whereon to deposit his own insignificant person, and blushing violently because Mme. de Pompadour had laughingly waved her fan in the direction of his monumental bed; M. le Duc, therefore, whilst adjusting a cushion behind the King's back, was able to reply hurriedly:

"Impossible, Sire!"

"And l'Anglais?"

"I have not yet tried."

"Ah! ah! ah!" laughed Pompadour merrily. "M. le Contrôleur-Général des Finances, are all Englishmen as modest as you?"

"I—I don't know, Madame. I don't know very many," he replied.

"Here is M. le Contrôleur too bashful to sit on the edge of his own bed in my presence," she continued, still laughing. "Nay, milor, I'll wager that you were reclining on those downy cushions when you were flirting with Mme. de Stainville."

"Only under the compulsion of my valet-de-chambre, Madame," he protested, "or I'd have got up hours ago."

"Is he such a tyrant, then?" asked Louis.

"Terrible, your Majesty."

"You are afraid of him?"

"I tremble at his look."

"Ah! it is well M. le Contrôleur-Général des Finances should tremble sometimes, even if only before his valet-de-chambre," sighed Louis XV with comic pathos.

"But, Sire, I tremble very often!" protested Lord Eglinton.

"I' faith he speaks truly," laughed Mme. de Pompadour, "since he trembles before his wife."

"And we tremble before M. le Contrôleur," concluded the King gaily.

"Before me, Sire?"

"Aye, indeed, since our Parliaments have made you our dragon."

"A good-tempered, meek sort of dragon, Sire, you'll graciously admit."

"That we will, milor, and gladly!" said Louis XV, now with somewhat too exuberant good-humour; "and you'll not have cause to regret that meekness, for your King hath remained your friend."

Then, as Lord Eglinton seemed either too much overcome by the amazing condescension, or too bashful to respond, his Majesty continued more sedately:

"We are about to prove our friendship, milor."

"Your Majesty—finds me—er—quite unprepared—er——" stammered milor, who in verity appeared distinctly confused, for his eyes roamed round the room as if in search of help or support in this interesting crisis.

"Nay! nay!" rejoined the King benignly, "this we understand, milor. It is not often the King of France chooses a friend amongst his subjects. For we look upon you as our subject now, M. le Contrôleur, since we have accepted your oath of allegiance. You have only just enough English blood left in your veins to make you doubly loyal and true to your King. Nay! nay! no thanks—we speak as our royal heart moves us. Just now we spoke of proofs of our friendship. Milor, tell us frankly, are you so very rich?"

The question came so abruptly at the end of the sentimental peroration that Lord Eglinton was completely thrown off his balance. He was not used to private and intimate conversations with King Louis; his wife saw to all affairs of State, and the present emergency found him unprepared.

"I—I believe so, Sire," he stammered.

"But surely not so rich," insisted the King, "that a million or so livres would come amiss? Hé!"?

"I don't rightly know, Sire; it a little depends."

"On what?"

"On the provenance of the million."

"More than one, good milor—two, mayhap," said the King exultantly.

Then he drew his chair in somewhat closer. Lord Eglinton had taken Mme. de Pompadour's advice and was sitting on the edge of the bed. We may presume that that edge was very hard and uncomfortable, for milor fidgeted and looked supremely unhappy. Anon the King's knees were close to his own, and Madame's brocaded skirt got entangled with his feet. The buzz of talk in the large room drowned the King's whispers effectually, the wide barrier of empty floor was an effectual check on eavesdropping. Obviously no one would hear what Louis was about to confide to his Minister; he leaned forward and dropped his voice so that Eglinton himself could scarcely hear, and had to bend his head so that he got Louis's hot, excited breath full on the cheek. Being General Comptroller of Finance and receiving the confidences of a King had its drawbacks at times.

"Milor," whispered his Majesty, "'tis a good affair we would propose, one which we could carry through without your help, but in which we would wish to initiate you, seeing that you are our friend."

"I listen, Sire."

"The Duke of Cumberland—you know him?"

"Yes."

"He has quelled the rebellion and humbled the standard of that arrogant Stuart Pretender."

"Your Majesty's friend—yes," said Eglinton innocently.

"Bah! our friend!" and Louis XV shrugged his shoulders, whilst Mme. de Pompadour gave a short contemptuous laugh.

"Oh! I am sorry! I thought——" said milor gently. "I pray your Majesty to continue."

"Charles Edward Stuart was no friend to us, milor," resumed

83

Louis decisively: "observe, I pray you, the trouble which he hath brought about our ears. We had had peace with England ere now, but for that accursed adventurer and his pretensions; and now that he has come to disaster and ruin——"

"I understand," said Eglinton, with a little sigh of sympathy. "It is indeed awkward for your Majesty; the solemn promise you gave him——"

"Bah, man! prate not to me of promises," interrupted Louis irritably. "I promised him nothing; he knows that well enough—the young fool!"

"Do not let us think of him, Sire; it seems to upset your Majesty."

"It does, milor, it does; for even my worst enemies concede that Louis the Well-beloved is a creature of sympathy."

"A heart of gold, Sire—a heart of gold—er—shall we join the ladies?"

"Milor," said the King abruptly, putting a firm hand on Eglinton's wrist, "we must not allow that young fool to thwart the external politics of France any longer. The Duke of Cumberland, though our own enemy on the field of battle, has shown that England trusts in our honour and loyalty even in the midst of war, but she wants a proof from us."

"Oh, let us give it, Sire, by all means. Prince Charles Edward Stuart——"

"Exactly, milor," said Louis XV quietly; "that is the proof which England wants."

"I am afraid I don't quite understand," said Lord Eglinton, a little bewildered. "You see, I am very stupid; and—and perhaps my wife——"

Then, as King Louis gave a sharp ejaculation of impatience, Mme. de Pompadour broke in, in tones which she knew how to render velvety and soothing to the ear, whilst her delicate fingers rested lightly on M. le Contrôleur's hand.

"It is quite simple, milor," she whispered just as confidentially as the King had done. "This Charles Edward Stuart is a perpetual worry to England. His Grace, the Duke of Cumberland has been accused of unnecessary cruelty because he has been forced to take severe measures for the suppression of that spirit of rebellion, which is only being fostered in Scotland because of that young Pretender's perpetual presence there. He fans smouldering revolt into flame, he incites passions, and creates misguided enthusiasms which lead to endless trouble to all!"

Then as she paused, somewhat breathless and eager, her

bright myosotis-coloured eyes anxiously scanning his face he said mildly:

"How beautifully you put things, Mme. la Marquise. I vow I have never heard such a perfect flood of eloquence."

"'Tis not a matter of Madame's eloquence," interposed Louis, with impatience, "though she hath grasped the subject with marvellous clearness of judgment."

"Then 'tis a matter of what, Sire?"

"The Duke of Cumberland has appealed to our loyalty. Though we are at war with England we bear no animus toward her reigning house, and have no wish to see King George's crown snatched from him by that beardless young adventurer, who has no more right to the throne of England than you, milor, to that of France."

"And his Grace of Cumberland has asked his Majesty's help," added Mme. de Pompadour.

"How strange! Just as Prince Charles Edward himself hath done."

"The Duke of Cumberland desires the person of the Pretender," she said, without heeding the interruption, "so that he may no longer incite misguided enthusiasts to rebellion, and cease to plunge Scotland and England into the throes of civil war."

"His Grace asks but little, methinks!" said Lord Eglinton slowly.

"Oh, England is always ready to pay for what she wants," said the Marquise.

"And on this occasion?" asked milor mildly.

"His Grace hath offered us, as man to man, fifteen millions livres for the person of the Pretender," said the King, with sudden decision, and looking M. le Contrôleur straight in the face.

"Ah! as man to man?"

Louis XV and Mme. la Marquise de Pompadour both drew a quick sigh of relief. M. le Contrôleur had taken the proposal with perfect quietude. He had not seemed startled, and his kindly face expressed nothing but gentle amazement, very natural under the circumstances, whilst his voice—even and placid as usual—was not above a whisper.

"As man to man," he repeated, and nodded his head several times, as if pondering over the meaning of this phrase.

How extremely fortunate! Milor had raised no objection! What a pity to have wasted quite so much thought, anxiety, and a wealth of eloquence over a matter which was so easily disposed of! Jeanne de Pompadour gave her royal patron an encouraging nod.

There was a world of wisdom in that nod and in the look which accompanied it. "He takes it so easily," that look seemed to say; "he thinks it quite natural. We must have his help, since we do not know where the fugitive Prince is in hiding. This little milor alone can tell us that, and give us a token by which Charles Edward would trustingly fall into the little ambush which we have prepared for him. But he thinks the affair quite simple. We need not offer him quite so large a share in the pleasant millions as we originally had intended."

All this and more Mme. de Pompadour's nod conveyed to the mind of Louis the Well-beloved, and he too nodded in response before he continued, speaking now more casually, in a calmer, more business-like tone.

"'Tis a fair offer," he said at last; "though the affair will not be quite so easy to conduct as his Grace supposes. He suggests our sending a ship to the coast of Scotland to meet the young adventurer and his friends, take them on board and convey them to an English port, where they will be handed over to the proper authorities. 'Tis fairly simple, methinks."

"Remarkably simple, your Majesty."

"Of course, we need a little help from you, milor. Oh, nothing much—advice as to the spot where our good ship will be most like to find Charles Edward Stuart—a token which if shown to that young firebrand will induce him to trust its bearer, and come on board himself with at least some of his friends. You follow me, milor?"

The question seemed necessary, for Lord Eglinton's face wore such a look of indifference as to astonish even the King, who had been prepared for some measure of protest, at any rate from this man who was being asked to betray his friend. Although Louis was at this period of his life quite deaf to every call of honour and loyalty through that constant, ever-present and exasperating want of money for the satisfaction of his extravagant caprices, nevertheless, there was Bourbon blood in him, and this cried out loudly now, that he was suggesting—nay, more, contemplating—a deed which would have put any of his subjects to shame, and which would have caused some of his most unscrupulous ancestors in mediæval times to writhe with humiliation in their graves. Therefore he had expected loud protest from Lord Eglinton, arguments more or less easy to combat, indignation of course; but this ready acceptance of this ignoble bargain—so strange is human nature!—for the moment quite horrified Louis. Milor took the selling of his friend as calmly as he would that of a horse.

"You follow me, milor?" reiterated the King.

"Yes, yes, Sire," replied Eglinton readily enough. "I follow you."

"You understand the service we ask of you?"

"Yes, yes, I understand."

"For these services, milor, you shall be amply rewarded. We would deem one million livres a fair amount to fall to your share."

"Your Majesty is generous," said Eglinton quite passively.

"We are just, milor," said the King, with a sigh of satisfaction.

M. le Contrôleur seemed satisfied, and there was little else to say. Louis XV began to regret that he had offered him quite so much. Apparently five hundred thousand would have been enough.

"Then we'll call that settled," concluded his Majesty, pushing back his chair preparatory to ending this conversation, which he had so dreaded and which had turned out so highly satisfactory. Pity about that million livres, of course! five hundred thousand might have done, certainly seven! Nathless, M. le Contrôleur's private fortune was not so large as popular rumour had it, or did Mme. Lydie actually hold the purse strings?

"C'est entendu, milor," repeated Louis once more. "We will see to commissioning the ship and to her secret orders. As you see, there is no risk—and we shall be glad to be in the good graces of M. le Duc de Cumberland. To oblige an enemy, eh, milor? an act of peace and good-will in the midst of war. Chivalry, what?—worthy of our ancestor Henri of Navarre! Methinks it will make history."

"I think so, too, Sire," said Eglinton, with obvious conviction.

"Ah! then we'll see to the completion of the affair; we—the King and M. le Duc d'Aumont. You are lucky, milor, your share of the work is so simple; as soon as the ship is ready to sail we'll call on you for the necessary instructions. Par ma foi! 'tis a fine business for us all, milor; one million in your pocket for a word and a token, the residue of the fifteen millions in our royal coffers, and the thanks of his Grace of Cumberland to boot, not to mention the moral satisfaction of having helped to quell an unpleasant rebellion, and of placing one's enemy under lasting obligation. All for the good of France!"

Louis the Well-beloved had risen; he was more than contented; an unctuous smile, a beaming graciousness of expression pervaded his entire countenance. He groped in the wide pocket of his coat, bringing forth a letter which bore a large red seal.

"His Grace's letter, milor," he said with final supreme condescension, and holding the document out to M. le Contrôleur, who took it without a word. "Do you glance through it, and see that we have not been mistaken, that the whole thing is clear, straightforward and——"

"And a damned, accursed, dirty piece of business, Sire!"

It was undoubtedly Lord Eglinton who had spoken, for his right hand, as if in response to his thoughts, was even now crushing the paper which it held, whilst the left was raised preparatory to tearing the infamous proposal to pieces. Yes, it had been milor's even, gentle voice which had uttered this sudden decisive condemnation in the same impassive tones, and still scarce audible even to these two people near him, without passion, without tremor, seemingly without emotion. Just a statement of an undisputable fact, a personal opinion in answer to a question put to him.

Louis, completely thrown off his balance, stared at milor as if he had been suddenly shaken out of a dream; for the moment he thought that his ears must have played him a trick, that he must have misunderstood the words so calmly uttered; instinctively his hand sought the support of the chair which he had just vacated. It seemed as if he needed a solid, a materialistic prop, else his body would have reeled as his brain was doing now. Mme. de Pompadour, too, had jumped to her feet, pushing her chair away with an angry, impatient movement. The disappointment was so keen and sudden, coming just at the moment when triumph seemed so complete. But whilst Louis stared somewhat blankly, at M. le Contrôleur, she, the woman, flashed rage, contempt, vengeance upon him.

He had tricked and fooled her, her as well as the King, leading them on to believe that he approved, the better to laugh at them both in his sleeve.

The contemptible, arrogant wretch!

He was still half sitting, half leaning against the edge of his bed, and staring straight out before him through the big bay window which gave on to the park, passively, gently, as if the matter had ceased to concern him, as if he were quite unconscious of the enormity of his action.

"A—a damned—what?—accursed!—what?——" stammered the King; "but, milor——"

"Nay, Sire, I pray you!" broke in a grave voice suddenly; "my lord seems to have angered your Majesty. Will you deign to explain?"

CHAPTER XV

DIPLOMACY

The buzz of talk was going on as loudly and incessantly as before. The whispered conversation around M. le Contrôleur's bedside had excited no violent curiosity. The first surprise occasioned by His Majesty's unparalleled condescension soon gave way to indifference; it was obvious that the King's assiduity beside the Minister of Finance was solely due to a more than normal desire for money, and these royal demands for renewed funds were too numerous to cause more than passing interest.

Eavesdropping was impossible without gross disrespect, the latter far more unpardonable than the most insatiable curiosity. Lydie alone, privileged above all, had apparently not heeded the barrier which isolated Louis XV, Pompadour and milor from the rest of the vast apartment, for she now stood at the foot of the bed— a graceful, imposing figure dressed in somewhat conventual gray, with one hand resting on the delicate panelling, her grave, luminous eyes fixed on the King's face.

Louis shook himself free from the stupor in which milor's unexpected words had plunged him. Surprise yielded now to vexation. Lydie's appearance, her interference in this matter, would be the final death-blow to his hopes. Those tantalizing millions had dangled close before his eyes, his royal hands had almost grasped them, his ears heard their delicious clink; milor's original attitude had brought them seemingly within his grasp. Now everything was changed. The whole affair would have to be argued out again at full length, and though le petit Anglais might prove amenable, Mme. Lydie was sure to be obdurate.

Louis XV scowled at the picture of youth and beauty presented by that elegant figure in dove-gray silk, with the proud head carried high, the unconscious look of power and of strength in the large gray eyes, so grave and so fixed. In his mind there had already flashed the thought that milor's sudden change of attitude— for it was a change, of that his Majesty had no doubt—was due to a subtle sense of fear which had made him conscious of his wife's presence, although from her position and his own he could not possibly have seen her approach.

This made him still more vexed with Lydie, and as she seemed calmly to be waiting for an explanation, he replied quite gruffly:

"Nay, madame, you mistake; I assure you milor and ourselves are perfectly at one—we were so until a few moments ago."

"Until I came," she said quietly. "I am glad of that, for 'twill be easy enough, I hope, to convince your Majesty that my presence can have made no difference to M. le Contrôleur's attitude of deep respect."

"Pardi, we hope not!" interposed Mme. de Pompadour acidly; "but we hope milor hath found his tongue at last and will do the convincing himself."

But Louis XV was not prepared to reopen the discussion in the presence of Mme. Lydie. He knew, quite as well as M. le Duc d'Aumont himself, that she would have nothing but contempt and horror for that infamous proposal, which he was more determined than ever to accept.

It was tiresome of course not to have the coöperation of Lord Eglinton; that weak fool now would, no doubt, be overruled by his wife. At the same time—and Louis hugged the thought as it sprang to his mind—there were other ways of obtaining possession of Charles Edward Stuart's person than the direct one which he had proposed to milor just now. The young Pretender was bound sooner or later to leave the shores of Scotland. Unbeknown to King Louis a ship might be sent by private friends to rescue the fugitive, but that ship could be intercepted on her way home, and, after all, Charles Edward was bound to land in France some day!—and then——

And there were other means besides of earning the tempting millions. But these would have to be thought out, planned and arranged; they would be difficult and not nearly so expeditious, which was a drawback when royal coffers were clamouring to be filled. Still, it would be distinctly unadvisable to broach the subject with Mme. la Marquise d'Eglinton, and unnecessarily humiliating, since a rebuff was sure to be the result.

Therefore, when—as if in placid defiance of Pompadour's challenge—Lord Eglinton handed the Duke of Cumberland's letter silently back to the King, the latter slipped it into his pocket with a gesture of ostentatious indifference.

"Nay! we need not trouble Mme. la Marquise with the discussion now," he said; "she is unacquainted with the subject of our present conversation, and it would be tedious to reiterate."

"I crave your pardon, Sire," rejoined Lydie, "if I have transgressed, but my zeal in the service of France and in that of your Majesty has rendered my senses preternaturally acute. My eyes see in the gloom, my ears hear across vast spaces."

"In a word, Mme. la Marquise has been listening!" said Pompadour, with a sneer.

"I did not listen," said Lydie quietly. "I only heard."

"Then you know?" said Louis, with well-assumed indifference.

"Oh, yes!"

She smiled at him as she replied. This was apparently a day of surprises, for the smile seemed distinctly encouraging.

"And—and what do you say?" asked his Majesty somewhat anxiously, yet emboldened by that encouraging smile.

Of a truth! was he about to find an ally there, where he expected most bitter opposition?

"Meseems that milor was somewhat hasty," replied Lydie quietly.

"Ah!"

It was a sigh of intense, deep, heartfelt, satisfaction breathed by Louis the Well-beloved, and unrestrainedly echoed by Mme. de Pompadour.

"This proposal, Sire," continued Lydie; "'tis from England, I understand?"

"From his Grace of Cumberland himself, Madame," assented the King, once more drawing the letter from out his pocket.

"May I be permitted to see it?" she asked.

For a moment Louis hesitated, then he gave her the letter. There was no risk in this, since she practically owned to knowing its contents.

And the whole affair would be so much easier, so much more expeditious with the coöperation of the Eglintons.

Lydie read the letter through, seemingly deeply engrossed in its contents. She never once raised her eyes to see how she was being watched. She knew quite well that the King's eyes were fixed eagerly upon her face, that Pompadour's cupidity and greed for the proposed millions were plainly writ upon her face. But she had not once looked at her husband. She did not look at him now. He had not spoken since that sudden burst of indignation, when his slender hand crushed the infamous document which she now studied so carefully, crushed it and would have torn it to ribbons in loathing and contempt.

When first she interposed he had turned and faced her. Since then she knew that his eyes had remained fixed on her face. She felt the gaze, yet cared not to return it. He was too weak, too simple to understand, and of her own actions she would be sole mistress; that had been the chief clause in the contract when she placed her hand in his.

Her intuitive knowledge of this Court in which she moved, her suspicions of this feeble monarch, whose extravagant caprices had led him to deeds at which in his earlier days he had been the first to blush, her dread of intrigues and treachery, all had whispered in her ear the word of prudence—"Temporize."

The whole infamous plan had been revealed to her through those same supernaturally keen senses, which her strong domineering nature had coerced, until they became the slaves of her will. Mingling with the crowd, her graceful body present in the chattering throng, her mind had remained fixed on that group beside the bed. She had noticed the King's expression of face when he engaged milor in conversation, his extraordinary bonhomie, his confidential attitude, his whispers, all backed and seconded by Pompadour. Gradually she manœuvred and, still forming a unit with the rest of the crowd, she had by degrees drawn nearer and nearer, until she saw her husband's movement, his almost imperceptible change of expression, as he clutched the letter which was handed him by the King.

Then she boldly entered the inner precincts; being privileged, she could do even that, without creating attention. Milor's words of contempt, the royal arms of England on the seal of the letter, coupled with her father's attitude with her just now, and his veiled suggestions, told her all she wanted to know. And quick as flashes of summer lightning her woman's intuition whispered words of wisdom in her ear.

"Know everything first—then temporize! Diplomacy will do more than defiance."

Having read the letter through, she of course knew all. It was simple enough—a monstrous proposal which the King of France was ready to adopt. She felt real physical nausea at contact with so much infamy.

But she folded the document neatly and carefully, then looked quietly at the King.

"The Duke of Cumberland is generous," she said, forcing herself to smile.

"Heu, heu!" assented Louis lightly, with a return of his wonted bonhomie. Matters were shaping themselves to a truly satisfactory end.

"Do I understand that your Majesty would desire us to accept his Grace's proposal?"

"What think you yourself, Madame?"

"It is worth considering," she mused.

"Parbleu! And you are a true woman!" exclaimed Louis XV, beaming with delight. "Full of wisdom as a statesman should be. To think that we could ever have mistrusted so clear a head and so sound a judgment."

"Your Majesty, I hope, will always remember that my sole desire is to serve France and her King!"

"Par ma foi! We'll not forget your help in this, Madame," he exclaimed whole-heartedly. "Then we may rely on your help?"

"What does your Majesty desire me to do?"

He came quite close to her, and she forced herself not to draw back one inch. For the sake of the fugitive prince and his friends, who had trusted in the honour of France; for the sake of that honour which, in her peculiar position, was as dear to her as her own, she would not flinch now; she would show no repulsion, no fear, though her whole being rose in revolt at contact with this man.

A man, not a king! Par Dieu, not a King of France!

His face to her looked hideous, the eyes seemed to leer, and there was lust for money, and ignoble treachery writ on every feature.

"We have explained it all to milor," whispered Louis under his breath; "a ship to be commissioned and sent to meet the Stuart. She will have secret orders—no one shall know but her captain—and he will be a man whom we can trust—a man whom we shall have to pay—you understand?"

"I understand."

"Then from you we want to know the place in Scotland where we will find Charles Edward—eh? And also a token—a ring, a word perhaps, by which that young adventurer will be made to trust his own person and that of his friends to our good ship. It is very simple, you see."

"Quite simple, your Majesty."

"The ship's orders will be that once the Stuart and his faction are on board, she shall make straight for the first English port—and—and—that is all!" he added complacently.

"Yes, that is all, your Majesty."

"And on the day that Charles Edward Stuart is handed over to the English authorities, there will be fifteen millions for your King, Madame, and a million livres pin money for the most able statesman in Europe."

And with consummate gallantry, Louis bowed very low and took her hand in his. It rested cold and inert between his hot fingers, but he was far too eager, far too triumphant to notice anything beyond the fact that he had succeeded in enlisting the help of Lydie d'Eglinton, without whom his project was bound to have been considerably delayed, if not completely frustrated. He had indeed not wasted this glorious morning.

"I am eternally your debtor, Madame!" he said gaily; "and 'tis well, believe me, to serve the King of France."

"I have done nothing as yet, Sire," she rejoined.

"Nay, but you will," he said confidently.

She bowed her head and he interpreted the movement according to his will. But he was impatient, longing to see this matter finally settled to his entire satisfaction.

"Will you not give me a definite answer now?"

"In the midst of so much chatter, Sire?" she said, forcing herself to smile gaily. "Nay, but 'tis a serious matter—and I must consult with my father."

Louis smiled contentedly. M. le Duc d'Aumont was at one with him in this. The letter had been originally sent to the Prime Minister, and the Duke, who was weak, who was a slave to the Bourbon dynasty, and who, alas! was also tainted with that horrible canker which was gradually affecting the whole of the aristocracy of France, the insatiable greed for money, had been bribed to agree with the King.

Therefore Louis was content. It was as well that Lydie should speak with the Duke. The worthy D'Aumont would dissipate her last lingering scruples.

"And your husband?" he added, casting a quick glance over his shoulder at milor, and smiling with good-natured sarcasm.

"Oh, my husband will think as I do," she replied evasively.

At thought of her father and the King's complacent smile, Lydie had winced. For a moment her outward calm threatened to forsake her. She felt as if she could not keep up this hideous comedy any longer. She would have screamed aloud with horror or contempt, aye! and deep sorrow, too, to think that her father wallowed in this mire.

She too cast a quick glance at milor. His eyes were no longer fixed on her face. He stood quietly beside Madame de Pompadour, who, leaving the King to settle with Lydie, had engaged Lord Eglinton in frivolous conversation. He was quite placid again, and in his face, gentle and diffident as usual, there was no longer the faintest trace of that sudden outburst of withering contempt.

The Duke of Cumberland's letter was still in her hand. It seemed to scorch her fingers with its loathsome pollution. But she clung to it, and after a violent effort at self control, she contrived to look Louis straight in the face and to give him a reassuring smile, as she slipped the letter into the bosom of her gown.

"I will consult with my father, Sire," she repeated, "and will read the letter when I am alone and undisturbed."

"And you will give me a final answer?"

"The day after to-morrow."

"Why not sooner?" he urged impatiently.

94

"The day after to-morrow," she reiterated with a smile. "I have much to think about, and—the only token which Charles Edward would trust without demur must come from Lord Eglinton."

"I understand," said the King knowingly. "Par ma foi! But we shall want patience. Two whole days! In the meanwhile we'll busy ourselves with preparations for the expedition. We had thought of Le Monarque. What say you?"

"Le Levantin would be swifter."

"Ah, yes! Le Levantin—and we can trust her captain. He is under deep obligation to Madame de Pompadour. And M. de Lugeac, Madame's nephew, you know—we had thought of him to carry the secret orders to Brest to the captain of Le Levantin directly she is ready to sail. Methinks we could trust him. His interests are bound up with ours. And there is another, too; but more of that anon. The secret orders will bear our own royal signature, and you might place them yourself, with the token, in our chosen messenger's hands."

Once more he gave her a gracious nod, and she curtseyed with all the deference, all the formality which the elaborate etiquette of the time demanded. Louis looked at her long and searchingly, but apparently there was nothing in the calm, serene face to disturb his present mood of complacent satisfaction. He put out his podgy hand to her; the short, thick fingers were covered with rings up to their first joint, and Lydie contrived to kiss the large signet—an emblem of that kingship to which she was true and loyal—without letting her lips come in contact with his flesh.

What happened during the next ten minutes she could not afterward have said. Her whole mind was in a turmoil of thought, and every time the infamous letter crackled beneath her corselet, she shuddered as with fear. Quite mechanically she saw the King's departure, and apparently she acted with perfect decorum and correctness. Equally, mechanically she saw the chattering throng gradually disperse. The vast room became more and more empty, the buzz less and less loud. She saw milor as through a mist, mostly with back bent, receiving the adieux of sycophants; she heard various murmurs in her own ears, mostly requests that she should remember and be ready to give, or at least to promise. She saw the procession of courtiers, of flatterers, of friends and enemies pass slowly before her; in the midst of them she vaguely distinguished Mme. de Stainville's brightly coloured gown.

La belle Irène lingered a long time beside milor. She was one of the last to leave, and though Lydie forced herself not to look in that direction, she could not help hearing the other woman's irritating giggle, and Lord Eglinton's even, pleasant voice framing compliments, that pandered to that brainless doll's insatiable vanity.

And this when he knew that his friend was about to be betrayed.

The taint! The horror! The pollution of it all!

Fortunately she had not seen her father, for her fortitude might have broken down if she read that same awful thought of treachery in his face that had so disgusted her when Louis stood beside her.

The last of that senseless, indifferent crowd had gone. The vast room was empty. Milor had accompanied Mme. de Stainville as far as the door. The murmur of talk and laughter came now only as a faint and lingering echo. Anon it died away in the distant corridors.

Lydie shivered as if with cold.

CHAPTER XVI

STRANGERS

And now she was alone.

Torpor had left her; even that intensity of loathing had gone, which for the past half-hour had numbed her very senses and caused her to move and speak like an irresponsible automaton. She felt as if she had indeed seen and touched a filthy, evil reptile, but that for the moment it had gone out of her sight. Presently it would creep out of its lair again, but by that time she would be prepared.

She must be prepared; therefore she no longer shuddered at the horror of it, but called her wits to her aid, her cool judgment and habitual quick mode of action, to combat the monster and render it powerless.

She knew of course that the King would not allow himself to be put off with vague promises. Within the two days' delay which she had asked of him he would begin to realize that she had only meant to temporise, and never had any intention of helping him in his nefarious schemes. Then he would begin to act for himself.

Having understood that she meant to circumvent him if she could, he was quite shrewd enough to devise some means of preventing those tempting millions from eluding his grasp. Though he did not know at the present moment where or how to lay his hands on Prince Charles Edward and his friends, he knew that they would of necessity seek the loneliness of the west coast of Scotland.

Vaguely that particular shore had always been spoken of in connection with any expedition for the succour of the unfortunate prince, and although the commissioning of ships was under the direct administration of the Comptrôlleur-Général of Finance, Louis, with the prospective millions dangling before him, could easily enough equip Le Levantin, and send her on a searching expedition without having recourse to State funds; whilst it was more than likely that Charles Edward, wearied of waiting, and in hourly fear of detection and capture, would be quite ready to trust himself and his friends to any French ship that happened to come on his track, whether her captain brought him a token from his friend or not.

All this and more would occur to King Louis, of course, in the event of her finally refusing him coöperation, or trying to put him off longer than a few days. Just as she had thought it all out, visualized his mind, as it were, so these various plans would present themselves to him sooner of later. It was a great thing to have gained two days. Forty-eight hours' start of that ignoble scheme would, she hoped, enable her to counteract it yet.

So much for King Louis and his probable schemes! Now her own plans.

To circumvent this awful treachery, to forestall it, that of course had become her task, and it should not be so difficult, given that two days' start and some one whom she could trust.

Plans now became a little clearer in her head; they seemed gradually to disentangle themselves from a maze of irrelevant thoughts.

Le Monarque was ready to start at any moment. Captain Barre, her commander, was the soul of honour. A messenger swift and sure and trustworthy must ride to Le Havre forthwith with orders to the captain to set sail at once, to reach that lonely spot on the west coast of Scotland known only to herself and to her husband, where Charles Edward Stuart and his friends were even now waiting for succour.

The signet-ring—Lord Eglinton's—entrusted to Captain Barre should ensure the fugitives' immediate confidence. There need be no delay, and with favourable wind and weather Le Monarque should have the Prince and his friends on board her before Le Levantin had been got ready to start.

Then Le Monarque should not return home direct; she should

skirt the Irish coast and make for Brittany by a circuitous route; a grave delay perhaps, but still the risks of being intercepted must be minimised at all costs.

A lonely village inland would afford shelter to the Young Pretender and his adherents for a while, until arrangements could be made for the final stage of their journey into safety—Austria, Spain, or any country in fact where Louis' treachery could not overtake them.

It was a big comprehensive scheme, of course; one which must be carried to its completion in defiance of King Louis. It was never good to incur the wrath of a Bourbon, and, unless the nation and the parliaments ranged themselves unequivocally on her side, it would probably mean the sudden ending of her own and her husband's career, the finality of all her dreams. But to this she hardly gave a thought.

The project itself was not difficult of execution, provided she had the coöperation of a man whom she could absolutely trust. This was the most important detail in connection with her plans, and it alone could ensure their success.

Her ally, whoever he might be, would have to start this very afternoon for Le Havre, taking with him the orders for Captain Barre and the signet ring which she would give him.

There were one hundred and fifty leagues between Versailles and Le Havre as the crow flies, and Lydie was fully aware of the measure of strength and endurance which a forced ride across country and without drawing rein would entail.

It would mean long gallops at breakneck speed, whilst slowly the summer's day yielded to the embrace of evening, and anon the glowing dusk paled and swooned into the arms of night. It would mean a swift and secret start at the hour when the scorching afternoon sun had not yet lifted its numbing weight from the journeyman's limbs and still lulled the brain of the student to drowsiness and the siesta; the hour when the luxurious idler was just waking from sleep, and the labourer out in the field stretched himself after the noonday rest.

It would mean above all youth and enthusiasm; for Le Havre must be reached ere the rising sun brought the first blush of dawn on cliffs, and crags, and sea; Le Monarque must set sail for Scotland ere France woke from her sleep.

Twelve hours in the saddle, a good mount, the strength of a young bullock, and the astuteness of a fox!

Lydie still sat in the window embrasure, her eyes closed, her graceful head with its wealth of chestnut hair resting against the delicate coloured cushions of her chair, her perfectly modelled arms bared to the elbow lying listlessly in her lap, one hand holding the infamous letter, written by the Duke of Cumberland to King Louis. She herself a picture of thoughtful repose, statuesque and cool.

It was characteristic of her whole personality that she sat thus quite calmly, thinking out the details of her plan, apparently neither flustered nor excited. The excitement was within, the desire to be up and doing, but she would have despised herself if she had been unable to conquer the outward expressions of her agitation, the longing to walk up and down, to tear up that ignoble letter, or to smash some inoffensive article that happened to be lying by.

Her thoughts then could not have been so clear. She could not have visualized the immediate future; the departure of Le Monarque at dawn—Captain Barre receiving the signet-ring—that breakneck ride to Le Havre.

Then gradually from out the rest of the picture one figure detached itself from her mind—her husband.

"Le petit Anglais," the friend of Charles Edward Stuart; weak, luxurious, tactless, but surely loyal.

Lydie half smiled when the thought first took shape. She knew so little of her husband. Just now, when she heard him condemn the King's treacherous proposals with such unequivocal words of contempt, she had half despised him for this blundering want of diplomatic art. Manlike he had been unable to disguise his loathing for Louis' perfidy, and by trying to proclaim his loyalty to his friend, all but precipitated the catastrophe that would have delivered Charles Edward Stuart into the hands of the English. But for Lydie's timely interference the King, angered and huffed, would have departed then and there and matured his own schemes before anything could be done to foil them.

But with her feeling of good-natured disdain, there had even then mingled a sensation of trust; this she recalled now when her mind went in search of the man in whom she could confide. She would in any case have to ask her husband for the token agreed on between him and the Stuart Prince, and also for final directions as to the exact spot where the fugitives would be most surely found by Captain Barre.

Then why should he not himself take both to Le Havre?

Again she smiled at the thought. The idea had occurred to her that she did not even know if milor could ride. And if perchance he did sit a horse well, had he the physical strength, the necessary endurance, for that flight across country, without a halt, with scarce a morsel of food on the way?

She knew so little about him. Their lives had been spent apart. One brief year of wedded life, and they were more strange to one another than even they had been before their marriage. He no doubt thought her hard and unfeminine, she of a truth deemed him weak and unmanly.

Still there was no one else, and with her usual determination she forced her well-schooled mind to dismiss all those thoughts of her husband which were disparaging to him. She tried not to see him as she had done a little while ago, giving himself over so readily to the artificial life of this Court of Versailles and its enervating etiquette, yielding to the whispered flatteries of Irène de Stainville, pandering to her vanity, admiring her femininity no doubt in direct contrast to his wife's more robust individuality.

Afterward, whenever she thought the whole matter over, she never could describe accurately the succession of events just as they occurred on that morning. She seemed after a while to have roused herself from her meditations, having fully made up her mind to carry her project through from beginning to end, and with that infamous letter still in her hand she rose from her chair and walked across the vast audience chamber, with the intention of going to her own study, there to think out quietly the final details of her plans.

Her mind was of course intent on the Stuart Prince and his friends: on Le Monarque and Captain Barre, and also very much now on her husband; but she could never recollect subsequently at what precise moment the actual voice of Lord Eglinton became mingled with her thoughts of him.

Certain it is that, when in crossing the room she passed close to the thronelike bedstead, whereupon her strangely perturbed imagination wilfully conjured up the picture of milor holding his court, with la belle Irène in a brilliant rose-coloured gown complacently receiving his marked attentions, she suddenly heard him speak:

"One second, I entreat you, Madame, if you can spare it!"

Her own hand at the moment was on that gilded knob of the door, through which she had been about to pass. His voice came from somewhere close behind her.

She turned slightly toward him, and saw him standing there, looking very fixedly at her, with a gaze which had something of entreaty in it, and also an unexplainable subtle something which at first she could not quite understand.

"I was going to my study, milor," she said, a little taken aback, for she certainly had not thought him in the room.

"Therefore I must crave your indulgence if I intrude," he said simply.

"Can I serve you in any way?"

"Your ladyship is pleased to be gracious——"

"Yes?"

She was accustomed to his diffident manner and to his halting speech, which usually had the knack of irritating her. But just now she seemed inclined to be kind. She felt distinctly pleased that he was here. To her keenly sensitive nature it seemed as if it had been her thoughts which had called to him, and that something in him responded to her wish that he should be the man to take her confidential message to the commander of Le Monarque.

Now his eyes dropped from her face and fixed themselves on the hand which had fallen loosely to her side.

"That paper which you hold, Madame——"

"Yes?"

"I pray you give it to me."

"To you? Why?" she asked, as the encouraging smile suddenly vanished from her face.

"Because I cannot bear the sight of Mme. la Marquise d'Eglinton, my wife, sullying her fingers one second longer by contact with this infamy."

He spoke very quietly, in that even, gentle, diffident voice of his, whilst his eyes once more riveted themselves on her face.

Instinctively she clutched the letter tighter, and her whole figure seemed to stiffen as she looked at him full now, a deep frown between her eyes, her whole attitude suggestive of haughty surprise and of lofty contempt. There was dead silence in the vast room save for the crackling of that paper, which to a keenly sensitive ear would have suggested the idea that the dainty hand which held it was not as steady as its owner would have wished.

It seemed suddenly as if with the speaking of a few words these two people, who had been almost strangers, had by a subtle process become antagonists, and were unconsciously measuring one another's strength, mistrustful of one another's hidden weapons. But already the woman was prepared for a conflict of will, a contest for that hitherto undisputed mastery, which she vaguely feared was being attacked, and which she would not give up, be the cost of defence what it may, whilst the man was still diffident, still vaguely hopeful that she would not fight, for his armour was vulnerable where hers was not, and she owned certain weapons which he knew himself too weak to combat.

"Therefore I proffer my request again, Madame," he said after a pause. "That paper——"

"A strong request, milor," said Lydie coldly.

"It is more than a request, Madame."

"A command perhaps?"

He did not reply; obviously he had noted the sneer, for a very

101

slight blush rose to his pale cheeks. Lydie, satisfied that the shaft had gone home, paused awhile, just long enough to let the subtle poison of her last words sink well in, then she resumed with calm indifference:

"You will forgive me, milor, when I venture to call your attention to the fact that hitherto I have considered myself to be the sole judge and mentor of my own conduct."

"Possibly this has worked very well in all matters, Madame," he replied, quite unruffled by her sarcasm, "but in this instance you see me compelled to ask you—reluctantly I admit—to give me that letter and then to vouchsafe me an explanation as to what you mean to do."

"You will receive it in due course, milor," she said haughtily; "for the moment I must ask you to excuse me. I am busy, and——"

She was conscious of an overwhelming feeling of irritation at his interference and, fearing to betray it beyond the bounds of courtesy, she wished to go away. But now he deliberately placed his hand on the knob, and stood between her and the door.

"Milor!" she protested.

"Yes, I am afraid I am very clumsy, Madame," he said quite gently. "Let us suppose that French good manners have never quite succeeded in getting the best of my English boorishness. I know it is against every rule of etiquette that I should stand between you and the door through which you desire to pass, but I have humbly asked for an explanation and also for that letter, and I cannot allow your ladyship to go until I have had it."

"Allow?" she said, with a short mocking laugh. "Surely, milor, you will not force me to refer to the compact to which you willingly subscribed when you asked me to be your wife?"

"'Tis not necessary, Madame, for I well remember it. I gave you a promise not to interfere with your life, such as you had chosen to organize it. I promised to leave you free in thought, action, and conduct, just as you had been before you honoured me by consenting to bear my name."

"Well, then, milor?" she asked.

"This is a different matter, Mme. la Marquise," he replied calmly, "since it concerns mine own honour and that of my name. Of that honour I claim to be the principal guardian."

Then as she seemed disinclined to vouchsafe a rejoinder he continued, with just a shade more vehemence in his tone:

"The proposal which His Majesty placed before me awhile ago, that same letter which you still hold in your hand, are such vile and noisome things that actual contact with them is pollution. As I see you now with that infamous document between those fingers which I have had the honour to kiss, it seems to me as if you were clutching a hideous and venomous reptile, the very sight of which should have been loathsome to you, and from which I should have wished to see you turn as you would from a slimy toad."

"As you did yourself, milor?" she said with a contemptuous shrug of the shoulders, thinking of his blunder, of the catastrophe which he all but precipitated, and which her more calm diplomacy had perhaps averted.

"As I did, though no doubt very clumsily," he admitted simply, "the moment I grasped its purport to the full. To see you, my wife—yes, my wife," he repeated with unusual firmness in answer to a subtle, indefinable expression which at his words had lit up her face, "to see you pause if only for one brief half hour with that infamy before your eyes, with that vile suggestion reaching and dwelling in your brain the man who made it—be he King of France, I care not—kissing those same fingers which held the abominable thing, was unspeakably horrible in my sight; it brought real physical agony to every one of my senses. I endured it only for so long as etiquette demanded, hoping against hope that every second which went by would witness your cry of indignation, your contempt for that vile and execrable letter which, had you not interposed, I myself would have flung in the lying face of that kingly traitor. But you smiled at him in response; you took the letter from him! My God, I saw you put it in the bosom of your gown!"

He paused a moment, as if ashamed of this outburst of passion, so different to his usual impassiveness. It seemed as if her haughty look, her ill-concealed contempt, was goading him on, beyond the bounds of restraint which he had meant to impose on himself. She no longer now made an attempt to go. She was standing straight before him, leaning slightly back against the portière—a curtain of rich, heavy silk of that subtle brilliant shade, 'twixt a scarlet and a crimson, which is only met with in certain species of geranium.

Against this glowing background her slim, erect figure, stiff with unbendable pride, stood out in vivid relief. The red of the silk cast ardent reflections into her chestnut hair, and against the creamy whiteness of her neck and ear. The sober, almost conventual gray of her gown, the primly folded kerchief at her throat, the billows of lace around the graceful arm formed an exquisite note of tender colour against that glaring geranium red. In one hand she still held the letter, the other rested firmly against the curtain. The head was thrown back, the lips slightly parted and curled in disdain, the eyes—half veiled—looked at him through long fringed lashes.

A picture worthy to inflame the passion of any man. Lord

Eglinton, with a mechanical movement of the hand across his forehead, seemed to brush away some painful and persistent thought.

"Nay, do not pause, milor," she said quietly. "Believe me, you interest me vastly."

He frowned and bit his lip.

"Your pardon, Madame," he rejoined more calmly now. "I was forgetting the limits of courtly manners. I have little more to say. I would not have troubled you with so much talk, knowing that my feeling in such matters can have no interest for your ladyship. When awhile ago this great bare room was at last free from the bent-backed, mouthing flatterers that surround you, I waited patiently for a spontaneous word from you, something to tell me that the honour of my name, one of the oldest in England, was not like to be stained by contact with the diplomatic by-ways of France. I had not then thought of asking for an explanation; I waited for you to speak. Instead of which I saw you take that miserable letter once more in your hand, sit and ponder over it without a thought or look for me. I saw your face, serene and placid, your attitude one of statesmanlike calm, as without a word or nod you prepared to pass out of my sight."

"Then you thought fit to demand from me an explanation of my conduct in a matter in which you swore most solemnly a year ago that you would never interfere?"

"Demand is a great word, Madame," he said, now quite gently. "I do not demand; I ask for an explanation on my knees."

And just as he had done a year ago when first she laid her hand in his and he made his profession of faith, he dropped on one knee and bent his head, until his aching brow almost touched her gown.

She looked down on him from the altitude of her domineering pride; she saw his broad shoulders, bent in perfect humility, his chestnut hair free from the conventional powder, the slender hands linked together now in a strangely nervous clasp, and she drew back because her skirt seemed perilously near his fingers.

Will the gods ever reveal the secret of a woman's heart? Lydie loathed the King's proposal, the letter which she held, just as much as Lord Eglinton did himself. Awhile ago she had hardly been able to think or to act coherently while she felt the contact of that noisome paper against her flesh. If she had smiled on Louis, if she had taken the letter away from him with vague promises that she would think the matter over, it had been solely because she knew the man with whom she had to deal better than did milor Eglinton, who had but little experience of the Court of Versailles, since he had kept away from it during the major part of his life. She had only meant to temporize with the King, because she felt sure that that was the only way to serve the Stuart Prince and to avert the treachery.

Nay, more, in her heart she felt that milor was right; she knew that when a thing is so vile and so abominable as Louis' proposed scheme, all contact with it is a pollution, and that it is impossible to finger slimy mud without some of it clinging to flesh or gown.

Yet with all that in her mind, a subtle perversity seemed suddenly to have crept into her heart, a perversity and also a bitter sense of injustice. She and her husband had been utter strangers since the day of their marriage, she had excluded him from her counsels, just as she had done from her heart and mind. She had never tried to understand him, and merely fostered that mild contempt which his diffidence and his meekness had originally roused in her. Yet at this moment when he so obviously misunderstood her, when he thought that her attitude with regard to the King's proposals was one of acceptance, or at least not of complete condemnation, her pride rose in violent revolt.

He had no right to think her so base. He had invaded her thoughts at the very moment when they dwelt on his friend and the best mode to save him; nay, more, was she not proposing to associate him, who now accused her so groundlessly, with her work of devotion and loyalty?

He should have known, he should have guessed, and now she hated him for his thoughts of her; she who had kept herself untainted in the midst of the worst corruption that ever infested a Court, whose purity of motives, whose upright judgments had procured her countless enemies amongst the imbecile and the infamous, she to be asked and begged to be loyal and to despise treachery!

Nay, she was too proud now to explain. An explanation would seem like a surrender, an acknowledgment—par Dieu of what? and certainly a humiliation.

According to milor, her husband, was there not one single upright and loyal soul in France except his own? No honour save that of his own name?

She laughed suddenly, laughed loudly and long. Manlike, he did not notice the forced ring of that merriment. He had blundered, of course, but this he did not know. In the simplicity of his heart he thought that she would have been ready to understand, that she would have explained and then agreed with him as to the best means of throwing the nefarious proposal back into the King's teeth.

At her laugh he sprang to his feet; every drop of blood seemed to have left his cheeks, which were now ashy pale.

"Nay, milor," she said with biting sarcasm, "but 'tis a mountain full of surprises that you display before my astonished fancy. Who had e'er suspected you of so much eloquence? I vow I do not understand how your lordship could have seen so much of my doings just now, seeing that at that moment you had eyes and ears only for Irène de Stainville."

"Mme. de Stainville hath naught to do with the present matter, Madame," he rejoined, "nor with my request for an explanation from you."

"I refuse to give it, milor," she said proudly, "and as I have no wish to spoil or mar your pleasures, so do I pray you to remember our bond, which is that you leave me free to act and speak, aye, and to guide the destinies of France if she have need of me, without interference from you."

And with that refinement of cruelty of which a woman's heart is sometimes capable at moments of acute crises, she carefully folded the English letter and once more slipped it into the bosom of her gown. She vouchsafed him no other look, but gathering her skirts round her she turned and left him. Calm and erect she walked the whole length of the room and then passed through another doorway finally out of his sight.

PART III

THE WOMAN

CHAPTER XVII

SPLENDID ISOLATION

M. Durand looked flustered when Lydie suddenly entered his sanctum. But she was hardly conscious of his presence, or even of where she was.

The vast audience chamber which she had just quitted so abruptly had only the two exits; the one close to which she had left milor standing, and the other which gave into this antechamber, where M. Durand usually sat for the express purpose of separating the wheat from the chaff—or, in other words, the suppliants who had letters of introduction or passports to "le petit lever" of M. le Contrôleur-Général, from those who had not.

It was not often that Mme. la Marquise came this way at all; no doubt this accounted in some measure for M. Durand's agitation when she opened the door so suddenly. Had Lydie been less absorbed in her own thoughts she would have noticed that his hands fidgeted quite nervously with the papers on his bureau, and that his pale watery eyes wandered with anxious restlessness from her face to the heavy portière which masked one of the doors. But, indeed, at this moment neither M. Durand nor his surroundings existed for her; she crossed the antechamber rapidly without seeing him. She only wanted to get away, to put the whole enfilade of the next reception rooms between herself and the scene which had just taken place.

Something was ringing in her ears. She could not say for certain whether she had really heard it, or whether her quivering nerves were playing her a trick; but a cry had come to her across the vastness of the great audience-chamber, and rang now even through the closed door.

A cry of acute agony; a cry as of an animal in pain. The word: "Lydie!" The tone: one of reproach, of appeal, of aching, wounded passion!

She fled from it, unwilling to admit its reality, unwilling to believe her ears. She felt too deeply wounded herself to care for the pain of another. She hoped, indeed, that she had grievously hurt his pride, his self-respect, that very love which he had once professed for her, and which apparently had ceased to be.

Once he had knelt at her feet, comparing her to the Madonna, to the saints whom Catholics revered yet dared not approach; then he talked of worship, and now he spoke of pollution, of stained honour, and asked her to keep herself free from taint. What right had he not to understand? If he still loved her, he would have understood. But constant intercourse with Irène de Stainville had blurred his inward vision; the image of the Madonna, serene and unapproachable, had become faded and out of focus, and he now groped earthwards for less unattainable ideals.

That this was in any way her fault Lydie would not admit. She had become his wife because he had asked her, and because he had been willing to cover her wounded vanity with the mantle of his adoration, and the glamour of his wealth and title. He knew her for what she was: statuesque and cold, either more or less than an ordinary woman, since she was wholly devoid of sentimentality; but with a purpose in her mind and a passion for work, for power and influence. Work for the good of France! Power to attain this end!

Thus he had found her, thus he had first learned to love her! She had denied him nothing that he had ever dared to ask. This had been a bond between them, which now he had tried to break; but if he had loved her as heretofore he would not have asked, he would have known. How, and by what subtle process of his mind Lydie did not care to analyze.

He would have known: he would have understood, if he still loved her.

These two phrases went hammering in her brain, a complement to that cry which still seemed to reach her senses, although the whole enfilade of reception rooms now stretched their vastness between her and that persistent echo.

Of course his love had been naught to her. It was nothing more at best than mute, somewhat dog-like adoration: a love that demanded nothing, that was content to be, to exist passively and to worship from afar.

Womanlike, she apprised it in inverse ratio to its obtrusiveness; the less that was asked of her, the less she thought it worth while to give. But the love had always been there. At great social functions, in the midst of a crowd or in the presence of royalty, whenever she looked across a room or over a sea of faces, she saw a pair of eyes which rested on her every movement with rapt attention and unspoken admiration.

Now she would have to forego that. The love was no longer there. On this she insisted, repeating it to herself over and over again, though this seemed to increase both the tension of her nerves, and the strange tendency to weakness, from which her proud spirit shrank in rebellion.

She was walking very rapidly now, and as she reached the monumental staircase, she ran down the steps without heeding the astonished glances of the army of flunkeys that stood about on landing and corridors. In a moment she was out on the terrace, breathing more freely as soon as she filled her lungs with the pure air of this glorious summer's day.

At first the light, the glare, the vibration of water and leaves under the kiss of the midday sun dazzled her eyes so that she could not see. But she heard the chirrup of the sparrows, the call of thrush and blackbird, and far away the hymn of praise of the skylark. Her nostrils drew in with glad intoxication the pungent fragrance of oak-leaved geraniums, and her heart called out joyfully to the secluded plantation of young beech trees there on her left, where she often used to wander.

Thither now she bent her steps. It was a favourite walk of hers, and a cherished spot, for she had it always before her when she sat in her own study at the angle of the West Wing. The tall windows of her private sanctum gave on this plantation, and whenever she felt wearied or disheartened with the great burden which she had taken on her shoulders, she would sit beside the open casements and rest her eyes on the brilliant emerald or copper of the leaves, and find rest and solace in the absolute peace they proclaimed.

And, at times like the present one, when the park was still deserted, she liked to wander in that miniature wood, crushing with delight the moist bed of moss under her feet, letting the dew-covered twigs fall back with a swish against her hands. She found her way to a tiny glade, where a rough garden seat invited repose. The glade was circular in shape, a perfect audience chamber, wherein to review a whole army of fancies. On the ground a thick carpet of brilliant green with designs of rich sienna formed by last year's leaves, and flecks of silver of young buds not yet scorched by the midday sun; all around, walls of parallel, slender trunks of a tender gray-green colour, with bold patches of glaring viridian and gold intermixed with dull blue shadows. And then a dado of tall bracken fantastic in shape and almost weird in outline, through which there peeped here and there, with insolent luxuriance, clumps of purple and snow-white foxgloves.

Lydie sank on to the rough bench, leaning well back and

109

resting her head against the hard, uneven back of the seat. Her eyes gazed straight upwards to a patch of vivid blue sky, almost crude and artificial-looking above the canopy of the beeches.

She felt unspeakably lonely, unspeakably forsaken. The sense of injustice oppressed her even more than the atmosphere of treachery.

Her father false and weak; her husband fickle and unjust! Prince Charles Edward abandoned, and she now powerless, probably, to carry through the work of rescue which she had planned! Until this moment she had not realized how much she had counted on her husband to help her. Now that she could no longer ask him to ride to Le Havre, and take her message to the commander of Le Monarque, she cast about her in vain for a substitute: some one whom she could trust. Her world was made up of sycophants, of flatterers, of pleasure-loving fops. Where was the man who would cover one hundred and eighty leagues in one night in order to redeem a promise made by France?

Her head ached with the agony of this thought. It was terrible to see her most cherished hope threatened with annihilation. Oh! had she been a man! . . .

Tears gathered in her eyes. At other times she would have scorned the weakness, now she welcomed it, for it seemed to lift the load of oppression from her heart. The glare of that vivid blue sky above weighed down her lids. She closed her eyes and for the space of a few seconds she seemed to forget everything; the world, and its treachery, the palace of Versailles, the fugitives in Scotland.

Everything except her loneliness, and the sound of that cry: "Lydie!"

CHAPTER XVIII

CLEVER TACTICS

As soon as M. Durand had recovered from the shock of Madame la Marquise's sudden invasion of his sanctum, he ran to the portière which he had been watching so anxiously, and, pushing it aside, he disclosed the door partially open.

"Monsieur le Comte de Stainville!" he called discreetly.

110

"Has she gone?" came in a whisper from the inner room.

"Yes! yes! I pray you enter, M. le Comte," said M. Durand, obsequiously holding the portière aside. "Madame la Marquise only passed through very quickly; she took notice of nothing, I assure you."

Gaston de Stainville cast a quick searching glance round the room as he entered, and fidgeted nervously with a lace handkerchief in his hand. No doubt his enforced sudden retreat at Lydie's approach had been humiliating to his pride. But he did not want to come on her too abruptly, and was chafing now because he needed a menial's help to further his desires.

"You were a fool, man, to place me in this awkward position," he said with a scowl directed at M. Durand's meek personality, "or else a knave, in which case ..."

"Ten thousand pardons, M. le Comte," rejoined the little man apologetically. "Madame la Marquise scarcely ever comes this way after le petit lever. She invariably retires to her study, and thither I should have had the honour to conduct you, according to your wish."

"You seem very sure that Madame la Marquise would have granted me a private audience."

"I would have done my best to obtain one for M. Le Comte," said M. Durand with becoming modesty, "and I think I should have succeeded ... with tact and diplomacy, Monsieur le Comte, we, who are privileged to ..."

"Yes, yes!" interrupted Gaston impatiently, "but now?"

"Ah! now it will be much more difficult. Madame la Marquise is not in her study, and ..."

"And you will want more pay," quoth Gaston with a sneer.

"Oh! Monsieur le Comte ..." protested Durand.

"Well! how much more?" said the Comte impatiently.

"What does M. le Comte desire?"

"To speak with Madame la Marquise quite alone."

"Heu! ... heu! ... it is difficult...."

But Gaston de Stainville's stock of patience was running low. He never had a great deal. With a violent oath he seized the little man by the collar.

"Two louis, you knave, for getting me that audience now, at once, or my flunkey's stick across your shoulders if you fool me any longer."

M. Durand apparently was not altogether unprepared for this outburst: perhaps his peculiar position had often subjected him to similar onslaughts on the part of irate and aristocratic suppliants. Anyway, he did not seem at all disturbed, and, as soon as the

Comte's grip on his collar relaxed, he readjusted his coat and his cravat, and holding out his thin hand, he said meekly:

"The two louis I pray you, Monsieur le Comte. And," he added, when Gaston, with another oath, finally placed the two gold pieces on the meagre palm, "will you deign to follow me?"

He led the way through the large folding doors and thence along the enfilade of gorgeous reception rooms, the corridors, landings and staircase which Lydie herself had traversed just now. Gaston de Stainville followed him at a close distance, acknowledging with a curt nod here and there the respectful salutations of the many lackeys whom he passed.

M. le Comte de Stainville was an important personage at Court: Madame de Pompadour's predilection for him was well known, and His Majesty himself was passing fond of the gallant gentleman's company, whilst Madame la Comtesse was believed to hold undisputed sway over M. le Contrôleur-Général des Finances.

Thus Gaston met with obsequiousness wherever he went, and this despite the fact that he was not lavish with money. M. Durand would have expected a much heavier bribe from any one else for this service which he was now rendering to the Comte.

Anon the two men reached the terrace. M. Durand then pointed with one claw-like finger to the spinney on the left.

"M. le Comte will find Madame la Marquise in yonder plantation," he said; "as for me, I dare not vacate my post any longer, for M. le Contrôleur might have need of me, nor would Monsieur le Comte care mayhap to be seen by Madame la Marquise in my company."

Gaston assented. He was glad to be rid of the mealy-mouthed creature, of whose necessary help in this matter he was heartily ashamed. Unlike Lydie, he was quite unconscious of the beauty of this August day: neither the birds nor the acrid scent of late summer flowers appealed to his fancy, and the clump of young beech trees only interested him in so far as he hoped to find Lydie there, alone.

When he reached the little glade, he caught sight of the graceful figure, half-sitting, half-reclining in the unconscious charm of sleep. Overcome by the heat and the glare, Lydie had dozed off momentarily.

Presently something caused her to open her eyes and she saw Gaston de Stainville standing there looking at her intently.

She was taken at a disadvantage, since she had undoubtedly been asleep—if only for a moment—and she was not quite sure if her pose, when Gaston first caught sight of her, was sufficiently dignified.

"I am afraid I have disturbed you," he said humbly.

"I was meditating," she replied coldly, as she smoothed down her skirts and mechanically put a hand to her hair, lest a curl had gone astray.

Then she made as if she would rise.

"Surely you are not going?" he pleaded.

"I have my work to do. I only stayed here a moment, in order to rest."

"And I am intruding?"

"Oh, scarcely," she replied quietly. "I was about to return to my work."

"Is it so urgent?"

"The business of a nation, M. le Comte, is always urgent."

"So urgent that you have no time now to give to old friends," he said bitterly.

She shrugged her shoulders with a quick, sarcastic laugh.

"Old friends? ... Oh! ..."

"Yes, old friends," he rejoined quietly. "We were children together, Lydie."

"Much has occurred since then, Monsieur le Comte."

"Only one great and awful fault, which meseems hath been its own expiation."

"Need we refer to that now?" she asked calmly.

"Indeed, indeed, we must," he replied earnestly. "Lydie, am I never to be forgiven?"

"Is there aught for me to forgive?"

"Yes. An error, a grave error ... a fault, if you will call it so ..."

"I prefer to call it a treachery," she said.

"Without one word of explanation, without listening to a single word from me. Is that just?"

"There is nothing that you could say now, Monsieur le Comte, that I should have the right to hear."

"Why so?" he said with sudden vehemence, as he came nearer to her, and in a measure barred the way by which she might have escaped. "Even a criminal at point of death is allowed to say a few words in self-defence. Yet I was no criminal. If I loved you, Lydie, was that wrong? ... I was an immeasurable fool, I own that," he added more calmly, being quick to note that he only angered her by his violence, "and it is impossible for a high-minded woman like yourself to understand the pitfalls which beset the path of a man, who has riches, good looks mayhap and a great name, all of which will tempt the cupidity of certain designing women, bent above all on matrimony, on influence and independence. Into one of these pitfalls I fell, Lydie ... fell clumsily, stupidly, I own, but not inexcusably."

113

"You seem to forget, M. le Comte," she said stiffly, "that you are speaking of your wife."

"Nay!" he said with a certain sad dignity, "I try not to forget it. I do not accuse, I merely state a fact, and do so before the woman whom I most honour in the world, who was the first recipient of my childish confidences, the first consoler of my boyhood's sorrows."

"That was when you were free, M. le Comte, and could bring your confidences to me; now they justly belong to another and ..."

"And by the heavens above me," he interrupted eagerly, "I do that other no wrong by bringing my sorrows to you and laying them with a prayer for consolation at your feet."

He noted that since that first desire to leave him, Lydie had made no other attempt to go. She was sitting in the angle of the rough garden seat, her graceful arm resting on the back, her cheek leaning against her hand. A gentle breeze stirred the little curls round her head, and now, when he spoke so earnestly and so sadly about his sorrow, a swift look of sympathy softened the haughty expression of her mouth.

Quick to notice it, Gaston nevertheless in no way relaxed his attitude of humble supplication; he stood before her with head bent, his eyes mostly riveted on the ground.

"There is so little consolation that I can give," she said more gently.

"There is a great one, if you will but try."

"What is it?"

"Do not cast me out from your life altogether. Am I such a despicable creature that you cannot now and then vouchsafe me one kind look? ... I did wrong you ... I know it. ... Call it treachery if you must, yet when I look back on that night, meseems I am worthy of your pity. Blinded by my overwhelming love for you, I forgot everything for one brief hour ... forgot that I had sunk deeply in a pitfall—by Heaven through no fault of mine own! ... forgot that another now had a claim on that love which never was mine to give, since it had always been wholly yours. ... Yes! I forgot! ... the music, the noise, the excitement of the night, your own beauty, Lydie, momentarily addled my brain. ... I forgot the past, I only lived for the present. Am I to blame because I am a man and that you are exquisitely fair?"

He forced himself not to raise his voice, not to appear eager or vehement. Lydie only saw before her a man whom she had once loved, who had grievously wronged her, but who now stood before her ashamed and humbled, asking with utmost respect for her forgiveness of the past.

"Let us speak of it no longer," she said, "believe me, Gaston, I have never borne you ill-will."

For the first time she had used his Christian name. The layer of ice was broken through, but the surface of the lake was still cold and smooth.

"Nay! but you avoid me," he rejoined seeking to meet her eyes, "you treat me with whole-hearted contempt, whilst I would lay down my life to serve you, and this in all deference and honour, as the martyrs of old laid down their life for their faith."

"Protestations, Gaston," she said with a quick sigh.

"Let me prove them true," he urged. "Lydie, I watched you just now, while you slept; it was some minutes and I saw much. Your lips were parted with constant sighs; there were tears at the points of your lashes. At that moment I would have gladly died if thereby I could have eased your heart from the obvious burden which it bore."

Emboldened by her silence, and by the softer expression of her face, he sat down close beside her, and anon placed his hand on hers. She withdrew it quietly and serenely as was her wont, but quite without anger.

She certainly felt no anger toward him. Strangely enough, the anger she did feel was all against her husband. That Gaston had seen her grief was in a measure humiliating to her pride, and this humiliation she owed to the great wrong done her by milor. And Gaston had been clever at choosing his words; he appealed to her pity and asked for forgiveness. There was no attempt on his part to justify himself, and his self-abasement broke down the barrier of resentment which up to now she had set up against him. His respectful homage soothed her wounded pride, and she felt really, sincerely sorry for him.

The fact that her own actions had been so gravely misunderstood also helped Gaston's cause; she felt that, after all, she too might have passed a hasty, unconsidered judgment on him, and knew now how acutely such a judgment can hurt.

And he spoke very earnestly, very simply: remember that she had loved him once, loved and trusted him. He had been the ideal of her girlhood, and though she had remorselessly hurled him down from his high pedestal since then, there remained nevertheless, somewhere in the depths of her heart, a lingering thought of tenderness for him.

"Lydie!" he now said appealingly.

"Yes?"

"Let me be the means of easing your heart from its load of sorrow. You spoke of my wife just now. See, I do not shirk the mention of her name. I swear to you by that early love for you which was the noblest, purest emotion of my life, that I do not wrong her by a single thought when I ask for your friendship. You are so immeasurably superior to all other women, Lydie, that in your presence passion itself becomes exalted and desire transformed into a craving for sacrifice."

"Oh! how I wish I could believe you, Gaston," she sighed.

"Try me!"

"How?"

"Let me guess what troubles you now. Oh! I am not the empty-headed fop that you would believe. I have ears and eyes, and if I hold aloof from Court intrigues, it is only because I see too much of their inner workings. Do you really believe that I do not see what goes on around me now? Do I not know how your noble sympathy must at this very moment be going out to the unfortunate young prince whom you honour with your friendship? Surely, surely, you cannot be a party to the criminal supineness which at this very moment besets France, and causes her to abandon him to his fate?"

"Not France, Gaston," she protested.

"And not you, surely. I would stake my life on your loyalty to a friend."

"Of course," she said simply.

"I knew it," he ejaculated triumphantly, as if this discovery had indeed caused him joyful surprise. "Every fibre in my soul told me that I would not appeal to you in vain. You are clever, Lydie, you are rich, you are powerful. I feel as if I could turn to you as to a man. Prince Charles Edward Stuart honoured me with his friendship: I am not presumptuous when I say that I stood in his heart second only to Lord Eglinton. ... But because I hold a secondary place I dared not thrust my advice, my prayers, my help forward, whilst I firmly believed that his greater friend was at work on his behalf. But now I can bear the suspense no longer. The crisis has become over-acute. The Stuart prince is in deadly danger, not only from supineness but from treachery."

Clever Gaston! how subtle and how shrewd! she would never have to come to meet him on this ground, but he called to her. He came to fetch her, as it were, and led her along the road. He did not offer to guide her faltering footsteps, he simulated lameness, and asked for assistance instead of offering it.

So clever was this move that Lydie was thrown off her guard. At the word "treachery" she looked eagerly into his eyes.

"What makes you think ... ?" she asked.

"Oh! I have scented it in the air for some days. The King himself wears an air of shamefacedness when the Stuart prince is mentioned. Madame de Pompadour lately hath talked freely of the completion of her château in the Parc aux Cerfs, as if money were forthcoming from some unexpected source; then a letter came from England, which His Majesty keeps hidden in his pocket, whilst whispered conversations are carried on between the King and Madame, which cease abruptly if any one comes within earshot. Then to-day ..."

"Yes? ... to-day?" she asked eagerly.

"I hardly dare speak of it."

"Why?"

"I fear it might give you pain."

"I am used to pain," she said simply, "and I would wish to know."

"I was in the antechamber when His Majesty arrived for le petit lever of M. le Contrôleur. I had had vague hopes of seeing you this morning, and lingered about the reception rooms somewhat listlessly, my thoughts dwelling on all the sad news which has lately come from Scotland. In the antechamber His Majesty was met by M. le Duc d'Aumont, your father."

He paused again as if loth to speak, but she said quite calmly:

"And you overheard something which the Duke, my father, said to the King, and which confirmed your suspicions. What was it?"

"It was His Majesty who spoke, obviously not aware that I was within earshot. He said quite airily: 'Oh! if we cannot persuade milor we must act independently of him. The Stuart will be tired by now of living in crags and will not be so chary of entrusting his valuable person to a comfortable French ship.' Then M. le Duc placed a hand on His Majesty's arm warning him of my presence and nothing more was said."

"Then you think that the King of France is about to deliver Prince Charles Edward Stuart to his enemies?" she asked calmly.

"I am sure of it: and the thought is more than I can bear. And I am not alone in this, Lydie. The whole of France will cry out in shame at such perfidy. Heaven knows what will come of it ultimately, but surely, surely we cannot allow that unfortunate young prince whom we all loved and fêted to be thus handed over to the English authorities! That is why I have dared intrude on you to-day. Lydie," he added now in a passionate appeal; "for the sake of that noble if misguided young prince, will you try and forget the terrible wrong which I in my madness and blindness once did you? Do not allow my sin to be expiated by him! ... I crave your help for him on my knees. ... Hate me an you will! despise me and punish me, but do not deny me your help for him!"

117

His voice, though sunk now almost to a whisper, was vibrating with passion. He half dropped on his knees, took the edge of her skirt between his fingers and raised it to his lips.

Clever, clever Gaston! he had indeed moved her. Her serenity had gone, and her cold impassiveness. She sat up, erect, palpitating with excitement, her eyes glowing, her lips parted, all her senses awake and thrilling with this unexpected hope.

"In what manner do you wish for my help, Gaston?"

"I think the King and M. le Duc will do nothing for a day or two at any rate. I hoped I could forestall them, with your help, Lydie, if you will give it. I am not rich, but I have realized some of my fortune: my intention was to charter a seaworthy boat, equip her as well as my means allowed and start for Scotland immediately, and then if possible to induce the prince to cross over with me to Ireland, or, with great good luck I might even bring him back as far as Brittany. But you see how helpless I was, for I dared not approach you, and I do not know where I can find the prince."

"And if I do not give you that help which you need?" she asked.

"I would still charter the vessel and start for Scotland," he replied quietly. "I cannot stay here, in inactivity whilst I feel that infamous treachery is being planned against a man with whom I have often broken bread. If you will not tell me where I can find Charles Edward Stuart, I will still equip a vessel and try and find him somehow. If I fail, I will not return, but at any rate I shall then not be a party or a witness to the everlasting shame of France!"

"Your expedition would require great pluck and endurance."

"I have both, and boundless enthusiasm to boot. Two or three friends will accompany me, and my intention was to start for Brest or Le Havre to-night. But if you will consent to help me, Lydie ..."

"Nay!" she interrupted eagerly. "I'll not help you. 'Tis you who shall help me!"

"Lydie!"

"The plan which you have formed I too had thought on it: the treachery of the King of France, my God! I knew it too. But my plans are more mature than yours, less noble and self-sacrificing, for, as you say, I have power and influence; yet with all that power I could not serve Prince Charles Edward as I would wish to do, because though I have pluck and endurance I am not a man."

"And you want me to help you? Thank God! thank God for that! Tell me what to do."

"To start for Le Havre—not Brest."

"Yes!"

"This afternoon ... reaching Le Havre before dawn."

"Yes."

"There to seek out Le Monarque. She lies in the harbour, and her commander is Captain Barre."

"Yes! yes!"

"You will hand him over a packet, which I will give you anon, and then return here as swiftly as you went."

"Is that all?" he asked in obvious disappointment, "and I who had hoped that you would ask me to give my life for you!"

"The faithful and speedy performance of this errand, Gaston, is worth the most sublime self-sacrifice, if this be purposeless. The packet will contain full instructions for Captain Barre how and where to find Prince Charles Edward. Le Monarque is ready equipped for the expedition, but ..." she paused a moment as if half ashamed of the admission, "I had no one whom I could entrust with the message."

Gaston de Stainville was too keen a diplomatist to venture on this delicate ground. He had never once mentioned her husband's name, fearing to scare her, or to sting her pride. He knew her to be far too loyal to allow condemnation of her lord by the lips of another man; all he said now was a conventional:

"I am ready!"

Then she rose and held out her hand to him. He bowed with great deference, and kissed the tips of her fingers. His face expressed nothing but the respectful desire to be of service, and not one thought of treachery disturbed Lydie's serenity. Historians have, we know, blamed her very severely for this unconditional yielding of another's secret into the keeping of a man who had already deceived her once; but it was the combination of circumstances which caused her to act thus, and Gaston's masterly move in asking for her help had completely subjugated her. She would have yielded to no other emotion, but that of compassion for him, and the desire to render him assistance in a cause which she herself had so deeply at heart. She had no love for Gaston and no amount of the usual protestations would have wrung a confidence from her. But he had so turned the tables that it appeared that he was confiding in her; and her pride, which had been so deeply humiliated that self-same morning, responded to his appeal. If she had had the least doubt or fear in her mind, she would not have given up her secret, but as he stood so coldly and impassively before her, without a trace of passion in his voice or look, she had absolutely no misgivings.

"I can be in the saddle at four o'clock," he said in the same unemotional tones, "when and how can I receive the packet from you?"

119

"Will you wait for me here?" she replied. "The packet is quite ready, and the walls of the palace have eyes and ears."

Thus they parted. She full of confidence and hope, not in any way attempting to disguise before him the joy and gratitude which she felt, he the more calm of the two, fearing to betray his sense of triumph, still trembling lest her present mood should change.

Her graceful figure quickly disappeared among the trees. He gave a sigh of intense satisfaction. His Majesty would be pleased, and Madame de Pompadour would be more than kind. Never for a moment did the least feeling of remorse trouble his complacent mind; the dominant thought in him was one of absolute triumph and pride at having succeeded in hoodwinking the keenest statesman in France. He sat down on the garden seat whereon had been fought that close duel between himself and the woman whom he had once already so heartlessly betrayed. He thought over every stage of the past scene and smiled somewhat grimly. He felt quite sure that he individually would never have trusted for the second time a woman who had once deceived him. But Lydie had no such misgivings; as she now sped through the park, she no longer saw its artificiality, its stunted rose trees and the stultified plantations. The air was invigorating to breathe, the fragrance of the flowers was sweet, the birds' twitter was delicious to the ear. There were good and beautiful things in this world, but the best of all was the loyalty of a friend.

CHAPTER XIX

A CRISIS

Lydie returned to the palace in a very different frame of mind than when, half an hour ago, she had run along corridor and staircase, her nerves on the jar, her whole being smarting under the sense of wrong and of injustice.

Hope had consoled her since then, and the thought that her own cherished plan need not fail for want of a loyal man's help had in a measure eased that strange obsession which had weighed on her heart, and caused foolish tears to start to her eyes. She was also conscious of a certain joy in thinking that the companion of her

120

childhood, the man who had been her earliest ideal was not so black a traitor as she had believed.

Gaston had spoken of pitfalls, he owned to having been deceived, and there is no woman living who will not readily admit that her successful rival is naught but a designing minx. Gaston had always been weak where women were concerned, and Lydie forgave him his weakness, simply because he had owned to it and because she liked to think of his fault as a weakness rather than as a deliberate treachery.

Now she only thought of her project. When first she had talked of commissioning Le Monarque, milor had entrusted her with all necessary directions by which Captain Barre could most easily reach the Stuart prince and his friends. It was but a very few weeks, nay days ago, that she had been quite convinced that the King himself would be foremost in the general desire to fit out an expedition for the rescue of the unfortunate Jacobites, and naturally the fitting-out of such an expedition would have been entrusted primarily to herself and incidentally to her husband.

These directions she still had. All she had to do now was to embody them in the secret orders which Gaston de Stainville would hand over to the Commander of Le Monarque. Further orders would be anent getting the prince and his friends on board, and the route to be taken homeward, the better to ensure their safety.

Beyond that she would need some sort of token which, when shown to Charles Edward Stuart by Captain Barre, would induce the young prince to trust himself and his friends unconditionally to Le Monarque. Lord Eglinton's signet ring had been spoken of for this object the day of the Young Pretender's departure, but now of course she could not ask milor for it. On the other hand she felt quite sure that a written word from her would answer the necessary purpose, a brief note sealed with the Eglinton arms.

The thought of the seal as an additional message of good faith first occurred to her when she once more reached the West Wing of the palace.

From the great square landing where she now stood, a monumental door on her right gave on her own suite of apartments. On the left was the long enfilade of reception rooms, with the vast audience chamber and milor's own withdrawing room beyond.

She deliberately turned to the left, and once more traversed the vast and gorgeous halls where, half an hour ago, she had suffered such keen humiliation and such overwhelming disappointment. She forced herself not to dwell on that scene again, and even closed her eyes with a vague fear that the mental vision might become materialized.

Beyond the audience chamber there were two or three more reception rooms, and from the last of these a door masked by a heavy portière, gave on milor's study. All these apartments were now deserted, save for a few flunkeys who stood about desultorily in the window embrasures. From one of them Lydie asked if M. le Contrôleur des Finances was within, but no one remembered having seen milor since the petit lever, and it was generally thought that he had gone to Trianon. Lydie hesitated a moment before she opened the door; she scarcely ever entered this portion of the palace and had never once been in milor's private rooms. But she wanted that seal with the Eglinton arms, and would not admit, even to herself, that her husband's presence or absence interested her in the least.

But on the threshold she paused. Milor was sitting at a gigantic escritoire placed squarely in front of the window. He had obviously been writing; at the slight sound of the creaking door and the swish of Lydie's skirts, he raised his head from his work and turned to look at her.

Immediately he rose.

"Your pardon for this intrusion, milor," she said coldly, "your lacqueys gave me to understand that you were from home."

"Is there anything that you desire?"

"Only a seal with the Eglinton arms," she replied quite casually, "I have need of it for a private communication."

He sought for the seal among the many costly objects which littered his table and handed it to her.

"I am sorry that you should have troubled to come so far for it," he said coldly, "one of my men would have taken it to your study."

"And I am sorry that I should have disturbed you," she rejoined. "I was told that you had gone to Trianon."

"I shall be on my way thither in a few moments, to place my resignation in the hands of His Majesty."

"Your resignation?"

"As I have had the honour to tell you."

"Then you will leave Versailles?"

"To make way for my successor, as soon as His Majesty hath appointed one."

"And you go ... whither?" she asked.

"Oh! what matter?" he replied carelessly, "so long as I no longer trouble your ladyship with my presence."

"Then you will have no objection if I return to my father until your future plans are more mature?"

"Objection?" he said with a pleasant little laugh. "Nay, Madame, you are pleased to joke."

She felt a little bewildered: this unexpected move on his part had somehow thrown all her plans out of gear. For the moment she scarcely had time to conjecture, even vaguely, what her own future actions would be if her husband no longer chose to hold an important position in the Ministry. The thought that his resignation would of necessity mean her own, suddenly rushed into her mind with overwhelming violence, but she was too confused at present to disentangle herself from the maze of conflicting emotions which assailed her, when first she realized the unexpected possibility.

She was toying with the seal, forgetful somehow of the purpose and the plans which it represented. These not being in jeopardy through milor's extraordinary conduct, she could afford to dismiss them from her mind.

It was the idea of her husband's resignation and her own future which troubled her, and strangely enough there was such an air of finality about his attitude that, for the moment, she was somewhat at a loss how to choose a line of argument with which to influence him. That she could make him alter his decision she never doubted for a moment, but since the first day of their married life he had never taken any initiative in an important matter, and his doing so at this moment found her at first wholly unprepared.

"Am I to understand that my wishes in so vital a decision are not to be consulted in any way?" she asked after a momentary pause.

"You will honour me, Madame, by making me acquainted with them," he replied.

"You must reconsider your resignation," she said decisively.

"That is not possible."

"I have much important business of the nation in hand which I could not hand over to your successor in an incomplete state," she said haughtily.

"There is no necessity for that, Madame, nor for depriving the nation of your able, guiding hand. The post of Comptroller of Finance need not be filled immediately. It can remain in abeyance and under your own matchless control, at the pleasure of His Majesty and M. le Duc d'Aumont, neither of whom will, I am sure, desire to make a change in an administration, which is entirely for the benefit of France."

She looked at him very keenly, through narrowed lids scanning his face and trying to read his intent. But there was obviously no look of sarcasm in his eyes, nor the hint of a sneer in the even placidity of his voice. Once more that unaccountable feeling of irritation seemed to overmaster her, the same sense of wrath and of injustice which had assailed her when she first spoke to him.

"But this is senseless, milor," she said impatiently. "You seem to forget that I am your wife, and that I have a right to your protection, and to a fitting home if I am to leave Versailles."

"I am not forgetting that you are my wife, Madame, but my protection is worth so little, scarcely worthy of your consideration. As for the rest, my château of Vincennes is entirely at your disposal; a retinue of servants is there awaiting your orders, and my notary will this day prepare the deed which I have commanded wherein I humbly ask you to accept the château, its lands and revenues as a gift from me, albeit these are wholly unworthy of your condescension."

"It is monstrous, milor, and I'll not accept it," she retorted. "Think you perchance I am so ready to play the rôle of a forsaken wife?"

A strange thought had been gradually creeping into her mind: a weird kind of calculation whereby she put certain events in juxtaposition to one another: the departure of Gaston de Stainville, for he had told her that he was prepared to go to Scotland whether she helped him in his expedition or not: then Irène would be temporarily free, almost a widow since Gaston's return under those circumstances would have been more than problematical; and now milor calmly expressing the determination to quit Versailles, and to give away his château and lands of Vincennes, forsooth, as a sop to the forsaken wife, whilst Madame de Stainville's provocative attitude this morning more than bore out this conclusion.

Lydie felt as if every drop of blood in her body rushed up violently to her cheeks, which suddenly blazed with anger, whilst his, at her suggestion, had become a shade more pale.

"I am free to suppose, milor, that Madame de Stainville has something to do with your sudden decision!" she said haughtily; "therefore, believe me, I have no longer a wish to combat it. As the welfare of France, the work which I have in hand, interests you so little, I will not trouble you by referring to such matters again. By all means place your resignation in His Majesty's hands. I understand that you desire to be free. I only hope that you will assist me in not washing too much of our matrimonial linen in public. I have many enemies and I must refuse to allow your whims and fantasies to annihilate the fruits of my past labours, for the good of my country. I will confer with Monsieur le Duc, my father; you will hear my final decision from him."

She turned once more toward the door. He had not spoken one word in interruption, as with a harsh and trenchant voice she thus hurled insult upon insult at him. She only saw that he looked very pale, although his face seemed to her singularly expressionless: whilst she herself was conscious of such unendurable agony, that she feared she must betray it in the quiver of her mouth, and the tears which threatened to come to her eyes.

When she ceased speaking, he bowed quite stiffly, but made no sign of wishing to defend himself. She left the room very hurriedly: in another second and she would have broken down. Sobs were choking her, an intolerable anguish wrung her heartstrings to that extent, that if she had had the power, she would have wounded him physically, as she hoped that she had done now mentally. Oh! if she had had the strength, if those sobs that would not be denied had not risen so persistently in her throat, she would have found words of such deadly outrage, as would at least have stung him and made him suffer as she was suffering now.

There are certain pains of the heart that are so agonizing, that only cruelty will assuage them. Lydie's strong, passionate nature perpetually held in check by the force of her great ambition and by her will to be masculine and firm in the great purpose of her life, had for once broken through the trammels which her masterful mind had fashioned round it. It ran riot now in her entire being. She was conscious of overwhelming, of indomitable hate.

With burning eyes and trembling lips she hurried through the rooms, and along the interminable corridors. The flunkeys stared at her as she passed, she looked so different to her usual composed and haughty self: her cheeks were flaming, her bosom heaving beneath the primly-folded kerchief, and at intervals a curious moan-like sound escaped her lips.

Thus she reached her own study, a small square room at the extreme end of the West Wing, two of its walls formed an angle of the structure, with great casement windows which gave on that secluded spinney, with its peaceful glade which she loved.

As soon as she entered the room her eyes fell on that distant beech plantation. A great sigh rose from her oppressed heart, for suddenly she had remembered her great purpose, the one project which was infinitely dear to her.

The graceful beech trees far away, with their undergrowth of bracken and foxgloves gleaming in the sun, recalled to her that Gaston was waiting in their midst for her message to Le Monarque.

Thank God, this great joy at least was not denied her. She still had the power and the will to accomplish this all-pervading object of her life: the rescue of the Stuart prince from the hands of his enemies and from the perfidy of his whilom friends.

This thought, the recollection of her talk with Gaston, the

125

work which still remained for her to do, eased the tension of her nerves and stilled the agonizing pain of her heart.

With a tremendous effort of will she chased away from her mental vision the picture of that pale, expressionless face, which seemed to haunt her. She forced herself to forget the humiliation, the injustice, the affront which she had suffered to-day, and not to hear the persistent echo of the deadly insults which she had uttered in response.

Her study was cool and dark; heavy curtains of soft-toned lavender fell beside the windows, partially shutting out the glare of the midday sun. Her secretaire stood in the centre of the room. She sat down near it and unlocked a secret drawer. For the next quarter of an hour her pen flew across two sheets of paper. She had in front of her a map of a certain portion of the West Coast of Scotland, with directions and other sundry notes carefully written in the margins, and she was writing out the orders for the commander of Le Monarque to reach that portion of the coast as quickly as possible, to seek out Prince Charles Stuart, who would probably be on the look-out for a French vessel, and having got him, and as many friends of his as accompanied him, safely aboard, to skirt the West Coast of Ireland and subsequently to reach Morlaix in Brittany, where the prince would disembark.

There was nothing flustered or undetermined about her actions, she never paused a moment to collect her thoughts for obedient to her will they were already arrayed in perfect order in her mind: she had only to transfer them to paper.

Having written out the orders for Captain Barre she carefully folded them, together with the map, and fastened and sealed them with the official seal of the Ministry of Finance: then she took one more sheet of paper and wrote in a bold clear hand:

"The bearer of this letter is sent to meet you by your true and faithful friends. You may trust yourself and those you care for unconditionally to him."

To this note she affixed a seal stamped with the Eglinton arms: and across the words themselves she wrote the name "Eglinton!"

There was no reason to fear for a moment that the Stuart prince would have any misgivings when he received this message of comfort and of hope.

Then with all the papers safely tied together and hidden in the folds of her corselet, she once more found her way down the great staircase and terraces and into the beech wood where M. de Stainville awaited her.

CHAPTER XX

A FAREWELL

Gaston de Stainville had been sitting idly on the garden seat, vaguely wondering why Lydie was so long absent, ignorant of course of the acute crisis through which she had just passed. For the last quarter of an hour of this weary waiting, anxiety began to assail him.

Women were so fickle and so capricious! which remark inwardly muttered came with singular inappropriateness from Gaston de Stainville. His keen judgment, however, fought his apprehensions. He knew quite well that Lydie was unlike other women, at once stronger and weaker than those of her own sex, more firm in her purpose, less bendable in her obstinacy. And he knew also that nothing could occur within the gorgeous walls of that palace to cause her to change her mind.

But as the moments sped on, his anxiety grew apace. He no longer could sit still, and began walking feverishly up and down the little glade, like an animal caged within limits too narrow for its activity. He dared not wander out of the wood, lest she should return and, not finding him there, think at once of doubting.

Thus when she once more appeared before him, he was not so calm as he would have wished, nor yet so keen in noting the subtle, indefinable change which had come over her entire personality. Desirous of masking his agitation, he knelt when she approached, and thus took the packet from her hand.

The action struck her as theatrical, her mind being filled with another picture, that of a man motionless and erect, with pale, expressionless face, which yet had meant so much more of reality to her.

And because of this theatricality in Gaston's attitude, she lost something of the fullness of joy of this supreme moment. She ought to have been happier, more radiant with hope for the future and with gratitude to him. She tried to say something enthusiastic, something more in keeping with the romance of this sudden and swift departure, the prospective ride to Le Havre, the spirit of self-sacrifice and courage which caused him to undertake this task, so different to his usual avocation of ease and luxury.

"I pray you, Gaston," she said, "guard the packet safely, and use your best endeavours to reach Le Havre ere the night hath yielded to a new dawn."

She could not say more just now, feeling that if she added words of encouragement or of praise, they would not ring true, and would seem as artificial as his posture at her feet.

"I will guard the packet with my life," he said earnestly, "and if perchance you wake to-night from dreams of the unfortunate prince, whom your devotion will save from death, send one thought wandering far away across the rich fields of Normandy, for they will be behind me by that time, and I will sight the port of Le Havre long before its church spires are tipped with gold."

"God speed you then!" she rejoined. "I'll not detain you!"

She chided herself for her coldness, noting that Gaston on the other hand seemed aglow now with excitement, as he unbuttoned his coat and slipped the papers into an inner pocket. Then he sprang to his feet and seemed ready to go.

Just at the moment of actual parting, when he asked for her hand to kiss, and she, giving it to him felt his lips trembling on her fingers, some measure of his excitement communicated itself to her, and she repeated more warmly:

"God speed you, Gaston, and farewell!"

"God bless you, Lydie, for this trust which you have deigned to place in me! Two days hence at even I shall have returned. Where shall I see you then?"

"In my study. Ask for an audience. I will see that it is granted."

The next moment he had gone; she saw the rich purple of his coat gradually vanish behind the tall bracken. Even then she had no misgivings. She thought that she had done right, and that she had taken the only course by which she could ensure the safety of the Stuart prince, to whom France, whom she guided through the tortuous paths of diplomacy, and for whose honour she felt herself to be primarily responsible, had pledged her word and her faith.

CHAPTER XXI

ROYAL THANKS

In one of the smaller rooms of the palace of Trianon, His Majesty King Louis XV received M. le Comte de Stainville in private audience. Madame la Marquise de Pompadour was present. She sat in an armchair, close beside the one occupied by His Majesty, her dainty feet resting on a footstool, her hand given up to her royal patron, so that he might occasionally imprint a kiss upon it.

Gaston de Stainville sat on a tabouret at a respectful distance. He had in his hand a letter with a seal attached to it and a map, which had a number of notes scribbled in the margin. His Majesty seemed in a superlatively good humour, and sat back in his chair, his fat body shaking now and again with bursts of merriment.

"Eh! eh! this gallant Count!" he said jovially, "par ma foi! to think that the minx deceived us and our Court all these years, with her prim ways and prudish manner. Even Her Majesty the Queen looks upon Madame Lydie as a pattern of all the virtues."

He leaned forward and beckoned to Gaston to draw his chair nearer.

"Voyons, M. le Comte," continued Louis with a humorous leer, "there is no need for quite so much discretion. We are all friends together ... eh? Tell us how you did it."

Gaston de Stainville did draw his chair nearer to His Majesty, such a proffered honour was not to be ignored. His face wore an air of provocative discretion and a fatuous smile curled his sensual lips.

"Nay," he said unctuously, "your Majesty who is galant homme par excellence will deign to grant me leave to keep inviolate the secret of how I succeeded in breaking through the barrier of prudery, set up by the most unapproachable woman in France. Enough that I did succeed: and that I have been made thrice happy by being allowed to place the result, with mine own hands, at the feet of the most adored of her sex."

And with an elegant and graceful flourish of the arm, he rose from his tabouret and immediately dropped on one knee at Madame's feet, offering her the letter and the map which he held. She took them from him, regarding him with a smile, which fortunately the amorous but highly jealous monarch failed to see; he had just taken the papers from Pompadour and was gloating over their contents.

"You had best see M. le Duc d'Aumont at once," said His Majesty with a quick return to gravity, as soon as Gaston de Stainville had once more resumed his seat. "Go back to the palace now, Monsieur le Comte, Madame will allow you to take her chair, and then by using our own private entrance on the South side, you will avoid being seen from the West Wing. Needless to say, I hope, that discretion and wariness must be your watchword until the affair is brought to a successful conclusion."

Gaston de Stainville bent himself nearly double, and placed one hand there, where his heart was supposed to be, all in token that he would be obedient to the letter and the spirit of every royal command.

"We do not think," said Louis, with somewhat forced carelessness, "that our subjects need know anything about this transaction."

"Certainly not, Sire," rejoined De Stainville most emphatically, whilst Madame too nodded very decisively.

"Most people have strange ideas about politics and diplomacy," continued the King. "Just as if those complicated arts could be conducted on lines of antiquated mediæval codes: therefore the whole business must be kept between our three selves now present, M. le Comte, and of course M. le Duc d'Aumont, who has helped us throughout, and without whom we could not now proceed."

"I quite understand, Sire," assented Gaston.

"We are of course presuming that your happy influence over Madame Lydie will not cease with her giving you those papers," said Louis with another of his unpleasant leers.

"I think not your Majesty."

"She will hold her tongue, I should imagine ... for very obvious reasons," said Madame with a malicious sneer.

"Anyhow you had best make our recommendations known to Monsieur le Duc d'Aumont. Tell him that we suggest not relying on Le Monarque even though she be ready to put to sea, as her commander may be, for aught we know a secret adherent of the Stuart. We should not care to trust him, since the Eglintons seem to have been already to do so. A delay of five or six days while Le Levantin is being commissioned is better than the taking of any risk. Though we are doing nothing that we are ashamed of," added Louis the Well-beloved airily, "we have no wish that the matter be bruited abroad, lest we be misunderstood."

We must suppose that Monsieur le Comte de Stainville had been denied at his birth the saving gift of a sense of humour, for in reply to this long tirade from the King, he said quite seriously and emphatically:

"Your Majesty need not be under the slightest apprehension. Neither M. le Duc d'Aumont, I feel sure, nor I myself will in any way endanger the absolute secrecy of the transaction, lest we be misunderstood. As for Madame Lydie ..." He paused a moment, whilst carefully examining his well-trimmed nails: a smile, wherein evil intent now fought with fatuity, played round the corners of his lips. "Madame Lydie will also hold her tongue," he concluded quietly.

"That is well!" assented the King. "M. le Duc d'Aumont will

130

see to the rest. In five or six days, Le Levantin should be ready. Her secret orders have been drafted and already bear our royal signature. Now with this map and directions, and the private note for the Stuart, all so kindly furnished by Madame Lydie, the expedition should be easy, and above all quite swift. The sooner the affair is concluded and the money paid over, the less likelihood there is of our subjects getting wind thereof. We must stipulate, M. le Comte, since you are the youngest partner in this undertaking and the least prominent in the public eye, that you take the secret orders yourself to Le Levantin. We should not feel safe if they were in any one else's hands."

"I thank your Majesty for this trust."

"For this special task, and for your work this afternoon, you shall be rewarded with two out of the fifteen millions promised by His Grace of Cumberland. M. le Duc d'Aumont will receive three, whilst we shall have the honour and pleasure of laying the remainder at the feet of Madame la Marquise de Pompadour."

He cast an amorous glance at Madame, who promptly rewarded him with a gracious smile.

"I think that is all which we need say for the present M. le Comte," concluded His Majesty; "within six days from now you should be on your way to Brest where Le Levantin should by then be waiting her orders and ready to put to sea. A month later, if wind, weather and circumstances favour us, that young adventurer will have been handed over to the English authorities and we, who had worked out the difficult diplomatic problems so carefully, will have shared between us the English millions."

With his habitual airy gesture, Louis now intimated that the audience was at an end. He was obviously more highly elated than he cared to show before Gaston, and was longing to talk over plans and projects for future pleasures and extravagances with the fair Marquise. Madame, who had the knack of conveying a great deal by a look, succeeded in intimating to Gaston that she would gladly have availed herself a little longer of his pleasant company, but that royal commands must prevail.

Gaston therefore rose and kissed each hand, as it was graciously extended to him.

"We are pleased with what you have done, Monsieur le Comte," said the King as M. de Stainville finally took his leave, "but tell me," he whispered slily, "did the unapproachable Lydie yield with the first kiss, or did she struggle much? ... eh? ... B-r-r ... my dear Comte, are your lips not frozen by contact with such an icicle?"

"Nay, your Majesty! all icicles are bound to melt sooner or

later!" said Gaston de Stainville with a smile which—had Lydie seen it—would have half killed her with shame.

And with that same smile of fatuity still lurking round his lips, he bowed himself out of the room.

CHAPTER XXII

PATERNAL ANXIETY

M. le Duc d'Aumont, Prime Minister of His Majesty King Louis XV of France, was exceedingly perturbed. He had just had two separate interviews, each of half an hour's duration, and he was now busy trying to dissociate what his daughter had told him in the first interview, from that which M. de Stainville had imparted to him in the second. And he was not succeeding.

The two sets of statements seemed inextricably linked together.

Lydie, certainly had been very strange and agitated in her manner, totally unlike herself: but this mood of course, though so very unusual in her, did not astonish M. le Duc so much, once he realized its cause.

It was the cause which was so singularly upsetting.

Milor Eglinton, his son-in-law, had sent in his resignation as Comptroller-General of Finance, and this without giving any reason for so sudden and decisive a step. At any rate Lydie herself professed to be ignorant of milor's motives for this extraordinary line of action as she was of his future purpose. All she knew—or all that she cared to tell her father—was that her husband had avowedly the intention of deserting her: he meant to quit Versailles immediately, thus vacating his post without a moment's notice, and leaving his wife, whom he had allowed to conduct all State affairs for him for over a year, to extricate herself, out of a tangle of work and an anomalous position, as best she might.

The only suggestion which milor had cared to put forward, with regard to her future, was that he was about to make her a free gift of his château and lands of Vincennes, the yearly revenues of which were close upon a million livres. This gift she desired not to accept.

In spite of strenuous and diplomatic efforts on his part, M. le Duc d'Aumont had been unable to obtain any further explanation of these extraordinary events from his daughter. Lydie had no intention whatever of deceiving her father and she had given him what she believed to be a perfectly faithful exposé of the situation. All that she had kept back from him was the immediate cause of the grave misunderstanding between herself and her husband, and we must do her the justice to state that she did not think that this was relevant to the ultimate issue.

Moreover, she was more than loath to mention the Stuart prince and his affairs again before M. le Duc. She knew that he was not in sympathy with her over this matter and she dreaded to know with absolute certainty that there was projected treachery afoot, and that he perhaps would have a hand in it. What Gaston de Stainville had conjectured, had seen and overheard, what she herself had guessed, was not to her mind quite conclusive as far as her father's share in the scheme was concerned.

She was deeply attached to her father, and her heart found readily enough a sufficiency of arguments which exonerated him from actual participation in such wanton perfidy. At any rate in this instance she chose ignorance rather than heartrending certainty, and as by her quick action and Gaston's timely and unexpected help, the actual treachery would be averted, she preferred to dismiss her father's problematical participation in it entirely from her mind.

Thus she told him nothing of milor's attitude with regard to the Duke of Cumberland's letter; in fact, she never once referred to the letter or to the Young Pretender; she merely gave M. le Duc to understand that her husband seemed desirous of living his future life altogether apart from hers.

M. le Duc d'Aumont was sorely disquieted: two eventualities presented themselves before him, and both were equally distasteful. One was the scandal which would of necessity spread around his daughter's name the moment her matrimonial differences with her husband became generally known. M. le Duc d'Aumont was too well acquainted with this Court of Versailles not to realize that Lydie's position, as a neglected wife, would subject her to a series of systematic attentions, which she could but regard in the light of insults.

On the other hand M. le Duc could not even begin to think of having to forego his daughter's help in the various matters relating to his own administration. He had been accustomed for some years now to consult her in all moments of grave crises, to rely on her judgment, on her able guidance, worth ten thousand times more to him than an army of masculine advisers.

In spite of the repeated sneers hurled at this era of "petticoat government," Lydie had been of immense service to him, and if she were suddenly to be withdrawn from his official life, he would feel very like Louis XIII had done on that memorable Journée des Dupes, when Richelieu left him for twenty-four hours to conduct the affairs of State alone. He would not have known where to begin.

But Lydie told him that her decision was irrevocable, or what was more to the point, milor had left her no alternative: his resignation was by now in His Majesty's hands, and he had not even suggested that Lydie should accompany him, when he quitted Versailles, in order to take up life as a private gentleman.

It was all very puzzling and very difficult. M. le Duc d'Aumont strongly deprecated the idea of his daughter vacating her official post, because of this sudden caprice of milor. He had need of her, and so had France, and the threads of national business could not be snapped in a moment. The post of Comptroller-General of Finance could remain in abeyance for awhile. After that one would see.

Then with regard to the proposed gifts of the château and revenues of Vincennes, M. le Duc d'Aumont would not hear of a refusal. Madame la Marquise d'Eglinton must have a private establishment worthy of her rank, and an occasional visit from milor would help to keep up an outward appearance of decorum, and to throw dust in the eyes of the scandal-mongers.

The interview with his daughter had upset M. le Duc d'Aumont very considerably. The whole thing had been so unexpected: it was difficult to imagine his usually so impassive and yielding son-in-law displaying any initiative of his own. M. le Duc was still puzzling over the situation when M. le Comte de Stainville, specially recommended by His Majesty himself, asked for a private audience.

And the next half-hour plunged M. le Duc into a perfect labyrinth of surmises, conjectures, doubts and fears. That Gaston de Stainville was possessed not only of full knowledge with regard to the Stuart prince's hiding-place, but also of a letter in Lydie's handwriting, addressed to the prince and sealed with her private seal, was sufficiently astonishing in itself, but the young man's thinly veiled innuendoes, his fatuous smiles, his obvious triumph, literally staggered M. le Duc, even though his palm itched with longing for contact with the insolent braggart's cheek. Every one of his beliefs was being forcibly uprooted; his daughter whom he had thought so unapproachable, so pure and so loyal! who had this very morning shamed him by her indignation at the very thought of this treachery, which she now so completely condoned! that she should have renounced her opinions, her enthusiasm for the sake of a man who had already betrayed her once, was more than M. le Duc could and would believe at first.

Yet the proofs were before him at this very moment. They had been placed in his hand by Gaston de Stainville: the map with the marginal notes, which Lydie had so often refused to show even to her own father, and the letter in her handwriting with the bold signature right across the contents, bidding the unfortunate young prince trust the traitor who would deliver him into the hands of his foes.

But M. le Duc would have had to be more than human not to be satisfied in a measure at the result of Gaston de Stainville's diplomacy; he stood in for a goodly share of the millions promised by England. But it was the diplomacy itself which horrified him. He had vainly tried to dissuade Lydie from chivalrous and misguided efforts on behalf of the young prince, or at any rate from active interference, if His Majesty had plans other than her own; but whilst she had rejected his merest suggestions on that subject with unutterable contempt, she had not only listened to Gaston de Stainville, but actually yielded her will and her enthusiasms to his pleadings.

M. le Duc sighed when he thought it all out. Though Lydie had done exactly what he himself wanted her to do, he hated the idea that she should have done it because Gaston de Stainville had persuaded her.

Later on in the afternoon when an excellently cooked dinner had softened his mood, he tried to put together the various pieces of the mental puzzle which confronted him.

Gaston de Stainville had obtained a certain ascendancy over Lydie, and Lydie had irretrievably quarrelled with her husband. Milor was determined to quit Versailles immediately; Lydie was equally bent on not relinquishing her position yet. Gaston de Stainville was obviously triumphant and somewhat openly bragged of his success, whilst milor kept to his own private apartments, and steadily forbade his door to every one.

It was indeed a very difficult problem for an indulgent father to solve. Fortunately for his own peace of mind, M. le Duc d'Aumont was not only indulgent to his own daughter whom he adored, but also to every one of her sex. He was above all a preux chevalier, who held that women were beings of exceptional temperament, not to be judged by the same standards as the coarser fibred male creatures; their beauty, their charm, the pleasure they afforded to the rest of mankind, placed them above criticism or even comment.

And of course Lydie was very beautiful ... and milor a fool ... and ... Gaston. ... Well! who could blame Gaston?

And it was most amazingly lucky that Lydie had given up her absurd ideas about that Stuart prince, and had thus helped those English millions to find their way comfortably across the Channel, into the pockets of His Majesty the King of France, and of one or two others, including her own doting father.

And after that M. le Duc d'Aumont gave up worrying any more about the matter.

CHAPTER XXIII

THE QUEEN'S SOIRÉE

What chronicler of true events will ever attempt to explain exactly how rumour succeeds in breaking through every bond with which privacy would desire to fetter her, and having obtained a perch on the swiftest of all currents of air, travels through infinite space, and anon, observing a glaringly public spot wherein to alight, she descends with amazing rapidity and mingles with the crowd.

Thus with the news anent milor Eglinton's resignation of the General Control of Finance.

By the time the Court assembled that evening for the Queen's reception, every one had heard of it, and also that milor, having had a violent quarrel with his wife, had quitted or was about to quit Versailles without further warning.

The news was indeed exceedingly welcome. Not from any ill-will toward Lord Eglinton, of course, who was very popular with the ladies and more than tolerated by the men, nor from any sense of triumph over Madame Lydie, although she had not quite so many friends as milor, but because it happened to be Thursday, and every Thursday Her Majesty the Queen held her Court from seven o'clock till nine o'clock: which function was so deadly dull, that there was quite an epidemic of dislocated jaws—caused by incessant yawning—among the favoured few who were both privileged and obliged to attend. A piece of real gossip, well-authenticated, and referring to a couple so highly placed as Lord and Lady Eglinton, was therefore a great boon. Even Her Majesty could not fail to be interested, as Lydie had always stood very highly in the good graces of the prim and melancholy Queen, whilst milor was one of that very small and very select circle which the exalted lady honoured with her conversation on public occasions.

Now on this same Thursday evening, Queen Marie Leszcynska entered her throne-room precisely at seven o'clock. Madame Lydie was with her as she entered, and it was at once supposed that Her Majesty was already acquainted with Lord Eglinton's decision, for she conversed with the neglected wife with obvious kindliness and sympathy.

His Majesty was expected in about a quarter of an hour. As Madame de Pompadour and her immediate entourage were excluded from these solemn functions, the King showed his disapproval of the absence of his friends by arriving as late as etiquette allowed, and by looking on at the presentations, and other paraphernalia of his wife's receptions, in morose and silent ennui.

This evening, however, the proceedings were distinctly enlivened by that subtle and cheerful breath of scandal, which hovered all over the room. Whilst noble dowagers presented débutante daughters to Her Majesty, and grave gentlemen explained to fledgling sons how to make a first bow to the King, groups of younger people congregated in distant corners, well away from the royal dais and discussed the great news of the day.

Lydie did not mingle with these groups. In addition to her many other dignities and functions, she was Grande Maréchale de la Cour to Queen Marie Leszcynska and on these solemn Thursday evenings her place was beside Her Majesty, and her duty to present such ladies of high rank who had either just arrived at Court from the country or who, for some other reason, had not yet had the honour of a personal audience.

Chief among these reasons was the Queen's own exclusiveness. The proud daughter of Stanislaus of Poland with her semi-religious education, her narrow outlook on life, her unfortunate experience of matrimony, had a wholesome horror of the frisky matrons and flirtatious minxes whom Louis XIV's taste had brought into vogue at the Court of France; and above all, she had an unconquerable aversion for the various scions of that mushroom nobility dragged from out the gutter by the catholic fancies of le Roi Soleil.

Though she could not help but receive some of these people at the monster Court functions, which the elaborate and rigid etiquette of the time imposed upon her, and whereat all the tatterdemalions that had e'er filched a handle for their name had, by that same unwritten dictum, the right of entry, she always proudly refused subsequently to recognize in private a presentation to herself, unless it was made by her special leave, at one of her own intimate audiences, and through the mediation either of her own Grande Maréchale de la Cour, or of one of her privileged lady friends.

Thus Madame la Comtesse de Stainville, though formally presented at the general Court by virtue of her husband's title and position, had never had the honour of an invitation to Her Majesty's private throne-room. Queen Marie had heard vague rumours anent the early reputation of "la belle brune de Bordeaux"; this very nick-name, freely bandied about, grated on her puritanic ear. Irène de Stainville, chafing under the restrictions which placed her on a level with the Pompadours of the present and the Montespans or La Vallières of the past, had more than once striven to enlist Lydie's help and protection in obtaining one of the coveted personal introductions to Her Majesty.

Lydie, however, had always put her off with polite but ambiguous promises, until to-day, when her heart, overfilled with gratitude for Gaston de Stainville, prompted her to do something which she knew must please him, and thus prove to him that she was thinking of him at the very time when he was risking his entire future and probably his life in an attempt to serve her.

Her own troubles and sorrows in no way interfered with the discharge of her social duties. Whilst she still occupied certain official positions at Court, she was determined to fill them adequately and with perfect dignity. A brief note to Irène de Stainville acquainted the latter lady with the pleasing fact, that Madame la Grande Maréchale would have much pleasure in introducing her personally to Her Majesty the Queen that very same evening, and "la belle brune de Bordeaux" was therefore present at this most exclusive of all functions on Thursday, August 13, 1746, and duly awaited the happy moment when she could make her curtsey before the proudest princess in all Europe, in the magnificent gown which had been prepared some time ago in view of this possible and delightful eventuality.

She stood somewhat isolated from the rest of the throng, between two or three of her most faithful admirers, holding herself aloof from the frivolity of the surrounding gossip and wearing a sphinx-like air of detachment and of hidden and sorrowful knowledge.

To every comment as to the non-appearance of her lord at the soirée, she had mutely replied by a slight shrug of the shoulders.

Up in the gallery, behind a screen of exotic plants, the band of musicians was playing one of M. Lulli's most famous compositions, the beautiful motet in E flat which, alone amongst the works of that master of melody, was sufficiently serious and sedate for the Queen's taste. Anon Her Majesty gave the signal that dancing might begin. She liked to watch it, if it was decorously performed, though she never joined in it herself. Therefore a measured and stately gavotte was danced by the young people every Thursday, and perhaps a majestic pavane afterward. But the minuet was thought unbecoming. Her Majesty sat in one of the heavy gilded chairs underneath the canopy, the other being reserved for King Louis.

Lydie watched the gavotte with dreamy, abstracted eyes; every now and then the Queen spoke to her, and the force of habit caused her to reply coherently and with that formality of expression, which Her Majesty liked to hear. But her mind was very far from her surroundings. It was accompanying Gaston de Stainville on his reckless ride through the rich plains of Normandy; her wishes sped him on his way, her gratitude for his noble self-sacrifice would have guarded him from the perils of the road.

The monotonous tune of the gavotte with its distinct and sharply defined beat, sounded to her like the measured clink of a horse's hoofs on rough hard ground. She was quite unconscious that, from every corner of the room, inquisitive and sarcastic eyes were watching all her movements.

CHAPTER XXIV

GOSSIP

Whilst the younger people danced, the older ones gossiped, and the absence of any known facts rendered the gossip doubly interesting.

There was one group most especially so engaged; at the further corner of the room, and with sixteen dancing pairs intervening between it and the royal daïs, there was little fear of Her Majesty overhearing any frivolous comments on the all-absorbing topic of the day, or of Madame Lydie herself being made aware of their existence.

Here Madame de la Beaume, a young and pretty matron, possessed of a good-looking husband who did not trouble her much with his company, was the centre of a gaily cackling little crowd, not unlike an assemblage of geese beside a stream at eventide. Young M. de Louvois was there and the old Duchesse de Pontchartrain, also M. Crébillon, the most inveterate scandal-monger of his time, and several others.

They all talked in whispers, glad that the music drowned every echo of this most enjoyable conversation.

"I have it from my coiffeur, whose son was on duty in an adjacent room, that there was a violent quarrel between them," said Madame de la Beaume with becoming mystery. "The man says that Madame Lydie screamed and raged for half an hour, then flew out of the room and along the passages like one possessed."

"These English are very peculiar people," said M. Crébillon sententiously. "I have it on M. de Voltaire's own authority that English husbands always beat their wives, and he spent some considerable time in England recently studying their manners and customs."

"We may take it for granted that milor Eglinton, though partly civilized through his French parentage, hath retained some of his native brutality," added another cavalier gravely.

"And it is quite natural that Madame Lydie would not tolerate his treatment of her," concluded the old Duchess.

"Ah!" sighed Madame de la Beaume pathetically, "I believe that English husbands beat their wives only out of jealousy. At least, so I have been told, whereas ours are too often unfaithful to feel any such violent and uncomfortable pangs."

"Surely," quoth young M. de Louvois, casting an admiring glance at Madame's bold décolletage, "you would not wish M. de la Beaume to lay hands on those beautiful shoulders."

"Heu! heu!" nodded Madame enigmatically.

M. Crébillon cast an inquisitorial look at Madame de Stainville, who was standing close by.

"Nay! from what I hear," he said mysteriously, "milor Eglinton had quite sufficient provocation for his jealousy, and like an Englishman he availed himself of the privileges which the customs of his own country grant him, and he frankly beat his wife."

Every one rallied round him, for he seemed to have fuller details than any one else, and Madame de la Beaume whispered eagerly:

"You mean M. de Stainville...."

"Hush—sh—sh," interrupted the old Duchess quickly, "here comes miladi."

The Dowager Marchioness of Eglinton, "miladi," as she was always called, was far too shrewd and too well versed in the manners and customs of her friends not to be fully aware of the gossip that was going on all round the room. Very irate at having been kept in ignorance of the facts which had caused her son's sudden decision, and Lydie's strange attitude, she was nevertheless determined that, whatever scandal was being bruited abroad, it should prove primarily to the detriment of her daughter-in-law's reputation.

Therefore, whenever, to-night, she noted groups congregated in corners, and conversations being obviously carried on in whispers, she boldly approached and joined in the gossip, depositing a poisoned shaft here and there with great cleverness, all the more easily as it was generally supposed that she knew a great deal more than she cared to say.

"Nay! I beg of you, Mesdames and Messieurs," she now said quite cheerfully, "do not let me interrupt your conversation. Alas! do I not know its subject? ... My poor son cannot be to blame in the unfortunate affair. Lydie, though she may be wholly innocent in the matter, is singularly obstinate."

"Then you really think that?——" queried Madame de la Beaume eagerly, and then paused, half afraid that she had said too much.

"Alas! what can I say?" rejoined miladi with a sigh. "I was brought up in the days when we women were taught obedience to our husband's wishes."

"Madame Lydie was not like to have learnt the first phrase of that wholesome lesson," quoth M. de Louvois with a smile.

"Exactly, cher Monsieur," assented miladi, as she sailed majestically on to another group.

"What did miladi mean exactly?" asked M. Crébillon.

"Oh! she is so kind-hearted, such an angel!" sighed pretty Madame de la Beaume, "she wanted to palliate Madame Lydie's conduct by suggesting that milor merely desired to forbid her future intercourse with M. de Stainville. ... I have heard that version of the quarrel already, but I must own that it bears but little resemblance to truth. We all know that so simple a request would not have led to a really serious breach between milor and his wife."

"It was more than that, of course, or milor would not have beaten her," came in unanswerable logic from M. Crébillon.

"Hush—sh—sh!" admonished the old Duchess, "here comes His Majesty."

"He looks wonderfully good-humoured," said Madame de la Beaume, "and doth not wear at all his usual Thursday's scowl."

"Then we may all be sure, Mesdames and Messieurs," said the irrepressible Crébillon, "that rumour hath not lied again."

"What rumour?"

"You have not heard?"

"No!" came from half a dozen eager and anxious lips.

"They say that His Majesty the King of France has agreed to deliver the Chevalier de Saint George to the English in consideration of a large sum of money."

"Impossible!"

"That cannot be true!"

"My valet had it from Monsieur de Stainville's man," protested M. Crébillon, "and he declares the rumour true."

"A King of France would never do such a thing."

"A palpable and clumsy lie!"

And the same people, who, five minutes ago, had hurled the mud of scandal at the white robes of an exceptionally high-minded and virtuous woman, recoiled with horror at the thought of any of it clinging to the person of that fat and pompous man, whom an evil fate had placed on the throne of France.

CHAPTER XXV

THE FIRST DOUBT

His Majesty certainly looked far less bored than he usually did on his royal consort's reception evenings. He entered the room with a good-natured smile on his face, which did not leave him, even whilst he kissed the frigid Queen's hand, and nodded to her entourage, every one of whom he cordially detested.

But when he caught sight of Lydie, he positively beamed at her, and astonished all the scandal-mongers by the surfeit of attentions which he bestowed on her. Directly after he had paid his respects to his wife and received the young scions of ancient aristocratic houses, that were being presented to him, he turned with great alacrity to Lydie and engaged her in close conversation.

"Will you honour us by stepping the pavane with us, Marquise?" he asked in sugary tones. "Alas! our dancing days should be over, yet par ma foi! we could yet tread another measure beside the tiniest feet in France."

Lydie would perhaps have been taken aback at the King's superlative amiability, but instinctively her mind reverted to the many occasions when he had thus tried to win her good graces, in the hope of obtaining concessions of money from the virtual chief of the Department of Finance. She saw that inquisitive eyes were watching her over-keenly as—unable to refuse the King's invitation—she placed a reluctant hand in his, and took her position beside him for the opening of the pavane.

She was essentially graceful even in the studied stiffness of her movements; a stiffness which she had practised and then made entirely her own, and which was somehow expressive of the unbendable hauteur of her moral character.

The stately pavane suited the movements of her willowy figure, which appeared quite untrammelled, easy and full of spring, even within the narrow confines of the fashionable corslet. She was dressed in white to-night and her young shoulders looked dazzling and creamy beside the matt tone of her brocaded gown. She never allowed the ridiculous coiffure, which had lately become the mode, to hide entirely the glory of her own chestnut hair, and its rich, warm colour gleamed through the powder, scantily sprinkled over it by an artist's hand.

She had not forgotten even for a moment the serious events of this never-to-be-forgotten day; but amongst the many memories which crowded in upon her, as, with slow step she trod the grave measure of the dance, none was more vivid than that of her husband's scorn, when he spoke of her own hand resting in that of the treacherous and perfidious monarch, who would have sold his friend for money. She wondered how he would act if he could see her now, her fingers, very frequently meeting those of King Louis during the elaborate figures of the dance.

Strangely enough, although everything milor had said to her at that interview had merely jarred upon her mood and irritated her nerves, without seemingly carrying any conviction, yet now, when she was obliged to touch so often the moist, hot palm of King Louis, she felt something of that intolerable physical repugnance which her husband had, as it were, brought to actuality by the vigour of his suggestions.

Otherwise she took little heed of her surroundings. During the preliminary movement of the dance, the march past, with its quaint, artificial gestures and steps and the slow majesty of its music, she could not help seeing the looks of malevolent curiosity, of satisfied childish envy, and of sarcastic triumph which were levelled at her from every corner of the room.

The special distinction bestowed on her by the King—who as a rule never danced at his wife's soirées—seemed in the minds of all these gossip-lovers to have confirmed the worst rumours, anent the cause of Lord Eglinton's unexpected resignation. His Majesty did

143

not suffer like his wife from an unconquerable horror of frisky matrons; on the contrary, his abhorrence was chiefly directed against the starchy dowagers and the prudish dévotes who formed the entourage of the Queen. The fact that he distinguished Lydie to-night so openly, showed that he no longer classed her among the latter.

"His Majesty hath at last found a kindred spirit in the unapproachable Marchioness," was the universal comment, which thoroughly satisfied the most virulent disseminator of ill-natured scandal.

Lydie knew enough of Court life to guess what would be said. Up to now she had been happily free from Louis's compromising flatteries, save at such times when he required money, but his attentions went no further—and they invariably ceased the moment he had obtained all that he wanted. But to-night he was unswerving in his adulation; and, in the brief pause between the second and third movement of the dance, he contrived to whisper in her ear:

"Ah, Madame! how you shame your King! Shall we ever be able to adequately express the full measure of our gratitude?"

"Gratitude, Sire?" she murmured, somewhat bewildered and rather coldly, "I do not understand ... why gratitude?"

"You are modest, Madame, as well as brave and good," he rejoined, taking one more opportunity of raising her hand to his lips. He had succeeded in gradually leading her into a window embrasure, somewhat away from the rest of the dancers. He did not admire the statuesque grace of Lydie in the least, and had always secretly sneered at her, for her masculine strength of will and the rigidity of her principles, but it had been impossible for any man, alive to a sense of what was beautiful, not to delight in the exquisitely harmonious picture formed by that elegant woman, in her stiff, white brocaded gown and with her young head crowned by its wreath of ardent hair, standing out brilliantly against the pale, buttercup colour of the damask curtain behind her. There was nothing forced therefore in the look of admiration with which the King now regarded Lydie; conscious of this, she deeply resented the look, and perhaps because of it, she was not quite so fully alive to the hidden meaning of his words as she otherwise might have been.

"And as beautiful as you are brave," added Louis unctuously. "It is not every woman who would thus have had the courage of her convictions, and so openly borne witness to the trust and loyalty which she felt."

"Indeed, Sire," she said coldly and suddenly beginning to feel vaguely puzzled, "I am afraid your Majesty is labouring under the misapprehension, that I have recently done something to deserve special royal thanks, whereas——"

"Whereas you have only followed the dictates of your heart," he rejoined gallantly, seeing that she had paused as if in search of a word, "and shown to the sceptics in this ill-natured Court that, beneath the rigid mask of iron determination, this exquisitely beautiful personality hid the true instincts of adorable womanhood."

The musicians now struck the opening chords to the third and final measure of the pavane. There is something dreamy and almost sad in this movement of the stately dance, and this melancholy is specially accentuated in the composition of Rameau, which the players were rendering with consummate art to-night. The King's unctuous words were still ringing unpleasantly in Lydie's ears, when he put out his hand, claiming hers for the dance.

Mechanically she followed him, her feet treading the measure quite independently of her mind, which had gone wandering in the land of dreams. A vague sense of uneasiness crept slowly but surely into her heart, she pondered over Louis's words, not knowing what to make of them, yet somehow beginning to fear them, or rather to fear that she might after all succeed in understanding their full meaning. She could not dismiss the certitude from her mind that he was, in some hidden sense, referring to the Stuart prince and his cause, when he spoke of "convictions" and of her "courage"; but at first she only thought that he meant, in a vague way, to recall her interference of this morning, Lord Eglinton's outburst of contempt, and her own promise to give the matter serious consideration.

This in a measure re-assured her. The King's words had already become hazy in her memory, as she had not paid serious attention to them at the time, and she gradually forced those vague fears within her to subside, and even smiled at her own cowardice in scenting danger where none existed.

Undoubtedly that was the true reason of the rapacious monarch's flatteries to-night; truth to tell, her mind had been so absorbed with actual events, her quarrel with her husband, the departure of Gaston, the proposed expedition of Le Monarque, that she had almost forgotten the promise which she had made to the King earlier in the day, with a view to gaining time.

"How admirably you dance, Madame," said King Louis, "the poetry of motion by all the saints! Ah! believe me, I cannot conquer altogether a feeling of unutterable envy!"

"Envy, Sire, of whom?—or of what?" she asked, forced to keep up a conversation which sickened her, since etiquette did not allow her to remain silent if the King desired to talk. "Methinks fate leaves your Majesty but little to wish for."

"Envy of the lucky man who obtained a certitude, whilst we had to be content with vague if gracious promises," he rejoined blandly.

She looked at him keenly, inquiringly, a deep line of doubt, even of fear now settling between her brows.

"Certitude of what, Sire?" she asked suddenly pausing in the dance and turning to look him straight in the eyes. "I humbly crave your Majesty's pardon, but meseems that we are at cross-purposes, and that your Majesty speaks of something which I, on the other hand, do not understand."

"Nay! nay! then we'll not refer to the subject again," rejoined Louis with consummate gallantry, "for of a truth we would not wish to lose one precious moment of this heavenly dance. Enough that you understand, Madame, that your King is grateful, and will show his gratitude, even though his heart burn with jealousy at the good fortune of another man!"

There was no mistaking the sly leer which appeared in his eye as he spoke. Lydie felt her cheeks flaming up with sudden wrath; wrath, which as quickly gave way to an awful, an unconquerable horror.

Still she did not suspect. Her feet once more trod the monotonous measure, but her heart beat wildly against the stiff corslet; the room began to whirl round before her eyes; a sickening sense of dizziness threatened to master her. Every drop of blood had left her cheeks, leaving them ashen pale.

She was afraid; and the fear was all the more terrible as she could not yet give it a name. But the sense of an awful catastrophe was upon her, impending, not yet materialized, but which would overwhelm her inevitably when it came.

CHAPTER XXVI

THE AWFUL CERTITUDE

Then all at once she understood!

There at the further end of the room, against the rich gold of the curtain, she saw Gaston de Stainville standing beside his wife and one or two other women, the centre of a gaily chattering crowd, he himself chattering with them, laughing and jesting, whilst from time to time his white and slender hand raised a gold-rimmed glass to his eye, with a gesture of fatuity and affectation.

Something in her look, though it had only lasted a few seconds, must then and there have compelled his own, for he suddenly dropped his glass, and their eyes met across the room; Lydie's inquiring, only just beginning to doubt, and fearful, as if begging for reassurance! his, mocking and malicious, triumphant too and self-flattering, whilst la belle Irène, intercepting this exchange of glances, laughed loudly and shrugged her bare shoulders.

Lydie was not that type of woman who faints, or screams at moments of acute mental agony. Even now, when the full horror of what she had so suddenly realized, assailed her with a crushing blow that would have stunned a weaker nature, she contrived to pull herself together and to continue the dance to the end. The King—beginning to feel bored in the company of this silent and obviously absent-minded woman—made no further effort at conversation. She had disappointed him; for Monsieur le Comte de Stainville's innuendoes had led him to hope that the beautiful marble statue had at last come to life and would henceforth become a valuable addition to the light-hearted circle of friends that rallied round him, helping to make him forget the ennui of his matrimonial and official life.

Thus the dance was concluded between them in silence. Louis was too dull and vapid to notice the change in his partner's attitude, the icy touch of her fingers, the deathly whiteness of her lips. But presently he, too, caught sight of Gaston de Stainville and immediately there crept into his face that malicious leer, which awhile ago had kindled Lydie's wrath.

Whether she noted it now or not, it were difficult to say. Only a great determination kept her from making a display before all these indifferent eyes, of the agonizing torture of her mind and heart.

With infinite relief, she made her final curtsey to her partner, and allowed him to lead her back to her official place beside the royal daïs. She could not see clearly, for her eyes had suddenly filled with burning tears of shame and bitter self-accusation. She bit her lips lest a cry of pain escaped them.

"You are ill, my dear! Come away!"

The voice—gentle and deeply concerned—was that of her father. She did not dare look at him, lest she should break down, but she allowed him to lead her away from the immediate noise and glare.

"What is it, Lydie?" queried M. le Duc again, more anxiously, as soon as they had reached a small and secluded alcove. "Has anything further happened? Par Dieu, if that man has again dared..."

"What man, father?" she interrupted.

Her voice had no tone in it, she wondered even if M. le Duc would hear, but he was talking ambiguously and she had had enough of misunderstandings to-day.

"What man?" rejoined Monsieur le Duc d'Aumont irritably. "Your husband of course. I have heard rumours about his behaviour to you, and by all the heathen gods ..."

He paused, astonished and almost awed, for Lydie had laughed suddenly, laughed loudly and long, and there was such a strange ring in that unnatural mirth, that Monsieur le Duc feared lest excitement had been too much for his daughter's brain.

"Lydie! what is it? You must tell me ... Lydie ..." he urged, "listen to me ... do you hear me, Lydie?"

She seemed to be collecting her scattered senses now, but great sobs of hysterical laughter still shook her from head to foot, and she leaned against her father's arm almost as if she feared to fall.

"Yes, father dear," she said fairly coherently, "I do hear you, and I pray you take no heed of me. Much hath occurred to-day to disturb me and my nerves seem to be on the jar. Perhaps I do not see quite clearly either. Father, tell me," she added with a voice almost steady, but harsh and trenchant, and with glowing eyes fixed on the Duke's face, "did I perceive Gaston de Stainville in the crowd just now?"

"You may have done, my dear," he replied with some hesitation. "I do not know."

She had been quick enough to note that, at mention of Gaston's name, his eyes suddenly wore a curious shamefaced expression and avoided meeting her own. She pressed her point more carelessly, feeling that there was something that he would only tell her, if she was perfectly calm and natural in her questionings.

"Then he is here?" she asked.

"Yes ... I believe so ... why do you ask?"

"I thought him gone," she said lightly, "that was all. Methought there was an errand he had meant to perform."

"Oh! there is no immediate hurry for that!"

Monsieur le Duc d'Amont, never a very keen observer, was feeling quite reassured by her calmer mood. His daughter had been overwrought. Events had crowded in upon her, thick and fast, some of them of an unpleasant nature: her final surrender to Gaston de

Stainville could not have occurred without a wrench; sentiment—he supposed—having conquered friendship and loyalty, no doubt remorse had held sway for awhile. He certainly thought his daughter quite at one with him and his confederates in the treacherous plan; it never entered his head for a moment to blame her for this volte-face, nor did he realize that Gaston's attitude had been one of lying infamy. He knew her for a pure-minded and exceptionally proud woman and his paternal heart had no fear that she would stoop to a vulgar intrigue, at the same time he had no reason to doubt that she had yielded to the persuasive powers of a man whom she had certainly loved at one time, who and of necessity would still exercise a certain influence over her.

And now she was no doubt anxious to know something of future plans she had probably not heard what had been decided with regard to the expedition, and perhaps fretted as to how her own actions had been interpreted by her father and the King. It was with a view to reassuring her on all these points that he now added:

"We are not thinking of sending Le Monarque."

"Ah? I thought that she would have been the most likely vessel..."

"Le Levantin will be safer," he explained, "but she will not be ready to put to sea for five or six days, so Gaston will not start until then; but you need have no fear, dear; the orders together with the map and the precious letter, which you have given him, are quite safe in his hands. He is too deeply concerned in the success of the expedition to think of betraying you, even if his regard were less genuine. ... And we are all deeply grateful to you, my dear ... It was all for the best..."

He patted her hand with kindly affection, much relieved now, for she seemed quite calm and the colour even was coming back to her cheeks: all the afternoon he had been dreading this meeting with his daughter, for he had not seen her since he learned from Gaston that she had yielded to his entreaties, and given him the map and letter which would help the King of France to betray his friend: now he was glad to find that—save for an unusual hysterical outburst—she took the whole matter as coolly as he did himself.

There is no doubt that there are moments in life when a crisis is so acute, a catastrophe so overwhelming, that all our faculties become completely deadened: our individuality goes out of us, and we become mere dolls moving automatically by muscular action and quite independently of our brain.

Thus it was with Lydie.

Her father's words could not be misunderstood. They left her without that last faint shadow of doubt which, almost unbeknown to

149

herself, had been her main support during the past few minutes of this intense agony. Now the tiny vestige of hope had vanished. Blank despair invaded her brain and she had the sensation as if sorrow had turned it into a pulpy mass, a great deal too bulky for her head, causing it to throb and to ache intolerably. Beyond that, the rest of herself as it were, became quite mechanical. She was glad that her father said nothing more about the scheme. She knew all that she wanted to know: Gaston's hideous, horrible treachery, the clumsy trap into which she had fallen, and above all the hopeless peril into which she had plunged the very man whom she had wished to save.

She had been the most perfidious traitor amongst them all, for the unfortunate prince had given her his friendship, and had trusted her more fully than he had others.

And then there was her husband!

Of him she would not think, for that way lay madness surely!

She managed to smile to her father, and to reassure him. Presently she would tell him all ... to-morrow perhaps, but not just yet ... She did not hate him somehow. She could not have hated him, for she knew him and had always loved him. But he was weak and easily misguided.

Heavens above! had anyone been more culpably weak, more misguided than she herself?

Monsieur le Duc, fully satisfied in his mind now by her outward calm, and the steady brilliance of her eyes, recalled her to her official duties.

"Dancing is over, Lydie," he said, "have you not a few presentations to Her Majesty to effect?"

"Oh yes!" she said perfectly naturally, "of a truth I had almost forgotten ... the first time for many years, eh? my dear father. . . How some people will gossip at this remissness of Madame la Grande Maréchale de la Cour ... will you conduct me straight away to Her Majesty? ... I hope she has not yet noticed my absence."

She leaned somewhat heavily on her father's arm, for she was afraid that she could not otherwise have walked quite straight. She fully realized what it meant when men talked of drunkenness amongst themselves. Copious libations must produce—she thought—just this same sensation of swaying and tottering, and hideous, painful giddiness.

Already Monsieur de Louvois, Her Majesty's Chamberlain, was waiting, whilst the ladies, who were to receive the honour of special presentation, were arraigned in a semi-circle to the left of the dais. Beneath the canopy the King and Queen were standing: Louis looking as usual insufferably bored, and the Queen calmly dignified, not a little disdainful, and closely scrutinizing the bevy of women—more or less gorgeously apparelled, some old, some young, mostly rather dowdy and stiff in their appearance—who were waiting to be introduced.

Quickly, and with a respectful curtsey indicative of apology, Lydie now took her stand beside her Royal mistress and the ceremony of presentations began. The chamberlain read out a name; one unit thereupon detached itself from the feminine group, approached with sedate steps to the foot of the throne, and made a deep obeisance, whilst Madame la Grande Maréchale said a few appropriate words, that were meant to individualize that unit in the mind of the Queen.

"Madame de Balincourt. Your Majesty will deign to remember the brave General who fought at Fontenoy. Madame has eschewed country life momentarily for the honour of being presented to your Majesty."

"Enchantée, Madame," the Queen would reply graciously, offering her hand for a respectful kiss.

"Madame Helvetius, the wife of our renowned scientist and philosopher. Your Majesty is acquainted with his works."

"Enchantée, Madame!"

"And Mademoiselle Helvetius, striving to become as learned as her distinguished father, and almost succeeding so 'tis said."

The Queen deigned to say a few special words to this shy débutante and to her mother, both primly clad in badly-fitting gowns which proclaimed the country dressmaker, but in their simplicity and gaucherie peculiarly pleasing to Her Majesty.

And thus the procession filed past. Elderly women and young girls, some twenty in all, mostly hailing from distant parts of France, where the noise and frivolity of the Court of Versailles had not even roused an echo. The Queen was very gracious. She liked this select little circle of somewhat dowdy provincials, who she felt would be quite at one with her in her desire for the regeneration of social France. The uglier and less fashionable were the women, the more drabby and ill-fitting their clothes, the sweeter and more encouraging became Her Majesty's smile. She asked lengthy questions from her Grande Maréchale, and seemed to take a malicious delight in irritating the King, by protracting this ceremony, which she knew bored him to distraction, until he could scarcely manage to smother the yawns which continually assailed his jaws.

Suddenly Lydie felt her limbs stiffen and her throat close as if iron fingers had gripped it. She had been saying the usual platitudes anent the wife, sister or aunt of some worthy general or country squire, when Monsieur de Louvois called out a name:

"Madame la Comtesse de Stainville."

And from out the group of dowdy country matrons and starchy-looking dévotes a brilliant figure now detached itself and glided forward with consummate grace. Irène de Stainville was approaching for presentation to the Queen, her eyes becomingly cast down, a rosy flush on her cheeks, for she was conscious that she was beautiful and that the King's wearied eyes had lighted up at sight of her.

There was something almost insolent in the gorgeousness of her gown: it was of a rich turquoise blue, that stood out, glaring and vivid against the buttercup-coloured hangings of the room. Her stiff corslet was frankly décolleté, displaying her fine shoulders and creamy bosom, on which reposed a delicately wrought turquoise necklet of exquisite design. Her hair was piled up over her head, in the monumental and outré style lately decreed by Dame Fashion, and the brocade of her panniers stood out in stiff folds each side of her, like balloon-shaped supports, on which her white arms rested with graceful ease. It seemed as if a gaudy, exotic butterfly had lost its way, and accidentally fluttered into an assembly of moths.

Gaston de Stainville stood a little behind his wife. Etiquette demanded that he should be near her, when she made her obeisance to the Queen. He, too, somehow, looked out of place among these more sedate cavaliers: there had always been a very distinct difference between the dress worn by the ladies and gentlemen of the Queen's entourage, and the more ornate style adopted by the gayer frequenters of the Court of Versailles. This difference was specially noticeable now, when this handsome young couple stood before Her Majesty, she not unlike a glittering jewel herself, he in a satin coat of pale mauve, that recalled the delicate shades of a bank of candytuft in mid-June.

The Queen no longer looked down from her daïs with an indulgent, somewhat melancholy smile. Her eyes—cold and gray as those of King Stanislaus had been—regarded with distinct disapproval these two people, who, in her rigid judgment, were naught but gaudily decked-out dolls, and who walked on high-heeled shoes that made an unpleasant noise on the polished floor.

Lydie had during the last agonizing half-hour wholly forgotten Irène de Stainville and the presentation which, on an impulse of gratitude toward Gaston, she had promised to bring about, and she certainly had not been prepared for this meeting, face to face, with the man who, for the second time in her life, had so bitterly and cruelly wronged her.

152

Gaston did not seem anxious to avoid her gaze. There was insolent triumph and mockery in every line of his attitude: in the head thrown a little to one side; in the eyes narrowed until they were slits, gazing at her over the barrier of his wife's elaborate coiffure: in the slender, well-kept hand toying with the gold-rimmed eyeglass, and above all in the sensual, sneering mouth, and the full lips parted in a smile.

Lydie was hardly conscious of Irène's presence, of any one in fact, save of Gaston de Stainville, of whom she had dreamed so romantically a few hours ago, speeding him on his way, praying—God help her!—that he might be well and safe. An intense bitterness surged up in her heart, a deadly contempt for him. Awhile ago she would not have believed that she could hate anyone so. She would at this moment have gladly bartered her life for the joy of doing him some awful injury. All softness, gentleness, went out of her nature, just while she looked at Gaston and caught his mocking smile.

It was the mockery that hurt her so! The awful humiliation of it all!

And there was also in Lydie that highly sensitive sense of loyalty, which revolted at the sight of these traitors approaching, with a smile of complacency on their lips, this proud Queen who was ignorant of their infamy.

Women have often been called petty in their hates: rightly perhaps! but let us remember that their power to punish is limited, and therefore they strike as best they can. Lydie, in spite of her influence and her high position, could do so little to punish Gaston, now that by his abominable treachery he had filched every trump card from her.

She had been such an unpardonable fool—and she knew it—that her very self-abasement whipped up her sense of retaliation, her desire for some sort of revenge, into veritable fury; and thus, when la belle Irène, triumphant in the pride of her universally acknowledged beauty, came to the foot of the Royal daïs, when—through some unexplainable and occult reason—a hush of expectancy descended on all spectators, Lydie's voice was suddenly raised, trenchant and decisive:

"This is an error on Monsieur le Chambellan's part," she said loudly, so that everyone in the vast audience-chamber might hear. "There is no one here to present this lady to Her Majesty!"

A gasp went round the room, a sigh of astonishment, of horror, of anticipation, and in the silence that immediately followed, the proverbial pin would have been heard to drop: every rustle of a silken gown, every creak of a shoe sounded clear and distinct, as did the quickly-suppressed sneer that escaped Gaston de Stainville's

153

lips and the frou-frou of his satin coat sleeve as he raised the gold-rimmed glass to his eye.

What were the joys of gossip in comparison with this unexpected sensation, which moreover would certainly be the prelude to an amazing scandal? Anon everyone drew instinctively nearer. All eyes were fixed on the several actors of this palpitating little scene.

Already Irène had straightened her graceful figure, with a quick jerk as if she had been struck. The terrible affront must have taken her completely unawares, but now that it had come, she instantly guessed its cause. Nevertheless there was nothing daunted or bashful about her attitude. The colour blazed into her cheeks, and her fine dark eyes responded to Lydie's scornful glance with one of defiance and of hate.

The Queen looked visibly annoyed. She disliked scenes and unpleasantness, and all incidents which disturbed the even placidity of her official life: the King, on the other hand, swore an unmistakable oath. Obviously he had already taken sides in favour of the gaily-plumaged butterfly against the duller moths, whilst Monsieur de Louvois looked hopelessly perturbed. He was very young and had only lately been appointed to the onerous position of Queen's Chamberlain. Though the post was no sinecure, a scandal such as threatened now, was quite unprecedented. He scented a violent passage of arms between two young and beautiful women, both of high social position, and manlike he would sooner have faced a charge of artillery than this duel between two pairs of rosy lips, wherein he feared that he might be called upon to arbitrate.

Lydie, alone among all those present, had retained her outward serenity. This was her hour, and she meant to press her triumph home to the full. All the pent-up horror and loathing which had well-nigh choked her during the whole of this terrible day, now rose clamouring and persistent in this opportunity for revenge. Though Gaston stood calm and mocking by, though Irène looked defiant and her cheeks flamed with wrath, they would glow with shame anon, for Lydie had deliberately aimed a blow at her vanity, the great and vulnerable spot in the armour of la belle brune de Bordeaux.

Lydie knew Marie Leszcynska well enough to be sure that the very breath of scandal, which she had deliberately blown on Gaston's wife, was enough to cause the rigid, puritanically-minded Queen to refuse all future intercourse with her. Rightly or wrongly, without further judgment or appeal, the Queen would condemn Irène unheard, and ban her and her husband for ever from her

154

intimacy, thus setting the mark of a certain social ostracism upon them, which they could never live down.

Less than three seconds had elapsed whilst these conflicting emotions assailed the various actors of this drawing-room drama. The Queen now turned with a frown half-inquiring, wholly disapproving toward the unfortunate Louvois.

"Monsieur le Chambellan," she said sternly, "how did this occur? We do not allow any error to creep in the list of presentations made to our Royal person."

These few words recalled Irène to the imminence of her peril. She would not allow herself to be humiliated without a protest, nor would she so readily fall a victim to Lydie's obvious desire for revenge. She too was shrewd enough to know that the Queen would never forgive, and certainly never forget, the esclandre of this presentation; but if she herself was destined to fall socially, at least she would drag her enemy down with her, and bury Lydie's influence, power and popularity beneath the ruins of her own ambitions.

"Your Majesty will deign I hope to pause a moment ere you sweep me from before your Royal eyes unheard," she said boldly; "the error is on the part of Madame la Grande Maréchale. My name was put on Monsieur le Chambellan's list by her orders."

But Marie Leszcynska would not at this juncture take any direct notice of Irène; until it was made quite clear that Madame la Comtesse de Stainville was a fit and proper person to be presented to the Queen of France, she absolutely ignored her very existence, lest a word from her be interpreted as implying encouragement, or at least recognition. Therefore she looked beyond Irène, straight at Monsieur de Louvois, and addressed herself directly to him.

"What are the true facts, Monsieur le Chambellan?" she said.

"I certainly ... er ... had the list as usual ... er ... from Madame la Grande Maréchale ... and ..." poor Monsieur de Louvois stammered in a fit of acute nervousness.

"Then 'tis from you, Madame la Marquise, that we require an explanation for this unseemly disturbance," rejoined Her Majesty turning her cold, gray eyes on Lydie.

"The explanation is quite simple, your Majesty," replied Lydie calmly. "It had been my intention to present Madame la Comtesse de Stainville to your Majesty, but since then events have occurred, which will compel me to ask Madame la Comtesse to find some other lady to perform the office for her."

"The explanation is not quite satisfactory to us," rejoined Her Majesty with all the rigid hauteur of which she possessed the stinging secret, "and it will have to be properly and officially amplified to-morrow. But this is neither the place nor the moment for discussing such matters. Monsieur de Louvois, I pray you to proceed with the other names on your list. The Queen has spoken!"

With these arrogant words culled from the book of etiquette peculiar to her own autocratic house, the daughter of the deposed King of Poland waved the incident aside as if it had never been. A quickly repressed murmur went all round the room. Lydie swept a deep and respectful curtsey before Her Majesty, and indicated by her own manner that, as far as she was concerned, the incident was now closed by royal command.

But Irène de Stainville's nature was not one that would allow the matter to be passed over so lightly. Whichever way the Queen might choose to act, she felt that at any rate the men must be on her side: and though King Louis himself was too indolent and egotistical to interfere actively on her behalf, and her own husband could not do more than pick a quarrel with some wholly innocent person, yet she was quite sure that she detected approval and encouragement to fight her own battles in the looks of undisguised admiration which the masculine element there present freely bestowed upon her. Monsieur le Duc d'Aumont, for one, looked stern disapproval at his daughter, whilst Monsieur de Louvois was visibly embarrassed.

It was, therefore, only a case of two female enemies, one of whom certainly was the Queen of France—a prejudiced and obstinate autocrat if ever there was one, within the narrow confines of her own intimate circle—and the other exceptionally highly placed, both in Court favour and in official status.

Still Irène de Stainville felt that her own beauty was at least as powerful an asset, when fighting for social prestige, as the political influence of her chief adversary.

Therefore when the Queen of France chose to speak as if Madame la Comtesse de Stainville did not even exist, and Monsieur de Louvois diffidently but firmly begged her to stand aside, she boldly refused.

"Nay! the Queen shall hear me," she said in a voice which trembled a little now with suppressed passion; "surely Her Majesty will not allow a jealous woman's caprice ..."

"Silence, wench," interrupted Marie Leszcynska with all the authority, the pride, the dictatorial will, which she had inherited from her Polish ancestors; "you forget that you are in the presence of your Queen."

"Nay, Madame, I do not forget it," said Irène, nothing daunted, and firmly holding her ground. "I remember it with every word I utter, and remember that the name of our Queen stands for purity and for justice. Your Majesty," she added, being quick to note

156

the slightly yielding look which, at her cleverly chosen words, crept in Marie Leszcynska's eyes, and gracefully dropping on her knees on the steps of the throne, "will you at least deign to hear me? I may not be worthy to kiss your Majesty's hand; we none of us are that, I presume, for you stand infinitely above us by right of your virtues and your dignity, but I swear to the Queen of France that I have done nothing to deserve this public affront."

She paused a moment, to assure herself that she held the attention of the Queen and of every one there present, then she fixed her dark eyes straight on Lydie and said loudly, so that her clear, somewhat shrill young voice rang out triumphantly through the room:

"My husband was made a tool of by Madame la Marquise d'Eglinton, for the purpose of selling the Stuart prince to England."

Once more there was dead silence in the vast reception hall, a few seconds during which the loudly accusing voice died away in an almost imperceptible echo, but in one heart at least those seconds might have been a hundred hours, for the wealth of misery they contained.

Lydie stood as if turned to stone. Though she had realized Gaston's treachery she had not thought that it would mean all this. The utter infamy of it left her paralyzed and helpless. She had delivered her soul, her mind, her honour, her integrity to the vilest traitor that ever darkened the face of the earth. If a year ago she had humiliated him, if to-day she had tried to thwart all his future ambitions, he was fully revenged now.

She did not hear even the loyal Queen's protest:

"It is false!" for Marie Leszcynska, sickened and horrified, was loth to believe the truth of this terrible indictment against the one woman she had always singled out for royal trust and royal friendship.

"It is true, your Majesty," said Irène firmly, as she once more rose to her feet. "Deign to ask Madame la Marquise d'Eglinton if to-day in the loneliness of the Park of Versailles, she did not place in the hands of Monsieur le Comte de Stainville the secret of the Stuart prince's hiding place so that he might be delivered over to the English for a large sum of money. Madame is beautiful and rich and influential, Monsieur de Stainville being a man, dared not refuse to obey her orders, but Monsieur de Stainville is also handsome and young, Madame honoured him with her regard, and I the wife was to be publicly ostracised and swept aside, for I was in the way, and might have an indiscreet tongue in my mouth. That, your Majesty, is the truth," concluded Irène now with triumphant calm; "deign to look into her face and mine and see which is the paler, she or I."

157

Marie Leszcynska had listened in silence at the awful accusation thus hurled by one woman against the other. At Irène's final words she turned and looked at Lydie, saw the marble-like hue of the face, the rigidity of the young form, the hopeless despair expressed in the half-closed eyes. It is but fair to say that the Queen even now did not altogether believe Madame de Stainville's story: she instinctively was still drawing a comparison between the gaudily apparelled doll with the shrill voice, and the impudently bared shoulders, and the proud, graceful woman in robes of virginal white, of whom, during all these years of public life, unkind tongues were only able to say that she was cold, rigid, dull, uninteresting perhaps, but whose vestal robes the breath of evil scandal had never dared to pollute.

The Queen did not feel that guilt was written now on that straight, pure brow, but she had a perfectly morbid horror of any esclandre occurring in her presence or at one of her Courts. Moreover, Irène had certainly struck one chord, which jarred horribly on the puritanical Queen's nerves, and unfortunately at the very moment when Madame de Stainville made this final poisoned suggestion, Marie Lesczynska's eyes happened to be resting on the King's face. In Louis' expression she caught the leer, the smile, half-mocking, half indulgent which was habitual to him when woman's frailty was discussed, and her whole pride rose in revolt at contact with these perpetual scandals, which disgraced the Court of Versailles, and which she was striving so hard to banish from her own entourage.

Because of this she felt angered now with every one quite indiscriminately. A few years ago her sense of justice would have caused her to sift this matter through, to test for herself the rights or wrongs of an obviously bitter quarrel; but lately this sense of justice had become blunted, through many affronts to her personal dignity as a Queen and as a wife. It had left her with a morbid egotistical regard for the majesty of her Court: this she felt had been attainted; and now she only longed to get away, and leave behind her all this vulgarity, these passions, these petty quarrels, which she so cordially abhorred.

"Enough," she said sternly; "our royal cheeks glow with shame at thought that this indecent brawl should have occurred in our presence. Your Majesty," she added turning haughtily to the King, "your arm, I pray; we cannot endure this noisy bickering, which is more fitting for the slums of Paris than for the throne-room of the Queen of France."

Louis' bewilderment was almost comical. It would have been utterly impossible for him, and quite unseemly in his wife's

158

presence, to interfere in what was obviously a feminine quarrel, even if he had desired to do so; and he had not altogether made up his mind how Madame la Comtesse de Stainville's indiscreet outburst would affect him personally, which was all that really interested him in the matter. On the whole he was inclined to think favourably of the new aspect of affairs. When the fact of the Stuart prince's betrayal into his enemies' hands became known—which it was bound to do sooner or later—it was not unpleasant that the first hint of the treachery should have come in such a form as to implicate Lydie, and that so deeply, that ever afterward the public, clinging to the old proverb that there is no smoke without fire, would look upon her as the prime mover in the nefarious scheme.

Louis the Well-beloved possessed, par excellence, the subtle knack of taking care of his august person, and above all of his august reputation. It would certainly be as well, for the sake of the future, that his over-indulgent subjects should foster the belief that, in this vile treachery, their King had been misled; more sinned against than sinning.

But of course he too was anxious to get away. That the present feminine altercation would lead to a more serious quarrel, he already guessed from the fact that his shrewd eyes had perceived Lord Eglinton standing close to one of the great doors at the further end of the room. Vaguely Louis wondered how much the husband had heard, and what he would do if he had heard everything. Then he mentally shrugged his shoulders, thinking that after all it did not matter what milor's future actions might be. Louis was quite convinced that Madame Lydie had thrown her bonnet over the mills, and that, as a gallant gentleman, milor would above all things have to hold his peace.

His Majesty therefore was not angered against any one. He smiled quite affably at the Comte and Comtesse de Stainville and bestowed a knowing wink on Lydie, who fortunately was too dazed to notice this final insult.

Every one else was silent and awed. The Queen now descended the steps of the daïs on the arm of the King. Irène was a little disappointed that nothing more was going to happen. She opened her lips, ready to speak again but Marie Leszcynska threw her such a haughty, scornful glance that Gaston de Stainville, realizing the futility—nay! the danger—of prolonging this scene, placed a peremptory hand on his wife's arm, forcibly drawing her away.

At the foot of the steps Her Majesty once more turned to Lydie.

"We shall expect an explanation from you, Marquise," she said haughtily, "but not to-night. See that our audience chamber is cleared from all this rabble."

And with this parting shot, hurled recklessly at her faithful adherents, just as much as at those who had offended her, the descendant of a proud line of Kings sailed majestically out of the room, whilst a loud "hush-sh-sh-sh ..." caused by the swish of brocaded skirts on the parquet floor as every one made a deep obeisance, accompanied the Royal lady in her short progress toward the door and then softly died away.

CHAPTER XXVII

A FALL

Irène de Stainville was quite right when she thought that sympathy would be on her side, in the grave affront which had been put upon her, and for which she had revenged herself somewhat drastically, but under the circumstances quite naturally.

Although in this circle—known as the Queen's set—the young Marchioness of Eglinton had always been looked up to as a leader and an especial favourite, the accusation which Irène had brought against her was so awful, her own attitude of passive acquiescence so incomprehensible, that it was small wonder that after the departure of Their Majesties, when the crowd broke up into isolated groups, most people there present held themselves aloof from her.

The words "a jealous woman's caprice," which at the outset had so angered the Queen, expressed fully the interpretation put upon Lydie's conduct by those who witnessed the scene from beginning to end. That Irène de Stainville had inflicted on her the humiliation of a terrible public indictment, was reckoned only as retributive human justice.

Lydie knew well enough that the crowd which surrounded her—though here usually composed of friends—was only too ready to believe evil, however crying, against a woman placed so highly in Royal and social favour as she herself had been for years. Already she could hear the murmur of condemnation round her, and that from people who should have known that she was quite incapable of committing the base treachery attributed to her.

160

Of course she had not denied it. She could not have denied it, in the face of the wording of the accusation itself.

And she felt herself hideously and morally guilty, guilty in the facts though not in the spirit. As Irène had put it crudely and simply, she had handed over to Gaston de Stainville in the privacy of the Park of Versailles the secret which would deliver the Stuart prince into the hands of his enemies.

How could she begin to explain to all these people that her motive had been good and pure, her orders to Gaston altogether different from those imputed to her by Irène? No one would have believed her explanation unless Gaston too spoke the truth. And Gaston meant to be an infamous liar to the end.

She had been the tool of that clique, it was they now who were ready to cast her aside, to break her power and ultimately to throw her on the heap of social refuse, where other traitors, liars and cheats mouldered away in obscurity.

Already she knew what the end would be, already she tasted the bitter fruit of waning popularity.

Quite a crowd of obvious sympathizers gathered round the Comte and Comtesse de Stainville. Gaston's avowedly base conduct was—it seems—to be condoned. At best he stood branded by his own wife—unwittingly perhaps—as having betrayed a woman who for right or wrong, had trusted him, but it is strange to record that, in this era of petticoat rule, the men were always more easily forgiven their faults than the women.

Lydie found herself almost alone, only Monsieur de Louvois came and spoke to her on an official matter, and presently Monsieur le Duc d'Aumont joined them.

"Will you let me take you back to your apartments, Lydie?" urged Monsieur le Duc. "I fear the excitement has seriously upset you."

"You think I have been to blame, father dear?" she asked quite gently.

"Oh! ..." he murmured vaguely.

"You did not speak up for me when that woman accused me..."

"My dear child," he said evasively, "you had not taken me into your confidence. I thought ..."

"You still think," she insisted, "that what Madame de Stainville said was true?"

"Isn't it?" he asked blandly.

He did not understand this mood of hers at all. Was she trying to deny? Impossible surely! She was a clever woman, and with the

161

map and her own letter, sealed and signed with her name, what was the good of denying?

"Your own letter and the map, my child," he added with gentle reproach, thinking that she feared to trust him completely.

"Ah yes! my own letter!" she murmured, "the map ... I had forgotten."

No! she did not mean to deny! She could not deny! ... Her own father believed her guilty ... and all she could have done would have been to urge the purity of her motive. Gaston had of course destroyed her orders to the command of Le Monarque and there was only the map ... and that awful, awful letter.

Monsieur le Duc thought that his daughter had been very unwise. Having trusted Gaston, and placed herself as it were in his hands, she was foolish to anger him. No man—if he have the faintest pretension to being called an honourable gentleman—however smitten he might be with another woman's charms, will allow his wife to be publicly insulted by her rival. No doubt Lydie had been jealous of Irène, whose somewhat indiscreet advances to milor Eglinton had aroused universal comment. But Lydie did not even pretend to care for her own husband and she had yielded her most treasured secret to Gaston de Stainville. There she should have remained content and not have provoked Irène's wrath, and even perhaps a revulsion of feeling in Gaston himself.

Unlike King Louis, Monsieur le Duc d'Aumont did not approve of his daughter's name being associated with the treacherous scheme from which he was ready enough to profit financially himself, although in the innermost depths of his heart he disapproved of it. He knew his Royal master well enough to be fully aware of the fact that, when the whole nefarious transaction came to light, Louis would find means of posing before the public as the unwilling tool of a gang of money-grabbers. When that happened, every scornful finger would of necessity—remembering the events of this night—point at Lydie, and incidentally at her father, as the prime movers of the scheme.

It had been far better to have conciliated Irène and not to have angered Gaston.

But women were strange creatures, and jealousy their most autocratic master. Even his daughter whom he had thought so exceptional, so clever and so clear-headed, was not free from the weaknesses of her sex.

"Methinks, my dear," he said kindly, "you have not acted as wisely as I should have expected. Madame de Stainville, on my honour, hath not wronged you so as to deserve a public affront, and Gaston himself only desired to serve you."

162

Monsieur le Duc must have raised his voice more than he intended, or else perhaps there had occurred quite suddenly in the crowd of sympathizers, that now stood in a dense group round Madame de Stainville, one of those inevitable moments of complete silence when angels are said to be fluttering round the room. Certain it is that Monsieur le Duc's words sang out somewhat loudly, and were heard by those whose names had been on his lips.

"Nay! I entreat you, Monsieur le Duc," came in light, bantering accents from Gaston de Stainville, "do not chide your fair daughter. Believe me, we who have suffered most are not inclined to be severe. As to me the psychology of Madame la Marquise's mood has been profoundly interesting, since it hath revealed her to the astonished gaze of her many admirers, as endowed with some of the weaknesses of her adorable sex. Why should we complain of these charming weaknesses? For though we might be very hard hit thereby, they are but expressions of flattery soothing to our pride."

The groups had parted somewhat as he spoke, leaving him face to face with Lydie, towards whom he advanced with an affected gait and mincing steps, looking at her with mocking eyes, whilst toying gracefully with the broad black ribbon that held his eyeglass.

But Gaston's were not the only sarcastic glances that were levelled at Lydie. His fatuous innuendoes were unmistakable, and bore out the broader and more shameful accusation hurled by Irène. Lydie's own attitude, her every action to-night, the expression of her face at this moment seemed to prove them true. She retreated a little as he advanced, and, doing so, she raised her head with that proud toss which was habitual to her.

Thus her eyes travelled swiftly across the room, and she saw her husband standing some distance away. She, too, like King Louis, wondered how much he had heard, how much he knew: and knowing all, what he meant to do. Instinctively when she caught sight of him, and then once more saw Gaston de Stainville drawing nearer to her, she remembered that warning which milor had given her that morning, and which she had thought so futile, anent the loathsome reptile that, once touched, would pollute for ever.

"Madame," said Gaston now, as he boldly approached her, "my friends here would tell me no doubt that, by every code of social honour, my duty is to punish you or someone who would represent you in this matter, for the affront done to my wife. But how can I do that since the offender is fair as well as frail? My desire is not to punish, but rather to thank you on my knees for the delicate compliment implied by your actions to-night. I knew that you honoured me by trusting in me," he added with obvious

163

significance, "but I had not hoped to provoke such flattering jealousy in the heart of the most statuesque woman in France."

A titter went round the room. Gaston's attitude seemed suddenly to have eased the tension, as of an impending tragedy, which had hung over the brilliant assembly for the last half hour. Monsieur le Comte was such a dreadful mauvais sujet but so delightful in his ways, so delicately refined in his wickedness! He was quite right to take the matter lightly, and a murmur of approval followed the titter, at the tact with which he had lifted the load of apprehension from the minds of the company.

Madame la Marquise d'Eglinton was something of a fool to take the matter so thoroughly au tragique. No doubt the affairs of the Stuart prince would right themselves presently, and she certainly should have had more regard for her willing and obviously devoted accomplice.

He looked so superlatively elegant and handsome now, the younger women sighed whilst they admired him. He pointed his toe and held out his tricorne in the manner prescribed by fashion for the making of a bow, and it was most unfortunate that he was so suddenly stopped in the very midst of his graceful flourish by a quiet and suave voice which came immediately from behind him.

"I would not do that, were I in your red-heeled shoes, my good Stainville. A slip on this highly-polished floor is certain to be the result."

But even before the gentle echo of these blandly spoken words had penetrated to the further ends of the room, Monsieur le Comte de Stainville had measured his full length face downward on the ground.

His fall was so instantaneous that he had not the time to save himself with his hands, and he was literally sprawling now at Lydie's feet with arms and legs stretched out, his face having come in violent contact with the polished floor. Quite close to him Lord Eglinton was standing, laughing softly and discreetly and looking down on the prostrate and distinctly inelegant figure of the handsome cavalier.

A ripple of merry laughter followed this unexpected turn of events. One or two spectators, who had stood quite close at the very moment that the catastrophe occurred, declared subsequently that milor had with a quick action of his foot thrown Monsieur de Stainville off his balance; the intense slipperiness of the parquet having merely done the rest.

Be that as it may, the laughter of necessity was prudently suppressed, for already Gaston had picked himself up and there was that in his face which warned all those present that the farce—such as it was—would prove the prelude to real and serious tragedy.

"There now," said Lord Eglinton blandly, "did I not warn you, Monsieur le Comte? Graceful flourishes are apt to be treacherous."

"Milor..." said Gaston, who was livid with rage.

"Hush—sh—sh," interrupted milor in the same even and gentle voice, "not in the presence of ladies. ... An you desire, Monsieur le Comte, I'll be at your service later on."

Then he turned toward his wife, bowing low, but not in the least as Gaston de Stainville would have bowed, for he had inherited from his father all the stiffness of manner peculiar to the Anglo-Saxon race.

Thus at this moment he looked distinctly gauche, though not without dignity, as, his back slightly bent, his left arm outstretched, he waited until Lydie chose to place her hand on his sleeve.

"Your seconds, milor," shouted Gaston, who seemed quite unable to control himself, and who had to be distinctly and even determinedly held back by two of his friends from springing then and there at Lord Eglinton's throat.

"They will wait on yours to-night, Monsieur le Comte," replied le petit Anglais affably. "Madame la Marquise, will you honour me?"

And Lydie took his arm and allowed him to lead her out of the room.

CHAPTER XXVIII

HUSBAND AND WIFE

Monsieur Achille was waiting in the vestibule of the Queen's apartments. As soon as Lord and Lady Eglinton appeared his majestic figure detached itself from the various groups of flunkeys, who stood about desultorily pending the breaking up of Her Majesty's Court; he had a cloak over his arm, and, at a sign from his master he approached and handed him the cloak which milor then placed round his wife's shoulders.

"Do you desire to sleep in Versailles to-night, Madame?" he asked, "my coach is below in case you wished to drive to Château d'Aumont."

165

"I thank you, milor," she said, "I would wish to remain in Versailles."

Then she added with a pathetic sigh of bitterness:

"My father would prefer it, I think. He is not prepared for my visit. And I do not interfere with your lordship's arrangements...."

"Not in the least, Madame," he rejoined quietly. "The corridors are interminable; would you like a chair?"

"No. ... Let us walk," she said curtly.

Without further comment he once more offered her his arm. She took it and together they descended the monumental staircase and then turned along the endless, vast corridors which lead to the West Wing. Monsieur Achille followed at a respectful distance, and behind him walked two flunkeys, also in the gorgeous scarlet and gold Eglinton livery, whilst two more bearing torches preceded Monsieur le Marquis and Madame, lighting them on their way.

On the way to the West Wing, milor talked lightly of many things: of Monsieur de Voltaire's latest comedy, and the quaint new fashion in headgear, of His Majesty the King of Prussia and of the pictures of Monsieur Claude Gelée. He joked about the Duchesse de Pontchartrain's attempts at juvenility and Monsieur Crébillon's pretensions to a place among the Immortals. Lydie answered in monosyllables; she could not bring herself to speak, although she quite appreciated milor's desire to appear natural and unconcerned before his own lacqueys.

A great resolution was taking root in her mind, and she only wanted the privacy and the familiarity of her own apartments to put it into execution. Thus they reached the West Wing.

Arrived in the antechamber whence her rooms branched off to the right and milor's to the left, Lord Eglinton stopped, disengaged her arm from his and was about to bid her an elaborate good-night, when she said abruptly:

"May I speak with you privately and in your own study, milor?"

"Certainly, Madame," he replied seemingly a little astonished at her request.

He dismissed all the flunkeys with the exception of Monsieur Achille, who led the way through the reception rooms toward milor's private suite. Lord and Lady Eglinton followed in silence now. The rooms seemed strangely silent and deserted, ghostlike too, for there was no artificial light, and the moon peered in through the tall windows, throwing patches of pale mauve and weird, translucent greens on the parquet floor and the brocade coverings of the chairs.

In milor's study, Monsieur Achille lighted the candles in two massive candelabra, which stood on the secrétaire, then, at a nod from his master, he walked backward out of the room.

The heavy portière fell back with a curious sound like a moan, and for the third time to-day husband and wife stood face to face alone. The gaucherie of his manner became at once apparent now: yet he seemed in no way bashful or ill as ease, only very stiff and awkward in his movements, as he drew a chair for her at a convenient angle, and when she had sat down, placed a cushion to her back and a footstool at her feet. He himself remained standing.

"I pray you sit, milor," she said with a quick sigh, that trembled as it escaped her lips, "and if I have not angered you beyond the bounds of your patience, I earnestly ask you to bear with me, for if I have been at fault I have also suffered much and ..."

"Madame," he said quite gently if somewhat coldly, "might I entreat of you not to insist on this interview if it distresses you very much; as to a fault ... on my honour, Madame, the very thought of self-accusation on your part seems to me wildly preposterous."

He did not sit as she had asked him to do, but stood looking down at her and thinking—thinking alas!—that she never had been quite so beautiful. She was almost as white as her gown, the powder still clung to her hair, which, in the dim light of the candles, chose to hide the glory of its ardent colour beneath the filmy artificial veil. She wore some exquisite pearls, his gift on the day of her marriage: row upon row of these exquisite gems fell on her throat and bosom, both as white, as glittering and pure as the priceless treasures from the deep.

The chair in which she sat was covered with damask of a rich dull gold, and against this background with its bright lights and impenetrably dark shadows, the white figure stood out like what he had always pictured her, a cold and unapproachable statue.

But to-night, though so still and white, the delicate marble had taken unto itself life: the life which means sorrow. All the haughtiness of the look had vanished; there were deep shadows under the eyes and lines of suffering round the perfectly chiselled lips.

Henry Dewhyrst, Marquis of Eglinton, was not yet thirty: he loved this exquisitely beautiful woman with all his heart and soul, and she had never been anything more to him than a perfectly carved image would be on the high altar of a cathedral. She had been neither helpmate nor wife, only an ideal, an intangible shadow which his love had not succeeded in materializing.

As he looked at her now, he wondered for the first time in the course of their married life, if it had been his own fault that they had remained such complete strangers: this was because for the first time to-day a great sorrow, a still greater shame had breathed life into the marble-like statue.

All at once he felt deeply, unutterably sorry for her; he had no thought of her wrongs toward him, only of those done to herself by her pride and the faults of the epoch in which she lived.

"Milor," she said trying to steady her voice, "it would ease me a little—and ease the painfulness of this interview—if you were to tell me at what precise moment you entered Her Majesty's throne-room to-night."

"I cannot say, Madame," he replied with the ghost of a smile; "I did not look at the clock, but I was in attendance on His Majesty and therefore ..."

"You heard what passed between Madame la Comtesse de Stainville and myself?" she interrupted hastily.

"Every word."

Somehow she felt relieved. She would have hated to recapitulate that vulgar scene, the mutual recriminations, the insults, culminating in Her Majesty's contemptuous exit from the room. She could not now see her husband's face, for he had contrived to stand so as to allow the light from the candelabra to fall full upon her, whilst he himself, silhouetted against the light, remained in the shadow; but there was a certain dignified repose about the whole figure, the white, slender hand resting lightly on the bureau, the broad shoulders square and straight, suggesting physical strength, and the simple, somewhat sober style and cut of the clothes.

The room too appeared as a complete contrast to the other apartments of the palace of Versailles, where the mincing fancies of Watteau and the artificialities of Boucher had swept aside the nobler conceptions of Girardon and Mansard. It was quite plainly furnished, with straight-back chairs and hangings of dull gold, and the leather covering of the bureau gave ample signs of wear.

The turmoil in Lydie's heart subsided, yielding itself to peace in the midst of these peaceful surroundings. She was able to conquer the tremor of her voice, the twitch of her lips, and to swallow down the burning tears of humiliation which blinded her eyes and obscured her judgment.

"Then, milor, it will indeed be easier for me. You understand of what I am charged, the awful load of disgrace and shame which by my own folly I have placed upon my shoulders ... you understand," and her voice, though steady, sunk to a whisper, "that I have proved unworthy of the confidence which the unfortunate Stuart prince, who was your friend, placed in me as well as in you?"

He did not reply, waiting for her to continue. Her head had

168

drooped and a heavy tear fell from her sunken lids upon her hands. To him who loved her, and whom she had so deeply wronged, there was a strange yet painful joy in watching her cry.

"What Madame de Stainville said to-night is true," she added tonelessly. "I gave into Monsieur de Stainville's hands the map, with full marginal notes and description of the place where the Stuart prince is hiding; I also gave him a letter written and signed by me, addressed to Prince Charles Edward Stuart, begging him to trust implicitly his own royal person and that of his friends to the bearer of my note. That letter and the plan are even now in the hands of His Majesty, who purposes to accept the proposals of His Grace the Duke of Cumberland, and to sell the Stuart prince to his foes for the sum of fifteen million livres. And that is all true."

Knowing men, the men of her world, she fully expected that this confession of hers would cause her husband's just wrath to break through that barrier of courteous good-breeding and self-restraint, imposed on all men of honour when in the presence of women, and which she firmly believed had alone prevented him from interfering between herself and Irène. She would not have been astonished if he had stormed and raged, loudly accused and condemned her, nay!—she had heard of such things—if he had laid hands on her. But when, hearing nothing, she looked up, she saw that he had scarcely moved, only the hand which still rested on the secrétaire trembled a little. Perhaps her look made him conscious of that, for he withdrew it, and then seemed to pull himself together, and draw himself up, straight and rigid like a soldier on parade.

"Having told you this, milor," she resumed after a slight pause, "I should like to add that I am fully aware that in your eyes there can be no excuse possible for what I did, since in doing it I have sacrificed the life of a man who trusted us—you and me, milor—more even than he did France. He and his friends, by my act, will leave the shelter of their retreat, and will be delivered into the hands of those who cannot do aught, for political and self-protective reasons, but send them to the scaffold. You see, milor, I do not palliate my offence, nor do I seek your pardon—although I know that you will look on what I have done as a disgrace brought by your wife upon your name. I deserve no pardon, and I ask for none. But if there is no excuse for my conduct, at least do I owe you an explanation, and for this I crave your attention if you would care to listen."

"Nay, Madame, you do but jest," he rejoined, "you owe me nothing ... not even an explanation."

"Yet you will listen?" she urged.

"It would be only painful to us both, Madame."

169

"You prefer to think of me as ignoble, treacherous and base," she said with sudden vehemence, "you do not wish to know for certain and from my own lips that Gaston de Stainville ..."

She paused abruptly and bit her lips, he watching her keenly, she not knowing that she was watched.

This was going to be a fight and he knew it, a dire conflict between distress and pride. At first he had hoped that she was prepared to yield, that she had sought this interview because the load of sorrow and of humiliation being more than she could bear, she had turned instinctively to the only man in the world who could ease and comfort her: whose boundless, untiring love was ready to share the present pain, as it had shrunk from participating in the glories of the past. But as she spoke, as she sat there before him now, white, passive, disdainful even in her self-abasement, he knew that his hour—Love's hour—had not yet struck. Pride was not yet conquered.

The dominant ruler of a lifetime will not abdicate very readily, and though distress and sorrow are powerful opponents, they are more transient, more easily cast aside than Pride.

"As you say, milor," she now said more quietly, "the matter is only painful to us both. I understand that your estimate of me is not an exalted one. You despise—you probably hate me! Well! so be it. Let us not think of our own feelings in this matter, milor! I entreat you to ignore my very existence for the time being, only thinking of the Stuart prince and of his dire peril!

"'Tis because of him I have begged for this interview," she resumed with just a thought of that commanding manner, which she was wont to assume whenever matters of public import were discussed: "I need not reiterate the fact that he is in deadly danger. Le Levantin, a fast brigantine, milor, is even now being equipped by His Majesty for the nefarious expedition. Le Levantin or perhaps Le Monarque—the latter is quite ready to sail at any time, and with the map and my letter it will be easy ... oh! so easy! ... Oh!" she added with a sudden uncontrollable outburst of passionate appeal, "milor, he was your friend ... can nothing be done? ... can nothing be done?"

"I do not know, madame," he replied coldly, "how should I?"

"But surely, surely you remember your promise to him, milor," she said impatient at his coldness, unable to understand this lack of enthusiasm. "You remember that night, in the Château d'Aumont—the banquet ... his farewell to you ... his trust, his confidence ... the assurance you gave him ..."

"So much has occurred since then, Madame," he said simply. "The guidance of affairs has been in your hands. ... I have lost what little grasp I ever had of the situation. ... As you know, I am neither

170

clever nor strong—and I have only too gladly relied on abler wits than mine own...."

"But your promise," she urged, with real passion ringing in her voice, "your promise to him...."

"I made a far more solemn one to you, madame, never to interfere in matters of State."

"I'll release you of that," she cried impulsively; "think, milor ... I entreat you to think! ... there must be some way out of this terrible labyrinth ... there must be some one whom you can trust ..."

She checked herself, and a quick hot blush rose to her cheeks. She thought that she had detected a quick flash in his eyes at these last words of hers, a flash which had caused that sudden rush of blood to her temples, but which was extinguished almost as soon as it arose: he said quite naturally and tonelessly:

"There is no one. How could there be?"

"But surely, surely," she repeated with growing, obstinate vehemence, "you can think of something to do ... you have the means ... you are rich ... have you no enthusiasms, milor?"

"Oh! ..." he said deprecatingly, "so few! ... they are scarce worthy of the name...."

"No thought how to help your friend who is in fear and peril of his life? ... Heavens above us, what are the men of France? Wooden dolls or ..."

"That what the women of France have made them, Madame," he said quietly.

"Then you have no thought, or initiative how to help your friend?" she retorted.

He had noted the ring of scorn in her voice, the return of that haughty and obstinate self-will, which would for ever stand between her and happiness. His expression suddenly hardened, as he looked at her flashing eyes and the contemptuous curl of the exquisite lips, all the gentleness went out of his face, the latent tenderness which she had wilfully ignored, and his voice, no longer softly mocking, became hard and bitter in its tones.

"I?" he said with a slight uplifting of his brow and a self-deprecating droop of the lip, "surely, Madame, you are pleased to jest. I am no statesman, no politician, I scarce have a sufficiency of brains to be a figure head in an administration. I have never been taught to think."

"You are mocking me, milor," she said haughtily.

"Nothing is further from my thoughts. I have far too much respect for your ladyship to venture on either mockery or individual thought."

She paused awhile, frowning and impatient, angered beyond

bounds, too, at his attitude, which she was quite clever enough to see did not represent the true state of his mind. No doubt he desired to punish her for her contempt of him that morning. She would have liked to read the expression in his face, to know something of what was going on behind that straight, handsome brow, and the eyes always so gentle, yet so irritating now in this semblance of humility. She thought certainly that the outline of the jaw suggested obstinacy—the obstinacy of the inherently weak. If she had not wanted his help so much, she would have left him then and there, in scorn and in wrath, only too glad that sentiment had not led her into more excuses or explanations—a prayer for forgiveness mayhap. She was not a little irritated with herself too, for she felt that she had made a wrong start: she was quite sure that his supineness, at any rate with regard to the fate of the Stuart prince, was assumed. There must be a way of appealing to that loyalty which she knew he cherished for his friend, some means of breaking down that barrier of resentment which he had evidently set up against her.

Oh! if it had been a few months ago, when he still loved her, before Irène de Stainville. . . She paused in this train of thought, her mind not daring to travel further along it; it was such a wide, such a glorious possibility that that one little "if" suggested, that her heart quivered with renewed agony, and the weak tears, of which she was so ashamed, insisted on coming to her eyes.

If only his love for her was not dead, how easy her task would have been! It would have fired him to enthusiasm now, caused him to forget his resentment against her in this great work yet to be accomplished, and instead of asking him for passive help she could have incited him to a deed of loyalty and of courage. But now she was too proud to continue her appeal: she thought that she had done her best, and had not even succeeded in breaking through the icy reserve and resentment which in his heart had taken the place of silent and humble worship.

"Milor," she said with sudden determination, and in the authoritative manner which was more habitual to her than the more emotional, passionately appealing mood, "with your leave we'll cease these unworthy bickerings. I may have been hasty in my actions this morning. If so I pray you not to vent your anger against your friend. If I have wronged you by taking you at your word, when a year ago you told me that you would never wish to interfere in my official work, well! I humbly beg you pardon, and again entreat you not to allow your friend to expiate the sins of your wife. You say that the men of France are what the women have made them; there I think that you are wrong—at least in this: that in your mind the word woman stands for those of the sex who are pure and loyal as well as those for who are not. It is not the women of France who have made the men, milor, rather it is the men who—looking to the Pompadours, the Irène de Stainvilles, not only for companionship and for pleasure, but also, heaven help them! for ideals—have made the women what they are! But enough of this. You no doubt think me wordy and tedious, and neither understand, nor wish to understand that there may be honour and chivalry in a far greater degree in the heart of a woman, than in that of the more selfish sex. I have asked for your advice in all simplicity and loyalty, acknowledging the sin I have committed and asking you to help me in atoning for it, in a way useful to your friend. This appeal for advice you have met with sneers and bitter mockery: on my soul, milor if I could now act without your assistance I would do so, for in all the humiliation which I have had to endure to-day, none has been more galling or more hard to bear believe me, than that which I must now endure through finding myself, in a matter essentially vital to my heart and even to my reason, dependent upon your help."

He could hear her voice trembling a little in spite of her efforts at self-control. He knew quite well that at this moment she spoke the truth, and these last words of hers, which for many a long day afterward rang persistently in his ears, represented to him ever afterward the very acme of mental—aye! and physical—pain which one human being could inflict on another. At the time it absolutely seemed unendurable: it seemed to him that under the blow, thus coldly dealt by those same beautiful lips, for which his own ached with an intensity of passionate longing, either his life or his reason must give way. The latter probably, for life is more tenacious and more cruel in its tenacity: yet if reason went, then Heaven alone could help him, for he would either kill her or outrage her beyond the hope of pardon.

"Therefore, milor," she resumed after a slight pause, unconscious evidently of the intense cruelty of her words, "I will beg of you not to make it harder for me than need be. I must ask this help from you, in order to succeed, if humanly possible, in outwitting the infamous work of a gang of traitors. Will you, at least, give me this help I need?"

"If it lies within my power," he replied; "I pray you to command Madame."

"I am thinking of sending a messenger post haste to the commander of Le Monarque with orders to set sail at once for Scotland," she continued in matter-of-fact tones. "I should want a fresh copy of the map where Prince Charles Edward is in hiding, and to make assurance doubly sure a letter from you to the prince, asking him to trust Captain Barre implicitly. Le Monarque I know can reach Scotland long ere Le Levantin is ready for sea, and my idea had been originally to commission her to take the prince and his friends on board, and then to skirt the west coast of Ireland, reaching Brittany or mayhap the Pyrenees by a circuitous route. I have firm belief that it is not too late to send this messenger, milor, and thus to put my original plan into execution. And if you will give me a new map and full directions and your signet ring for the prince, I feel confident that I can find someone whom I could thoroughly trust ..."

"There is no one whom you could thoroughly trust with such an errand, Madame!" he said drily.

"I must risk that, milor. The crisis has become so acute that I must do something to avert that awful catastrophe."

"Betrayal would be the inevitable result."

"I entreat you to leave that to me," she urged firmly. "I know I can find someone, all I ask is for the map, and a word and signet ring from you."

She was leaning forward now, eager and enthusiastic again, self-willed and domineering, determined that he should do what she wished. Her eyes were glowing, the marble was indeed endowed with life; she gleamed like a jewel, white and fragile-looking, in this dull and sombre room, and he forgetting for the moment her cruelty of awhile ago was loth to let her go, to speak the harsh words which anon would have to be said, and which would send her resentful, contemptuous, perhaps heartbroken, out of his sight again.

Would it not have been ten thousand times more simple to throw pride, just anger, reason to the winds, to fall at those exquisite feet, to encircle that glittering marble with passionately tremulous arms, to swear fealty, slavery, obedience to her whims.

How she would smile, and how softly and tenderly would the flush of victory tinge those pale cheeks with delicate rose! to see it gradually chase away the pearl-like tone of her skin, to see her eyes brighten at his word, to feel perhaps the tiny hand tremble with joy as it lay for sheer gratitude a few brief seconds in his, was not that well worth the barren victory of a man's pride over a woman's self-will?

She had thought that he would have yielded at her first word, would at once have fawned at her feet, kissing her hand, swearing that he was her slave. He had done it once ... a year ago, and why not now again? Then she had smiled on him, had allowed him to kneel, to kiss her gown, anon had yielded her cold fingers to his kiss; he had reaped a year of misery for that one moment's joy, and now, just for the space of a few seconds he was again assailed with an awful temptation to throw prudence and pride away, to enjoy one golden hour—less perhaps—but glorious and fulsome whilst it lasted, until it gave way once more to humiliation, far worse to bear than heretofore.

The temptation for those few brief seconds was overwhelming, and 'twas fortunate that he stood in shadow, else she had seen signs of an awful conflict in that young and handsome face which she had been wont to see so gentle and so placid. But he knew that in her, pride had by now absolutely got the upper hand: sorrow had laid down her arms and constituted herself a prisoner of war, following meekly behind the triumphal chariot of her conquering rival.

And because of that, because he knew that there was not one spark yet in her heart which Love had kindled, that Love itself was still lying dormant within her, gagged and bound even in his sleep, kept in subjection thus pinioned and helpless by masterful self-will and by obstinate pride, he would not yield to the temptation of culling the Dead Sea fruit, that would inevitably turn to ashes, even as his lips first tasted its fleeting, if intoxicating savour.

She had half risen from her chair leaning across the bureau, eager, excited, tremulous, sure of victory. Paper and pen lay close to her hand, smiling she pointed to these:

"Oh! I pray you, milor," she said with passionate fervour, "do not delay! Every hour, every minute is precious ... I swear to you that I'll find a messenger. He'll not know the purport of his errand. ... Oh! I assure you I'll play the part of indifference to perfection! ... The packet to the commander of Le Monarque will seem of the most insignificant kind. ... I'll not even order the messenger to hurry ... just to guard the packet as inviolate as any secret of State. ... Nay! hundreds of such messages have to be trusted to indifferent hands, in the course of a single transaction of the nation's business. Believe me, milor, there is not cause for fear! Le Monarque can put to sea within an hour of receiving my orders, and Prince Charles Edward Stuart and his friends will be safely out of reach, ere Le Levantin unfurls her sails, and pins to her masthead the pennant of traitors...."

"But you do not speak, milor," she said suddenly changing the tone of her voice, all eagerness gone from her manner, a strange, nameless anxiety gripping her heart, "will you not do this little I ask? ..."

"It is impossible, Madame," he said curtly.

"Impossible? ... Why? ..."

Her voice now was harsh, trenchant, as it had been when she

175

hurled a loud insult at Gaston de Stainville through his wife. She was on her feet, tall and erect; a statue once more, white to the lips, cold and haughty, rigid too, save for the slight trembling of her hands and the tremulous quiver of her mouth when she spoke.

As he did not reply to her question, she said impatiently:

"Will you give me a reason for this unexplainable refusal, milor?"

"No. I refuse, that is all."

"This is not your last word?"

"It is my last word."

"Would you have me think that you are at one with the treacherous scheme, milor? and that you do not desire the safety of the Stuart prince?"

She had raised her voice, boldly accusing him, inwardly knowing that the accusation was groundless, yet wishing to goad him now into passion, into explanation, above all into acquiescence if it still lay in her power to force it.

But he took the insult with apparent calm, shrugged his shoulders and said quietly:

"As you please."

"Or is it ... is it that you do not trust me? ... that you think I...?"

She could not finish the sentence, nor put into words the awful suggestion which had sprung like a stinging viper straight across the train of her thoughts. Her eyes dazed and burning tried to pierce the gloom wherein he stood, but the flickering light of the candles only threw weird, fantastic gleams upon his face, which suddenly seemed strange, unknown, incomprehensible to her. His figure appeared preternaturally tall, the sober gray of his coat looked like the pall of an avenging ghost. He was silent and had made no sign of protest, when she framed the terrible query.

A bitter, an awful humiliation overwhelmed her. She felt as if right within her heart something had snapped and crumbled, which nothing on earth could ever set up again.

She said nothing more, but she could not altogether repress a heartbroken moan, which rose from the intensity of her mental agony.

Then she turned and with head thrown back, with silent, trembling lips and half-closed eyes she walked slowly out of the room.

176

CHAPTER XXIX

THE FATE OF THE STUART PRINCE

Lydie hardly knew how she reached her apartments. Earlier in the day she had thought once or twice that she had reached the deepest abyss of sorrow and humiliation into which it was possible for a woman of pride to descend. When her husband first asked an explanation from her, and taxed her with lending an ear to the King's base proposals; when she found that her own father, whom she respected and loved, had himself delved deeply in the mire of treachery; when she stood face to face with Gaston de Stainville and realized that he was an infamous liar and she a weak, confiding fool; when Irène had accused her publicly of scheming that which she would have given her life's blood to avert, all these were moments when she felt that the shame of them was more than she could bear.

Yet how simple and childish, how paltry seemed the agony of those mental tortures in comparison with that she endured now.

She felt as if she had received a blow in the face, a blow which had left a hideous, disfiguring mark on her which everyone henceforth would see: the scarlet letter of ignominy with which in the New World beyond the seas a puritanic inquisition branded the shameless outcasts. By her husband's silence rather than by his words she had been branded with a mark of infamy.

Ye saints and angels above, how terribly it hurt!

Yet why did she suffer so? Was it only because she had failed to obtain that which she almost begged for on her knees? Lydie, proud, dictatorial, domineering Lydie, felt that she had humiliated herself beyond what she would have thought possible less than twelve hours ago, and she had been refused.

Was it that, that made her heart, her head, her very limbs ache with almost unendurable agony?

Her mind—though almost on the verge of madness—retained just one glimmer of reason. It answered "No! the pain has deeper roots, more mysterious, at present incomprehensible, and death-dealing in their tenacity."

Her husband thought that if he entrusted her with a letter for the Stuart prince, she might use that letter for treacherous ends. That was the reason of his refusal. He so hated, so despised her that his mind classed her as one of the most ignoble of her sex!

Well! Awhile ago, in the Queen's antechamber, Irène de Stainville had publicly accused her of selling her royal friend for gold. Most people there had believed Irène readily enough! That had hurt too, but not so much.

Then why this? Why these terrible thoughts which went hammering in her mind? whispers of peace to escape from this racking torture? peace that could only be found in death!

"Great God, am I going mad?"

Monsieur Achille had been accompanying Madame la Marquise on her way along the corridors; he was carrying a candelabrum, wherein four wax candles spluttered and flickered in the incessant draught. Lydie had been unconscious of the man's presence, but she had followed the light mechanically, her eyes fixed on the four yellowish flames which looked like mocking mouths that laughed, and emitted a trail of black smoke, foul as the pestilential breath of shame.

Arrived at the door of her own antechamber, she was met by one of her liveried servants, who told her that Monsieur le Duc d'Aumont was within and awaiting to see her. To her hastily put query, the man replied that Monsieur le Duc had arrived about half an hour ago, and, hearing that Madame la Marquise was closeted with milor, he had elected to wait.

This visit from her father at this hour of the night meant a grave crisis, of course. At once Lydie's mind flew back to the Stuart prince. She had almost forgotten him since she left her husband's room. It seemed as if the overwhelming misery of that silent and deadly indictment had weighed down all other thoughts, until they sank into complete insignificance.

Vaguely, too, she had the sensation that there was no immediate necessity for her to rack her overtired brain to-night on the subject of the Jacobite's fate. She had at least six clear days before her, before Le Levantin, which was to start on the dire expedition, could be ready to put to sea. There was Le Monarque, on the other hand, quite ready to sail within an hour of receiving her orders. And Captain Barre was an honest man, a gallant sailor; he would only be too willing to make top speed in order to circumvent a treacherous plot, which he would abhor if he knew of it.

True, Lydie had now no means of locating the fugitives exactly, but with a six days' start of Le Levantin this want of precise knowledge need not necessarily prove fatal. She could trust to her memory somewhat, for she had repeatedly studied and fingered the map; she could draw something approximate from memory, and Captain Barre's determination and enthusiasm would surely do the rest.

These suggestions all rushed into her mind directly she heard that her father had come to visit her at this late hour. At first her desire was to avoid seeing him at risk even of offending him: but in spite of all that she had gone through, Lydie still retained sufficient presence of mind not to allow any impulse to rule her at such a critical moment. She forced herself to reflect on the Stuart prince and on him alone, on his danger and the treacherous plot against him, for at least twenty seconds, time enough to realize that it was absolutely necessary that she should see her father, in order to glean from him if possible every detail of the proposed expedition. She would indeed be helpless if she remained in ignorance of what had been planned between the King, Gaston, and her father. Perhaps—who knows?—in accordance with the habits of a lifetime, the Duke might even at this moment be anxious to consult his daughter—his helpmeet in all such matters—as to the final arrangements for the equipment of Le Levantin.

Satisfied with her conclusions, she therefore went straight into the boudoir where the lacquey said that Monsieur le Duc was waiting.

The first look at his benign face proved to her that he, at least, was not in any trouble. Whatever his daughter's views on the subject might be, he evidently was not altogether dissatisfied with the events of the day. He still wore a perturbed look, certainly; the scene which had occurred in Her Majesty's throne-room would not tend to decrease his mental worry; but beyond the slightly troubled look in his kindly eyes, and the obvious solicitude with which he took her hand and led her to a low divan, he seemed fairly serene.

"Well?" he said in a tone of anxious query.

"Well, father dear?"

"Your husband ... what did he say?"

She looked at him, a little bewildered, with a stupid, vacant stare which puzzled him.

"What should he have said, father dear?" she asked. "I do not understand."

"About the fracas to-night, my child. Was he there when Irène de Stainville spoke up so indiscreetly?"

"No ... no ... I mean yes ..." she said vaguely, "yes, milor was there; he heard every word which Irène de Stainville said."

"Well? What did he say?" he repeated with marked impatience. "Lydie, my child, this is not like you. ... Cannot you see that I am anxious? ... I have been waiting here for over an half hour in a perfect agony of uncertainty. ... Your servants told me you were closeted with milor. ... You must tell me what he said."

"He said nothing, father," she replied simply.

"Nothing?"

"Nothing."

Monsieur le Duc looked at her very keenly, but her eyes were clear now and met his straight and full. There was obviously no deceit there, no desire to conceal more serious matters from him. He shrugged his shoulders, in token that he gave up all desire to understand. His son-in-law had always been a shadowy personality to him, and this attitude of his now, in face of the public scandal resting on his wife's name, was quite beyond Monsieur le Duc's comprehension.

Had Lydie told him that her husband had heaped torrents of abuse on her, and had concluded a noisy scene by striking her, he would have been very angry, but he would have understood.

"Hm!" he said placidly, "these English are mad, of a truth; we men of honour here cannot really comprehend them. Nevertheless, my dear Lydie, I suppose I, as your father, must be thankful that he did not lay hands on you, for English husbands are notoriously brutal. You are quite sure that you have nothing to complain of in your husband's conduct?"

"Quite sure, father dear."

"I had come prepared to take you away with me. My coach is below and I am driving to Château d'Aumont to-night. Would you like to come?"

"Not to-night, dear," she replied serenely, and her father was glad to note that a slight smile hovered round her lips. "I am a little tired, and will go straight to bed. ... But to-morrow I'll come."

"Permanently?"

"If you will have me."

"Well! until you go to your Château of Vincennes, you know my views on that subject?"

"Yes, father dear. ... We will talk of that another time. ... I am very tired to-night."

"I understand that, my child," said Monsieur le Duc rather fussily now, and clearing his throat, as if there was something which still oppressed him and of which he would have liked to speak before leaving her.

There was that awkward pause, the result of a want of mutual understanding between two people who hitherto have been all in all to each other, but whom certain untoward events have suddenly drawn apart. Lydie sincerely wished that her father would go. She had much to think about, a great deal to do, and the strain of keeping up a semblance of serenity was very trying to her overwrought nerves. He on the other hand felt uncomfortable in her presence: he left quite angry with himself for not being able to discuss freely with her the subject matter which was uppermost in his mind. There were one or two details in connection with the expedition to the Scottish coast that he very much wanted to talk over with his daughter. The habits of a lifetime gave him the desire to consult her about these details, just as he had been wont to do on all public and official matters. He had come to her apartments chiefly for that purpose. Was she not at one with him, with the King and Gaston over the scheme? She had given substantial proof that she favoured the expedition. His Majesty had thanked her for her help: she had rendered such assistance as now made the whole affair not only feasible but easy of accomplishment.

It was therefore passing strange that Monsieur le Duc d'Aumont still felt an unaccountable bashfulness in her presence when referring to the Stuart prince at all.

So he went to work in a circuitous way, for there was another matter that troubled him, but less so than the expedition: therefore, perhaps, he spoke of it first.

"I presume, my dear child," he said lightly, "that you are sufficiently a woman of the world to understand that some sort of reparation is due from your husband to Monsieur de Stainville."

"Reparation? ..." she asked. "For what?"

Again she stared at him blankly, and with that vague expression of puzzlement which irritated whilst it half-frightened him.

"You were there, my dear," he said impatiently, "you know ... and of course you must have seen ..."

"What?"

"Milor jeered at Gaston, then tripped him up with his foot, so that Monsieur de Stainville measured his full length on the floor."

"I did not notice...." she said simply.

"But many people did ... enough at all events to give Monsieur de Stainville the initiative in the necessary reparation. He was the insulted party."

"Oh! a duel, you mean," she said indifferently, "yes, I suppose my husband will fight Monsieur de Stainville if His Majesty will grant them leave."

"Gaston will not appeal to His Majesty, and milor cannot very well refuse to meet him. The King has oft declared his intention of permanently suppressing all duelling just as it has been done in England. Even to-night after the unfortunate fracas, when I had the honour of paying my final respects, His Majesty said to me: 'If milor Eglinton and Monsieur de Stainville fight and one of them is killed, we'll hang the survivor!'"

"Then they'll not fight, you think?"

Monsieur le Duc stared at his daughter. Such complete

indifference as to her husband's actions in so grave a matter passed the bounds of correct behaviour.

"Mais oui! they will fight, my dear!" he said sternly. "You know as well as I do that Gaston could not pocket the slight put upon him by milor without covering himself with ridicule. But the duel need not be serious ... a scratch or two and no more. ... Gaston is a perfect swordsman ... he never misses his man," added the Duke hesitatingly. "Is milor clever with the foils?"

"I do not know."

"He has never fought a duel to your knowledge?"

"I think never."

"Whilst Gaston's skill is famous. ... But, my dear, you need have no anxiety. ... It was also with a view to reassuring you on the subject that I have sought you so late. ... You will believe your father's word, Lydie, if he tells you that your husband is in no grave danger at the hands of Gaston."

"I thank you, father dear," she rejoined with the same natural, even tone of voice which should have tranquillised him as to her mental condition, but which somehow failed to do so.

"Gaston must take up the matter ... you understand that. ... It is quite public and ... he would be laughed at if he appealed for leave to fight from His Majesty ... the matter was not serious and the result will be likewise. ... Gaston will administer a slight punishment to milor ... such a perfect swordsman, you understand, can select the very place on his opponent's body where he will inflict the scratch ... it will be the shoulder perhaps ... or ... or ... the cheek ... nothing to be anxious about..."

"I am not anxious, father dear," she said with a serene smile, amused in spite of herself at his many circumlocutions, his obvious confusion, and his still quite apparent wish to speak of one more matter which seemed to be weighing on his mind.

"Is that all that you wished to say to me, dear?" she said gently, "for if so I can assure you that you need not be troubled on my account. I am neither anxious nor upset. ... Milor I feel confident will take tender care of his shoulder ... or of his cheek just as he does of his comfort and of his ... his dignity."

"And you will not take it amiss from me, my dear, if I do not offer to be one of your husband's seconds in the affair?" he asked suddenly, throwing off his hesitation and speaking more frankly.

"Certainly not, father dear. ... I feel sure that milor himself would not have suggested it...."

"My position near His Majesty ... you understand, my dear," he explained volubly, "and also my ... our association with Gaston...."

182

"Certainly—certainly," she repeated, emphasizing her words, "our association with Gaston...."

"And he really is acting like a perfect gentleman ... a man of honour...."

"Indeed?"

"His enthusiasm, his courage, and devotion have been quite marvellous. And though we shall primarily owe the success of our enterprise to you, my dear, yet His Majesty feels as I do, that we also owe much to Monsieur de Stainville. Ah! mon Dieu! what it is to be young!"

"What has Monsieur de Stainville done, dear, to arouse your special enthusiasm?" she asked.

"You shall judge of it yourself, my dear. After the esclandre provoked by Irène to-night, the publicity given to our scheme, we held a hurried boudoir meeting, at which His Majesty and Madame de Pompadour were present, as well as myself and Gaston. We all felt that you too should have been there, dear, but you had gone with milor, and ...."

"Yes, yes, never mind about me, father," she interrupted impatiently, seeing that he was getting lost in the mazes of his polite apologies. "You held a boudoir meeting. What did you decide? ...."

"That after the publicity given to the main idea of our scheme, you understand," he rejoined, "it would be no longer safe to wait for its execution until Le Levantin was ready for sea. Something had to be risked, of course, but on the whole we all thought that now that the matter had become 'le secret de Polichinelle' a six days' delay would be dangerous, if not fatal to success. You were not there, Lydie," he repeated diffidently, "we could not consult you...."

"No, no! Then what did you decide?"

"That we must send Le Monarque off at once."

"Le Monarque? ... at once? ...."

"Yes! she is quite ready, so you told me this morning. And though we feared that Captain Barre might be too firm an adherent of the Stuart cause to be altogether reliable, still—as we had your own letter—we finally decided that we had better trust him now, rather than wait for Le Levantin. ... I think we did right, do you not? ... Lydie. ... Lydie ... child, what is it?"

The desperately anxious query had its justification in Lydie's terrible pallor, the wild dilation of her pupils, the dark purple rings which circled her eyes.

As her father spoke she had risen from the divan, and now she seemed unable to stand; she was trembling from head to foot, her hands were held out before her, as in a pathetic appeal for physical support. In a moment his arm was round her, and with gentle force

183

he drew her back to the couch, pressing her head against his shoulder.

"Lydie ... Lydie, dear ... I am sure you are ill."

But already she had recovered from this sudden attack of faintness and dizziness, of which, with characteristic impatience for all feminine weaknesses, she was now thoroughly ashamed. Her nervous system had received so many severe shocks in the course of this terrible and memorable day, that it was small wonder that this last awful blow struck her physically as well as mentally.

"No, no, dear father," she said as lightly as she could for she still felt very faint and ill, "I am quite well, I assure you ... please ... please ..." she urged earnestly, "do not worry about me now, but tell me quite clearly—and as briefly as you can—exactly what are your plans at this moment ... yours and Gaston's, with regard to the expedition against the Stuart prince ... you spoke of a duel just now ... and then of Monsieur de Stainville's enthusiasm and courage. ... I ... I am a little confused ... and I would like to understand."

"I will tell you as briefly as I can, my dear," he rejoined, not feeling altogether reassured, and regarding her with loving anxiety. "We decided that, instead of waiting for Le Levantin to be ready for sea, we would send Le Monarque, and instruct Captain Barre in accordance with the plan and the letter which you gave us, and the secret orders framed by His Majesty and myself. Le Monarque having got the Stuart and his friends on board will make straight for the north-west coast of England, and land the Jacobites at the first possible port, where they can be handed over to the English authorities. Once this was settled, Gaston immediately offered to start for Le Havre at dawn with the secret orders. We are not really afraid of Captain Barre's possible disloyalty—and, of course, he is compelled to obey orders or suffer for his insubordination, which he is not likely to contemplate. On the whole I think we may safely say that we run far less risk by sending Le Monarque than by waiting for Le Levantin: and Gaston has full powers to promise Captain Barre a heavy bribe in accordance with the speed which Le Monarque will make. After that His Majesty was pleased to dismiss Monsieur de Stainville and myself, being most specially gratified with Gaston's enthusiastic offer to ride at breakneck speed to Le Havre, as soon as he could get to horse. Outside the boudoir, Gaston explained to me, however, that he could not shirk the duel with Lord Eglinton: his seconds, Monsieur de Belle-Isle and Monsieur de Lugeac, already had his instructions and would wait on milor to-night: to put it off now would be to cover himself with ridicule and to risk social ostracism; the affront put upon his wife could not be allowed to rest until after his own return. But the duel could take place at dawn, and then he could get to horse half an hour later. ... So you see, my dear, that the duel cannot—because of these weighty reasons—have any serious consequences. As for our expedition, methinks everything now is most satisfactorily arranged, as Gaston swears that he will reach Le Havre ere the shades of the evening fall upon the sea."

Lydie had listened quite quietly to this long explanation, taking in every detail of the project, lest anything should escape her. Her father could indeed be completely reassured. She was perfectly calm, apparently cheerful, and when he had finished speaking she thanked him quite naturally and expressed approval of all that had been done.

"Everything is beautifully planned and arranged, my dear father," she said pleasantly, "methinks I cannot do better than take a rest. I fear I have been overwrought all day and have caused you much anxiety. All is for the best now, is it not? ... Shall we both go to bed?"

Monsieur le Duc sighed with satisfaction. He seemed to have found a long-lost daughter. This was the one he knew, self-possessed, clear-headed, a comfort and a guide.

He drew her to him and kissed her tenderly, and if there was a suggestion of shrinking, of withdrawal in the young body, he was certainly too preoccupied to notice it. He bade her "good-night," and then with obvious relief and a light, elastic step, he finally went out of the room.

CHAPTER XXX

M. DE STAINVILLE'S SECONDS

When Monsieur Achille, having escorted Madame la Marquise as far as her apartments, once more retraced his sedate footsteps toward those occupied by Lord Eglinton, he was much surprised to find the worthy Baptiste Durand in the octagonal room which gave immediately on milor's study.

The wizened little man looked singularly upset; he had a couple of heavy books under his arm: and two large white quills, one behind each ear, gave him the look of a frightened stork.

It was long past the usual hour when M. Durand laden with his bulky books habitually entered the Marquis's private room and remained closeted therein with milor until long past midnight. Every evening at the self-same hour he came to the octagonal room, passed the time of day with Monsieur Achille and then went in, to milor: he always carried a leather bag filled with papers neatly tied in bundles, and he wore a somewhat anxious look when he entered and one of relief when he finally departed. Monsieur Achille had often bent his broad and majestic back, in order to bring his ear down to the level of the keyhole of the door, through which Monsieur Durand invariably disappeared at ten o'clock in the evening; but all the satisfaction which his curiosity obtained was the sound of two voices, one steady and low and the other somewhat shrill, without any individual or comprehensible sentence detaching itself from the irritating babel.

And when M. Durand came out of the room after midnight, he bade Monsieur Achille a curt good-night and invariably refused any information with regard to the work he did for milor at that late hour of the night.

When closely pressed he would vaguely say: "Accounts!" which of course was ridiculous. Monsieur Achille had never heard of a nobleman troubling himself about accounts, at the time when most people of consideration were either at petits soupers or else comfortably in bed.

As time went on Monsieur Achille ceased to take any interest in these nightly proceedings; they were so monotonous and so regular, that they were no longer exciting. But to-night everything seemed changed. M. Durand instead of marching straight through with his books into the study, stood in the middle of the room, a veritable picture of helpless perturbation.

"Why, M. Durand," said Achille greatly astonished, "what ails you? You look as if you had seen a ghost."

"Sh!—-sh!—-sh!" whispered the timorous little man, indicating with a jerk of his lean shoulder the distant door of the study, "do you hear that?"

Monsieur Achille bent his ear to listen. But strive how he might he could hear nothing but the great bracket-clock on the wall ticking monotonously. He shrugged his shoulders to indicate that the worthy Baptiste had been dreaming, but there was a certain look in the wizened face which caused him to tiptoe toward the study door and once more to bring his ear down to the level of the keyhole.

Then he shook his head, and tiptoed back to the centre of the room.

"I can hear nothing," he whispered. "Are you sure he is in there?"

"Quite, quite sure," replied Durand.

"Then why don't you go in as usual?"

"I ... I can't!"

"Why not?"

"I ... I don't know. ... I seemed to hear such a funny sound as if..." he paused a moment searching for the words that would best render his impression of what he had heard. Finding none apparently, he reiterated:

"It is a very funny sound."

"Perhaps milor was asleep and snoring," suggested the practical Achille.

"No, no," protested Durand very energetically.

"Or ill ..."

"Ah yes! ... perhaps ..." stammered the little man, "perhaps milor is ill."

"Then I'll to him at once."

And before M. Durand could prevent him—which undoubtedly he would have done—Achille had gone back to the study door and loudly knocked thereat.

At first there was no answer. M. Achille knocked again, and yet again, until a voice from within suddenly said:

"Who is it?"

"Achille, M. le Marquise!" responded the worthy with alacrity.

"I want nothing," said the voice. "Tell Durand that I shall not need him to-night."

M. Durand nearly dropped his heavy books on the floor.

"Not want me!" he ejaculated; "we shall get terribly in arrears!"

"Will milor go to bed?" again queried M. Achille.

"No!" came somewhat impatiently from within. "Do not wait up for me. If I want you later I will ring."

Achille looked at M. Durand and the worthy Baptiste returned the look of puzzlement and wonder. Both shrugged their shoulders.

"There's nothing to be done, my good Baptiste," said Achille at last; "you had best take your paraphernalia away and go to bed. I know that tone of voice, I have heard it once before when ... but never mind that," he added abruptly checking himself, as if he feared to commit an indiscretion, "enough that I know if milor says, in that tone of voice, that he does not want you and that you are to go away—well then, my good Durand, he does not want you and you are to go away. ... Do you see?"

187

And having delivered himself of this phrase of unanswerable logic he pointed toward the door.

M. Durand was about to take his friend's sound advice, when a loud ring broke in upon the silence which had fallen over this portion of the stately palace.

"A visitor at this late hour," mused Monsieur Achille. "Ma foi! methinks perhaps milor was expecting a fair and tardy visitor. ... eh, M. Durand? ... and that perhaps this was the reason why you and I were to go away ... eh? ... and why you were not wanted to-night, ... What?"

M. Durand was doubtful as to that, but there was no time to discuss that little matter, for a second ring, louder and more peremptory than the first, caused M. Achille to pull himself together, to flick at his cravat, and to readjust the set of his coat, whilst M. Durand loath to retire before he knew something of the tardy visitor, withdrew with books, bag and papers into a dark corner of the room.

Already the sound of approaching footsteps drew nearer; the visitor had been admitted and was now being escorted through the reception rooms by the two footmen carrying torches. The next moment the doors leading to the official suite of apartments were thrown open, M. Achille put himself in position in the centre of the room, whilst a loud voice from the distant hall announced:

"M. le Marquis de Belle-Isle! M. le Comte de Lugeac!"

Achille's broad back was bent nearly double. The names were well known to him and represented, if not exactly the flower of aristocratic France, at least the invisible power which swayed her destinies. M. le Marquis de Belle-Isle was Madame de Pompadour's best friend, and M. de Lugeac was her nephew.

"Your master ... is he within?"

It was M. de Belle-Isle who spoke; his voice was loud and peremptory, the voice of a man who only recently had been in a position to command.

"Milor is ... er ... within, M. le Marquis," said Achille with slight hesitation. It is not often that he was taken aback when in the exercise of his duties, but the situation was undoubtedly delicate, and he had not yet made up his mind exactly how he ought to deal with it.

Neither of the two gentlemen, however, seemed to have any intention of leaving him much longer in doubt.

"Go and tell him at once," said M. de Lugeac, "that Monsieur le Marquis de Belle-Isle and myself will have to trouble him for about two minutes."

Then as Achille seemed to be hesitating—for he did not move

188

with any alacrity and his well-kept hand stroked his smooth, heavy chin—M. de Belle-Isle added more loudly:

"Go knave! and at once. ... Par le diable, man! ... how dare you hesitate?"

Indeed Monsieur Achille dared do that no longer. M. le Marquis de Belle-Isle was not a gentleman to be trifled with so he shrugged his majestic shoulders, and rubbed his hands together in token that the affair had passed out of their keeping, and that he no longer held himself responsible for any unpleasant consequences which might accrue from such unparalleled intrusion.

He strode with becoming majesty to the study door, his broad, straight back emphasising the protest of his whole attitude. Once more he knocked, but more loudly, less diffidently than before.

The voice from within queried with marked impatience:

"What is it now?"

"An urgent call, Monsieur le Marquis!" replied Achille in a firm voice.

"I can see no one. I am busy," said the voice from within.

M. de Belle-Isle felt that this little scene was not quite dignified; neither he nor M. de Lugeac was accustomed to stand behind a lacquey's back, parleying with a man through closed doors: therefore when Monsieur Achille turned to him now with a look which strove to indicate respectfully but firmly that the incident was closed, he pushed him roughly aside and himself called loudly:

"Pardi, Marquis, methinks you are over-anxious to forbid your door to-night. I, André de Belle-Isle and my friend le Comte de Lugeac desire a word with you. We represent M. le Comte de Stainville, and unless you are closeted with a lady, I summon you to open this door."

Then as the door remained obstinately closed—too long at any rate for M. le Marquis's impatience—he boldly placed his hand on the knob and threw it open. The heavy panels flew back, revealing Lord Eglinton sitting at his secrétaire writing. His head was resting on his hand, but he turned to look at the two gentlemen, as they stood, momentarily silent and subdued in the doorway itself. He rose to greet them, but stared at them somewhat astonished and not a little haughtily, and he made no motion requesting them to enter.

"We crave your pardon, milor," began Monsieur de Belle-Isle, feeling, as he afterward explained, unaccountably bashful and crestfallen, "we would not have intruded, M. de Lugeac and I, only that there was a slight formality omitted this evening without which we cannot proceed and which we must pray you to fulfill."

"What formality, Monsieur?" asked milor courteously. "I am afraid I do not understand."

"The whole incident occurred very rapidly, we must admit," continued M. de Belle-Isle still standing in the doorway, still unwilling apparently to intrude any further on this man whom he had known for some time, yet who seemed to have become an utter stranger to him now: haughty, grave and courteous, with an extraordinary look of aloofness in the face which repelled the very suggestion of familiarity. "And that is no doubt the reason, milor, why you omitted to name your seconds to Monsieur de Stainville."

"My seconds?" repeated milor. "I am afraid you must think me very stupid ... but I still do not understand ..."

"But surely, milor ..." protested M. de Belle-Isle, a little taken aback.

"Would you be so kind as to explain? ... if it is necessary."

"Necessary? Pardi, I should not have thought that it had been necessary. You, milor, in yourself also and through Madame la Marquise your wife have insulted M. le Comte de Stainville and Madame la Comtesse too. We represent M. le Comte de Stainville in this affair, wherein we presume that you are prepared to give him satisfaction. And we have come to-night, milor, to ask you kindly to name your own representatives so that we may arrange the details of this encounter in the manner pre-eminently satisfactory to M. le Comte de Stainville, since he is the aggrieved party."

Gradually M. de Belle-Isle had raised his voice. His feeling of bashfulness had entirely left him and he felt not a little wrathful at this strange rôle which he was being made to play. It was quite unheard of that a gentleman who had so grossly insulted another, as Lord Eglinton had insulted M. de Stainville, should require such lengthy explanations as to what the next course of events would necessarily be.

"Therefore, milor," he continued with some acerbity as Lord Eglinton had vouchsafed no reply to his tirade, "we pray you to name your seconds to us, without delay, so that we may no longer intrude upon your privacy."

"I need not do that, M. le Marquis," said milor quietly. "I require no seconds."

"No seconds?" gasped the two gentlemen with one breath.

"I am not going to fight M. de Stainville."

If Lord Eglinton had suddenly declared his intention of dethroning King Louis and placing the crown of France on his own head, he could not more have astonished his two interlocutors. Both M. de Belle-Isle and M. de Lugeac were in fact absolutely speechless: in all their vast experience of Court life such a situation had never occurred before, and literally neither of them knew exactly how to deal with it. M. de Lugeac, young and arrogant, was the first to recover his presence of mind. Like his successful relative Jeanne Poisson de Pompadour he had been born in the slums of Paris, his exalted fortune, following so quickly in the wake of the ex-victualler's wife, had given him an assurance and an amount of impudence which the older de Belle-Isle lacked, and which stood him in good stead in the present crisis.

"Are we to look on this as a formal refusal, milor?" he now asked boldly.

"As you please."

"You will not give M. le Comte de Stainville the satisfaction usually agreed upon between men of honour?"

"I will not fight M. de Stainville," repeated milor quietly. "I am busy with other things."

"But milor," here interposed M. de Belle-Isle testily: "you cannot have reflected on the consequences of such an act, which I myself at this moment would hardly dare to characterize."

"You will excuse me, gentlemen," said Lord Eglinton with seeming irrelevance, "but is there any necessity for prolonging this interview?"

"None at all," sneered M. de Lugeac. "It is not our business to comment on milor's conduct ... at present," he added with audacious significance.

But M. de Belle-Isle, who, in spite of his undignified adherence to the Pompadour and her faction, was a sprig of the old noblesse of France, was loath to see the humiliation of a high-born gentleman—whatever his faults might be—before such an upstart as de Lugeac. A kindly instinct, not altogether unexplainable, caused him to say encouragingly:

"Let me assure you, milor—though perhaps in this I am overstepping my official powers—that M. le Comte de Stainville has no desire to deal harshly with you. The fact that he is the most noted swordsman in France may perhaps be influencing you at this moment, but will you trust to my old experience when I assure you that M. le Comte's noted skill is your very best safeguard? He will be quite content to inflict a slight punishment on you—being a past master with his sword he can do that easily, without causing you graver injury. I am telling you this in confidence of course, because I know that these are his intentions. Moreover he starts on an important journey to-morrow and would propose a very brief encounter with you at dawn, in one of the spinneys of the Park. A mere scratch, I assure you, you need fear no more. Less he could not in all honour concede."

A whimsical smile played round the corners of milor's mouth, chasing momentarily the graver expression of his face.

"Your assurance is more than kind, M. de Belle-Isle," he said with perfect courtesy, "but I can only repeat what I said just now, that I will not fight M. de Stainville."

"And instead of repeating what I said just now, milor ..." said de Lugeac with a wicked leer.

"You will elect to hold your tongue," said M. de Belle-Isle authoritatively, placing his hand on the younger man's wrist.

De Lugeac, who lived in perpetual fear of doing or saying something which would inevitably betray his plebeian origin, meekly obeyed M. de Belle-Isle's command. The latter, though very bewildered, would be sure to know the correct way in which gentlemen should behave under these amazing circumstances.

Lord Eglinton standing beside his secrétaire, his face in shadow, was obviously waiting for these intruders to go. M. de Belle-Isle shrugged his shoulders partly in puzzlement, partly in contempt; then he nodded casually to milor, turned on his heel, and walked out of the doorway into the octagonal room beyond, whilst M. de Lugeac imitated as best he could the careless nod and the look of contempt of his older friend. M. Achille stepping forward now closed the study doors behind the two gentlemen, shutting out the picture of that grave, haughty man who had just played the part of coward with such absolute perfection.

"Bah! these English!" said young de Lugeac, as he made the gesture of spitting on the ground. "I had not believed it, par tous les diables! had I not heard with mine own ears."

But de Belle-Isle gravely shook his head.

"I fear me the young man is only putting off the evil day. His skin will have to be tough indeed if he can put up with ... well! with what he will get when this business becomes known."

"And it will become known," asserted de Lugeac spitefully. He had always hated what he called the English faction. Madame Lydie always snubbed him unmercifully, and milor had hitherto most conveniently ignored his very existence. "By G—d I hope that my glove will be the first to touch his cheek."

"Sh!—sh!—sh!" admonished de Belle-Isle, nodding toward Achille who was busy with the candelabrum.

"Nay! what do I care," retorted the other; "had you not restrained me I'd have called him a dirty coward then and there."

"That had been most incorrect, my good Lugeac," rejoined de Belle-Isle drily, and wilfully ignoring the language which, in moments of passion, so plainly betrayed the vulgar origin. "The right to insult Lord Eglinton belongs primarily to Gaston de Stainville, and afterward only to his friends."

And although M. le Marquis de Belle-Isle expressed himself in more elegant words than his plebeian friend, there was none the less spite and evil intent in the expression of his face as he spoke.

Then giving a sign to Achille to precede them with the light, the two representatives of M. le Comte de Stainville finally strode out of the apartments of the ex-Comptroller General of Finance.

M. Durand, with his bulky books and his papers under his arms, followed meekly, repeatedly shaking his head.

CHAPTER XXXI

THE FINAL DISAPPOINTMENT

Lydie waited a few moments while her father's brisk steps died away along the stone-flagged corridors. In the silence of the evening, the quietude which rested on this distant portion of the palace, she could hear his brief word of command to the valet who had been stationed in the antechamber; then the Duke's quick, alert descent down the marble staircase, and finally the call for his coach oft repeated, when he reached the terrace and began skirting the building on his way to the main paved yard, where, no doubt, his horses were awaiting his return.

When everything in and around the palace seemed quiet again, Lydie rang for her maid.

"A dark hood and cloak," she ordered as soon as the girl appeared, and speaking very rapidly.

"Madame la Marquise goes out again?" asked the maid a little anxiously, seeing that the hour was late and she herself very sleepy.

"Only within the palace," replied Lydie. "Quick, girl! the cloak!"

Within two or three minutes she was enveloped from head to foot in a cloak of dark woollen material, that effectually hid the beautiful gown beneath. Then she bade the girl wait for her in her boudoir, and, not heeding the latter's anxious protestations, she walked quickly out of the room.

The corridors and reception halls were now quite deserted. Even from the main building of the palace, where the King himself was wont to sup copiously and long, there no longer came the faintest echo of revelry, of laughter or of music. The vast château built at the cost of a nation's heart's blood, kept up at the cost of her tears and her humiliation, now lay wrapped in sleep.

In this remote West Wing the silence was almost oppressive. From her own apartments Lydie could reach those occupied by milor, without going through the ante-chamber and corridors, where a few night-watchmen were always stationed. Thus she could pass unperceived; a dark, ghost-like figure, silent and swift, gliding through an enchanted castle, inhabited mayhap only by a sleeping beauty and her Court. From outside not a sound, save the occasional hoot of an owl or the flap of a bat's wings against the projecting masonry.

Lydie drew her cloak closely round her figure; though the August night was hot and heavy with the acrid scent of late summer flowers she felt an inward shivering, whilst her temples throbbed and her eyes seemed made of glowing charcoal. A few more rooms to traverse, a few moments longer wherein to keep her trembling knees from giving way beneath her, and she would be in milor's rooms.

She was a little astonished to find them just as deserted as the rest of the palace. The great audience chamber with its monumental bed, the antechamber wherein M. Durand's wizened figure always sat enthroned behind the huge secrétaire, and the worthy Baptiste himself was wont to hold intrusive callers at bay, all these rooms were empty, silent and sombre.

At last she reached the octagonal room, out of which opened the study. Here, too, darkness reigned supreme save for a thin streak of light which gleamed, thin and weird, from beneath the study door. Darkness itself fought with absolute stillness. Lydie came forward, walking as if in her sleep.

She called to milor's valet: "Achille!" but only in a whisper, lest milor from within should hear. Then as there was no sound, no movement, she called once more:

"Achille! is milor still awake? Achille! are you here?"

She had raised her voice a little, thinking the man might be asleep. But no sound answered her, save from outside the cry of a bird frightened by some midnight prowler.

Then she walked up to the door. There behind it, in that inner sanctum hung with curtains of dull gold, the man still sat whom she had so often, so determinedly wronged, and who had wounded her to-night with a cruelty and a surety of hand which had left her broken of spirit, bruised of heart, a suffering and passionate woman. She put her hand on the knob of the door. Nothing stirred within; milor was writing mayhap! Perhaps he had dropped asleep!

And Gaston preparing to ride to Le Havre in order to send the swiftest ship to do its deed of treachery!

No! no! anything but that!

At this moment Lydie had nerved herself to endure every rebuff, to suffer any humiliation, to throw herself at her husband's feet, embrace his knees if need be, beg, pray and entreat for money, for help, anything that might even now perhaps avert the terrible catastrophe.

Boldly now she knocked at the door.

"Milor! milor! open! ... it is I! ... ! Lydie. ... !"

Then as there was no answer from within she knocked louder still.

"Milor! Milor! awake! Milor! in the name of Heaven I entreat you to let me speak with you!"

At first she had thought that he slept, then that obstinate resentment caused him to deny her admittance. She tried to turn the knob of the door, but it did not yield.

"Milor! Milor!" she cried again, and then again.

Naught but silence was the reply.

Excitement grew upon her now, a febrile nervousness which caused her to pull at the lock, to bruise her fingers against the gilt ornaments of the panel, whilst her voice, hoarse and broken with sobs, rent with its echoes the peace and solemnity of the night.

"Milor! Milor!"

She had fallen on her knees, exhausted mentally and physically, the blood beating against her temples until the blackness around her seemed to have become a vivid red. In her ear was a sound like that of a tempestuous sea breaking against gigantic rocks, with voices calling at intervals, voices of dying men, loudly accusing her of treachery. The minutes were speeding by! Anon would come the dawn when Gaston would to horse, bearing the hideous message which would mean her lifelong infamy and the death of those who trusted her.

"Milor! milor! awake!" She now put her lips to the keyhole, breathing the words through the tiny orifice, hoping that he would hear. "Gaston will start at dawn ... They will send Le Monarque, and she is ready to put to sea ... Milor! your friend is in deadly peril. . . ! I entreat you to let me enter!"

She beat her hands against the door, wounding her delicate flesh. She was not conscious of what she was doing. A mystic veil divided her reasoning powers from that terrible mental picture which glowed before her through the blood-red darkness. The lonely shore, the angry sea, the French ship Le Monarque flying the pennant of traitors!

Then suddenly an astonished and deeply horrified voice broke in upon her ears.

"Madame la Marquise, in the name of Heaven! Madame la Marquise!"

She heard quick footsteps behind her, and left off hammering against the door, left off screaming and moaning, but she had not the power to raise herself from her knees.

"Madame la Marquise," came in respectful, yet frightened accents, "will Madame la Marquise deign to allow me to raise her—I fear Madame la Marquise is not well!"

She recognized the voice of Achille, milor's valet, yet it never entered her mind to feel ashamed at being found by a lacquey, thus kneeling before her husband's door. The worthy Achille was very upset. Etiquette forbade him to touch Madame la Marquise, but could he leave her there? in that position? He advanced timidly. His behaviour was superlatively correct even in this terrible emergency, and there was nothing in his deferential attitude to indicate that he thought anything abnormal had occurred.

"I thought I heard Madame la Marquise calling," he said, "and I thought perhaps Madame la Marquise would wish to speak with milor ..."

But at the word she quickly interrupted him; rising to her feet even as she spoke.

"Yes! yes ... ! milor ... I do wish to speak with him ... open the door, Achille ... quick ..."

"The door is locked on the outside, Madame la Marquise, but I have the key by me," said M. Achille gravely. "I had fortunately recollected that mayhap milor had forgotten to put out the lights, and would in any case have come to see that all was safe ... if Madame la Marquise will deign to permit me ..."

It was a little difficult to reconcile utmost respect of movement and demeanour with the endeavour to open the door against which Madame la Marquise was still standing. However, everything that was deferential and correct was possible to Monsieur Achille; he fitted the key in the lock and the next moment had thrown the door wide open, whilst he himself stood immediately aside to enable Madame la Marquise to enter.

Four candles were burning in one of the candelabra; milor had evidently forgotten to extinguish them. Everything else in the room was perfectly tidy. On the secrétaire there were two or three heavy books similar to those Monsieur Durand usually carried about with him when he had to interview milor, also the inkpot and sand-well, with two or three quills methodically laid on a silver tray. One window must have been open behind the drawn curtains, for

196

the heavy damask hangings waved gently in the sudden current of air, caused by the opening of the door. The candles too, flickered weirdly in the draught. In the centre of the room was the armchair on which Lydie had sat a while ago, the cushion of red embroidery which milor had put to her back, and below the little footstool covered in gold brocade on which her foot had rested ... a while ago.

And beside the secrétaire his own empty chair, and on the table the spot where his hand had rested, white and slightly tremulous, when she proffered her self-accusation.

"Milor?" she murmured inquiringly, turning glowing eyes, dilated with the intensity of disappointment and despair on the impassive face of Achille, "milor ... ? where is milor?"

"Milor has been gone some little time, Madame la Marquise," replied Achille.

"Gone? Whither?"

"I do not know, Madame la Marquise ... Milor did not tell me ... Two gentlemen called to see him at about ten o'clock; as soon as they had gone milor asked for his outdoor clothes and Hector booted and spurred him ... whilst I dressed his hair and tied his cravat ... Milor has been gone about half an hour, I think."

"Enough ... that will do!"

That is all that she contrived to say. This final disappointment had been beyond the endurance of her nerves. Physically now she completely broke down, a mist gathered before her eyes, the candles seemed to flicker more and more weirdly until their lights assumed strange ghoul-like shapes which drew nearer to her and nearer; faces in the gloom grinned at her and seemed to mock, the walls of the room closed in around her, her senses reeled, her very brain felt as if it throbbed with pain, and without a cry or moan, only with one long sigh of infinite weariness, she sank lifeless to the ground.

CHAPTER XXXII

THE DAWN

M. le Comte de Stainville only shrugged his shoulders when M. de Belle-Isle and young de Lugeac brought him milor's reply.

"Bah!" he said with a sneer, "he'll have to fight me later on or

I'll hound him out of France! Never fear, gentlemen, we'll have our meed of fun very soon."

On the whole Gaston was not sorry that this stupid so-called "affair of honour" would not force him to rise before dawn. He had no special ill-will against le petit Anglais, for whom he had always tried to cultivate a modicum of contempt. He had not always succeeded in this praiseworthy endeavour, for milor as a rule chose to ignore M. de Stainville, as far as, and often more than, courtesy permitted.

The two men had not often met since the memorable evening when milor snatched the golden prize which Gaston had so clumsily cast aside. Their tastes were very dissimilar, and so was their entourage. Milor was officially considered to belong to the Queen's set, whilst Gaston clung to the more entertaining company of Madame de Pompadour and her friends; nor had M. de Stainville had the bad grace to interfere with his wife's obvious predeliction for Lord Eglinton's company.

The memorable day which was just drawing to its close had seen many changes—changes that were almost upheavals of old traditions and of habitual conditions of court life. Gaston had deceived and then hideously outraged the woman whom long ago he had already wronged. A year ago she had humiliated him, had snatched from him the golden prize which his ambition had coveted, and which she made him understand that he could not obtain without her. To-day had been his hour; he had dragged her down to the very mire in which he himself had grovelled, he had laid her pride to dust and shaken the pinnacle of virtue and integrity on which she stood.

That she had partly revenged herself by a public affront against Irène mattered little to Gaston. He had long ago ceased to care for la belle brune de Bordeaux, the beautiful girl who had enchained his early affections and thereby become a bar to his boundless ambition. The social ostracism—applicable only by a certain set of puritanical dévotes—and the disdain of Queen Marie Leszcynska which his wife might have to endure would be more than compensated by the gratitude of Pompadour and of His Majesty himself, for the services rendered by Gaston in the cause of the proffered English millions.

But for him the expedition against the Stuart prince could never have been undertaken; at any rate, it had been fraught with great difficulties; delays and subsequent failure would probably have resulted. Gaston de Stainville felt sure that in the future he could take care that the King should never forget his services.

After his wife's indiscreet outburst he feared once more for the success of the plan. Remembering Lydie's reliance on Le Monarque and her commander, he declared himself prepared to start for Le Havre immediately. He was quite ready to display that endurance and enthusiasm, in the breakneck ride across the fields of Normandy, which Lydie had thought to find in him for the good of a noble cause.

Gaston de Stainville's pockets were always empty; the two millions which the King had promised him would be more than welcome. His Majesty had even offered to supplement these by an additional half million if Le Monarque sailed out of Le Havre before sunset on the morrow.

The incident of the duel with milor would have delayed matters and—who knows—perhaps have made that pleasant half million somewhat problematical. Therefore Gaston received the news of the refusal with a sardonic grin, but not with real impatience.

He felt really no great ill-will toward Lord Eglinton; but for that incident when he was forcibly made to measure his length on the parquet floor, Gaston would have willingly extended a condescending hand to the man whose wife he had so infamously wronged.

The incident itself had angered him only to the extent of desiring to inflict a physical punishment on milor. Sure of his own wrist as the most perfect swordsman in France, he had fondled the thought of slicing off a finger or two, mayhap a thumb, from the hand of le petit Anglais, or better still of gashing milor's face across nose and cheek so as to mar for ever those good looks which the ladies of Versailles had so openly admired.

Well! all these pleasant little occurrences could happen yet. M. de Stainville was quite sure that on his return from Le Havre he could provoke the Englishman to fight. Milor might be something of a coward—obviously he was one, else he had accepted so mild a challenge—but he could not always refuse to fight in the face of certain provocation, which would mean complete social ruin if disregarded.

The hour was late by the time Gaston de Stainville had bade good-night to Belle-Isle and Lugeac. Together the three men had drunk copiously, had laughed much and sneered continually at the pusillanimous Englishman.

"This comes of allowing all these aliens to settle amongst us," said de Lugeac impudently; "soon there will be neither honour nor chivalry left in France."

Whereupon de Stainville and Belle-Isle, both of whom bore ancient, aristocratic names, bethought themselves that it was time to break up the little party and to turn their backs on this arrogant gutter-snipe.

The three men separated at midnight. De Lugeac had a room in the palace, and Stainville and Belle-Isle repaired to their respective lodgings in the little town itself.

Soon after dawn Gaston de Stainville was on horseback. He started alone, for that extra half million was dangling before his eyes, and he was afraid that companionship—even that of a servant—might cause unlooked-for delay. He had a hundred and eighty leagues by road and field to cover, and soon the day would become very hot. He meant to reach Le Havre before five o'clock in the afternoon; within an hour after that, he could have handed over his instructions to Captain Barre, and seen Le Monarque unfurl her sails and glide gracefully out of the harbour: an argosy anon to be laden with golden freight.

The little town of Versailles had scarce opened its eyes to the new day when the clink of a horse's hoofs on her cobble stones roused her from her morning sleep.

A few farmers, bringing in their produce from their gardens, gazed with keen interest at the beautiful animal and her gallant rider. The hour was indeed early for such a fine gentleman to be about.

Soon the rough paving of the town was left behind; the sun, who at first had hidden his newly-awakened glory behind a bank of clouds, now burnt his way through these heavy veils, and threw across the morning sky living flames of rose, of orange, and of vivid gold and tipped the towers and spires of distant Paris with innumerable tongues of fire.

Far away the clock of Notre Dame tolled the hour of five. Gaston cursed inwardly. It was later than he thought, later than he had intended to make a start. That business of the duel had kept him up longer than usual and he had felt lazy and tired in the morning. Now he would have to make top speed, and he did not feel as alert, nor so well prepared for the fatigues of a long day's ride, as he would have been two years ago, before the enervating dissipations of court life at Versailles had undermined the activity of his youth.

Fortunately the ground was soft and dry, the air keen and pure, and Gaston spurred his horse to a canter across the fields.

CHAPTER XXXIII

THE RIDE

It is one hundred and fifty leagues from Versailles to the harbour of Le Havre as the crow flies, one hundred and eighty most like by road and across fields.

Gaston had twelve hours in which to cover the ground, a good horse, and the enthusiasm born of empty pockets when two and a half million livres loom temptingly at the end of the journey.

The fields, after the corn harvest, were excellent for a gallop, yielding just sufficiently to the mare's hoofs to give her a pleasant foothold, but not in any way spongy, with good stubble to give resistance and the sandy soil below to prevent the slightest jar. Riding under such conditions, in the cool hours of the morning, was distinctly pleasant.

Gaston reached Nantes soon after seven, having covered close on forty leagues of his journey without unduly tiring Belle Amie. He was a good rider and knew how to ease her, and there was Arab blood in her. She made light of the work, and enjoyed her gallops, being of the breed that never shows fatigue, own daughter to Jedran who had carried Maurice de Saxe on his famous ride from Paris to Saargemund, three hundred leagues in eighteen hours.

At Nantes, Stainville partook of a frugal breakfast, and Belle Amie had a rest and a mouthful of corn. He was again to horse within half an hour, crossing the Seine here by the newly constructed stone bridge, thence on toward Elboeuf. By ten o'clock the sun was high in the heavens and was pouring heat like molten lead down on horse and rider. Progress had become much slower. Several halts had to be made at tiny wayside inns for a cooling drink and a rub down for Belle Amie. The enjoyment had gone out of the ride. It was heavy, arduous work, beside which despatch riding, with message of life and death, was mere child's play.

But this was not a case of life and death, but of that which was far dearer to Gaston than life without it. Money! money at the end of it all! even if Belle Amie dropped on the roadside and he himself had to cover the rest of the distance on foot. An extra half million if La Monarque set sail before sunset to-day.

At Rouen, horse and rider had to part company. Belle Amie, who had covered close on a hundred leagues, and most of it in the full glare of the midday sun, wanted at least a couple of hours rest if she was to get to Le Havre at all, and this her rider was unwilling to give her. At the posting hostelry, which stands immediately at the rear of the cathedral, Stainville bargained for a fresh horse, and left Belle Amie in charge of mine host to be tended and cared for against his return, probably on the morrow.

Here, too, he partook of a light midday meal whilst the horse was being got ready for him. A good, solid Normandy mare this time, a perfect contrast to Belle Amie, short and thick in the legs, with a broad crupper, and a sleepy look in her eye. But she was a comfortable mount as Gaston soon found out, with a smooth, even canter, and though her stride was short, she got over the ground quickly enough. It was still very hot, but the roads beyond Rouen were sandy and light; the lanes were quite stoneless and shaded by tall trees; the Normandy mare settled down along them to an easy amble. She had not the spirit of Belle Amie but she made up in stolidity what she had lacked in swiftness. Gaston's first impatience at the slowness of her gait soon yielded to content, for she needed no checking, and urging being useless—since she could go no faster—the rider was soon able to let his mind rest and even to sink into semi-somnolence, trusting himself to the horse entirely.

At half-past five the towers of Notre Dame du Havre were in sight; an hour later than Gaston had dared to hope, but still far from the hour of sunset, and if he could infuse a sufficiency of enthusiasm into the commander of Le Monarque, the gallant ship could still negotiate the harbour before dusk, the tide being favourable, and be out in the open ere the first stars appeared in the heavens.

The little seaport town, whose tortuous, unpaved, and narrow streets were ankle deep in slimy mud in spite of the persistent heat and dryness of the day, appeared to Gaston like the golden city of his dreams. On his left the wide mouth of the Seine, with her lonely shore beyond, was lost in the gathering mist, which rose rapidly now after the intense heat of the day. On his right, a few isolated houses were dotted here and there, built of mud, thatched and plastered over, and with diminutive windows not more than a few inches square, because of the tax which was heavy; they testified to the squalor and misery of their inhabitants, a few families earning an uncertain livelihood with their nets. Soon along the length of the river, as it gradually widened toward its mouth, a few isolated craft came to view; fishing boats these mostly, with here and there a graceful brigantine laden with timber, and a few barges which did a precarious coasting-trade with salted fish and the meagre farm produce of the environs.

Gaston de Stainville took no heed of these, though the scene—

if somewhat mournful and desolate—had a certain charm of rich colouring and hazy outline in the glow of the afternoon sun. The heat had altogether abated, and the damp which rose from the spongy soil, peculiar to the bed of the river, was already making itself felt. Gaston shivered beneath the light cloth coat which he had donned in the morning, in view of the fatigues of a hot summer's day. His eyes peered anxiously ahead and to the left of him. His mare, who had borne him stolidly for over five hours, was quite ready to give way; there was no Arab blood in her to cause her to go on until she dropped. She had settled down to a very slow jog-trot, which was supremely uncomfortable to the rider, whose tired back could scarcely endure this continuous jar. Fortunately the straggling, outlying portions of the townlet were already far behind; the little mud houses appeared quite frequently now, and from them, wizened figures came out to the doorway; women in ragged kirtles and children half-naked but for a meagre shift, gazed, wide-eyed, at the mud-bespattered cavalier and his obviously worn-out mount.

From the fine old belfry the chime had long tolled the half hour. Gaston vainly tried to spur the mare to a final effort. She had reached a stage of fatigue when blows would not have quickened her steps, whilst her rider, roused from his own somnolent weariness, was suddenly alert and eager. Goal was indeed in sight. The mud huts even had been left behind, and one or two stone houses testified to the importance of the town and the well-being of its inhabitants; the first inn—a miserable wooden construction quite uninviting even after a day's ride—had already been passed. Ahead was the church of Notre Dame, the fish market, and the residence of the governor; beyond were some low wooden buildings, suggestive of barracks, whilst the Seine, ever widening until her further shore was finally lost in the mist, now showed an ever-varying panorama of light and heavy craft upon her breast; brigantines, and fishing boats, and the new-fashioned top-sail schooners, and far ahead, majestic and sedate, one or two three-deckers of His Majesty's own navy.

Gaston strained his eyes, wondering which of these was Le Monarque!

CHAPTER XXXIV

"LE MONARQUE"

A few minutes later he had reached the principal inn of the town, "L'Auberge des Trois Matelots," immediately opposite the rough wooden jetty, and from the bay window of which Gaston immediately thought that a magnificent view must be obtainable of the stretch of the river and the English Channel far away.

He turned into the gate. The house itself was low, one-storied only, and built entirely of wood round a central court-yard, which was as deep in slime as the rest of the town of Le Havre. Opposite Gaston as he rode in, were some primitive stablings, and on his right some equally primitive open sheds; the remaining two sides apparently stood for the main portion of the building, as several doors gave upon a covered verandah, to which some four or five steps gave access.

A weary-eyed ostler in a blue blouse and huge wooden sabots, from which bunches of straw protruded at the heel came leisurely forward when Gaston drew rein. He seemed to have emerged from nowhere in particular, risen out of the mud mayhap, but he held the mare none too clumsily when M. le Comte dismounted.

The next moment a portly figure appeared in one of the doorways under the verandah, clad precisely like the ostler, save for the gorgeous scarlet kerchief round the gargantuan neck, whilst another, equally bright in hue, peeped out of the pocket of the blouse.

Above the scarlet neckerchief a round face, red as a Normandy apple, was turned meditatively on the mud-stained cavalier, whilst a pair of small, beady eyes blinked drowsily at the afternoon sun.

"See that the mare gets a good rub down at once, then a feed of corn with a dash of eau-de-vie in it, a litter of straw, and a drink of water; she is done to death," said Gaston, peremptorily to the sleepy-looking ostler. "I'll be round in a quarter of an hour to see if she is comfortable, and give you a taste of my whip if she is not."

The ostler did not reply, neither did he touch his forelock in token of obedience. He smothered a yawn and with slow, dragging steps he led the over-tired mare toward the rough stabling in the rear. Gaston then turned toward the verandah and to the few wooden steps which led up to the doorway, wherein the apple-faced man still stood with his hands behind him, drowsily blinking at the unexpected visitor.

"Are you the innkeeper?" asked Gaston curtly.

"Yes, M'sieu," replied the other with great deliberation.

"I shall want a good room for the night, and a well-cooked supper. See to it at once."

Mine host's placidity gave way somewhat at these peremptory orders, which were accompanied by a loud and significant tapping of a whip across a riding boot. But the placidity did not yield to eagerness, only to a certain effort at sulky protest, as Gaston, having mounted the steps, now stood facing him in his own doorway.

"My house is full, M'sieu ..." he began.

"I am on the King's business," shouted Gaston now with angry impatience, "so none of this nonsense. Understand?"

Evidently mine host not only understood, but thought it best to obey with as good grace as he could muster. He stepped aside still somewhat grudgingly, and allowed Gaston de Stainville to enter: but he did not condescend to bow nor did he bid M'sieu the visitor welcome in his house.

Gaston however was not minded to notice the fat man's sulky temper. The moodiness of provincial innkeepers had become proverbial in France; they seemed to look upon all guests, who brought money into their pockets, as arrogant intruders, and treated them accordingly.

"See to a decent supper at once," repeated de Stainville now with that peremptoriness which he knew would alone ensure civility, "and send a wench into my room to see that it is properly aired, and that clean linen is put upon the bed."

The warning was no doubt necessary, judging by the appearance of the room in which Gaston now found himself. It was low and stuffy in the extreme. He was conscious of nothing else for the moment, as only two diminutive windows, hermetically closed, admitted a tiny modicum of light through four dirty and thick panes of rough glass. On the left there was a door evidently leading to another and larger room from which—as this door was ajar—came the sound of voices and also suffocating gusts of very pungent tobacco.

Obviously there was some light and air in that further room, whereas here it seemed to Gaston as if only cave-dwellers and moles could live and breathe.

"You had best serve my supper in there," he said, pointing with his riding whip toward that half-open door, and without waiting for the protests which mine host was obviously preparing himself to make, he strode boldly toward it and pushed it fully open.

The place was certainly very different to the one which he had just quitted. The floor was strewn with clean white sand, and, though the air was thick with the fumes of that same pungent tobacco, which already had offended Gaston's nostrils, it was not hopelessly unpleasant, as the deep and square oriel window at the extreme end of this long, low room was wide open, freely admitting the sweet, salt breeze which blew straight from the English Channel; affording too—as Gaston had originally surmised—a magnificent view of a panorama which embraced the mouth of the Seine, the rough harbour and tiny jetty, with the many small craft lying at anchor on the calm bosom of the river, and the graceful schooners and majestic three-deckers further away, all lit by the slanting rays of the slowly-sinking sun.

Gaston, without hesitation, walked straight up to a bench and trestle table, which to his pleasurable surprise he found was unoccupied. These were just inside the bay of the window, and he deliberately placed his hat, coat and whip upon the table in token that he took possession of it. Then he once more turned to mine host, who, much torn between respect for a man who travelled on the King's business—a nobleman mayhap—and pride of peasant at contact with an unwelcome visitor, had slowly followed Gaston, lolling with that peculiar gait which betrays the ex-sailor whilst firm if deferential protest was writ all over his rubicund countenance.

Jean Marie Palisson was born at Le Havre; he had been armateur ere the welcome death of a relative put him in possession of the most frequented inn in the town together with a very comfortable competence, and the best furnished cellars this side of Rouen. He greatly resented the appearance of a stranger in the midst of his usual habitués, which distinguished circle embraced M. le Général commanding the fortress, M. the Military Governor of the port, M. the Civil Governor of the town, MM. the commanders on His Majesty's ships, not to speak of M. le Maire, and M. le Député of the Parliament of Rouen, in fact all the notabilities and dignitaries of the town and the harbour.

These gentlemen were wont to assemble in this the best room of "Les Trois Matelots" at five o'clock, "l'heure de l'apéritif," when eau-de-vie, punch or mulled wine were consumed, in order to coax recalcitrant appetites to a pleasurable anticipation of supper. It was an understood thing, between the worthy Jean Marie Palisson and his distinguished customers, that no strangers were to be admitted within this inner sanctum, save by the vote of the majority, nor had it ever occurred before that any one had thus forced an entrance past that magic door which mine host guarded with jealous care.

Now when Gaston thus arrogantly took possession of the best table in the best portion of the best room in "Les Trois Matelots," Jean Marie was so taken aback, and so awed by the masterfulness which could rise to such complete disregard of the etiquette pertaining to the social circles of Le Havre, that he found himself unable to do aught but shrug his broad shoulders at intervals, and blink his beady eyes in token of helpless distress.

And this in spite of the fact that several pairs of eyebrows were lifted in token of pained surprise.

Gaston was equally unconscious of the disapproval which his entry had evoked, as of Jean Marie's want of alacrity in his service. When he entered, he noted that the several occupants of the room were gentlemen like himself, and he always felt thoroughly at home and unabashed amongst his kind: as for the landlord of a tumbledown provincial inn, Gaston thought him quite unworthy of close attention. He sat himself down on the edge of the table, dangling one well-booted leg with easy nonchalance, and from this elevated position he surveyed leisurely and with no small amount of impertinence, the company there assembled. He had scarce time to note the scowling looks of haughty disapproval which were levelled at him from every side, when the door was vigorously pushed open and an aggressively cheerful young man, loud of voice, jocose of manner, boisterously entered the room.

"Par ma foi! my worthy Jean Marie," he said in stentorian tones, "is this the latest fashion in Le Havre? the host not at the door to receive his guests? ... Hé! ..." he added, suddenly realizing the presence of a stranger in the room, "whom have we here?"

But already, at the first words uttered by the newcomer, Gaston de Stainville had jumped to his feet, and as soon as the young man ceased talking, he went forward to greet him.

"None other than Gaston de Stainville, my good Mortémar, and pleased indeed to look into a friend's face."

"Gaston de Stainville!" exclaimed the other gaily, "par tous les diables! but this is a surprise! Who would have thought to see you in this damned and God-forsaken hole!"

"The King's business, my good Mortémar," said Gaston, "and if you'll forgive me I'll see to it at once and then we'll sup together, eh? ... Palsambleu! and I who thought I'd die of ennui during this enforced halt on this lonely shore."

"Ennui? perish the thought! Gentlemen," added the young Comte de Mortémar, with a graceful flourish of the arm which embraced the entire company, "allow me to present unto you the most accomplished cavalier of the day, whom I have the honour to call my friend, and whom I hope we will all have the honour to call our guest to-night, M. le Comte Gaston Amédé de Stainville."

Gaston had no cause now to complain of want of welcome. Once the stranger duly accredited and presented by a member of the intimate circle, he was cheered to the echo. Every one rose to greet him, many pressed forward to shake him by the hand: the presence of a cavalier of Versailles with all the Court gossip, the little intrigues, the laughable anecdotes which he would of necessity bring with him was indeed a veritable God-send to the little official world of Le Havre, who spent most of its life in mortal ennui.

"As for thee, my good Jean Marie," now interposed Mortémar with mock severity, "let me tell thee at once that if within an hour this table here doth not groan under the weight of the finest and best cooked capon that Normandy can produce, neither I nor these gentlemen here will e'er darken thy doors again. What say you, gentlemen?"

There was loudly expressed assent, accompanied by much laughter and vigorous clinking of pewter mugs against the deal tables.

"And in the meanwhile," continued Mortémar, who seemed to have taken the lead in this general desire to bid the visitor a substantial welcome, "a bowl of punch with half a glass of eau-de-vie and a dozen prunes soaked in kirsch therein. Never fear, friend Stainville," he added, slapping Gaston boisterously on the shoulder, "I tell you mine host knows how to brew a bowl of punch, which will send you reeling under one of his tables in less than half an hour."

A round of applause greeted this cheerful sally.

"Nay, in that case," said Gaston, on whom the strenuous fatigues of the day were telling severely after the preliminary excitement of arrival, "I'll to my business, ere your good cheer, friend, render me quite helpless."

"Perish the thought of business," retorted Mortémar. "Your head in a bucket of cold water after the punch, and you can meet the most astute notary on even ground and beat him at his own game. The punch, knave!" he shouted to the fat landlord, "the punch, this instant, M. le Comte de Stainville is wearied and is waiting for refreshment."

But Gaston's frame of mind was far too grave, his purpose far too important, to allow himself to be led into delaying business with Captain Barre a moment longer than was necessary. Mortémar and his convivial friends could not know that half a million livres would be the price paid for that bowl of punch, since it might mean an hour's carousing and the full of dusk before Le Monarque received her orders. He was deadly fatigued undoubtedly, faint too from the heat and want of proper food, but when money was at stake Gaston de Stainville always displayed an enthusiasm and an amount of courageous endurance worthy of a better cause.

"A thousand thanks, my good Mortémar, and to you all,

gentlemen," he now said courteously but firmly, "do not, I beseech you, think me churlish if I must momentarily refuse your kind hospitality. One glass of eau-de-vie to give me a modicum of strength, and I must to my business first. Gentlemen, I see by your coats that most of you serve the King in some capacity or other, you know as well as I do that the laws which govern the King's commands cannot be broken. I will not be gone long, half an hour at most; after that I am at your commands, and will be the most grateful as well as the most joyous of you all."

"Well spoken, friend Stainville," declared Mortémar "and you, Jean Marie, serve a small refreshment to M. le Comte immediately. Nay, friend," he added pleasantly, "I fear I have been importunate ... 'twas the joy of seeing so elegant a cavalier grace this unhallowed spot."

Every one nodded approval; as Gaston had surmised, there were soldiers, sailors there present, all of whom understood duty and obedience to the King's commands.

"Perhaps some of us could be of assistance to M. le Comte de Stainville," suggested a grave gentleman who wore His Majesty's colours. "If he is a stranger at Le Havre he might be glad of help."

"Indeed well said," spoke another; "could one of us here accompany you anywhere, Monsieur le Comte?"

"I am more than grateful, gentlemen," replied Gaston, to whom the host was even now offering a cup of mulled wine. He drank the liquor at one draught, then set down the cup ere he spoke further:

"And gladly will I accept these kindly offers of assistance," he now said. "I am indeed a stranger here, and did feel doubtful how I could most speedily accomplish my business. I must have speech with Captain Barre, gentlemen, commanding His Majesty's ship Le Monarque and that with as little delay as possible...."

To his intense astonishment he was interrupted by a ringing laugh from his friend Mortémar.

"Nay, then my good Stainville," said the lively young man, "you'll have plenty of time for that bowl of punch, aye! and for getting right royally drunk and fully sober again if your business is with Captain Barre."

"What do you mean?" queried Gaston with a sudden frown.

"Le Monarque sailed out of Le Havre an hour ago; methinks you can still see her sails against the evening sun."

And the young man pointed through the open window out toward the West. Mechanically Gaston's eyes followed the direction in which his friend pointed. There, far away in the mist-laden distance, a graceful three-decker, with sails unfurled, was distinctly visible in the glow of the setting sun. She was gaily riding the waves, the soft south-easterly breeze having carried her swiftly and lightly already far out to sea.

Gaston felt an awful dizziness in his head. An icy sweat broke out upon his brow, he passed a hand across his eyes for he did not feel that he could trust them.

"That is not Le Monarque," he murmured.

"By my faith, but it is," said Mortémar, a little perturbed, for he had not thought to be conveying evil news. "I was bidding her captain 'God-speed' myself little more than an hour ago. A gallant sailor, and a personal friend," he added, "and he seemed mighty glad to get on the way."

"Whither was he bound?" asked Gaston mechanically.

"Nay! that I do not know. Barre had received secret orders only an hour before he started...."

But now Gaston felt his senses reeling.

"She must be stopped! ... she must be stopped!" he shouted wildly. "I have orders for her ... she must be stopped, at any cost!"

And breaking through the compact group of his newly found friends he made a wild dash for the door.

But the excitement, the terrible keenness of this disappointment had been too much for him, after the strenuous fatigues and the overpowering heat of the day. The dizziness turned to an intolerable feeling of sickness, the walls of the room spun round and round him, he felt as if a stunning blow had been dealt him on the head, and with a final shriek of "Stop her!" he staggered and would have fallen headlong, but that a pair of willing arms were there to break his fall.

CHAPTER XXXV

THE STRANGER

It was M. des Coutures—a middle-aged man, military governor of Le Havre—who had caught Gaston de Stainville in his arms when the latter all but lost consciousness. A dozen willing pairs of hands were now ready to administer to the guest's comforts, from the loosening of his cravat to the pulling off of his heavy riding boots.

"The mulled wine was too heavy for him," said M. le Maire Valledieu, "no doubt he had been fasting some hours and his stomach refused to deal with it."

"Tell the kitchen wench to hurry with that supper, Jean Marie," said Mortémar to mine host, "he'll be himself again when he has eaten."

"If there's a plate of soup ready, bring that," added M. Valledieu. "Anything's better than an empty paunch."

"I thank you, friends," now murmured Stainville feebly. "I fear me I must have turned giddy ... the heat and ...”

He was recovering quickly enough. It had been mere dizziness caused by fatigue; and then that awful blow which had staggered him physically as well as mentally! His newly found friends had dragged him back to the table close to the open window: the keen sea-breeze quickly restored him to complete consciousness.

Already he had turned his head slowly round to watch that fast disappearing three-decker, gleaming golden now in the distant haze.

His argosy which he had hoped to see returning from her voyage laden with golden freight! Somehow as first the hulk and then the graceful sails were gradually merged into the Western glow, Gaston knew—by one of those inexplicable yet absolutely unerring instincts which baffle the materialist—that all hopes of those coveted millions were vanishing as surely as did the ship now from before his gaze. He was still weak in body as well as in mind, and it was as if in a dream, that he listened to de Mortémar's carelessly given explanations of the event which meant the wreckage of so many fondly cherished hopes.

"Captain Barre broke his fast in this very room this morning," said the young man lightly, "several of these gentlemen here, as well as myself, had speech with him. He had no idea then that he would have to start on a voyage quite so soon. He left here at eleven o'clock and went back to his ship. An hour later when I was strolling along the shore I met him again. He seemed in a vast hurry and told me in a few curt words that Le Monarque had received orders to be under way as soon as the tide permitted."

"You did not ask him whither the ship was bound?" queried Gaston, speaking hoarsely like a man who has been drinking.

"He could not tell me," replied the other, "her orders were secret."

"Do you know who was the bearer of these secret orders?"

"No, but I heard later that a stranger had ridden into Le Havre at midday to-day. His mare—a beautiful creature so I understand—

dropped not far from here; she had been ridden to her death, poor thing; and her rider, so they say, was near to dropping too."

"I saw him," here interposed a young soldier, "he was just outside that God-forsaken hole, 'Le Gros Normand' and politely asked me if it were the best inn in Le Havre."

"I hope you told him it was," said des Coutures with a growl, "we want no stranger here."

"Nor do we want Le Havre to have a reputation for dirt and discomfort," corrected M. le Maire.

"And I certainly could not allow a gentlemen—for he was that—I'll lay any wager on it, with any one—to be made superlatively uncomfortable on the broken beds of 'Le Gros Normand,'" asserted the young soldier hotly.

"You advised him to come here?" gasped Mortémar with genuine horror. He was the chief of that clique which desired to exclude, with utmost rigour from the sacred precincts of "Les Trois Matelots," every stranger not properly accredited.

"Ma foi! what would you have me do?" retorted the other sulkily.

"You did quite right, Lieutenant le Tellier," rejoined M. le Maire, who was jealous of the reputation of Le Havre. "Gentlemen must be under no misapprehension with regard to the refinement and hospitality of this town."

The entrance of mine host carrying a steaming bowl of soup broke up the conversation for awhile. Jean Marie was followed by a fat and jovial-looking wench, who quickly spread a white cloth for Monsieur le Comte's supper and generally administered to his wants.

De Mortémar, Général des Coutures, and M. le Maire Valledieu had constituted themselves the nominal hosts of Gaston. They too sat round the table, and anon when Jean Marie brought huge jugs of red wine, they fell to and entertained their guest, plying him with meat and drink.

This broke up the company somewhat. The other gentlemen had withdrawn with all the respect which Frenchmen always feel for the solemnity of a meal; they had once more assumed their old places at the various tables about the room. But no one thought yet of returning home: "l'heure de l'apéritif" was being indefinitely prolonged.

Conversation naturally drifted back again and again to Le Monarque and her secret orders. Every one scented mystery, for was it not strange that a noble cavalier like Monsieur le Comte de Stainville should have ridden all the way from Versailles on the King's business, in order to have speech with the commander of one of His Majesty's own ships, only to find that he had been forestalled? The good ship had apparently received orders which the King knew naught about, else His Majesty had not sent Monsieur de Stainville all this way on a fool's errand.

Eager, prying eyes watched him as he began to eat and drink, dreamily at first, almost drowsily. Obviously he was absorbed in thought. He too must be racking his brains as to who the stranger might be who had so unexpectedly forestalled him.

His three genial hosts plied him continually with wine and soon the traces of fatigue in him began to yield to his usual alertness and vigour. The well-cooked food, the rich liquors were putting life back into his veins. And with renewed life came a seething, an ungovernable wrath.

He had lost a fortune, the gratitude of the King, the goodwill of Pompadour, two and a half millions of money through the interference of a stranger!

He tried to think, to imagine, to argue with himself. Treacherous and false himself, he at once suspected treachery. He imagined that some sycophant, hanging to the Pompadour's skirts, had succeeded in winning her good graces sufficiently to be allowed to do this errand for her, instead of himself.

Or had the King played him false, and sent another messenger to do the delicate business and to share in the spoils?

Or had Lydie ... ? But no! this was impossible! What could she have done at a late hour of the night? How could she have found a messenger whom she could trust? when earlier in the day she had herself admitted that there was no one in whom she could confide, and thus turned almost unwillingly to the friend of her childhood.

Jean Marie's favoured customers sat at the various tables sipping their eau-de-vie; some had produced dice and cards, whilst others were content to loll about, still hoping to hear piquant anecdotes of that distant Court of Versailles, toward which they all sighed so longingly.

But the elegant guest was proving a disappointment. Even after the second bumper of wine Gaston de Stainville's tongue had not loosened. He was speculating on the identity of that mysterious stranger, and would not allow his moodiness to yield to the joys of good cheer. To-morrow he would have to ride back to Versailles hardly more leisurely than he had come, for he must find out the truth of how he came to be forestalled. But he could not start before dawn, even though fiery impatience and wrath burned in his veins.

To all inquisitive queries and pointed chaff he replied with a sulky growl, and very soon the delight of meeting an interesting stranger gave place to irritation at his sullen mood. He was drinking heavily, and did not seem cheerful in his cups, and anon even Mortémar's boisterous hilarity gave way before his persistent gloom.

After an hour or two the company started yawning: every one had had enough of this silent and ill-tempered stranger, who not only had brought no new life and animation into the sleepy town, but was ill repaying the lavish hospitality of "Les Trois Matelots" by his reticence and sulky humour.

One by one now the habitués departed, nodding genially to mine host, as they settled for their consommations, and bidding as hearty a good-night to the stranger as their disappointment would allow.

De Mortémar and Valledieu had tried to lure M. le Comte de Stainville to hazard or even to a more sober game of piquet, but the latter had persistently refused and sat with legs stretched out before him, hands buried in breeches' pockets, his head drooping on his chest, and a meditative scowl between his eyes.

The wine had apparently quite dulled his brilliant wit, and now he only replied in curt monosyllables to queries addressed directly to him.

Anon Valledieu and old Général de Coutures pleading the ties of family and home, begged to be excused. Now de Mortémar alone was left to entertain his surly guest, bored to distraction, and dislocating his jaws in the vain efforts which he made to smother persistent yawns.

It was then close on half-past seven. The final glory of the setting sun had yielded to the magic wand of night which had changed the vivid crimson and orange first to delicate greens and mauves and then to the deep, the gorgeous blue of a summer's evening sky. The stars one by one gleamed in the firmament, and soon the crescent moon, chaste and cold, added her incomparable glory to the beauty and the silent peace of the night.

Tiny lights appeared at masthead or prow of the many craft lying at anchor in the roadsteads, and from far away through the open window there came wafted, on the sweet salt breeze, the melancholy sound of an old Normandy ditty sung by a pair of youthful throats.

Fatigue and gloom had oppressed Gaston at first, now it was unconquerable rage, seething and terrible, which caused him to remain silent. De Mortémar was racking his brains for an excuse to break up this wearisome tête-à-tête without overstepping the bounds of good-breeding, whilst cursing his own impetuosity which had prompted him to take this surly guest under his wing.

Jean Marie now entered with the candles, causing a welcome

214

diversion. He placed one massive pewter candelabrum on the table occupied by Gaston and de Mortémar: the other he carried to the further end of the room. Having placed that down too, he lolled back toward de Mortémar. His rubicund face looked troubled, great beads of perspiration stood out upon his forehead, and his fat fingers wandered along the velvety surface of his round, closely-cropped crown.

"M'sieu le Comte ..." he began hesitatingly.

"What is it?" asked Mortémar smothering a yawn.

"A stranger, M'sieu le Comte ..." stammered Jean Marie.

"What, another? ... I mean," added the young man with a nervous little laugh, feeling that the sudden exclamation of undisguised annoyance was not altogether courteous to his guest, "I mean a ... an ... an ... unknown stranger? ... altogether different to M. le Comte de Stainville, of course!"

"A stranger, M'sieu," repeated Jean Marie curtly. "He came at midday...."

"And you told us nothing about him?"

"I did not think it was necessary, nor that the stranger would trouble M'sieu le Comte. He asked for a clean room and a bed and said nothing about supper at the time. ... He seemed very tired and gave me a couple of louis, just if as they were half livres."

"No doubt 'twas the stranger with whom Lieutenant Tellier had speech outside 'Le Gros Normand!'" suggested de Mortémar.

"Mayhap! mayhap!" rejoined Jean Marie thoughtfully. "I took him up a bowl of sack and half a cold capon, but what he wanted most was a large wash-tub and plenty of water ... it seems he needed a bath!"

"Then he was English," commented Mortémar decisively.

But at these words, Gaston, who had been listening with half an ear to mine host's explanations, roused himself from his heavy torpor.

The stranger who had forestalled him and sent Le Monarque on her secret voyage to-day was English!

Then it was . . .

"Where is that stranger now?" he demanded peremptorily.

"That's just it, M'sieu le Comte!" replied Jean Marie, obstinately ignoring Gaston and still addressing de Mortémar, "he slept all the afternoon. Now he wants some supper. He throws louis about as if they were dirt, and I can't serve him in there!" he added with unanswerable logic and pointing to the stuffy room in the rear.

"Pardi! ..." began Mortémar.

But Gaston de Stainville was fully alert now; with sudden vigour he jumped to his feet and brought his fist crashing down on

215

the table so that the candelabrum, the mugs, and decanters of wine shook under the blow.

"I beseech you, friend, admit the stranger into this room without delay," he said loudly. "Ma foi! you have found me dull and listless, ill-humoured in spite of your lavish hospitality; I swear to you by all the devils in hell that you'll not yawn once for the next half-hour, and that Gaston de Stainville and the mysterious stranger, who thwarts his will and forestalls his orders, will afford you a measure of amusement such as you'll never forget."

His face was flushed, and his eyes, somewhat hazy from the copiousness of his libations, had an evil leer in them and an inward glow of deadly hate. There was no longer any weakness, nor yet ill-humour, visible in his attitude. His hands were clenched, one resting on the table, the other roughly pushing back the chair on which he had been sitting.

"Admit the stranger, friend host!" he shouted savagely. "I'll vouch for it that your patron will not regret his presence in this room."

"Ma foi! I trust not," said a quiet voice, which seemed to come suddenly from out the gloom. "Gentlemen, your servant!"

Mortémar turned toward the door, whence had proceeded that gentle, courteous voice. Lord Eglinton was standing under the lintel, elegantly attired in full riding dress, with top boots and closely-fitting coat. He wore no sword, and carried a heavy cloak on his arm.

He made a comprehensive bow which included every one there present, then he stepped forward into the room.

CHAPTER XXXVI

REVENGE

We must surmise that surprise and rage had rendered Gaston speechless for the moment.

Of all the conjectures which had racked his brains for the past two hours none had come near this amazing reality. Gaston was no fool, and in one vivid flash he saw before his mental vision not only his own discomfiture, the annihilation of all his hopes, but also the failure of King Louis' plans, the relegation of those fifteen millions back into the pockets of His Grace the Duke of Cumberland.

That Eglinton had not ridden to Le Havre on the King's business but on his own, that he had not sent Le Monarque to Scotland in order that he might share in those millions was of course obvious.

No! no! it was clear enough! Lydie having found that Gaston had failed her, had turned to her husband for help: and he, still nominally Comptroller-General of Finance, had found it quite easy to send Captain Barre on his way with secret orders to find Charles Edward Stuart and ensure the safety of the Jacobites at once and at any cost.

Milor was immensely rich; that had helped him too, of course; bribes, promises, presents of money were nothing to him. Mentally he was weak—reasoned Gaston's vanity—and Lydie had commanded him.

But physically he was as strong as a horse, impervious to fatigue, and whilst Gaston rested last night preparing for his journey, le petit Anglais was in the saddle at midnight and had killed a horse under him ere de Stainville was midway.

What King Louis' attitude would be over this disappointment it were premature to conjecture. Royal disfavour coupled with Pompadour's ill-humour would make itself felt on innocent and guilty alike.

That he himself was a ruined man and that, through the interference of that weak-kneed young fop, whom it had been the fashion in Versailles mildly to despise, was the one great, all-absorbing fact which seemed to turn Gaston's blood into living fire within his veins.

And the man who had thus deliberately snatched a couple of millions or more from his grip stood there, not twenty paces away, calm, somewhat gauche in manner, yet with that certain stiff dignity peculiar to Englishmen of high rank, and withal apparently unconscious of the fact that the rival whom he had deprived of a fortune was in this same room with him, burning with rage and thirsting for revenge.

Gaston watched his enemy for awhile as he now settled himself at the table, with Jean Marie ministering obsequiously to his wants. Soon mine host had arranged everything to his guest's liking, had placed a dish of stewed veal before him, a bottle of wine, some nice fresh bread, then retired walking backwards, so wonderfully deferential was he to the man who dealt with gold as others would with tin.

One grim thought had now risen in Stainville's mind, the

217

revival of a memory, half-faded: an insult, a challenge, refused by that man, who had thwarted him!

A coward? Eh?

These English would not fight! 'twas well known; in battle, yes! but not in single combat, not in a meeting 'twixt gentlemen, after a heady bottle of wine when tempers wax hot, and swords skip almost of themselves out of the scabbard.

Aye! he would ride a hundred and eighty leagues, to frustrate a plan, or nathless to dip into the well-filled coffers of the Jacobite Alliance—such things were possible—but he would not fight!

Gaston hugged the thought! it was grim but delicious! revenge, bitter, awful, complete revenge was there, quite easy of accomplishment. Fortune was lost to him, but not revenge! Not before his hand had struck the cheek of his enemy.

This was his right. No one could blame him. Not even the King, sworn foe of duelling though he might profess to be.

A long laugh now broke from Gaston's burning throat! Was it not all ridiculous, senseless, and puerile?

His Majesty the King, Pompadour, the Duc d'Aumont, Prime Minister of France, and he himself, Gaston de Stainville, the most ruthlessly ambitious man in the kingdom, all fooled, stupidly fooled and tricked by that man, who was too great a coward to meet the rival whom he had insulted.

At Gaston's laugh Eglinton turned to look in his direction, and his eyes met those of de Mortémar fixed intently upon him.

"Surely it is M. le Contrôleur-Général," said the latter, jumping to his feet.

He had paid no heed to his guest's curious outburst of merriment, putting it down as another expression of his strange humour, else to the potency of Jean Marie's wine; but he had been deeply interested in the elegant figure of the stranger, that perfect type of a high-born gentleman which the young man was quick enough to recognise. The face, the quaintly awkward manner, brought back certain recollections of two days spent at the Court of Versailles.

Now when Eglinton turned toward him, he at once recognised the handsome face, and those kind eyes, which always looked grave and perfectly straight at an interlocutor.

"Milor Eglinton, a thousand pardons," he now said as he moved quickly across the room. "I had failed to recognise you at first, and had little thought of seeing so great a personage in this sleepy old town."

Eglinton too had risen at his first words and had stepped forward, with his habitual courtesy, to greet the young man. De

218

Mortémar's hand was cordially stretched out toward him, the next moment he would have clasped that of the young Englishman, when with one bound and a rush across the room and with one wild shout of rage, Gaston de Stainville overtook his friend and, catching hold of his arm, he drew him roughly back.

"Nay! de Mortémar, my friend," he cried loudly, "be warned in time lest your honest hand come in contact with that of a coward."

His words echoed along the vast, empty room. Then there was dead silence. Instinctively Mortémar had stepped back as if he had been stung. He did not of course understand the meaning of it all, and was so taken aback that he could no nothing but stare amazed at the figure of the young man before him. Eglinton's placidity had in no sense given way before the deadly insult; only his face had become pale as death, but the eyes still looked grave, earnest and straight at his enemy.

"Aye! a coward," said Gaston, who during these few moments of silence had fought the trembling of his limbs, the quiver of his voice. He saw the calm of the other man and with a mighty effort smothered the cryings of his rage, leaving cool contempt free play. "Or will you deny here, before my friend le Comte de Mortémar, who was about to touch your hand, that last night having insulted me you refused to give me satisfaction? Coward! you have no right to touch another's hand ... the hand of an honourable gentleman. ... Coward! ... Do you hear me? I'll say it again—coward—and coward again ere I shout it on the house-tops of Versailles—coward!—even now when my hand has struck your cheek—coward!"

How it all happened Mortémar himself could not afterward have said, the movement must have been extraordinarily quick, for even as the last word "Coward!" rose to Gaston's lips it was drowned in an involuntary cry of agony, whilst his hand, raised ready to strike, was held in a grip which indeed seemed like one of steel.

"'Tis done, man! 'tis done!" said the gentle, perfectly even voice, "but in the name of Heaven provoke me no further, or it will be murder instead of fight. There!" he added, releasing the other man's wrist, who staggered back faint and giddy with the pain, "'tis true that I refused to meet you in combat yester e'en; the life of my friend, lonely and betrayed, out there in far-off Scotland, had been the price of delay if I did not ride out of Versailles before cock-crow, but now 'tis another matter," he added lightly, "and I am at your service."

"Aye!" sneered Gaston, still writhing with pain, "at my service now, when you hope that my broken wrist will ensure your impunity."

"Nay, sir, but at your service across the width of this table," responded Eglinton coldly, "a pair of pistols, one unloaded. ... And we'll both use the left hand."

An exclamation of protest broke from Mortémar's lips.

"Impossible! ..."

"Why so, Monsieur le Comte?"

"'Twere murder, milor!"

"Does M. le Comte de Stainville protest?" queried the other calmly.

"No! damn you! ... Where are the pistols?"

"Yours, M. le Comte, an you will; surely you have not ridden all the way from Versailles without a pair in your holster."

"Well guessed, milor," quoth Gaston lightly. "Mortémar, I pray you, in the pocket of my coat ... a pair of pistols."

Mortémar tried again to protest.

"Silence!" said Gaston savagely, "do you not see that I must kill him?"

"'Tis obvious as the crescent moon yonder, M. de Mortémar," said Eglinton with a whimsical smile. "I entreat you, the pistols."

The young man obeyed in silence. He strode across the room to the place lately vacated by Gaston, and near which his cloak was lying close to his hat and whip. Mortémar groped in the pockets: he found the two pistols and then rejoined the antagonists.

"I used one against a couple of footpads in the early dawn," said Gaston, as he took the weapons from Mortémar's hands and placed them on the table.

"'Twas lucky, Monsieur le Comte," rejoined Eglinton gravely, "then all we need do is to throw for the choice."

"Dice," said Stainville curtly.

On a table close by there was a dice-box, left there by one of Jean Marie's customers: Mortémar, without a word, handed it to Eglinton. He could not understand the placidity of the man: Gaston's attitude was simple enough, primitive animal rage, blinding him to the possibility of immediate death; excitement too, giving him a sense of bravado, an arrogant disregard of the consequences of his own provocation.

Eglinton was within his rights. He was now the insulted party, he could make his own conditions, but did he wish to die? or was he so supremely indifferent to life that he could view with perfect serenity that pair of pistols, one of which death-dealing of a surety across a narrow table, and that box of dice the arbiter of his fate?

Of a truth Eglinton was perfectly indifferent as to the issue of the combat. He did not care if he killed Gaston, nor did he care to live. Lydie hated him, so what mattered if the sky was blue, or if the sun ceased to shed radiance over the earth?

It was the supreme indifference of a man who with life had nothing else to lose.

His hand was absolutely steady as he took the dice-box and threw:

"Blank!" murmured Mortémar under his breath, as he saw the result of the throw. Yet the face of milor was as impassive as before, even though now by all the rules of chance Gaston's was the winning hand.

"Three!" he said calmly, as the dice once more rolled on to the table. "Monsieur le Comte, the choice of weapon rests with you."

Once more Mortémar tried to interpose. This was monstrous! horrible! a shocking, brutal murder!

"Monsieur de Stainville knows his own weapons," he said impulsively, "he discharged one this morning and ..."

"Milor should have thought of this before!" retorted Stainville savagely.

"The remark did not come from me, Monsieur," rejoined Eglinton passively, "an you will choose your weapon, I am fully satisfied."

But his grave eyes found occasion to send a kindly glance of gratitude to young de Mortémar. The latter felt a tightening of his very heart strings: he would at this moment have willingly given his fortune to avert the awful catastrophe.

"Mortémar, an you interfere," said Gaston, divining his thoughts, "I'll brand you as a meddler before the Court of Versailles. An you are afraid to see bloodshed, get you gone in the name of hell."

By all the unwritten laws which governed such affairs of honour, Mortémar could not interfere. He did not know the right or wrong of the original enmity between these two men, but had already guessed that mere disappointment with regard to the voyage of Le Monarque had not been sufficient to kindle such deadly hate: vaguely he surmised that somewhere in the background lurked the rustle of a silk petticoat.

Without the slightest hesitation now Gaston took one of the pistols in his left hand: his right still caused him excruciating pain; and every time he felt the agony, his eyes gleamed with more intense savagery, the lust of a certain revenge.

He had worked himself up into a passion of hate. Money has the power to do that sometimes; that vanished hope of fortune had killed every instinct in the man, save that of desire for vengeance. He was sure of himself. The pistols were his as de Mortémar had said, and he had handled them but a few hours ago: he could apprise their weight—loaded or unloaded—and he was quite satisfied.

It was hatred alone that prompted him to a final thrust, a blow, he thought, to a dying man. Eglinton was as good as dead, with the muzzle of a loaded pistol a foot away from his breast, and an empty weapon in his own hand; but his serenity irritated Gaston; the blood which tingled in his own veins, which had rushed to his head almost obscuring his vision clamoured for a sight of a shrinking enemy, not of a wooden puppet, calm, impassive even before certain death.

The agony as he lifted the half-broken wrist to his coat was intolerable, but he almost welcomed it now, for it added a strange, lustful joy to the excitement of this deed. His eyes, glowing and restless with fumes of wine and passion of hate, were fixed upon the marble-like face of his enemy. Then from the breast-pocket of his coat, he drew a packet of papers.

And although he was nigh giddy with the pain in his wrist, he clutched that packet tightly, toyed with it for a while, smoothed out the creases with a hand which shook with the intensity of his excitement, the intensity of his triumph.

The proofs in Madame la Marquise d'Eglinton's own writing that she was at one with the gang who meant to sell the Stuart prince for gold! The map revealing his hiding-place! and her letter to him bidding him trust the bearer whose orders—now affixed to map and letter—were that he deliver the young Pretender into the hands of the English authorities.

That these orders to Le Monarque had been forestalled by milor Eglinton could not exonerate Madame la Marquise from having been at one with Gaston de Stainville and Madame de Pompadour, and others who might remain nameless, in the blackest treachery ever planned against a trusting friend.

No wonder Gaston de Stainville forgot physical suffering when he toyed lovingly with this packet of papers in his hand, the consummation of his revenge.

At last 'twas done. A subtle, indefinable change had come over the calm face of Lord Eglinton, an ashen grey hue which had chased the former pallor of the cheeks, and the slender hand, which held the pistol, trembled almost imperceptibly.

Serenity had given way at sight of that packet of papers.

"Friend de Mortémar," said Gaston lightly, but with glowing eyes still fixed on his opponent, "the chances of my demise being at least equal to those of milor's—seeing that I know not, on my honour, which is the loaded pistol, and that methinks at this moment I can read murder in his eye—I pray you to take charge of this packet. It is a sacred trust. In case of my death promise me that you will deliver it into the hands of my wife, and into no other. Madame la Comtesse de Stainville will know how to deal with it."

The young Comte de Mortémar took the packet from Gaston.

"I will do as you desire," he said coldly.

"You promise that no one shall touch these papers except my wife, Irène Comtesse de Stainville," reiterated Gaston solemnly.

"On my word of honour," rejoined the young man.

The request was perfectly proper and natural, very usual in such cases; de Mortémar could not help but comply. He could not know that the fulfilment of this promise would mean public dishonour to an innocent and noble woman, and the supreme revenge of a baffled traitor.

If Gaston expected protest, rage, or excitement from his foe he was certainly disappointed. Eglinton had all the characteristics of his race, perfect sang-froid in the face of the inevitable, and an almost morbid consciousness of pride and dignity. He could not filch those papers from Gaston nor prevent de Mortémar from accepting and fulfilling a trust, which had all the appearance of being sacred.

He knew that by this act he had wrested a fortune from a man whose fetish was money, and the power which money gives: true that being an honest man himself, he had never thought of such an infamous revenge.

If he died now Heaven help his proud Lydie! but if he lived then Heaven help them both!

CHAPTER XXXVII

THE LETTER

De Mortémar had stowed the packet carefully away inside his coat, Gaston keenly watching his antagonist the while.

"Are you ready, milor?" he asked now with marked insolence of manner.

"At your service," replied the other quietly. "M. de Mortémar, will you give the word?"

The two men stood opposite to one another, a table not four

feet wide between them. Each held a pistol in his left hand. Of these one was loaded, the other not. De Mortémar had cleared the table, pushing aside the decanter of wine, the tureen of soup, the glasses. The window was still open, and from that outside world which to these men here present seemed so far away, there came the sound of the old church belfry tolling the hour of eight, and still from afar that melancholy tune, the Norman ditty sung by young throats:

"C'est les Normands, qu'à dit ma mère,
"C'est les Normands qu'ont conquis l'Angleterre!"

"Fire!" said de Mortémar.

Two arms were raised. Eye was fixed to eye for one brief second, then lowered for the aim. There was a slight dull sound, then a terrible curse muttered below the breath, as the pistol which Gaston de Stainville had vainly tried to fire dropped from his hand.

Had his excitement blinded him when he chose his weapon, or was it just fate, ruthless, inscrutable, that had placed the loaded pistol in Lord Eglinton's hand?

"A blank!" he shouted with a blasphemous oath. "À vous, milor! Curse you, why don't you fire?"

"Fire, milor, in Heaven's name," said Mortémar, who was as pale as death. "'Tis cruelty to prolong."

But Eglinton too had dropped his arm.

"M. le Comte de Stainville," he said calmly, "before I use this weapon against you, as I would against a mad dog, I'll propose a bargain for your acceptance."

"You'd buy that packet of precious documents from me, eh?" sneered Gaston savagely, "nay, milor, 'tis no use offering millions to a dying man. ... Shoot, shoot, milor! the widowed Comtesse de Stainville will deal with those documents and no one else. ... They are not for sale, I tell you, not for all your millions now!"

"Not even for this pistol, M. le Comte?"

And calm, serene with that whimsical smile again playing round the corners of his expressive mouth, Lord Eglinton offered the loaded pistol to his enemy.

"My life? ..." stammered Gaston, "you would? ..."

"Nay, mine, M. le Comte," rejoined milor. "I'll not stir from this spot. I offer you this pistol and you shall use it at your pleasure, after you have handed me that packet of letters."

Instinctively Gaston had drawn back, lost in a maze of surprise.

"An you'll not take the weapon, M. le Comte," said Eglinton decisively, "I shoot."

There was a moment's silence, whilst Gaston's pride fought a grim battle with that awful instinct of self-preservation, that strange love of fleeting life to which poor mortals cling.

Men were not cowards in those days; life was cheap and oft sold for the gratification of petty vanity, yet who shall blame Gaston if, with certain death before him, he chose to forego his revenge?

"Give me that pistol, milor," he said dully, "de Mortémar, hand over that packet to Lord Eglinton."

He took the pistol from milor, and it was his own hand that trembled.

Silently de Mortémar obeyed. Milor took the packet of papers from him, then held them one by one to the flame of the candle: first the map, then the letter which bore Lydie's name writ so boldly across it. The black ash curled and fell from his hand on to the table, he gripped the paper until his seared fingers could hold it no longer.

Then he once more stood up, turning straight toward Gaston.

"I am ready, M. le Comte," he said simply.

Gaston raised his left arm and fired. There was a wild, an agonized shriek which came from a woman's throat, coupled with one of horror from de Mortémar's lips, as le petit Anglais stood for the space of a few seconds, quite still, firm and upright, with scarce a change upon his calm face, then sank forward without a groan.

"Madame, you are hurt!" shouted de Mortémar, who was almost dazed with surprise at the sight of a woman at this awful and supreme moment. He had just seen her, in the vivid flash when Gaston raised his arm and fired: she had rushed forward then, with the obvious intention of throwing herself before the murderous weapon, and now was making pathetic and vain efforts to raise her husband's inanimate body from the table against which he had fallen.

"Coward! coward!" she sobbed in anguish, "you have stilled the bravest heart in France!"

"Pray God that I have not," murmured Gaston fervently, as, impelled by some invisible force, he threw the pistol from him, then sank on his knees and buried his face in his hands.

But Mortémar had soon recovered his presence of mind, and had already reached his wounded friend, calling quickly to Jean Marie who apparently had followed in the wake of Madame la Marquise in her wild rush from her coach to the inner room.

Together the two men succeeded in lifting Lord Eglinton and in gently insinuating his body backward into a recumbent position. Thus Lydie—still on her knees—received her lord in her arms. Her eyes were fixed upon his pallid face with passionate intensity. It seemed as if she would wrest from those closed lids the secret of life or death.

"He'll not die? ..." she whispered wildly; "tell me that he'll not die!"

A deep red stain was visible on the left side, spreading on the fine cloth of the coat. With clumsy though willing fingers, Mortémar was doing his best to get the waistcoat open, and to stop temporarily the rapid flow of blood with Lydie's scarf, which she had wrenched from her shoulders.

"Quick, Jean Marie! the leech!" he ordered, "and have the rooms prepared ..."

Then, as Jean Marie obeyed with unusual alacrity and anon his stentorian voice calling to ostler and maids echoed through the silence of the house, Lydie's eyes met those of the young man.

"Madame! Madame! I beseech you," he said appalled at the terrible look of agony expressed on the beautiful, marble-like face, "let me attend you ... I vow that you are hurt."

"No! no!" she rejoined quickly, "only my hand ... I tried to clutch the weapon ... but 'twas too late ..."

But she yielded her hand to him. The shot had indeed pierced the fleshy portion between thumb and forefinger, leaving an ugly gash: the wound was bleeding profusely and already she felt giddy and sick. De Mortémar bound up the little hand with his handkerchief as best he could. She hardly heeded him, beyond that persistent appeal, terrible in its heartrending pathos:

"He'll not die ... tell me that he'll not die."

Whilst not five paces away, Gaston de Stainville still knelt, praying that the ugly stain of murder should not for ever sully his hand.

CHAPTER XXXVIII

THE HOME IN ENGLAND

The first words which milor uttered when presently consciousness returned were:

"The letter ... Madonna ... 'tis destroyed ... I swear...."

He was then lying in Jean Marie's best bed, between lavender-scented sheets. On his right a tiny open window afforded a glimpse of sea and sky, and of many graceful craft gently lolling on the breast of the waves, but on his left, when anon he turned his eyes that way, there was a picture which of a truth was not of this earth, and vaguely, with the childish and foolish fancy of a sick man who hath gazed on the dark portals, he allowed himself to think that all the old tales of his babyhood, about the first glimpse of paradise after death, must indeed be true.

He was dead and this was paradise.

What he saw was a woman's face, with grave anxious eyes fixed upon him, and a woman's smile which revealed an infinity of love and promised an infinity of happiness.

"Madonna!" he murmured feebly. Then he closed his eyes again, for he was weak from loss of blood and from days and nights of fever and delirium, and he was so afraid that the vision might vanish if he gazed at it too long.

The leech—a kindly man—visited him frequently. Apparently the wound was destined to heal. Life was to begin anew, with its sorrows, its disappointments, its humiliations, mayhap.

Yet a memory haunted him persistently—a vision, oh! 'twas a mere flash—of his madonna standing with her dear, white hand outstretched, betwixt him and death.

It was a vision, of course; such as are vouchsafed to the dying: and the other picture?—nay! that was a fevered dream; there had been no tender, grave eyes that watched him, no woman's smile to promise happiness.

One day M. le Duc d'Aumont came to visit him. He had posted straight from Paris, and was singularly urbane and anxious when he pressed the sick man's hand.

"You must make a quick recovery, milor," he said cordially; "par Dieu! you are the hero of the hour. Mortémar hath talked his fill."

"I trust not," rejoined Eglinton gravely.

M. le Duc looked conscious and perturbed.

"Nay! he is a gallant youth," he said reassuringly, "and knows exactly how to hold his tongue, but Belle-Isle and de Lugeac had to be taught a lesson ... and 'twas well learned I'll warrant you. ... As for Gaston...."

"Yes! M. le Duc? what of M. le Comte de Stainville?"

"He hath left the Court momentarily ... somewhat in disgrace ... 'twas a monstrous encounter, milor," added the Duke gravely. "Had Gaston killed you it had been murder, for you never meant to shoot, so says de Mortémar."

The sick man's head turned restlessly on the pillow.

"De Mortémar's tongue hath run away with him," he said impatiently.

"The account of the duel ... nothing more, on my honour," rejoined the Duke. "No woman's name has been mentioned, but I fear me the Court and public have got wind of the story of a conspiracy against the Stuart prince, and connect the duel with that event—hence your popularity, milor," continued the older man with a sigh, "and Gaston's disgrace."

"His Majesty's whipping-boy, eh? the scapegoat in the aborted conspiracy?"

"Poor Gaston! You bear him much ill-will, milor, no doubt?"

"I? None, on my honour."

M. le Duc hesitated a while, a troubled look appeared on his handsome face.

"Lydie," he said tentatively. "Milor, she left Paris that night alone ... and travelled night and day to reach Le Havre in time to help you and to thwart Gaston ... she had been foolish of course, but her motives were pure ... milor, she is my child and ..."

"She is my wife, M. le Duc," interrupted Lord Eglinton gravely; "I need no assurance of her purity even from her father."

There was such implicit trust, such complete faith expressed in those few simple words, that instinctively M. le Duc d'Aumont felt ashamed that he could ever have misunderstood his daughter. He was silent for a moment or two, then he said more lightly:

"His Majesty is much angered of course."

"Against me, I hope," rejoined Eglinton.

"Aye!" sighed the Duke. "King Louis is poorer by fifteen million livres by your act, milor."

"And richer by the kingdom of honour. As for the millions, M. le Duc, I'll place them myself at His Majesty's service. My château and dependencies of Choisy are worth that," added milor lightly. "As soon as this feeble hand can hold a pen, I'll hand them over to the crown of France as a free gift."

"You will do that, milor?" gasped the Duke, who could scarce believe his ears.

"'Tis my firm intention," rejoined the sick man with a smile.

A great weight had been lifted from M. le Duc's mind. Royal displeasure would indeed have descended impartially on all the friends of "le petit Anglais" and above all on milor's father-in-law, whose very presence at Court would of a surety have become distasteful to the disappointed monarch. Now this unparalleled generosity would more than restore Louis' confidence in a Prime Minister whose chief virtue consisted in possessing so wealthy and magnanimous a son-in-law.

Indeed we know that M. le Duc d'Aumont continued for some time after these memorable days to enjoy the confidence and gratitude of Louis the Well-beloved and to bask in the sunshine of Madame de Pompadour's smiles, whilst the gift of the château and dependencies of Choisy by Milor the Marquis of Eglinton to the crown of France was made the subject of a public fête at Versailles and of an ode by M. Jolyot Crébillon of the Institut de France, writ especially for the occasion.

But after the visit of M. le Duc d'Aumont at his bedside in the "auberge des Trois Matelots" the munificent donor of fifteen millions livres felt over-wearied of life.

The dream which had soothed his fevered sleep no longer haunted his waking moments, and memory had much ado to feed love of life with the rememberance of one happy moment.

Milor the Marquis of Eglinton closed his eyes, sighing for that dream. The little room was so still, so peaceful, and from the tiny window a gentle breeze from across the English Channel fanned his aching brow, bringing back with its soothing murmur the memory of that stately home in England, for which his father had so often sighed.

How peaceful it must be there among the hills!

The breeze murmured more persistently, and anon with its dreamlike sound there mingled the frou-frou of a woman's skirts.

The sick man ventured to open his eyes.

Lydie, his wife, was kneeling beside his bed, her delicate hands clasped under her chin, her eyes large, glowing and ever grave fixed upon his face.

"Am I on earth?" he murmured quaintly.

"Of a truth, milor," she replied, and her voice was like the most exquisite music he had ever heard; it was earnest and serious like her own self, but there was a tremor in it which rendered it unspeakably soft.

"The leech saith there's no longer any danger for your life," she added.

He was silent for awhile, as if he were meditating on a grave matter, then he said quietly:

"Would you have me live, Lydie?"

And as she did not reply, he repeated his question again:

"Do you wish me to live, Lydie?"

She fought with the tears, which against her will gathered in her eyes.

"Milor, milor, are you not cruel now?" she whispered through those tears.

"Cruel of a truth," he replied earnestly, "since you would have saved me at peril of your own dear life. ... Yet would I gladly die to see you happy."

"Will you not rather live, milor?" she said with a smile of infinite tenderness, "for then only could I taste happiness."

"Yet if I lived, you would have to give up so much that you love."

"That is impossible, milor, for I only love one thing."

"Your work in France?" he asked.

"No. My life with you."

Her hands dropped on to the coverlet, and he grasped them in his own. How oft had she drawn away at his touch. Now she yielded, drawing nearer to him, still on her knees.

"Would you come to England with me, Lydie? to my home in England, amongst the hills of Sussex, far from Court life and from politics? Would you follow me thither?"

"To the uttermost ends of the world, good milor," she replied.

THE END

www.ingramcontent.com/pod-product-compliance
Lightning Source LLC
Chambersburg PA
CBHW011521240626
47154CB00009B/2914